A Hollow Soul

A Soul Saga

Raquel Gabrielle

Dark Storm LLC

Published in the United States by Dark Storm LLC

Visit us on the web! www.RaquelGabrielle.com

ISBN: 978-1-958970-00-3

eBook ISBN: 978-1-958970-01-0

Cover art and design by Kyla Sixkiller

Printed in the United States of America

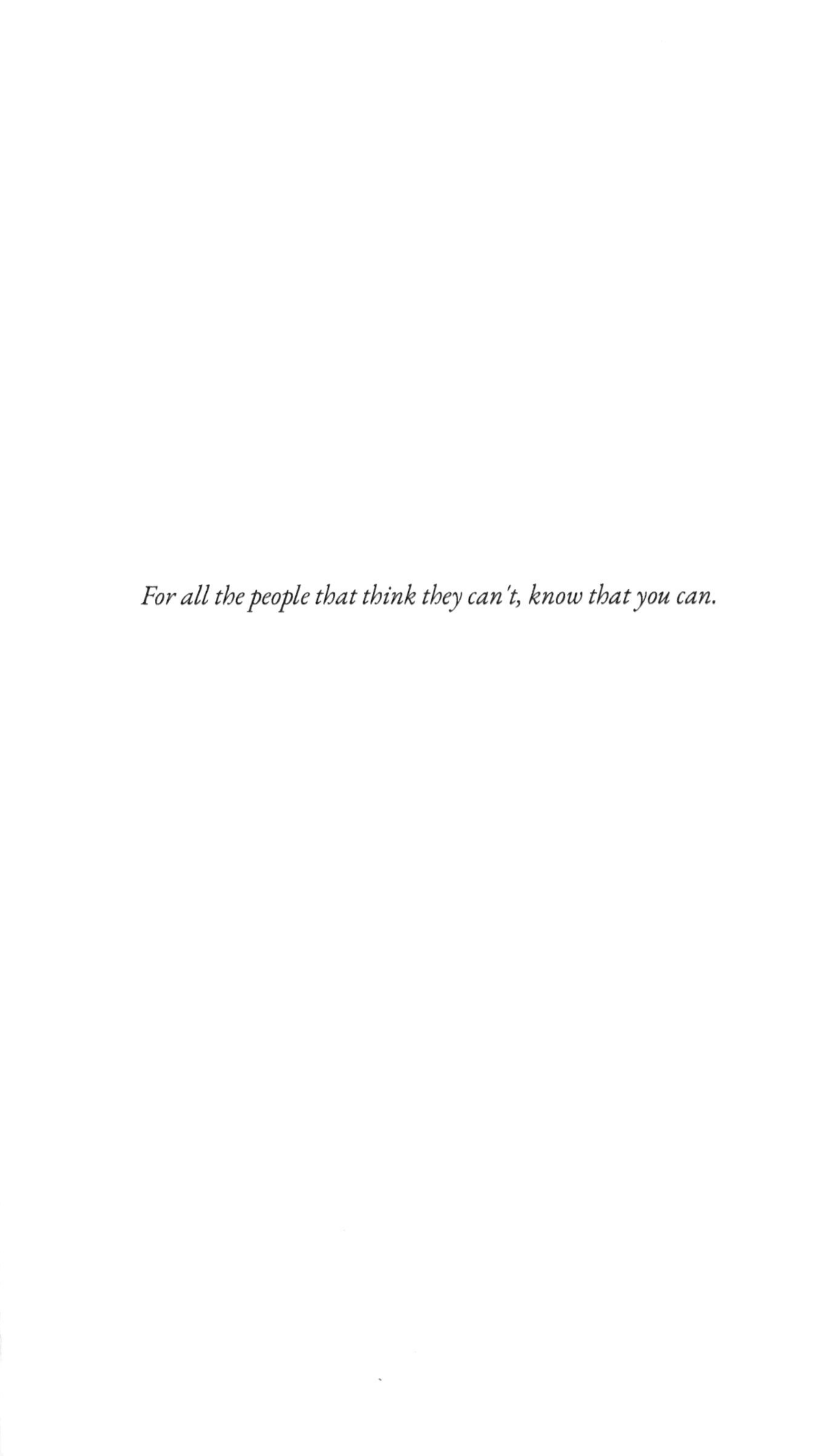

For all the people that think they can't, know that you can.

CHAPTER 1

"ALEXIA?"

I swivel my head to the right, eyes landing on the doctor in front of me. She is dressed conservatively in a peach pant suit. Her blonde hair is tied into a tight bun, and she is leaning back in her chair with her legs crossed, pen in hand waiting to write her notes and prepared to judge me.

I roll my eyes.

"I am Doctor Sorenson. Do you remember me?"

"Of course, I remember you," I spit out. "That is not how it works, and you know it," I say bitterly.

She ignores my comment. "It has been a few weeks since the incident." She pauses, waiting to see if I say anything. "Are you recalling any memories from that time or is it all still blank?"

My anger unfurls as I glare pointedly at her. She stares back at me with a bored look; she must have too many others that give her a hard time. She has built up a wall to our bullshit. I huff and lean back in the chair. I think back over the time I have been here. Though it has only been a couple of weeks I pretty much remember every minute of this place.

Right now, I am caught between waiting to be assigned to either a nuthouse or a prison cell. The first few days I was here I was restrained for my own protection, they said.

They think I don't hear them whisper but I hear them just fine. This place is a real step down from where I used to live. I think back to those memories and am saddened by where I am now.

"Alexia? Do you remember anything before you came here?" she insists.

I gaze outside the big window behind Doctor Sorenson watching the wind whip the leaves back and forth. "You already know that answer."

"You must try to remember something—a smell, a sound, an image, anything?" She straightens her back. "If you don't give me something to help you with, you know where you are going to end up. I won't be able to help you from prison."

I catch her frowning out of my peripheral as I stare out the window, ignoring her.

She purses her lips. "Do you want to go to jail for what you did?"

"I didn't do it," I say lamely.

"You were covered in blood and grime; you were in the middle of it all and are the only one left alive. How could it be anyone else?'"

As those words hit, I rub my temples, easing the ache that starts to throb between my eyes. I shake my head trying to dislodge the pain and memories, but they do not come. I could not give them what I did not know. "What does it matter if you think I am a danger, lock me up and throw away the key, then." I am tired of the questions, I am tired of not having answers myself, I pick at my nails that are ragged and ruined.

She eases back releasing the tension. "Okay, maybe we will try some easier questions first. How about that?" She waits for me to nod in acceptance. "Where did you go to school? You are 23 years old. Even if you were not going to a college, you should still remember a high school you went to, or if you were homeschooled." She looks down at the paper, reading what is written there, waiting on my answer.

"You're not going to find anything. I was homeschooled. I was taking a couple of years off to travel, and then would figure out what I wanted to major in and figure out what college I wanted to go to. That was what the traveling was for. I wanted to know where I wanted to set down my roots." I prop my head on my resting hand. "I don't know why you want to keep on harping on things like this, I have explained and went over this all previously."

Her lips press together to form a grim line. "Yes, you have, but there is no record of that. There is no record of you, Alexia Kremer. The only records we have are of the tests that we have run and anything from your stay here. It's as if you have fallen from the sky. There isn't a record of you on any virtual learning platforms or even around that neighborhood where we found you. There are no pictures of you at that house there is nothing."

A shiver runs down my spine and my head begins to throb in time with my racing heart. "No, that doesn't make sensc... No... What are you saying?" I groan as I rub at my temple.

She sets her notes to the side and uncrosses her legs, sitting up straight and leaning forward. "We tested you when you first came here. There were no drugs in your system. Have you done them in the past, though, can you recall? This could explain the memory lapses or the amnesia." She looks on with sad, knowing eyes.

I glare at her; she wants to seem like she cares, but I know she doesn't. "As I have said before, no I have not done drugs!" I burst. "Why will you not believe!"

I tug at my reddish-brown hair and tug on it until it hurts. I hiss in pain, rubbing at my head again.

"I don't know what more I can give you. Everyone forgets their younger years, why am I different? There has to be something of me somewhere." My lower lip quivers.

Doctor Sorenson stands up and walks over to me, gingerly taking my hand that is tugging at my hair in hers and eases it down so I don't harm myself more. "You must see it from our perspective. This looks extremely suspicious. We weren't able to find anything of yours in that house—not a picture or a paper with your name on it. We should have found something showing that you belong there. There were no personal artifacts that would belong to a young adult."

I pull my hand away from hers, but keep them down and fold them in my lap in front of me and scratch at my cuticles. "No, that can't be right. That doesn't sound right. Where have I been all this time?" I try to think back just over the last couple of months and am met with darkness and pain, my head shakes back and forth not believing what I am hearing.

"Exactly!" Doctor Sorenson paces. "It doesn't seem right either something so horrific happened to you that you are blocking out everything or you literally were on something that screwed you up this much." She taps her fingers against her pink lips in thought.

Her pacing makes me nervous as I watch her walk back and forth. My eyes snag on one of my fingernails; I gnaw at them. "I only know that house that I was in so I had to belong there." I try to think of something, anything to give them. "Blue walls. The room I lived in had blue walls," I suggest, unsure of the words I just spoke.

"There were no blue painted walls in any of the rooms in that house. There were no rooms that held a young girl's things that would have been your size." Her eyes turn sad as they look at me with sympathy. "Did they possibly kidnap you? There were a number of weird things in that house."

I shudder in revulsion and pick up my feet, bringing them closer to my center and hugging my knees to my face. I tap my head against my knees. "What? Those people... You think they kidnapped me?" Air comes in and out of my lungs in a rush. "Why would you say that!" I squeak out.

"It didn't appear as if you lived there and the things, we saw would not be pleasant for anyone young, unless you were into that kind of scene. We are trying to understand, to help you get back to your family, if you have one. You seem genuinely confused. We want to help." The doctor steps away and sits down, trying to bring the room back under control with calming vibes. "There are so many holes in your story that we think something else may have happened to you, something sinister that is keeping your mind from remembering." She gives a sad smile as she hints at something darker. "We just need to know what side that may have been, I can only do that if you help me help you."

I peek my eyes up from my knees and glare at her. "I don't know what you are hinting at, just spit it out!"

The pain in my head doubles as I think back to those weeks before I came here. Red paints my vision, screams pierce my ears and a lone name rings through the pain— *Alexia Kremer!*

"I knew my name when you found me," I whisper.

"Yes, or the name you have given yourself, again we have no record of an Alexia Kremer matching your description." She pouts in frustration.

"I can only give you what I know."

She nods in agreement. "I would like to try something new that we have not yet tried, if you would allow it."

I give her a look of questioning.

"Have you ever heard or done hypnotherapy?" I shake my head. "It essentially is where we put you under, kind of in a deep, deep sleep, and your mind is more able to accept or remember things that your waking mind is not ready for."

I straighten out of the ball I was curled into and even stand up and move away from her putting more distance between us. "Will it hurt?" I rub at my temple and scratch the back of my neck.

No, something whispers to me. My eyes go to the right and then back to the left; nothing is there other than the doctor and me. No one said that.

She notes my nervous energy and halfway sits on the arm of the chair instead.

I take another step back, my back hits the wall behind me. A puff of breath escapes my lips. The walls feel as if they are coming closer and closer and bend in toward me.

"Alexia," she says calmly.

My eyes move over to her. She is not moving closer, just talking to me calmly. "Yes," I squeeze out between a wheeze.

"It is not painful at all, it is like going to sleep and being in a dream state, kind of like watching a movie. You like movies, right?"

I shrug at that, but don't interrupt.

"It will play out like a movie where your mind is able to unlock things it usually cannot. We can finally make progress with some things you don't remember."

My breath comes in short puffs as my chest heaves up and down. I'm not sure I like the sound of that, of being so vulnerable.

"Relax, Alexia... relax."

My anger spikes again. "You know when someone tells you to relax, usually the opposite occurs," I throw at her.

"It will be okay. I will count down, and you will become sleepy and remember the past memories that you have forgotten," Doctor Sorenson says in a calm manner ignoring my outburst.

"Why do you always ignore me when I get angry?" I puff out. I squeeze my hands into fists wanting to throw a punch. I walk slowly instead to the chair, hesitating each step.

"Would it help to harp on those facts or would it help more to get past those emotions and work on what the real issues are?" she says matter-of-factly.

My eyes scan the room and my breathing becomes easier as I take in that information. I ease down slowly into the chair.

"Plus, most of the people that come through my office need me to get them riled up or upset, they are needing someone to cut through that to the issue at hand and help them fix what is needed," she states.

"I do want answers," I whisper. My eyes turn down, looking at the carpet. "You seem nice, and I get it—you are doing your job. I am not trying to make your job harder; I really am trying to remember."

"I believe you, believe me I am just trying to help you." Her face softens. "Please just try this, I feel like this will help."

I take a deep breath. "Fine," and breathe out once again. Trying to calm everything inside. "We will try this." I glare at her, my eyes distrusting her. "But if this doesn't work, *I am done*." I enunciate each syllable of the last three words.

She nods and gets up slowly from her half sitting position and walks over to the chaise that is seated closer to the door. She turns her chair around, so it is facing me. "Please lie here instead of sitting in that uncomfortable chair. It will help you relax, and you will have to trust me to go into a deep sleep."

I nod and get up, staggering my steps slowly, trying to take extra time to get there unsure of if I wanted to open the can of worms that my head was obviously keeping from me.

"Good, good. Lean back, not too cold, are you?"

I give her a weird expression and shake my head and huff as I lie down, propping my feet up. I swish the pillows around behind me to get in the right spot. "Now what?" I look at her pointedly. I set my hands next to my legs then clasp them over my flat stomach.

She walks away, and the tapping of her pointed shoes brings her to stand at her desk. A clicking starts.

"What is that?" My fists curl up and my body tenses. I ease up to see what she is doing.

"A metronome. It helps keep a steady rhythm or beat so you can remain calm, and your heart stays in tempo with it to keep you that way." She nods and walks back towards the chair. Sitting down as well, she grabs the pad of paper and waits for me to unwind once again.

I sit back and lean against the pillowed softness, releasing the tension in my hands. I still keep them clasped over my stomach and try to sink into the pillows behind me. "When will it start?" I ask, listening to the tick tock of the noise.

"When it needs to," she says simply.

"Hmmm," I hum. I close my eyes, shutting out everything just for a moment. It feels nice to just rest and relax regardless of if we get something from it or not.

"Five..." Doctor Sorenson breathes out.

My hands loosen their grip and just rest on my shirt, the fabric soft against my scratchy palms.

"Four..." she says slowly.

My head leans to the side, and I breathe in deeper.

"Three..." she whispers.

I feel myself start to float away and grow very heavy.

"Two..." The clicking of the metronome goes back and forth.

I yawn and exhale and feel myself succumbing to the darkness.

"One..." she says with soft finality. "Alexia... Open your eyes, what do you see right now?"

My eyes spring open at her command. I look around and cannot see much of anything. "I am in a sea of darkness. I can barely see my hands. It feels like I am floating though."

"Are you afraid?"

"No, it's nice actually." I smile. "It's peaceful, I hope this is how it feels when one departs from life."

"I hope so, too," she agrees. "Do you hear anything?"

"No..." I concentrate and try to hear something, anything. "I don't think so," my voice stutters.

"Just rest and relax, no worries if you don't just let me know if you do." She urges.

I chuckle and laugh a little, moving my left-hand underneath me.

"What was that?" she questions.

"Nothing, just a tickle." A chuckle dies in my throat as I concentrate back on listening.

"Do you feel..."

"Wait. I hear something..." I tip my head the other direction hoping to hear better. "It's muffled." I scratch at my ears and rub them.

"Keep with it," Doctor Sorenson says.

I tug on my lobes, trying to open up my ears.

"Can you hear me, Alexia?" a voice booms. My hands shake as I lower them back down.

"I can," I whisper back so as not to scare the voice off.

"Can what, Alexia?" Doctor Sorenson asks.

"I heard someone," I say, still whispering. "I think I did."

"It's okay, just let it go. If it wants to talk again, it will, but don't chase after it. Just feel, hear, and see what you can for now."

I sink into the darkness. "I would rather like to know what happens, or what is supposed to happen, that is." I sigh.

"Unfortunately, this is your mind's space, anything can happen if you want it to. But know you are safe and if for any reason things seem to be upsetting you or if you don't want to do it anymore just say so and I will stop things," she says with sincerity.

"Okay," I utter. My breath shakes as I exhale.

"I, again, am here for you. Your best interest is what I have in my mind at all times."

"Uh huh."

"Though you may not think it, you are in control. I can't force you to say, see, or hear what you do not really want to."

My body rolls as if a wave has hit me, and I scramble my hands to the side to keep me seated in place. "What is going on?"

"What do you mean?" Doctor Sorenson asks.

"I was just lying here in my sea of darkness, and it rolled me. Didn't I move?" I sit up, trying to get a better idea of what is around me.

"Not everything that happens to you happens in the real world, your mind feels it but your body is safe here. Alexia nothing that is in your mind will happen to you physically."

"But."

"Alexia. Hear me, nothing that happens in your mind will happen to you physically. You will experience things, but they will not affect you here in the waking world." She puts force behind her words.

"I guess," I whine.

"You must know it to be true," she says stronger.

"Yes, it is true," I repeat.

"What is the first memory that you can remember?"

My face scrunches up, thinking back. "I remember my time here. I remember the car ride to here."

"Remember further back to the earliest memory that you have, one that is the furthest to reach."

"I... I..." I search through the fog trying to find a light to stick with. An image begins to manifest. "There are colors that are swirled together."

"Good, stay with that. Are they forming anything?"

"Uhhh, not sure."

"Keep calm, just breathe and let the image come to you, don't force the memory," she says with a serene voice.

Her serene voice soothes me deeper into concentration and my heartbeat begins to slow. "It's kind of hard to see as if mist or fog is covering it."

After a few minutes, she speaks up. "Perhaps if you envisioned wind clearing away the fog that deters you then you could see it clearer. You are the only one that can stop you from seeing what you want."

I do as she says, too, and the image clears out a bit. Dark colors swirl above me. They move in motion and take on a form. It is close but just out of arm's reach. "I see someone."

"What are they doing? Can you reach them?"

I reach out my arms, feeling the cool touches of a frosty wind that are no longer just in my thoughts. The wind whips at my chubby arms, and the shadow takes shape in that of a woman. "My arms are too little. There is a woman with dark hair above me," I say loudly to compensate for the wind that is howling in my ears.

The woman's head whips back and forth. She emits a distorted scream. "Make her stop!" I shout. "She is screaming."

"Why is she screaming? What is she doing? What does she look like?"

The piercing scream grows louder. "I can't!" I shrink down trying to move away from the harsh sound.

"Shhhh," she soothes. "Take a step back. Whatever is happening to you is not real. Remember, this is just a memory."

I step away from the form and step out where I am on even ground with the woman, she is no longer looking down at me. "There the sound isn't as bad. I am next to what looks like a crib.

Would that be me?" I look at myself but only see a shadow around me. "Why is there a shadow around me? I can't see my baby self?"

"It could be because you don't know what you looked like as a baby. It could be a way to explain the missing memories. We will come back to that another time for now just focus on the scene."

"The woman is backing up away from me, or child me. Her hair is dark and cascades around her, the wind is tossing it back and forth." My eyes roam around seeing if she is in the middle of a storm. "She looks like she is in the middle of a tornado."

"Good go on."

I hear her scratching down notes on her paper.

After she is done writing she notices I have not spoken yet. "Can you see what she is wearing or what her face looks like?" she prompts.

I try to move forward, forcing the picture to be clear. "Every time I move closer, the picture dissolves and becomes fuzzy." I say clearly frustrated.

I try to pull the memory to me, forcing it to become clear, it is fighting me as if it doesn't want to be remembered. I grab at it with both hands as if it were an actual picture and it slips and slides right through my fingers, the memory runs away from me as if it had legs of its own.

"No," I say defeated. "It is gone... I tried."

"Okay." Sorenson sighs. "Relax, let the memory go and let the rest of it lift away from you, go back to your sea of darkness where you were most comfortable."

I slump back into the floating abyss of serenity. I shrink away from the difficulty of trying to remember something that seems to be blocked and does not want to be remembered. "I wish I could just stay here," I whisper.

"If only." The doctor chuckles softly.

"No worries or people to harass me about anything." I sigh. "It would be a dream come true."

"I want you to remember the night your parents passed away," she says in a soft, hushed voice. "Do you think you can do that?"

The question echoes around me. I am ripped from my solitude of darkness and thrown into a nightmare of blood and guts strewn about as if it were a Jackson Pollock painting. "What is this!" I screech.

"What is what? What are you seeing?"

"There are bodies and blood everywhere!" I hiss. I don't breathe in, not wanting to smell the rotten bodies. I shake my head trying to dislodge the scent. "I want out! There is blood." The blood inches closer to my bare feet.

"You aren't really there. Be still and calm. This is a memory. It happened in the past, remove yourself from the picture like you did the last time," she says.

"As if it is that simple," I taunt.

I try to shove myself away as I did last time and end up nowhere quickly. The blood still is working its way towards me. My head twitches to the side as I see red dots appear out of my periphery. "My hands are covered in blood," I say.

My voice is edged in terror, but I try to hold it together. I pull up my arm and see the blood cascade down to my elbow and drip down onto the hardwood floors.

"Don't focus on that, what do you hear or smell? Focus on something else other than sight?" She stutters, and scribbles furiously.

I sniff and almost lose what little I have in my stomach. "That is horrendous!" I yell. "I can smell bile and waste, but the tang of blood is strong." The blood sticks to my fingers as I swish them around. Sweat runs down the middle of my back and forehead. I feel no cool wind; it is hot and humid. "I am so hot," I say sadly. "I don't know if I can do this."

"You can, I believe in you. Remember, you are not actually doing this right now. I just want to understand what happened. Is the blood fresh?"

"Yes, it is still dripping off my hands."

"Is all the blood bright red or dark and black."

I look around and try to move on my tiptoes edging around the pools of blood and bodies. "Some of the blood is bright and fresh, some of it is darker, but that is closer to the front of the room. I can't get there not without stepping *on* someone or *in* something." I shudder at the thought.

Though the heat permeates me, I am frozen on the inside. I dare not hug myself and rub my arms. I look down, and the blood looks as if it were trying to swallow me whole, making me into this color instead of who I really am. I move my fingers, keeping them mobile, watching the drops that slide down my fingers. They make dots on the brown wood floor.

"I need you to move closer to the front. See if you notice anyone or see anyone you remember. I have a picture of the homeowners and we need to make sure that is who you remember."

"Why didn't you ask me before we started?" I ask suspiciously.

"You didn't remember anything. It would have been useless. Plus, we don't want you to create false memories," she says factually. "I will need you to describe them if you can."

I cringe as inch forward dipping my toes in the warm blood. "It's just water, it's just water," I repeat to myself. "Though water does not cling to the skin and coat everything in crimson." My throat closes off making impossible to swallow.

"That's it, keep going," she urges. Furious scratching hangs in the air as she writes her notes once more.

I edge to the side to go around a couple of bodies that were blocking my way, taking care to step carefully and not slip. The fireplace is on the left with pictures on a mantle. "I have pictures." I stop and stare at each of their faces. "There is a man and a woman that are standing next to each other." My eyes squint to try to bring the picture into focus. "Those are my parents!" I say excitedly. "See I belong here." I hold on to the edge of the mantel to keep my balance.

"Are there any pictures of you? Where are you looking?"

My eyes swing around for more pictures, there are a few on a side table but they only hold my parents. "No." I bite my tongue.

"Okay I want you to think really hard on this. What are their names?" she waits.

I look at the pictures willing the names to come to me. A twinge of pain arches up into my head and my arm. I grab onto my arm, my hand slipping from the blood. A rough voice pours out of my mouth as I fall to my knees, my forehead bangs against the wall next to the fireplace. My eyes keep pinned on the pictures.

"Why?" I whine.

Pain arcs through me as shadows dance in front of my eyes covering their faces. I peer down and the shadows flow out from beneath me. They cover my arm fully where the blood was. It elongates and stretches into a demonic claw with sharp tips.

"What the fuck is going on!" I scrambled away from the wall, jumping to my feet.

"Do you remember?"

My right-hand shakes, trying to make the darkness and claw disappear. I glance down to my left and find it unscathed, clear with no shadows wrapping around it. "Get me out of here!" I bellow. Whispers surround me as I dance away.

"You have to remember," she urges.

I move the claw back and forth in front of my face and swipe the claw across my other arm. I barely press down and feel it slice across my bicep. "Ahhh. It's sharp," I hiss.

"What is sharp, a knife? Do you have a knife?" she whispers.

I shake my head, but do not utter anymore. Blood drips down the gash I created. "Like butter, strong like steel," I utter.

"Do you have a weapon?"

"No," I bite out.

"Then what is sharp?"

I bite my tongue, refusing to let the words out, my inner voice bubbles out. "Shadows."

"Shadows?" she questions. "Are you sure?"

"Yes," I say, simply not wanting to keep going, it would just be more incriminating.

I glare at the claw, concentrating on it, trying to peer into the darkness. I see the darkness retract away from my fingers and fade away. Both of my hands shake after the black shadow is gone.

"Why? How!?"

My mind races, trying to wrap my mind around it. It refuses to understand what just happened. "This can't be real."

"Your mind might be covering something up, if you describe what is happening, I might be able to explain."

"It is too crazy. I can't do this. Please don't make me."

Doctor Sorenson hum's to herself a bit but continues on. "It's okay, let's keep moving with this but we will come back to it at another time."

My mind fights for some semblance of normalcy. "There is no way I wasn't on something. What else could it have been? This could not have really happened."

"When you came in, we tested you for drugs as I have stated. We didn't find anything but that doesn't mean that there wasn't something there and burned out before we could test for it. Or it could be something we didn't think to test for," she huffs in annoyance.

This puts me at ease, and I continue on looking around at the scene before me. Dark shadows pull in close. "There are shadows everywhere."

"Shadows?" she asks.

The shadows pull together. "They look like ink, and are very dark and act like liquid."

"What happens next in this memory?"

The ink pulls together from every corner of the room and makes a tall human form. "He is pure darkness," I answer, my voice low and flat.

"Who is he?" she asks eagerly. "How do you know it is a he?"

The light pulls away from his inky form. "His essence is all male there is no question or doubt." He stands at full height and towers over me, he floats above the mess of the living room, not making a sound. "He doesn't touch the ground," I whisper.

"Who is he? Your mind must be protecting you from this person," she edges.

He floats in front of me, but there is no anger, and he is not menacing. He makes arms appear out of his form and caresses my back.

"He cares. He is trying to calm me... I think."

"What do you mean? Remember, I am not seeing what you are, so I only have your words to go on," she seethes with a bit of frustration.

"I felt better the instant he started caressing my back."

He continues to brush away the rage and darkness that clouds my mind.

The name pulls out of me. "Thanks, Shade."

Shade?

"Where did the name come from?" I ask.

"Who is Shade? Are you starting to remember? Are you not afraid of him?"

"Not exactly," I stutter in silence. "I don't know the name or what it may mean. No, he brings peace."

"Continue," she barks.

"Shade." I whisper the name over and over again trying to dislodge something in my mind. "Please work with me, I need... No, I must remember."

A sharp pain breaks over my head. "Aghhhh not again." My hands come up and touch my head as it fractures in two. I see flashbacks of a boy who lives down the street. "Shade! Come back, I'm sorry!"

The boy is cast in shadows "Was this my childhood best friend?" I ask myself.

Flashes move through my mind; I am chasing after his shadowy form. "*I'm sorry. I know you can't speak and can only communicate by nodding or shaking your head,*" I cry. "*I wasn't making fun, I swear.*"

"He is a boy from my childhood I believe," I hiss between shallow breaths, breathing through the pain.

"Shade." She scratches notes down once again.

"He doesn't speak." I shake my head slightly reiterating what I see to Doctor Sorenson.

"Anything else that you can remember?"

I keep quiet and continue to concentrate on what is before me. The memory fades, and I am back in the house full of bodies. "No going back now, I want to figure this out," I say with anger in my voice so maybe the shadowy form will believe me along with the doctor. "I am going to let things play out and see what exactly happens," I say, more to convince myself than anyone.

Shade's shadow-like head bobs in agreement with me as if he could hear me and tell what I am saying even now instead of then. His form shrinks down as he hovers in the air. He brushes over the slash on my bicep with one of his inky dark wisps that look like a hand. He caresses my arm as he slides it over the cut and continues to dwindle in size.

"Why is he so small now?" I ask as I see him continue to shrink.

He floats over my arm in his inky form, which is so small now, and continues up my arm to my shoulder.

"It's acting like a tattoo now. The shadow is laying down on my skin!" I grab onto my shoulder. "I don't have a tattoo, do I?"

"Not that we have found," she says in a crisp voice. "Remember, we did a full work up when you came in, so we checked for these things so no, no tattoos."

I feel him flutter there against my left shoulder blade, but settle down. "It's like he is hiding," I state. "Or keeping close to follow me wherever I go." The blood is becoming dry and sticky on my hands. The pool of blood reaches my toes. "Get it away," I call out, as I scramble away. I don't want the color to swallow me whole.

As I climb backwards, I don't notice the bodies that are piled behind me. I fall back on my butt, tripping over them. My eyes come to rest on what is settled near my feet.

"This thing doesn't even look like a body," I spit out as my stomach begins to roll.

My eyes stare at it, wanting to make sense of what is before me. I stare and cannot move from it until the puzzle is figured out.

"It is shredded to pieces. There is a torso but everything else, I am less sure about."

"Are you able to see more of the body?" she asks.

"I can't not look at it," I say in answer.

"Man or woman, and where is your location?" she asks quickly.

Though I can see around me, my eyes stay glued on the body at my feet. "About five or six paces away from the fireplace. Woman... I think it's slender, but the top half is missing... Oh God, there are bones sticking out of it."

I quickly look away and breathe in deeply and out through my nose. My eyes land on an arm and hand a few inches away.

"There is a man's hand attached to an arm, but that is all."

My feet are coated in blood, so I carefully get to my feet and try not to slip. I look towards the ceiling, not wanting to see the bodies before me.

A red-light blinks on and off in quick succession. I turn slowly back to the front of the room, away from the fireplace. It pulls me like a moth to a flame.

"There is a light," I say in a dreamlike state. I walk toward it, not even paying attention where I am stepping. "I must go."

"What is the light coming from?" she asks.

It continues to blink on and off, but I bring my hand up to block my eyes a bit. "Is that an altar?"

"It could be, there was one there at the house. What are you seeing?"

"There are knives and cups, a book..."

"And what about the blinking lights? What is that coming out of?"

I feel as if I am crawling through this memory. As I grow closer to the altar, my body begins to slow down as if it is fighting me on this. I am a step away after what seems like hours and I finally see where the light is coming from.

"It looks like a black skull. It's not Halloween, is it?" I say in confusion.

"Hmmm." Nothing else comes from her.

My lips pinch in anger, but I keep moving forward, wanting to touch the skull or handle it.

"I need answers.".

My arms reach out and my fingers run over the rough edges of the eye socket. The red light turns off, and the dark eye socket stares at me.

"The light stopped after I touched it."

"Where did you go with the skull? Or what happened?" she asks.

I pick up the dark skull, flipping it over to study it. "Would I be able to tell if it was real or not?" I question.

"The skull? Not without further testing."

I nod and go to set it down. *Remember,* is pushed into my mind, and I stumble back, still having a hold of the skull, clutching it to me.

The voice is a whisper barely even heard. *Shade is your protector. He will guide you and keep you safe.* Another thought pushes into me. *The bad people no longer have a hold on you. But you are still not out of danger.* The thought echoes through my mind.

"Danger?" I echo.

"Danger? Are you in danger?" she asks. "I need something, Alexia. You have to tell me what is going on."

Don't forget. A final thought echoes away from me, as if whispering from somewhere far away.

"How can I remember? I mustn't forget!" I exclaim; my voice catches.

"Why would you want to remember, is a better question? It sounds like your mind is protecting you from something horrible," she says sadly.

As I think over the memory, I say, "Unfortunately, once you see something and understand it is hard to unsee it, no matter how hard you try to forget."

"What happened?" she asks softly.

"I forgot everything. Nothing I remember is correct. How can I or someone cause me to forget everything that I am?" I spiral. "I will probably forget even this memory if no others have stuck with me."

"Alexia, are you still with me? You are not making any sense. What gives you that idea?" Doctor Sorenson questions. Her pitch in her voice sounds like she is slightly irritated with me for not answering any of her questions.

"How do I keep from forgetting?" I shoot right back at her, ignoring her questions. "I need to remember all of this. What is keeping me from remembering, do you think I will forget this all once again?" I say in a panicked voice.

"Alexia, I need you to calm down and answer my questions. I will help you remember but I can only do that if you tell me what is going on," she says in a stern voice.

I exhale loudly. "Yes, I remember some of the night, but not enough to piece together what happened. These people were bad, I know that much." I try to distance myself by walking away from the memory tired of looking at disfigured bodies. I didn't need to keep seeing this horror show. "Or I was told that much."

"How do you know they were bad? Who told you? Do you remember anything leading up to their deaths?" she asks, getting a little short with me. Her voice is breathless with anticipation of getting somewhere with this questioning.

"A claw—mine, I think. A shadow… that disappears into a tattoo. A skull, the altar… Nothing about this is right. What were they into?"

"That is what we are trying to figure out," she states calmly.

"I don't want to forget," I cry out. My arm flails to my shoulder blade where the black shadow disappeared. "You are supposed to protect me! Don't let me forget!" I scream out.

"Alexia, it's okay, you will remember. Shade is either made up, protecting your mind and is actually not letting you remember, or Shade is a real living person and might actually have the answers to what happened to you, to this place, to everything!" she bursts out with me.

A blanket of darkness falls down on me and smothers me as if I am a flame. I try pushing against the darkness with my hands and mind, trying to find a way out. "No, I need more. I needed to go back to my memories."

"What is happening?" she says breathlessly, her voice very close now.

I feel her hands on me.

"Your body is convulsing. I need you to stay calm, your mind is trying to reject this," Dr. Sorenson says calmly.

"I don't understand." My teeth bite down on my tongue as I try to speak. My pain breaks through the choking darkness.

"Your memories can be like a dream. You can create things in it to try to help you or hinder you as your mind sees fit," she rushes out. "This will take patience and time; it doesn't just happen overnight. With practice it can help you and give you the control you need."

"That doesn't really help me now does it?" I say in a rage, the darkness eases up and stops outright choking.

"Calm down," she waits. "More now. You have stopped seizing, but I don't want you to go through that again. Nothing is wrong, you just need to try to think of a less difficult memory, one that isn't as hard to remember or one less strenuous on the mind, like what did you do yesterday?" she presses on.

"I.... I..." I stutter as I try to do what she asks of me. I search for other memories swimming through the darkness, searching for a light. My head begins to feel pressure on the sides, I am pushed and tumble blindly forward into the darkness. "It knows. Something knows!"

"There is no bad guy here, it is only your mind. You are doing this to yourself. Take charge and be in control."

"Easy for you to say!" I growl. My head is aching. A deep throb runs through my mind pushing me to give up. "Your head isn't the one that feels like it is going to explode, now, is it?" I say haughtily. "Shade!" My mind is splintering in two, and I am slowly losing my grip on reality.

"Shade can't protect you. He is not real."

"What's real?" I utter in defeat; my body and mind go lax. "Does anything exist?" I feel almost broken.

Doctor Sorenson said these things weren't real, but they feel real to me. How were they affecting me if they weren't? Confusion clouds my thoughts and makes me struggle with reality just that much more.

I laugh as I feel something move up my wrist toward my upper arm. My body is still in a cocoon of darkness, but the pressure isn't as bad here. It eases as I start to lose hope and give up. "What's that?"

"What's what?" Her voice has moved from further back.

"Are you touching me?" I question looking over my body, but give up as I cannot see anything in the dark.

"No, what are you feeling?"

"Like something is tickling me." I breathe out. Am I not alone? Is Shade here? I will have to find out for myself later... If I remember.

"Nothing is touching you here," she states, moving back over me to double check. "Is Shade there?"

I berate myself for ever telling her that name; she is like a dog with a bone. "I don't know. I think he may be trying to help though," I quickly say, hoping she will ease up.

"Tell me about where you are now. What is happening? What do you see?"

"I am in a sea of darkness again, but now it feels more like a blanket smothering me rather than open like the sea when I first got here. It feels more menacing, like something is watching me in the dark."

"Okay, let's keep going. Let's see how far we can push this."

"How far are you willing to go?" I ask exasperated. "Can't you just accept defeat?" I know I can. I wanted to stop before she killed me for the information that I held. I get it that she wants to figure out what was going on, but at what expense?

Whatever it is, seems to be listening to me, and it descends on me, the menacing anger dissipated. With it growing closer to me, I want to let it all go and fall away. Give into the darkness and accept my fate.

"I am losing," I say. "I'm tired." The fight went out of me just as quickly as it came.

"No, you are so close," she urges.

The blanket keeps wrapping around me tightly, suffocating me. I try to clear my throat to get some air, but it closes up as well. "I need out," I whisper.

"I will pull you out if needed. I need to know what is happening."

It won't let me speak anymore; it has closed off everything. I have to wait until she decides to pull me out or I die. I try to struggle or claw at the cloth, but it just moves with my hands. Those sharp claws are nowhere in sight and neither was Shade. "I thought you were my protector," I whisper with what breath I have left.

"I am here. Is everything okay?" Doctor Sorenson asks worriedly. Something must have spooked her because her voice came closer. "Alexia?" She leans over and is touching my unresponsive body. "You will begin to wake up as I count down and will remember everything that has occurred," she says rapidly. "Five, four, three, two, and one."

I gasp and come up into a sitting position. I wrap my arms around my torso and try to catch my breath. A pressure tightens on my right side; I grip my side, forcing it to stop throbbing. Something flutters against my fingertips. *Tattoo?*

"Are you okay?" she asks, her fingers run over as she takes my wrist in her hands and checks my pulse.

I glare at her from the dark curtain of my hair. "What was that?" I ask, still trying to catch my breath.

"You were so close!" she exclaims. "You were so close to remembering. If you could only get out of your own way," she says sternly.

"That didn't feel like I was fighting myself. It felt as if something wanted me to stop searching my memories no matter the consequences." I cringe at the sharp pain that hammers at the back of my head.

She gives me a vehement look. "You are the only one who could force you out of your own head. There is nothing weird happening here. Yes, you might have been in some weird stuff with those people. There were a lot of supernatural items that we found in the house, but that does not mean it is actually real." She walks back and stops the ticking of the metronome, and the room becomes silent.

"Perhaps you just need some rest, and then we can try again in the morning."

"I am not doing that again." I throw out my hand to the chair as I quickly get up and stand away from it. "You almost killed me!"

"You're exaggerating," she states as she leans against her glass desk.

"I am not." The thumping in my head drums in tempo with my racing heart. I try to slow my breathing and take a few steps to the door. My eyesight dims at the edges and grows fuzzy. I stumble into her chair on my way to the door. "What is wrong with me?"

"What's wrong?" she asks at the same time. She comes forward.

I stagger away from her. "No..." I do not want her to touch me again. "I'm... Okay. Yeah." I nod my head and walk slowly to the door. "I just think it was a lot today, and I need to rest."

"Mary," Doctor Sorenson calls out as I open the door. A tall, thin, blonde-haired woman stands close to the door. "Will you please make sure Alexia gets to her room, okay? She is a little shaky on her feet."

"Of course." Mary nods and her arms curl around me, guiding me back to my room.

Mary doesn't say much as she helps me. The building we are in is not that big and doesn't have very many rooms. This is not a place meant to stay at, just a go between. A place that houses people like me, dealing with ongoing investigations.

Later, I will be judged by the evidence gathered where they will send me to prison. The evidence I could already see piling against me.

As I round the doorway to my room, my stomach drops. "I am going to be sick." I race out of her arms and into my room, not even stopping to turn on the lights.

They pop on a short time after I hit the bathroom that is off of my room. I miss a step and run into the sink. It slams into me, and my breath exits in a whoosh. I dry heave as the air leaves me.

"Whoa there." Her arms are around me again and help me toward the toilet. She sets me down gently and pulls up the lid. "Careful."

I empty my stomach contents into the toilet. I hear the rushing water start shortly after. She grabs a washcloth and wrings it through a few times. I see her outside of my periphery, but it is hard to keep my eyes on her as my stomach curls in on itself.

After a few minutes, the cold rag touches the back of my neck and feels very nice and refreshing. "Thank you," I utter as I hit the flusher and sit back against the bathroom wall.

"You're welcome." She throws a hand out to help me up. "Let's get your face washed and then into bed. You had too much excitement today."

I nod and do as she says. She will not push me or force me into anything I don't want to. She, unlike the doctor, only wants to help. I wash my face and fall into the waiting bed. It is not long before my eyes shut, and I am out almost as soon as my head hits the pillow.

Chapter 2

I WAKE UP TO someone shaking my shoulder, the sun is beaming into the only window in the room. "Hey, girl. It's time to get up. Dr. Sorenson is ready for you," a bulky man hollers.

"Where's Mary?" I ask as I rub the sleep from my eyes.

"Her shift ended earlier this morning."

"What time is it?" I moan. I would rather have Mary here than this behemoth of a man.

"It's already noon." This giant looks at me as if I am crazy.

"What?" I scramble up into a sitting position to look out the window. The sun is high in the sky. "How could I sleep so long? I slept through breakfast and my early morning session."

"Yeah, Mary said you got sick and to let you rest, but the doctor is wanting to check on you and make sure you get something in your stomach." He gives a sad look. He shrugs and backs away from me. "We will stop by the doctor first, though."

I nod my head and get to my feet, shoving them in the authorized slippers they distributed to me when I got here. My stomach cramps up, causing me to double over in pain. I can't tell if it is just from hunger or from nerves. I go slowly, trying to hold my stomach, keeping it in place.

I shuffle after the man that woke me up, as he is moving through the doorway and down the corridor already. I smack my lips together, trying to make them less dry. We pass by a small room that is set up for lunch.

"Since you almost lost it back there, we will stop and get you something first, then go to Doctor Sorenson. She won't mind." He smiles and waits by the door, letting me pick something to eat and drink from the lunch items that they still have available.

I look up at him; his frame is huge and tree-like compared to my 5-foot-2 slight frame. On quiet feet, I slide across the linoleum floor to grab some bread and water to get rid of my cottonmouth.

"Where is everyone?" I ask as I see only us around.

"It's towards the end of lunch. Everyone already came and got what they needed." He nods to the lady that is waiting to clean up after my selection.

I nod as well. "Thank you."

Some of the people here are like me, fine and able to walk around freely. There are a few, though, that were locked up. That is what happened to me when I first came here.

Those weeks were horrendous. Constantly being strapped down. I shudder at what I went through. Though I do understand why they did it; I was half crazed and out of my mind. My eyes slide back up to the guard who now looks bored with my sluggish and slow movements. He stomps off down the hallway expecting me to follow in his wake.

I nibble on my bread, hoping it will soak up the sourness I still feel in my stomach. As we come to the door, I guzzle a bit of my water down. He gives one lone solid knock before walking into Doctor Sorenson's office.

"Good afternoon, Alexia."

"Hey," I mumble. I pad my way to the overstuffed chair and drop myself into it, already feeling exhaustion seep into my bones. I lean my head back.

Doctor Sorenson nods. "Thank you," she says in dismissal. She turns back to me after she watches him close the door. "Okay, so yesterday we tried hypnotherapy, and it looks like we got somewhere with that. How are you feeling today? Mary said you weren't doing too well." She frowns as she walks closer and leans against the desk, which is closer to the chair I chose.

"Yeah, I am okay. I think that it was a little much all at once," I say, wanting to continue, but also wanting to let her know so she could keep it slow.

She nods. "Okay, I just wanted to make sure you were well enough to go on today."

I nod once again, but keep my words to myself.

"I am going to go over what you said and saw yesterday, there may be possibilities or thoughts you may have on the scene that you saw. Get more of an understanding. Then maybe you won't be so afraid to try it again and will know how your mind can play tricks on you." She smiles and walks over to sit in the chair opposite of me.

"Fair enough."

"Okay, yesterday you said you saw a claw or a shadow? Can you explain exactly what you saw? You seemed really confused and frightened at that part, and that was after you saw all the bodies piled around you." She sits on the edge of her seat and grabs a pen and pad of paper, poised to write everything down.

"Huh?" A high-pitched whining noise sounds in my right ear. It isn't painful, just annoying to listen to while trying to understand what the doctor is saying.

She looks at me, and then back to her notes. "A claw and or a shadow? You talked about it yesterday."

"Was it a shadow claw, or just a claw and shadow separately?" I rub my ear, hoping the incessant noise will stop soon.

"Don't you remember?" she asks suspiciously. "Do you remember Shade? You called out for him many times. He was this shadow creature in your mind."

"Shade?" I rub my head. "He is a long-time friend that lives down the way from me. I don't know why I would call out his name though?" I reply in confusion, though happy to be able to answer one of her questions finally. The whistling in my ear lowers and eases.

"Hmmm. Was he there with you in the house?"

"I.... I... Dunno." I think back and am hit with a roadblock.

"Okay, let's start at the beginning. It started off with a very distant memory of a woman... and then moved to the night of the murders. What about the claw or shadow thing that you saw? Was there someone there with you in the house when the murders occurred, maybe Shade?" she questions again.

The sharp piercing noise picks up again in both of my ears. "What are you talking about?" I bellow, not able to concentrate. "What claw? What shadow?" I pull on my ears, trying to open up the ear canal so the ringing will stop.

"You called out his name many times, but right before I woke you, you said he was supposed to protect you." Her kind but hard eyes fall on me, noticing my discomfort. "Is something wrong are you not remembering again?"

"There is this high pitched, shrill ringing in my ear." Her face falls as she sees that I am not being cooperative and wanting to answer her questions. "I am trying."

"Perhaps you should see a doctor since you are having a lot of headaches lately. I can schedule you with them tomorrow. Maybe they can give you something for that."

I feel heat rush to my cheeks. "I don't need more drugs! I need answers!" I say through clenched teeth. I rise out of the chair as I cross my arms and grip my sides. My stomach rolls with unease. "It just seems like every time I try to remember something, my head starts hurting or my ears start messing with me."

Doctor Sorenson leans back into her chair, her eyes wide, as I pace in front of her. "Alexia, please, you need to calm down. Don't you see that this is very suspicious behavior saying you want answers and to help, but then having these things come up that block our help or block us from learning what really happened? You have to see it from our perspective."

"Calm down!?" I glance at her with a fierce, shrewd look. "You expect me to stay calm with everything that is happening! I am so tired of this place and you people. I just want to go. I want my life back!" I rage.

"We are trying to give that back to you, but you don't even know where home or your life is. We don't know where that is for you. That's the point of this—we don't see that you have had a life before we found you at that house," she says in a calm and hushed tone.

"How could I not have had a life? I told you what I could remember. If you can't figure out what's going on, maybe it's because you are looking in the wrong places!"

She eases up from her chair, leaning against the front of her desk. "Perhaps if you could tell us more about this shadow you saw, that would help us look in another direction. You are showing signs of abuse. Even when you came in there were marks on your arm like from a syringe, but no drugs that we could trace. We want to know who this shadow person is so maybe we can help get you the answers you need." She stands up and backs away towards her desk, backing away from me giving me space.

"I don't know where you're getting this shadow person from. I already told you guys I don't remember anything from the night my parents died." I circle around the room and yank on my short stringy hair that is pulled up into a ponytail. "I can't understand this, am I not making sense?"

The high-pitched noise comes back with a loud screech, like gears rubbing together.

"Parents? They cannot be your parents. Don't you remember what we talked about yesterday? What do you remember after coming in here to talk?" she asks slowly.

"I..." I think over yesterday. "I remember talking about trying to remember, and that we did hypnotherapy."

"Good, and what else?"

"Umm," I say nervously. "There was darkness." I look up to read her facial features; they push me forward for more. "A house?" I say less sure, her face falls. "Why can I not remember? You were supposed to help me remember!" I yell.

"This is progress, but you shouldn't be forgetting things this soon. We barely touched on the horror of what happened in that house, and your mind is still blacking out everything that has to do with that." She scratches a note on her desk. "Interesting though it is, we need answers."

"I don't know what you are talking about! Stop lying to me! I don't remember any of this," I hiss in anger, stepping towards her menacingly.

She quickly hops back on her desk and reaches for some buttons on her desk phone and yells frantically into the receiver. "I need someone in here right away! Patient is becoming too agitated."

I stare at her with wide, fearful eyes. "I didn't do anything. Why are you doing this!?" I yell. Why are they blaming me again for something I didn't do? I back away from her and the door. "I thought we were past this."

The door bangs open, and the intimidating orderly is back with another person to help him. They both hold onto black square boxes moving towards me, crowding me into a corner.

I glance between the two of them still backing up, my back connects hard against the wall behind me. "I didn't do anything," I whine. I search the room for somewhere to run away from all this or somewhere to hide.

They advance on me slowly, knowing they have me cornered.

They crowd me against the wall.

"Why aren't you listening to me?" I raise my hands to protect my face and head. "Stop. Pl..."

The giant beasts move forward, cutting me off and places the black boxes against my body. Electricity seizes through my body and mind. I drop to the floor and bang my head against the wall on my way down. There was no grace to falling when you had no control of your limbs.

My body goes numb and limp. My throat convulses and tries to form words to my rambling thoughts. They hit me again; their faces break out into smiles as my pain brings them happiness. I feel drool run over my chin and can barely keep my eyes open.

I can no longer move, just endure the fire that crackles along my veins from the two jolts I received. The excruciating pain of it was made worse by not being able to voice that pain; it was all internalized. I scream through my head.

The headache I started to get before now has died down and is finally quiet through this whole experience. No sounds ring through my ears or mind. All I can hear is the rushing of my blood through my veins.

The darkness crawls into my vision; fingers come at me as they stop shocking me. His fingers blur into a blob of skin as it grows closer, picking me up effortlessly between the two hulking figures.

Oh, how I wish for a shadow creature all my own, like the one the doctor talked about. If I had one, it could cause some damage to these people who said they were helping me but were not.

"I'm trying," I dribble out between partially open lips. It came out more IIIIIIIII tieeeeee.

Doctor Sorenson comes over to look at me between the two hulking figures that have me easily hoisted between them. "Yes, I know you were trying," she says sweetly enough. "But we have run out of time, and you did not try hard enough unfortunately. This facility is only temporary, and since you have only gotten worse and are not remembering anything at all, we will have to relocate you. I am sorry," she states as she sees a tear roll down my cheek. "But we are going to have to place you in a more permanent and secure location, one that can handle your issues and help you to remember. Maybe after a longer sentence you will finally be able to tell us some answers."

I sneer as much as I can muster, but don't meet her icy gaze and steel façade. I am a problem she thought she could fix to help her career along, but when it came down to it, she didn't care one way or the other. If I couldn't essentially help her move up, then she needed to move onto someone who could. Isn't that what the world is coming to these days? Think, watch, and help out yourself first, and all others be damned.

"What.... does... mean?" I dribble out.

"It means that you will be shipped out in the morning to a facility called..." She walks back to her desk for a moment to flip through some notes she has there. "Hopewood. There they have better equipment to help you in remembering the things needed to prove whether you are innocent or if you are guilty."

Lock me up and throw away the key is more like it so they never have to look at me or even think of me again. I had hoped that this was all just a big misunderstanding, that I could just try to get back to my life or some semblance of it. Since I am an adult, even if I didn't remember, I could still get out of here and remember on my own time and live the life I want.

Regardless, if the memory loss was due to post traumatic stress or something else, nothing was adding up. I could remember some things, but they felt fuzzy. When thinking of my parents' things didn't make sense, I remember what it should have been like but every time I think of my past memories a headache comes on and it is better if I am not in pain. Why fight it when they aren't going to believe me anyway.

I silently hang my head in defeat, having my dark, russet-colored hair hide my anger and sadness towards the people that said they would help me, but, in the end, were just another great disappointment. Instead, they seem to just want a scapegoat, a person to frame for the murders. I didn't know how to shove that in their faces since they were holding all the cards; if there was only some way, I could prove to them that I wasn't some sort of killer.

Doctor Sorenson shakes her head. "We are going to have to make sure she is in a quiet place. This has been incredibly traumatic and stimulating for her. I don't want her hurting herself or anyone else either. We will put her in the quiet zone. Jud, you will keep an eye on her till your replacement comes in. Then ask George to take over for you. She will need all night care in case she gets agitated again."

She speaks to the smaller man, not the mountain that had brought me in.

"Of course, ma'am." He nods his head. "You know, I oversee everyone in this place. I will make sure she is taken care of."

"Good, good." She gives a sad smile to me, and then looks away.

Drool starts to dry over my cheek, my fingers are still numb and twitch back and forth. They quickly usher me through the door and down the halls, trying to be as quiet as possible. They avoid the passages where people tend to linger.

My lips tingle and start to loosen up. "Why did you do that?" I cry.

Both guards look down but Jud glares at the other. "Hush. You were becoming irrational and eccentric. We had to—to get you under control. The doctors don't ask us to help out unless things have gotten out of hand."

"Was I attacking her?" I try to give a logical argument.

"Not from what I could see, no." He looks down once again, then away as they come to a door and slow.

"Jud, don't listen to her," the other orderly says, forcing me into the crook of his arm as he gets the door with his other hand.

"I know, we have heard this all before." He rolls his eyes.

They both muscle me through the door and into the room. There is a bed with colored plastic wrapped around it. They don't strain too much as they lift me onto the bed. Jud presses down on my shoulders while the other man messes with something next to my legs. A thick strap pulls up into my vision. They tighten the strap to the side, corralling my thighs. Once the other man is done with my legs, Jud reaches for an identical strap for my hands.

"What are you doing?" I screech. I try to move my arms and legs to get out, but it comes across as me fidgeting.

"You heard the doctor. We have to make sure you are not a danger to us or anyone else. Another Doctor will be in to make sure you are calmed for the rest of your stay, until we can transfer you over to Hopewood," Jud says as the other guard comes up and takes his place so he can place a larger strap across my chest.

"I am not a danger! Not to you or anyone else."

A guy in a white lab coat comes in and gets some gloves from a drawer nearby. "This one gave Doctor Sorenson some trouble?" he asks. He has wrinkles all over his face and hunches a bit.

"Yes, sir." Jud nods. The other guard leaves quickly, but Jud stays and stands near the door. "Would you like me to stay here to help or wait outside, Doctor?"

The older guy mumbles to himself and is staring at my chart since he had come in, he realizes Jud had spoken and looks up. His white beard twitches back and forth. "Oh, of course, ol' boy. I don't think I will need your help with this one. She is just a wisp of a girl. You can just stand outside, enjoy your time. I know you don't much care for these types." He nods and shoos him out of the room.

Jud doesn't take much to go out the door; he stands next to it, the glass easy to see through. The door was not as solid as the one to Doctor Sorenson's room. "I'll keep an eye out here. Wave at me if you need my help." Jud nods to the doctor and stands across the way to keep guard.

The doctor closes the door quietly and shuffles across the way. "You must have done something horrific. Or had the potential to do so." He flips a switch, and the lights dim.

My fingers still tingle, but I wiggle them easily enough. "I didn't do anything," I yell. "Come back here, you cowards."

"Oh, dearie me, he can't hear you, darlin'." He hums to himself as he grabs a few utensils and needles. His hands shake a bit as he puts them on a tray near me.

"What do you mean he can't hear me? He is right outside." I pick my head up off the bed they have me tied down to and can barely see him through the window.

The older man chuckles and points to the side. "You see that door there?"

I nod my head, still feeling like Jell-O.

"When I close that, the room becomes soundproof. Yes, he can see us, but no, he can't hear us. That is why he asked me to wave at him if I need him." He waves but nods so that Jud can see him but knows not to come in.

"Why do you need soundproof?" I whimper.

"Can't have you disturbing any of the folks around here." He smiles as he raises one of the sharp scalpels to the light.

"You can't. That will leave marks on me!" I hiss. The strap digs into my side, keeping me from taking a full breath of air.

"Honey, that won't matter. Here, they will take my side, and if there are marks left on you, good ol' Jud out there can vouch for me. You tell them what I did, and it will be your word against mine. And since you threw a temper tantrum earlier, things aren't looking well for you are they, dearie?"

"Why are you doing this? Doesn't anyone want to help me?" A few tears escape as I thrash back and forth, trying to loosen the bonds that hold me.

"No, not at all. You are the worst of the worst. You killed five people in that house, or if you did not, then you helped with that. We know all about you, and I don't play into your amnesia ploy. I do this because I am good at it. I couldn't get away with this in normal instances, but since I deal with the lowest of the low, eyes become turned." He smiles and gives a little hop as he walks over to me with a sharp instrument in hand. "Also, being a good ol' boy and elderly to boot helps with these types of things."

He walks up and glides the sharp point against my skin; it barely grazes.

"Won't Jud see the blood? Won't he see what you are doing to me?" I shiver as it skates down my skin.

"Hmmm, you might be right." He places the scalpel down and out of reach and leans back against the table next to him and thinks. He snaps his fingers as an idea comes to him. "I got it!" he exclaims. He walks over to the window and waves his fingers at Jud as he opens the door a little. "I am going to close the partition to give her some privacy. You understand, right? The little lady is a bit shy; you see."

"Yeah, I get it." He rubs the back of his neck, noticeably uncomfortable. "I will see your shadows still, and you can always just come to the door if you need help. I will be here until my shift is done, of course." He keeps looking down at the floor.

"Good man," the doctor boasts. Once he has the door firmly shut, he smiles as he lowers the partition, Jud's silhouette still can be seen from inside the room. "There, problem solved. Glad I had your help for that." He smirks.

"Guess I'm not all bad," I spit out sarcastically.

"We should probably start with that tongue of yours. It is too wicked for your own good." He walks back over to his tools to look over them and grabs the forceps and scalpel. He clicks the forceps shut and then back open again in front of me.

I screech in terror and kick my heels against the plastic, causing it to crinkle and tear. I kick again and push my feet against the table, trying to break free, but all it does is cause my slippers to fall off.

"Hush now, my sweet, it is not going to be that bad. Careful or you will give yourself a heart attack, and then we will have to cut you open even more." He grins with glee. He gives me a look and then goes back to his tools and grabs a syringe. "Perhaps we better put you in a calmer state just in case, don't need you getting overworked." He smiles as he comes across and depresses the plunger into my arm and goes back to his selection to get the tools he had before.

He doesn't go to my mouth like I thought he would. I keep it clamped shut in case. He takes a hold of my shirt and pulls it up slowly uncovering my stomach, he caresses the sharp edge of the scalpel against my skin and pushes ever so gently. I pull my head down hard, wanting to see what he is doing every step of the way. A bright line of red appears where he slices, as he pulls down and the tension increases. The pain does not come right away, but as the air hits the sliced skin, a stinging sensation zings through my abdomen.

"You fucker!" I yell. His hand raises up holding still.

"Such language for someone so young as you, though you are malnourished and look as if you have not seen sunlight for some time." He pokes at my creamy skin, but does not bring the scalpel down again. The lights flicker.

I feel something slither over my arm. "What the hell are you doing now?" My breathe comes in and out quickly as I wiggle around to get a better view. My eyes focus on the scalpel and if he will bring it down once again. His eyes meet mine, then glance over to my shoulder widening in shock.

"What, what are you looking at?" I thrust my head to the left and then the right trying to see better.

"What is this witchery?" He gasps and moves closer with the blade and forceps. He brings clamps down on my arm. I look between him and my arm as he pinches it very hard with the tool. "What are you? Are you even human?" He whispers as he holds something to my arm and pokes at it with the point of the knife.

"Owww, that is still me," I burst, trying to move away as much as possible. "Is that a tattoo? I don't have a tattoo, do I? A flower tattoo, is that it?" I utter in astonishment.

"Your chart didn't mention a tattoo." He gives a look of confusion. "Did you do this?" He strokes his white beard and thinks to himself a moment. "I don't recall a tattoo being there just a moment ago."

A flutter races down my arm, we stare at each other, not sure what was happening. "What the hell!" I squeal. "Get it off me!" I shriek trying to move and fling it away.

He shrewdly dissects it and tries to hold on to it with the clamp he still has in his hands. He pinches at my skin as it races down slicing here and there trying to stop its progression. "What are you?"

I stare in terror, not able to make a sound. With each slice he takes, chills run through my body.

"Stop that!" I finally am able to yell. The tattoo moves and slithers away; the cuts and pinching doesn't affect its descent. I scream at the top of my lungs, my voice fading at the end, and my throat tightens, going silent.

The lights flicker once more as it peels off of my skin. It drops down to the floor and enlarges to a bigger, scarier shape. I whimper, not trusting or wanting to draw attention to myself. I watch as this shadow creature arcs up, making itself huge and terrifying. It looks like a huge black blob with many tentacles that look razor sharp.

"What the hell is that?" I whisper to myself, not wanting to talk too loudly.

Neither entity in the room pays me any attention. The black shadow slithers over to the doctor, who is still trying to slice at the creature. For an elderly man, he sure is spry.

"This is amazing!" he calls out as he turns to his tray and extracts a couple of other large sharp tools and throws them at the creature.

The creature parts where the weapons land, and they fall to the floor. A tentacle shoots out and wraps around the doctor's throat, choking off whatever he might have been about to say. He grabs for the creature, trying to pry the tentacle-like appendage off his neck. The creature could have substance and then not at any given moment. The doctor's fingers glide right through the shadows even though they hold onto his neck.

I look around for something, anything to get me out of this predicament. I glance down, and one of the scalpels that the doctor had been holding is right next to my hand. My fingers inch over and pick it up being careful not to drop it or slice into myself.

"I have already been cut enough," I whisper.

I drop my eyes to the scalpel and only concentrate on this task. The cool metal twirls around my fingers angling the blade up so it is pointing up towards my wrist and the cuff. I work on slicing it through the leather strap. My fingers slip, and it flips onto my thigh, sticking into me. My breath hisses in pain and I fight myself from jarring it loose and causing my only source of salvation to fall.

I slowly extract it from my leg, working on twisting the blade back up to start back on the strap. My body shivers and moves along with my fingers, sawing through the leather strap.

I startle when I hear a loud bang and see the doctor crumpled on the ground near the door. It causes the partition to go up a bit, the scalpel at that time cuts through and releases my left arm. I pull it up as the strap loosens.

Jud looks up as the partition raises and he sees my arm partially raised in the air with the scalpel. My eyes widen at what he is seeing.

"Shit." I scrabble with my right wrist cuff trying to untie it from the bed.

A groan emits from the door, my head swivels, shocked that he is still alive. The doctor is slowly coming to. The dark blob moves closer to him on the floor hovering over him. I peer around him and see Jud move forward toward the door. He notices the shadow creature as he reaches the door. His mouth hangs open a bit as he looks up at the tall figure.

"Help," I yell, before I remember that he can't hear me. The shadow creature looks back toward me as it reaches the doctor, as if asking a question.

"What are you? What do you want?" I question.

The doorknob twists and turns frantically, but won't open. Jud is blocked. He bangs on the door, trying to force his way through. The dark from raises all its tentacle-like appendages and strikes, piercing through the doctor and the wood that is behind him. Jud jumps back away from the pierced wood and stands there staring at the carnage before him.

"Call this thing off!" A muffled yell from Jud pierces through the now open holes in the door as the shadow retracts his form.

It slinks back from the door and fully turns to me after watching the doctor draw his last breaths. Jud kicks at the door, forcing the door to budge.

"It is not mine to call off!" I yell.

The shadow comes towards me.

"Stay away," I yell. I lift my top half off the bed and scoot down to my ankles to undo the straps there. My fingers scramble over the buckles.

It moves forward, creeping up to me. I release one ankle and kick out before it gets closer. I hit a solid mass and cringe as my ankle twitches in pain.

"What the fuck!" I yowl.

It catches my foot before I can reel back for another kick and places my foot down on the bed. I am paralyzed to do anything; I do not want to move to anger it. Or else I may end up like the doctor.

A small whimper pulls out of me as it removes the other cuff from my leg. I pull my feet away from the tendrils. Its inky black tentacles slide over the padded plastic, the purple color contrasting with the darkness.

A loud crunch sounds from the doorway. I look back over, and Jud has kicked his way in. He shoulders his way squeezing through the blood-soaked door and the doctors form slumps to the side as the door pushes him.

"What did you do?" Jud asks. He bends down to check on the doctor's pulse but shakes his head and turns back to the shadow creature. "You literally killed all of those people, didn't you?" Jud marches up to me passing by the Shadow creature as if it didn't exist or wasn't scared of it.

"Do you not see it?" My eyes widen in horror. Maybe I am crazy, maybe this isn't happening. "What did that doctor give me?" My mouth tastes like cotton, and the floor starts to dip. I move backwards and do not find more bed to hold onto. I'm about to go overboard when a hand reaches out to mine.

Jud pulls me back up straight.

As his hand touches mine, I hear a clear almost lyrical voice ring out. "Shade, the shadow creature is Shade, he will protect you."

Jud lets go just as quickly, and I fall back, not having found my balance yet. My head bangs on the hard floor as I fall.

I groan and roll over to my side. The ground moves even with me lying there, so I stay low not wanting to chance falling again. I barely move my head to the side and have to shut my eyes, my head is killing me as the world tries to right itself and spins in defiance.

"What are you?" I peel open my eyes to see Jud ask the Shadow creature. "Is your name Shade?" Shade nods in response. "Are you a shade?" Jud asks as he comes forward peering up at it with pinched eyes. "Did she tie you to her? No that's not it. Or are you something she constructed? Hmm. Not that either."

The creature shakes his head as Jud asks questions.

"How do you know its name? What did you do to me? Did you hear that?" I ask, feeling as if my mouth would barely cooperate.

"That voice was from you, a memory I am guessing. I see the truth in things," he throws out behind him, keeping his eyes focused on the black creature that is engulfing the room. It changes into a snake-like form and strikes out against Jud.

"Watch out," I call.

I watch as Shade passes right through Jud and falls to the floor behind him, hovering over me. I squeak back in fear.

"I didn't mean for it to attack," I whisper.

It tears back around and faces Jud once again and charges at him, but yet again passes through him with no damage done.

"Call that brute off." Jud walks back to me, hovering over me now, fists raised.

"It is not mine to control. I don't know what it is or what you are talking about." I lay my head down, too tired and scared to want to deal with this. "Why can it not touch you?" I scramble for a thought that makes sense.

"I am a Null, meaning magic or spells cannot touch me. It also makes seeing or telling the truth from someone easier, which is my other specialty." He points to Shade who has run into the wall and is hovering over by the cupboards. "He is a spell, something that is pure magic so he can't touch me, magic slides over me as if I don't exist. Your memory, part of the truth power I told you about, gave me its name—Shade. I can see the truth when I touch things, so if there was a spell placed on you, I would see through it, or if there was a glamor in place, I will see past it," he explains.

"Glamor, magic. What?" I squint at him.

Shade tears through the cabinets and finds anything and everything he can get his tentacles on. He throws them directly at Jud. Jud moves back and forth, dodging what is thrown. They sail over me and crash into the wall. Luckily, I am lying down and none fall or hit me directly.

"Do you want to hurt your master?" Jud crouches down low so that if he were hit, he would hit me as well.

Shade raises the bottle he holds in his tentacle, but stops before throwing. It shakes its head no as if it understood the question.

"So, you do understand me?"

It shakes its head yes.

My eyes grow heavy with the weight of it all, so I struggle to raise my head to continue to listen to Jud. It causes the world to tip, so I crawl over to the wall, pushing the medical supplies out of the way.

Jud looks at the creature, studying it. "You can only hurt me with other objects. I do not plan on hurting your master," he states.

The creature lowers the jar as if it is listening to him.

I pull my body across the cool floor into a sitting position so I can see both easily and lean back against the wall without too much effort to keep me up right.

"Why are you talking to it? Doesn't he need destroying?" I call out.

Jud glares at me. "Are you dense?" he yells. "This thing is yours. I can't affect the spell—only you can do that. I do not have any magic. I just negate it and see the truth." He rushes to my paperwork on the side table near where the bed that I was originally on. "It says here that you were going to be escorted to a place called Hopewood." He shakes his head. "We are going to have to change that. We can't have this thing on the loose. I have a better place where you will get the help you need." He scribbles furiously and keeps an eye on the door to make sure no one else happens across the room.

"What are you talking about? You can see it right—just kill it." I wave my hand at the shadow. "Are you in league with it? Is it a demon?" I mumble. "I wanna be left alone, I'm tired."

"What did he give you?" Jud flips through the papers, but does not come towards me to check on me or help. He makes sure there is enough space between us and keeps an eye on the shadow creature. He frowns. "You protect her, correct?"

Shade nods in agreement.

"He does not!" I yell. "No one does," I complain. "He has done a horrible job so far if I am in this place with you people."

He rolls his eyes at me and turns back to Shade. "If you want to actually help her, you can't kill in this place again. You have to let her get to this other place, Morning Star. I am guessing you only come out if she is hurt or something to that effect?"

Shade nods but slower this time.

"I am always hurt." I cry, not making much sense anymore.

"You need to allow me to take her to this new place where she will be able to help herself learn more about everything, regardless of what it leads to. I don't know if you are just a spell or something else tied to her, forced to do this but this will help."

Shade floats above the floor and just stays there, not moving.

"She obviously does not have any recollection of you or what your purpose is. This place will help. It is for our kind, whatever that may be," Jud continues.

"Bad, Alexia, you don't know anything," I call, shaking a finger. "I'll show you all what I am made of. I put a spell on you."

"Go back to your master. She will have to sleep this off and then will be transferred tomorrow." Jud looks back at the body that is by the door. He walks over quickly to the window and closes the partition again. "I will have to do something with this." He taps his belt and grabs the phone from it. He taps on it a few times and then places it to his ear. "I need cleaners, quick." He waits a few moments. "Report will be ready by end of night. Transfer will need to occur tomorrow." He nods once and then places the phone back on his belt that it was attached to.

Shade flows over to Jud and stands in front of him. Jud stares back, waiting.

"Shade can't touch him. Dunnanananah," I sing.

He shrinks down to a small black worm and slinks back towards me.

"No don't," I cry, but am having a hard time making my limbs listen to me to try to fight.

The worm stops to wait till I calm down. I glare at it. "How kind of you to not freak me out any more than I am." My head lists to one side, the drugs making it hard to stay frightened or angry.

Jud kneels next to me and puts his hands under my chin, making me look him in the eyes. "Listen to me." He waits till my eyes are focused on his. "Shade is a spell that is meant to protect you. I am not sure of what else it is meant to do or the extent of its power, but know that much is true. Careful with what you ask of it or what you feed into it."

I shake my head. "I can't. I have no control over it. No control, bye, bye." Tears stream down my face.

"This place you will go to will help you."

My eyes droop down as I grow very sleepy. "Right. Hopewood." I yawn.

"No, not that place."

"Uh huh," I mumble as my eyes refuse to open back up.

He rests my head against the cabinet and wall carefully. "Sleep for now," he whispers.

That is the last thing I hear before I am out once again.

Chapter 3

T HE NEXT MORNING, I sit handcuffed to the back seat of a van. The vehicle itself is black in color and doesn't have any design or writing to call attention to it. The only thing that caught me by surprise was that the license plates were missing when they brought me to the van.

Since it is a car that transports crazy people to other locations, there might be a reason for that. I'm not sure, and I'm sure not going to ask about it either. Perhaps it is for our protection. I didn't want to anger anyone more than I had already, I didn't need another jolt of electricity. My mind still seemed in a daze.

I sit here feeling as if I am the worst sort of criminal, the bottom of the barrel. "Why?" I ask myself. "Why am I being transferred like this?"

I have never given them any reason to hate me, treating me as if I were a mass murderer or went on a killing spree. I knew that it looked like that, I did, but I didn't cause those people's deaths.

The van gives a jolt side to side as we make a turn, the ride to my final resting place not especially significant. A few hours later, the road becomes bumpy and uneven as if we were traveling down a gravel or dirt road instead. This went on for the remaining part of the trip.

"Makes sense," I say to myself since they wouldn't want crazy people close to others or able to mix with normal people. "Are you going to be silent the whole trip?" I ask Jud.

He looks at me and then nods.

There are no windows for me to peer out of to see where I am, to see my surroundings to even know where I am located. The only thing that I can tell is the gravel road we travel down is quiet and long. I can't even tell if it is night or day; the front part of the van is blocked off by a wall. It is literally just me and Jud with nothing to stare at but each other.

When the van comes to a slow halt, I hear a loud shout ring out from the front of the van. "Ready!"

The doors open up slowly, letting a head poke around the edge of the door making sure I am still fastened into my seat. Jud stays where he is, waiting for him to be acknowledged. My look of confusion does nothing to deter his cautious activity.

"This the one?" the man at the door asks.

"Yep, a real handful, she is. Do you guys need help?" Jud moves to stand up.

"Nah we got her," he states.

The man pushes the door open all the way, showing me that it is sunset and we have been traveling for the better part of the day. The man's head is attached to a slight body as he skitters into the back of the van with me. He rubs his hands together in excitement.

"What are you, a mouse?" I hiss.

"No, worse—a rat!" he snaps. Jud chuckles and throws the keys to release me. He twitches his mustache back and forth under his nose.

"I can believe it." I lob back at him.

He pulls out long black gloves with silver embroidery. The silver stitching is very elegant and neat and reminds me of scroll work, like something from long ago.

"Are you going to a ball?" I scoff.

A tall, slender man relaxes back by the opening of the van and gives a jolt of laughter, but quickly covers it with a cough. He is slightly behind the rat. He ducks back out, avoiding us.

"No, these are for you, itchy witchy." His nose twitches once again.

"Witch... I am offended that you think I am that powerful." If my hands were free, I would pop them in his face.

"No, you aren't very powerful, are you?" He eyes me up and down. His beady eyes laugh at me as he smiles, his mouth full of crooked and stained teeth.

I cringe away from him, trying to create more distance between us. The small space in the back of the van between Jud and this scrawny thing is giving me anxiety. "Can you all not crowd me?" Air puffs out of my chest as I shrink down, but the cuffs catch against the metal plate that they are locked into and attached to the seats.

Rat man dangles the keys between his fingers, showing me who has the power. I squint my eyes shut, hoping he will disappear.

He pulls my wrists to him gripping them hard, he pulls them as far as the cuffs will stretch. My eyes open in surprise and glance back at Jud who just sits there, his eyes closed, acting as if he is in slumber.

"You did not fall asleep that quickly," I seethe.

"Hurry up, Doug, I don't want to be doing this all day," the man bellows from outside the van at the back.

Doug's smile becomes even toothier, as if he likes seeing me uncomfortable. "You don't want me to hurry up, do you, precious?" he whispers.

"Maybe, the other one is more handsome than you," I hiss right back at him. Of course, there had to be two guards. I saw the other one earlier but did not get too good of a look at him.

"I like my lunch with a bit of a bite." He snaps right back as he jerks me closer and rubs my wrists raw with the chains, pulling taught between them.

I hiss in pain, which makes him happy, and he releases the tension, giving some slack once again.

Doug slowly moves through the motions, but finally unlocks the chains holding me to the seat of the bench. "She's a talker, Toby," he yells back out of the van.

"Great, you deal with her then," he hurls back at his partner, and I hear the crunch of gravel as he walks away.

"Good news, Toby hates talkers. We now have more privacy. He will keep his distance." He gives a toothy grin once again. He slides his thin bony fingers around my bicep, squeezing extremely hard.

I glare at him as I feel something start to move around from my back, detaching. I glance at the shadows, and around me, that sunset casts into the back of the van with us. "You don't want to do that," I warn.

I was able to remember most of what happened yesterday when Jud came to get me this morning. The drugs did not make me forget. I had never had that before where I remembered things clear from the day before.

"We are not alone."

Shade peers out from the shadows. He elongates his form not waiting for me to be in pain this time, the threat was there.

"Aww, you care. Don't worry, princess. Jud here can keep a secret. That is why he is in the human realm making sure our kind doesn't leak over." He pulls my body against his. "Jud brought you to the right place. He knows what you are and why you need to be here, and how we can better deal with you." His pointy nails dig into my skin; if he were not wearing gloves then they would be biting into me.

Jud's voice echoes behind me; I turn to him as he speaks. "I see things that most do not," he growls. "People who get away with things that they cause even though they say they don't." He looks directly at me. "They deserve what they get."

"What do you know?" I shoot back.

"I have seen your darkness," is all he says before he rests his head back and closes his eyes once more.

I shake my head and look back at Doug, and Shade, who is behind him. He didn't warn Doug of Shade. He knew he was there and could see him, why didn't he? What did he know or was it all a ploy and he was really talking to Doug? I didn't know enough about this place or the people that were here.

I watch as Shade elongates his form. He creates black wings like a bat, but one that encompasses the whole back end of the van. He could easily wrap the wingspan around both Doug and me, consuming us with his darkness. Doug is distracted and calling out something to his partner, Toby.

I smirk and can't wait till Doug glances back and sees the shadow staring at him. "Make him cower like he did to me," I whisper in a very low voice, hoping Shade heard or understands.

Shade helped me when none other would, for now my trust is with him.

Doug's fingers slide up and down my arm in a suggestive manner, and he pulls me against the front of his body, pinning me there. He does not turn to see Shade.

My eyes widen in horror, and I try to fall away from him, but he pulls me in closer.

Doug squeaks out in anticipation and excitement of my fear.

Shade slithers closer to Doug. his bat-like wing covers over his arm to rip him away from me. Since he could only affect physical things and not communicate, he has to resort to violence.

Bright piercing light blots out the whole back van.

"What the hell?" I yell, my hands reach up to cover my eyes

Doug laughs out a bellowing sound. "Bitch thought she could get the upper hand," he barks to no one in particular.

Shade's darkness shrinks back from the light. The light keeps up, glaring and bright until he moves away. I glance at the gloves that guard Doug's arms.

"These gloves have protective spell work written in the stitching to shield me against darker spells and any tricks that you may have up your sleeves. Jud here warned us you have a dark creature with you and gave us all the tools to combat and help you during your stay with us." He smiles back. He peeks at the wisp of darkness that slithers over my skin, going back to where Shade rests. "Sorry, itchy witchy, your magic won't work on me at the moment," he taunts. He points a long finger at me, shaking it back and forth. "Maybe save a spell for me later though when I visit." He winks.

"In your dreams," I croak, trying to stay strong and ruthless.

"Don't think you will catch us without these gloves as protection. All guards that are working with you are ordered to wear these, you will not be able to use your power on them the way you did back at the last place," he grits out.

"How could you do this to me, Jud? You seemed so nice before."

"We just met. I don't know you, and you don't know me. I am surrounded by dangerous people, and I needed to keep you calm. Why would I not be nice until you were where I needed you to be?" He stretches his legs out and crosses them at the ankle.

"Let's get going, troublemaker. Others are waiting to destroy and break you down."

"Is everyone in there like me? Do they have the same power?" I ask in awe, now more curious than ever to get inside and see what was next. Maybe learn how to use the power or what it is in the first place. Perhaps learn how to use some of these powers to keep people from harming me.

"Not all," he quips. "Some, yes. But most are other forms of creatures that have turned their back on their true purpose. Doesn't matter though, all will be explained later. Not my circus, not my monkeys." Doug's eyes stare back, laughing as if I am something worthless.

Doug loosens his grip on me towards the back of the van so I will be able to get down from the back.

Was Shade just a spell then, or was he something or someone that is tied to me because of a spell? These are all questions running through my mind. Nothing makes sense. But since I got shocked, memories from that point on have started sticking, but none from my past are coming back to me yet. If I would have forgotten anything from yesterday, it would have been Shade.

I feel Shade flutter against the back of my shoulder. I jump and shriek.

"What's going on in there?" Toby bellows, coming closer to the van

"Nothing," Doug reiterates. "Just jumpy, this one." He presses his hands into my arms harder.

I'm going to have to get used to his movements on my body. I shake my head as Doug gives me a look of wonder. Did it hurt when Shade touched the gloves earlier? I roll my head back and forth, trying to make him calm down. Shade couldn't keep moving so much, or it would cause me to squirm.

"What's wrong itchy witchy?" Doug gives a shrewd look. He hops down out of the van, skirting around me since I don't jump down first.

Doug hovers between the doors, blocking my way, in case I want to try something and run. "Nothing, just these cuffs are hurting me a bit," I weep.

"Lies," Jud smoothly says as one of his eyes opens up. The sun glinting over him makes him squint.

I glare back at him, but he doesn't offer any more than that. The other guard, Toby, moves up to the side of the van, keeping his eyes downcast.

"We ready?" Toby asks, his brown hair hanging over his eyes. His slim form is not as tall as the other two. He doesn't look like he belongs here with Doug; he doesn't seem like the type to cause pain, he seems... no, *feels* different.

I give him a questioning look but shake my head. What was I thinking? He had to be just like them? They all were against me here, I had to remember that. I look down at the other guard and his arms and hands were also covered in the black gloves.

"Yeah..." Doug glares up at me. "Get out of there, itchy witchy," he growls, reaching out to grab onto my bicep, and pulls me down out of the van.

I stumble forward and barely have time for my legs to catch me as I am thrown out. I crouch low on the gravel road. Toby bends down and grasps the other bicep so I am between the both of them with no way to escape.

"Tell him to relax!" I yell at Toby. His hands hold me but have no bite.

Doug's fingers were crushing. "Yeah, tell me Toby." Doug laughs.

Toby glares at me, and then casts his eyes to the side.

"He's new blood, itchy witchy, he can't and won't help you." He presses into me more, as he also pulls me forward.

The two guards pin me between them, caging me and corralling me towards the huge red brick building. The first thing I notice is a lack of fences, but perhaps they don't need one since this place is surrounded by dense woods and wilderness.

There were huge mountains in the distance, and the trees all around that are encompassing the huge castle-like structure.

"I wouldn't get any ideas about wanting to leave. Unless one knows how to survive in the wilderness with minimal resources and doesn't mind the cool temperatures at night then by all means think away." Doug smiles wickedly, his eyes track mine as I look around. "Someone is bound to run across your dead body eventually. Maybe years down the line. We are out in the middle of nowhere and in a different world entirely!" He laughs.

The building is old with the brick edges worn down and deep grooves in the grout. Despite its apparent age it is well taken care of; no bricks out of place or cracks in the windows. Its exterior has a dark charm that reminds me of those haunted houses during Halloween. Large barren trees hold dead branches and spider webs. Raggedy brown bushes dot the exterior taking away any reminder that this place once held life.

As the guards take me up the stairs and through the wide double doors, I feel utterly defeated. I stop noticing what is around me after the third—or was it the fourth—turn. I shake my head to myself and only notice that all the hallways are painstakingly blinding and bright, producing a white hue.

Every hallway smells strongly of cleaning products. Which could be a good thing if you knew the place was clean, but it could also be covering up something more sinister. The walls are white, the ceiling is white, and even the tiles beneath my sneakers are white.

The absence of color is like the absence of minds that they hold here. Surprisingly, the only sort of color that is in the hallways is the light brown wooden doors.

"Heh. Go figure. Would have thought they would be white as well," I whisper to myself.

Toby looks over at me, then glances to Doug, and then stares straight forward once again. The two men muscle me in front of one of the many doors we pass and Doug gives a sharp knock against the solid oak door. They wait stiffly, as I fidget to stand as still as possible between them.

The door sweeps open, and a tall man stands in front of me. He looks down his nose with an innocent smile plastered all over his plump face. He wipes his beefy hands on his rotund belly and reaches toward me, his right palm out to shake. I gently take a hold of his hand and give it a quick shake before swiftly letting go.

"Well, who do we have here?" he asks.

Doug speaks up first. "This is the new transfer, Alexia. We received her paperwork yesterday. The council said to bring her straight to you to get started, and to get her acquainted with the day-to-day routine as soon as she arrived."

"Ahhh, quite right," he says after a bit of hesitancy. "Come in. Come in." He motions to the two guards.

They both push me in briskly and bow in unison. "We must be getting back to our post, orders and all." They force me forward, and Doug grabs the door, pushing Toby back and closing the door behind him silently. I stare at the door for a little while, unsure of what to do next.

So far, each doctor I have dealt with has not been helpful at all. They didn't even bother to unlock the cuffs that were still on my wrists. I jangle them a bit; they still dig into my skin. With the slack in the chain, I shrug and rearrange my shirt on my neck, pulling my short sleeves back in place. I turn to face the doctor to see what the next steps were.

"Welcome. Alexia, right?" he questions me as he slowly walks back to his desk and opens a drawer to remove some keys.

I nod, glancing back at the closed door, wanting to make sure the door stays closed at my back. "And you are?" I ask slowly. "They never said your name." I stare at him and eye the key in his hand; my fingers begin to tremble.

"I am the psychoanalyst here, Doctor Helm, but you can call me Quintan. I am the lead psychiatrist here at Morning Star and will be talking with you while you are here in our care." Quintan moves towards me and picks at one of the keys, his hands do not shake as they remove the metal cuffs from my wrists. "Better?" He moves back in the direction of his extravagant chair behind his even more ginormous desk.

I cock my head to the left in confusion as I follow him and stand in front of the desk. "No, I am not better." I throw up my fingers in quotation marks. "Did you say Morning Star? Is that the name of this place?" I stutter through.

"Yes!" he exclaims good-naturedly. He frowns then at my bewilderment. "Is something the matter?" He sits down in the big chair. It engulfs his form as he searches through the papers on his desk. Before picking up a form he throws the keys back in a desk drawer to the left.

"Doctor Sorenson said yesterday that I was supposed to be transferred to a place called Hopewood," I stated. "Did I hear incorrectly? There was a time when I might have," I hedge, unsure of my memories. "I thought she said Hopewood." I try thinking back over the last couple of days trying to discern what was real and what was made up.

He frowns and looks down at the papers scattered from a thick file folder. He pulls it over to him and flips through many of the pages held within and some that are not attached to the file as well. "It would seem you were supposed to transfer there." He looks up, worried, then continues. "It looks like there was a change, and a recorded incident which made this change required. The humans must have thought we could help you more here than at Hopewood. Jud is one of our many agents that keeps an eye out for people like you. Ones that don't necessarily know what they are or maybe can do and have become dangerous for one reason or another. Given what he saw the other night made it more than enough reason to have him make that change. That is why we made sure he was in a high enough position to make those decisions. He oversees security, so anything he encounters, he can make the changes. To here at Morning Star," he states with a flourish.

"Humans? What am I? Where are we? Doug said we weren't even on Earth. I thought I was just being transferred somewhere for a longer stay, not that I needed a specialist for anything other than hypnotherapy, or that is what Doctor Sorenson started with me." I scowl at the papers trying to discern the words they hold even though they were upside down to me and mostly covered.

My eyes scramble to focus on something real and physical. I breathe in and out quickly, not sure what all of this means. Was I forgetting again?

"I am actually surprised we didn't get you right away, or sooner, at least. Our agents out there are usually fairly good at catching our people in the Earth realm before you are fully incorporated into the human database," he states, ignoring my questions. "You see, our realm here only connects to your Earthly realm, there are others of course." He waves a hand next to his face as if that thought didn't matter. "But Earth is the only place our world can connect to."

"Human database?" I question, picking up on something. "What the hell is going on?" I shriek, demanding him to pay attention to what I am going through.

He looks up and gives me a quizzical scan. "Yes, otherworldly people, such as yourself, cannot be held in regular prisons or mental institutions, so they are taken to places such as this one, depending on the situation. You are here so we can determine whether you are truly a danger or just need help adjusting. Sometimes accidents can happen." He reads through the papers. "We will also need to know what faction or side you belong to. Your blood will be able to tell us if you belong to the light or dark side."

"Wait..." I back up, hitting the chair behind me, plopping down hard into the leather seat. "What do you mean otherworldly? What do you think I am if not human?" I laugh., My fingers run through the top of my hair, but stop before it gets to my ponytail. I continue to pull my hand back and start again; the scratching soothed me.

He balks at my confusion and rapid questions. "The people that were killed in your presence. Now, I only say that because you do not remember enough to know if you were a part of it. Anyway, the people that were killed were part of a white-light group and were registered witches."

"My parents?" I question.

"They were not your parents," he states coldly. "This was discussed in your session with Dr. Sorenson. Do you not remember that?"

"They were my parents," I state just as coldly.

"Know this to be true. They were not your parents. From what we know so far, we can't tell if you have just a spell placed on you or if you are a witch yourself." He eyes me, preparing for an outburst or waiting to see what I do next.

My mouth drops open, and the room begins to spin, causing me to lurch forward, almost falling out of the chair. I clutch on to the plush leather, keeping myself upright and grounded. I breathe in deeply, letting out shallow breaths.

"I am not a witch," I say with confidence that I do not feel. "Why should I trust you anyway? None of you have given me a reason to trust you. I have been in isolation, I have been locked up, I have seen things, I have been told everything I know to be true is not. What should I believe and why should I?" I spill out.

"No, you most likely aren't. If you were a witch, you would not have been kept in that house for as long as you were. Though you do have a spell attached to you." He reads from a paper. "Jud made sure we knew about that part and were prepared for it. We are not sure what you are yet. That is why this place is here, to help you figure that out along with the other parts of your missing memory."

"I don't remember much. Doctor Stenson just started with me before we even really got anywhere. I remember being at my parent's house," I growl as he looks up and rush on, so Quintan doesn't interrupt. "Not how I got there or where I came from, because to me that is the place I grew up and lived. I remember the shadow that came out from me yesterday, and a claw, though that is hazy—perhaps from a dream. I don't remember much more than that. Maybe someone put a curse on me, and it went wrong. Maybe I am normal, and you have everything wrong," I say with hopeful intent.

Quintan sits forward carefully and pulls the pile of papers together. "That could be a possibility, but then we must find out why and get to the bottom of it. But if you do have powers, and they are just forming and new to you, you are not properly able to handle them, and will need all our help here to get you through this transition. No need to worry. Deaths like those witches went through can happen when a newling comes into their own." He gives a frown. "Being from our side of the world, they should have known that. You are a lot older than usual for someone to come into their powers."

I shake my head. "That can't be. I don't remember." My hands begin to tremble, as I wrap them around my middle holding myself tight. "Are you sure the people that are dead were part of a white light group?" I eye him carefully.

"These factions consider them sort of like a side in war. Some are good, some are not so good, light does not necessarily mean good, and dark does not mean bad. They were part of the side that was labeled as white-light. They are basically a group that represent good and follow light, but some believe that in order to make light the winner that some bad things have to happen. The other side of the coin is a group called dark-shadow. They are of course the path that follows a darker and more sinister path, but some really good people can be a part of that side as well."

My eyes skim over my shoulder when he talks about the dark shadow group, reminding me of Shade. "So, what does that make you? What side are you on? Do you have to be on a side? Why would my parents be a part of something like this—this war?" I question.

"I am a mage." He lights a bit of purple fire between his fingers when he says that, and it quickly dissipates. "I can help you recall and retain the memories you have forgotten." He pulls his weight from the chair, straining his arm muscles.

I feel my eyes grow big at the little flicker of the flame. "You didn't say what side you were on," I reply, staring at him. I regain my composure and frown at him.

He gets up and stands in front of his chair, not moving. "Some of us choose not to follow a certain side, some of us are here to do other things," he states cryptically.

I nod. "Keep your secrets, for now. Though you should keep in mind trust is earned."

He stumbles forward, catching his shoe on the side of his huge desk. I move forward quickly, wanting to help him, but stop before I round the desk, clenching my fists closed.

"Do you think that is such a good idea?" I question, doubting how he could help me when he could barely help himself.

He waves me away with a flick of his wrist and stalks over to me. "Of course. We must start right away." His grubby fingers reach out towards me, corralling me backwards towards a chair.

I glance up at him nervously. "What are you going to do?" I ask, the back of my legs hit the seat of the chair, and I drop down.

"This process is mostly painless, depending on what I find. For the most part, though, I place my fingertips against your temples. There might be a purple haze or fire that emits from me. Don't worry, though, that is just part of my life essence or force, if you will. Just sit back and close your eyes."

I look at him as if he is crazy and grip the edges of the chair's arms. My fingernails turn white as I dig them into the chair. "You mean the same fingers that just had fire between them just a minute ago?" I peer around him, trying to find a way around.

He simply nods. "Yes. I can do other things than just dig into your mind. I was showing you the flame, so you had proof of magic, in case you didn't believe me," he states calmly. "Being around humans and no magic it is hard for some to catch on."

"Other than everyone thinking they are better than others without magic. What is the difference between a mage and a witch though?" I keep him talking, trying to avoid the inevitable. Trying to gain all the knowledge I could in this strange new place.

I don't know how long I will be in this reality or if I would even remember this for later. How did I manage to remember Shade but nothing else?

"Witches use outside sources with their own energies to fuel the spells or powers they have and what they want them to do. Mages use their own life force only to create the magic that needs to be done. That is why you will see many mages with vials, trinkets, or other little things that can hold spells within. You will always see a mage have a stock of these on their person or near them at all times, since they have a limited amount of power that they can wield on their own." He waves his arm towards the glass cabinets and cases behind the desk that hold many shelves and rows of such items.

My eyes scan the cabinets, my fingers itching to look at them and maybe use them to get me out of this place. I look back to him with distrust in my eyes. I have to know what happened to me and my past, what I may or may not have done.

"You will help me get answers? Actual answers?" I ask, my eyes steady on him. "Why should I trust you?" My tone and gaze never waver.

"Yes, actual answers. Unlike the other doctor that just talked. I can actually get in there to see if it is a spell that is causing you to forget, or if it is just your mind. If it is then that is easy enough to fix." He snaps his fingers as if it would be just that easy. His eyes raise to mine. "You don't have to trust me. We can do it the hard way and take a long time, but you will have to stay here for as long as it takes. Also, if it is a spell that is in place keeping you from that information, then you most likely won't overcome this on your own." He lays the facts down, but his tone is steady and calm. He drops his eyes and leans back against the desk waiting.

My breath eases out of me as he gives me room to think. "So, I may never be able to keep my memories?" I ask confused. "I remember the shadow creature from yesterday. Perhaps it is because they shocked me that I have started to remember." I stop and try to think of what it is I want to say.

"The taser," Quintan supplies.

I pick at the brown leather seat with my fingers. "I think that is when I started to not forget." I shrug off. "The shadow thing also helps, but I have no memory of it other than a childhood friend named Shade." My legs begin to bounce in time with my nerves.

"He might be another spell. Is he about?" He gives me a moment, but silence answers him. "We may look at that another time, but for now, we will stick with just your mind, we don't want to activate or agitate it. I think with the electric jolt you received earlier, you will be able to remember memories from that point forward, but before that incident took place the spell would still block the other memories from you." He shakes his head. "There will be no retrieving those memories unless we go in and get to the bottom of things."

Settling back into the chair and keep my eyes on the glass cases that hold vials and trinkets. I force my eyes to stare straight ahead of me as he walks quietly around. I feel his clammy fingers touch my temples causing me to jump, purple fog dusts down around me. Flames start to lick my skin, but there is no heat that comes with that touch. My back eases into the chair more since pain does not follow and I close my eyes. A small pinch and warming sensation begins to ease its way down the nape of my neck, pinpricks rupture there at the base of my skull.

Quintan whispers in a trance-like state, "No matter what you feel, I need you to keep very still. I think I have found what is blocking your memories."

I tense at his words. "What happens if I don't stay still?" I hedge, remaining as still as possible, but unable to unclench my muscles.

"I could either slip and not have what I am looking for anymore, which could cause pain to you or it could backfire on myself," he bites out.

I bite my lips as the heat begins to increase, I concentrate on my arms and torso and force myself not to move. The pressure begins to press on the sides of my head. Drips of sweat slide down my temples and my back as the heat continues to intensify. A stray tear escapes from my eye and rolls down my cheek. I force my hands to stay at my sides rather than acknowledge it.

The pain in my head feels like a distant memory as a shadow begins to cover me and I float in the darkness. A big dark blanket falls against me. I bring my fingertips to the edge of its darkness and slide them down.

I push an instinctual thought towards it. *I need this. I need answers.*

The blanket floats away and leaves me to the deep sea of raw searing pain that flows down my spine, making me want to arch my back in answer. I dig my fingers deep into my thighs, pressing them there curling them under, so I am almost sitting on top of them so they wouldn't betray me and try to reach out to dislodge Quintan. Something else is in the darkness waiting for me, waiting to grab me at my most vulnerable. I am unsure of what is going on. Quintan said it shouldn't have been that painful.

"Hello? Quintan, are you there?" My voice wavers, the darkness surrounds me, and I can't even feel the chair I am sitting on anymore.

Burning purple symbols appear all around me against the darkness. The pain still zings through me, though I can't see what causes it. "Am I in my mind again?" I scream. The pain dulls a bit as if in answer, the symbols burn brighter. "Quintan, your magic is purple—is this you?" I ask, hesitating, unsure if I want the darkness to answer me.

The symbols around me close in. I back up, but notice them closing in on me from all sides. I move to crawl under one of the symbols, but they lower, mimicking my movement, keeping me in its circle. They close around me, so I bring my arms up in defense, but they slow down and just keep a small circle around me.

I move to the left and right and watch as it moves with me. "Is this like some sort of protection ring?"

The symbols around me act as a torch to light the darkness searching for something, anything around. I notice tunnels branching off. "What is this a maze?" I say in wonderment and worry. I walk over to the hard surface and notice the symbols disappear behind the rock, my palm lands on one of the walls. It is smooth, but I can't tell if it is stone or something else. The darkness is pure, and the purple light doesn't light it up fully.

"Which way do I go?" My head flicks back and forth, circling around, trying to stick to the edges to see how many tunnels there are. "Eeny meeny miny mo." My fingers skip from tunnel to tunnel, and as I end the song, I land on one at random.

I take care to try to not bump into the walls and go slow. The darkness seems deeper as I move through the passageways. I keep my eyes mostly on the ground choosing which tunnel to go down by another song.

"Left, left, left, right, left."

I stomp my feet in tempo with the words.

"Hello?" I gurgle out, sniffling. Though there is light it does not bring down the creep factor. "Quintan, where are you?" I bring my arms around my middle. "Should I really be talking out loud? Something could find me here, though what could be in my mind hunting me? Shouldn't it just be me?" I argue with myself. "Stupid Quintan, didn't prepare me for this at all."

A loud screech echoes in the distance. "How is my mind this dark? What is that?" I puff out and then draw another breath in just as quickly. My heart races at the noises that are starting to echo off the walls.

The purple symbols grow brighter and stop moving with me. I stop suddenly, not sure if I want to keep going. The pain is just starting to dim and not be as prominent.

"Quintan, what am I supposed to do? Why did your symbols stop?"

I reach my hand out tentatively through the symbols moving past them. Quintan latches onto my shoulder squeezing it tight, his breath coming in gulps.

I jump physically, but help him steady himself. "Quintan, what is it, why are you so shaken?" My voice raises up an octave higher.

The words come out shaky as he keeps hanging on to my frame. "The mind is a dangerous thing. It does not enjoy anyone else being inside other than who is supposed to be here." His eyes rest on mine for a moment. "My magic didn't come through with me, it went to you..." He seems baffled by this.

"Is that not normal?" I ask, still unsure what was really going on.

"Nothing about this is normal." He raises his left arm and coughs into it. His form wavers ever so slightly, the air is still and stagnant. "But I finally found you." His form flickers again.

"Are you sure you're, okay? You seem to be flickering like a candle that is about to go out." I step away from him a bit.

Quintan looks down at himself and watches his form flicker once more. "We must hurry," he mutters to himself as he casts his eyes around.

I watch him and the shadows around us and notice some of the dark pits that branch off of the tunnels are blocked by an orange red light. "What are these? They look like the scrollwork on the gloves Doug was wearing when he brought me into this place."

He scrunches his face and leans away from me, taking some of his weight off. "This spell, whatever it is, is extraordinarily strong. I will not be able to hold it back for very long. It seems the memories that are closer to your present self are stronger and reinforced by the spell which is blocking you from knowing what has happened to you recently. We will have to continue on and hopefully we can come across some of your older memories and they won't be as guarded as these ones. That way we can get some answers, we may have to come back with more power if the spell is strong throughout." He edges forward slowly; his powers sluggishly follow him.

I creep forward with him at a slow pace, wanting to stay safe in the circle of the spell. "Should we not just stop now and go back for more power, were you not attacked? Shouldn't we leave and be more prepared and get more of what we need?" I ask as we keep moving. I hold onto his sleeve more for me, but also to make sure he doesn't just pop out of existence, since his form still flutters in and out.

"No, after this it will take me some time to gain enough momentum to come back here so while we are here, we should get all that we can out of it," he states with confidence.

"What happens if you disappear altogether?" I whisper, huddling closer to him. "Will your protection spell stop? How do I get out?"

"The spell is what pulled us both in, so if I am cast out, it most likely will cast you out." He keeps moving forward, but at a slower pace, not wanting to bump into me with his girth. "And if I pop out, my magic may continue to stay with you. I am not sure since it came to you instead of to me as it should have." He stops a bit to take a full look at me, as if deciding something.

"And if I don't come out of it?" My teeth chatter, I turn away from him, not liking the weight of his eyes.

"Let's not think of things like that." He waves his hand and shakes his head, easing away from me and taking his weight off of me. "The power of thought is strong where we are right now." He mutters, his eyes keep scanning to keep an eye out around us. "Thoughts go a long way here, for this place to be so dark like this your mind must have lots of dark thoughts running through it. You have not experienced much happiness in your lifetime, have you?" he asks.

I nod, but don't raise my eyes. "Is there a way I can help navigate this place, so we can find the older memories faster?" I question.

"It is your mind. Only you can find the memories you need, but remember this memory needs to be far enough in the past, where the spell is weak where we will be able to get through. I also suggest you hurry; the spell is draining me." He flickers in and out in quick succession.

"Is that how I found you so quickly? Because I wanted to find you?"

"Most likely." He pushes me forward, so that I would be in the lead of where we went.

I glance around, keeping track of the many different tunnels branching out all around us. Some of the passageways have scroll work that burns brightly, and others are dimmer, but still there. I think back to what I would want to know or remember, it could not be anything recent so I couldn't find out if or what killed those people at that house.

"If I died in a memory or in here, what would happen to me in reality?" I walk forward, not basing my way on anything other than just a feeling. I sway back and forth, letting my body take control of what my mind didn't want to lock on to.

"Positive thoughts, remember?" His voice wavers as he lets me get further away. "We don't want to think about something like that right now."

I peer at him with one eye. My body freezes mid sway.

"Answer truthfully, Quintan." I open up my other eye so both of them are staring straight through him. "We are not alone down here." I smile.

"Honestly, I do not know. I have never come across something like this before in my lifetime, perhaps we can ask others that might have or if you are up to it testing things. Let's put a pin in that for now, but later we can talk about what we want to do." He nods vigorously and continues to walk at a slower pace.

My body begins to sway once again and pick another entrance at random. "What do I want to know?" I chatter to myself, my fingers dance in the air around me as my arms swing around. I spin off another tunnel to my left. "You said those people that were in that house were not my parents. Who were they then?"

A cold wind blasts me in the face. The wind comes from a dull lit cave with that magic writing scrolling in front of it. I look to the right and stop dead still. Quintan bumps into me, casting me forward.

He makes me stumble forward, I half fall, my palms scraping against the rough floor. I stand up from my crouch and feel the barrier of scroll work behind me, glancing behind me, I see how close I am. I clap my hands together removing the dirt, my breath hisses out as I bump the scratches on my hands.

"Why have you stopped? Are you okay?" He blusters about, righting himself then coming to look over me. He pulls me back into the center of his spell and symbols, and peers down at my palms. "Not too bad," he whispers and grumbles something under his breath.

I glare up and take my palms away from him. "Then maybe I should run into you and knock you over." I point behind me. "I believe this is a memory we should try; you know the one you almost knocked me into."

"I'm sorry, okay?" He heaves and fixes his shirt and pants that were ruffled. He shies away from my sight and goes to inspect the scroll work of the spell.

"Okay," I say. My anger falls just as quickly as it rises. My head and palms drop down as I move aside, I feel bad as I move behind him giving him room to inspect the spell. The entry glows a very dull red, almost black, and constantly flickers in and out. "This has to be the right memory that we can get into, it's almost dead, the light of the spell is off more than it is on," I say as I bounce my feet up and down. "Finally, some answers," I breathe.

I reach out to the scroll work, and the symbols light up against my touch, but only barely. There is a slight warming sensation against my roughened palms, but it isn't too uncomfortable. "This feels like a memory I need to see." My fingers dance around in the warmth.

He nods and waits till I am done then touches his own fingers against it, it does not light up like it does to my touch. "I think this one will work. Though I think you could have gotten in this one yourself. I was hoping the memory would have been in some relation to what happened to you but we will start here for now. We can always come back and see others." He looks around a bit nervously.

I brush my fingers against the spell again and it lights up, but then dies once again, not able to stay lit the whole time.

"Perhaps you may not be able to get through without my help especially when it is lit," Quintan states.

"I feel like this memory will help. Anything is progress, forward, right?" I look hopefully at him before turning my gaze to the memory wanting past the spell so badly. I stretch my hands and body against the barrier.

I caress the scroll work trying to ask it to forgive me as if it were a living thing with feelings.

"Are you sure you haven't already been in this memory before?" He hesitates. "I am seeing damage to the spell's edges, as if someone punched through it at some time."

"The doctor said that I remembered something from long ago but didn't really touch on what it was, and we did the hypnotherapy before I was shocked, so I don't really remember too much." I say my face drops in sadness by what the spell is doing and causing me to forget. "I don't think Doctor Sorenson thought it was very important either," I tell him.

Quintan tuts at me. "There, there. If you think this is what you need, then so be it. This is your memory and your mind. Only you can tell what will be right for you." He rubs his sides, wiping his hands.

I squeeze my hands into fists, more focused now and wanting to persevere and move forward. "Let's do this then." I punch one of my fists forward.

Quintan bats my arm out of the way before I throw another punch and hurt myself. Instead, he holds onto my lower arm, linking us together. He pushes us through the cave entry. He waits for the light to pulse again and moves us forward when it blinks out.

His symbols continue around us moving with us, cutting through the spell. It lets us pass through easily. Quintan stops and stands in the doorway, his palms spread outward and his legs spread shoulder width apart, as if he is ready to carry the weight of the world or something equally as heavy.

"I cannot come into your memory with you and hold this way secure at the same time. So, I will give you as much time to gather what you need, but be quick or else I might have to yank you out, which will not be pleasant at all." He has a wicked look in his eye, though his form continues to flicker his symbols that protect him do not, and they hold the way.

I nod, understanding. I turn to disappear into my memory wanting the answers to reveal themselves to me. As I walk forward, I am pushed from behind into a room where a baby cries and coos in a crib. I look at my hands and feet and notice I am still myself.

"Weird," I exclaim as I move further into the room.

I look around the room and walk over to the baby in the crib. "Is that me?" I ask no one in particular.

"Alexia! You little scoundrel." A woman calls out as she approaches the crib.

I shrink away to the other side of the crib keeping away from the woman, not sure if she could see or hear me or if I could interact with things here. She did not look my way so I don't duck behind things and just keep an eye out to not knock into anything or make much noise.

The wind rushes through huge open windows tossing sheer curtains around. They billow out the baby stares at the curtains floating in the wind, the baby laughs out again as her eyes track to the woman who is above her.

There are hardwood floors beneath my shoes and the space looks expensive. But the memory holds only these features, everything outside of the baby and the woman is fuzzy around the edges like it is an imperfect picture or a memory that is not fully formed.

The woman's hair tosses around as she bends over the crib to caress the baby's cheek. "There, there little one. Mother is here. Was Flit playing with you again?" she asks, glancing around her, eyes not seizing on anything.

"Mother," I utter. I reach out and place a hand over my mouth, not sure if I can keep my words inside.

I back up a bit, staring at her over the crib. I take in her features, her long brown hair that is wavy where mine is stringy. Her dark eyes that match mine. She frowns, tugging at the blanket to pull it up over the little one.

"Mother, that frown, seems familiar." My face scrunches in thought.

I move around the crib to get a closer look at the woman who says she is my real mother, wanting to be closer to the warmth that pours out of her. She scoots the crib away. I look down and notice the wheels that it rolls on.

"Convenient," I call, a bit louder.

She laughs.

I give a grim look. "Can you hear me?" I stutter, following her with the baby.

She either ignores the question or does not hear it. She moves the crib next to an extravagant chair. I stop and stare as I notice two thrones sitting up there near her and the baby. One is grander than the other and is built on things that look like skulls.

"Are those skulls?" I ask in horror, the chair itself is simple and is solid black with green emeralds embedded into the eye sockets of the skulls.

The one next to that chair is a bit smaller, less intimidating. And the woman pulls the crib up next to the chair and sits down sitting on the edge of the seat as she peers over the crib. Her chair, though smaller, is no less elegant, hers is a dark green made of vines.

In between the tightly coiled vines are black jewels. They glitter darkly, both of the chairs hold a part of each other. There is a red cushion where she perches upon otherwise the chairs look unyielding and hard.

The woman pulls the baby closer to her. She tugs down one of the sides of the crib so she has a better view of the baby and can maneuver the blankets to better cover her. Her long deep brown hair pools over the side over her shoulder as she leans down, blowing raspberries and tickling the little one's tummy. Her hair is a dark chocolate and swings over her face hiding it from my view.

I draw closer, wanting this, wanting a family to call my own. Needing to chisel her face to my memory so I will not forget. The baby laughs once again as she tickles it.

"What is this?" I question as the scene keeps moving. "Why would this help?" I want this to all make sense, but I am just shown a piece of the puzzle and have no idea of how these fit into the bigger picture.

The woman jerks back up and touches the little one on the nose. "All will make sense soon, won't it, my love?"

"Sera," a stern voice emits from behind me.

I spin around and retract myself from between them, cowering behind the two chairs they are low enough to peer over and can still see everything, making sure to keep myself safe and at a distance.

"Ivan," she says just as sternly, piercing him with her dark eyes.

I stare at the man; his intense blue eyes laugh at her.

"You promised." He cocks his head to the side. "They must be able to have a look at their new heir, my sweet." He gives a happy grin as he sees Sera caressing the little one's blanket. He walks up to the other throne and sits down all the way, relaxing into his chair as if he owns it and has sat there for many hours. His reddish hair is cut short, and he is clean shaven. He puts out a palm for her hand.

She smiles at him and places her hand in his. "They can't have her, Ivan." She frowns as she glances back, the little one is dozing off at their low voices. "Let's leave this all together and start again. They don't need us," she utters. "This is too much for someone so small." She worries over the blanket covering the baby.

I frown in confusion and really take a good look around the lavish room noticing others coming into my view. They ghost in as they come closer to the thrones. I shrink back even more behind the chairs, focus on the horror in front of them. This was not a normal king and queen, with normal people. Their loyal subjects, some of them are grotesque in features. Some are glorious and lovely, but they are creatures of stories.

"What the fuck is this place?" I say under my breath. "What are all these things?"

Sera laughs again.

"What is it, my sweet?" Ivan pauses.

"Oh, nothing, you brute. I was just thinking about all these people. They will look to Alexia to lead them. What if she does not want to lead them though?" A sad smile turns down the corners of her mouth. "What if she doesn't know *how* to lead them?"

Ivan perks up and reaches over Sera and pulls the baby closer in front of both of them. "She is strong." He plays with the baby's hand and waits for her to take his finger in his fist and squeeze it. "She is the best of both of us," he says simply. "We will teach her and help her grow into whoever or whatever she wants to be, in our own way." He smiles, his face aglow with happiness.

"What if she does not understand? Or more so hates us for it." Tears trickle down her face; her fingers pull at the blanket that covers the little one but does not pull the baby towards her.

Ivan growls at something in front of them, the ghosts move back becoming less corporeal and harder to see. "We have to do it this way, you know that. The seer explained all would be lost if we did not. We have to trust in things, and believe that they will be okay in the end. I am sorry for the part I have played in this but know you are the light to my darkness." He holds out his palm and cups her cheek taking the pad of his thumb and wiping it across her cheek taking the tear with it.

"And you are the darkness to my light." She recites back to him as she takes his palm and kisses the center of it. "Know this, little one," she speaks down at the babe. "We are here for you, regardless of what you think and know. Though we might not be physically known, we will be pushing things to guide you."

It was as if she were talking to me directly, but not. "This is not real," I balk.

Sera places her hand on her flat stomach as another tear tracks down her cheek. Her face turns to me. "Oh, but it is," she says before she turns her head away from me.

My mouth hangs open as I kick away from the chairs, scooting as quickly as I can from them, only stopping when neither one of them move toward me. How could she hear me, and he could not? This is just a memory, is it not?

Many questions were reeling through my mind at once, not being able to control what was happening. My lungs heave in and out as I just watch them talk to one another in hushed tones. My back presses up against the wall very hard.

Sera speaks up though once they finish muttering over the small baby, so I can hear them even from where I am. "Ivan, sweet she is getting fussy. We need to lay her down soon. Shall we give her the gift now before anyone else visits her tonight?" She looks out at the people before her, they are still mostly hidden in the mist. Ivan tsks at her, but pushes the crib closer to Sera.

"Go on, be quick," he urges.

"I'll be but a moment," she says to the crowd as she picks up the little one. Sera caresses Ivan with her eyes doing what her hands could not.

Ivan growls out. "Woman, you are a danger."

She gives a hoot of laughter and pulls away.

Ivan pulls himself out of the chair and in a big booming voice talks to the mass of people. "All right calm yourself! She is changing the babe. Do you want a stinky infant on you?" he says gruffly.

Sera laughs as she takes the baby away into a room behind the thrones. I slowly get up and rush after her, keeping enough distance between us. Before going through the door fully, I do a double take back at Ivan not wanting to forget him. This was my father. He seems so strong. I lower my head and follow Sera out.

"Shhh…" Sera whispers out. "Lexi, no giving away our secret, no crying now." The baby gurgles and offers a small cry in protest.

I come in fully and edge back in the corner the furthest I can get from Sera afraid that she will grab onto me or say something once again to my questions. I keep quiet.

"I am going to deliver you the greatest gift my power can bestow on you, a warrior to protect you when you may need it most." She looks over her shoulder to my corner.

I glance behind me to the door that is next to me to see if someone is coming.

She turns back to the baby. "Your life will not be easy being of mixed blood of light and dark. We will try regardless of where we are to protect you as much as we can, as well as teach you to protect yourself. Your father is of Darkness, and I am of Light. Both can mix to create a most wonderful thing." Her fingers tickle the little one's belly. "Beliefs are all that worry them, but our blood is the same, know this to be true." She closes her hand in a fist while the other is cradling me close to her body. She begins to hum and sway in tune to the beat she sings.

She opens her fist slowly letting something pool into the middle of her palm. Shadows grow around her. She forces the shadow into a small round like ball and presses against the skin of the little one's cheek. The baby pats at her own face, trying to pull it off and see what is there. The shadow inches down her face and disappears into the onesie that the baby has on, scurrying away from the child's searching hands.

"This shadow will grow with you and protect you, little one. He will also be the answer for you when the darkness becomes too much."

A loud commotion emits from the grand room beyond. The wind picks up, throwing Sera's hair haphazardly around. I quickly look through the door that we came through to see what is going on. Sera bumps into a table as the wind picks up once again. I turn back to see her shoving things out of the way in a cupboard hidden in the table.

Something passes through my arm, things flying about and ghostly people in a state of panic fluttering about the room. The room becomes utter chaos. A group of people are making great strides to this hidden room, coming right for us. I see at the head of the line an angry young woman; her hair is cut short and there are more harsh angles where Sera is soft.

"Who *are* you?" I grow closer to the woman that is all hard edges. "You seem familiar."

Her eyes flick to Sera then back at the people following her.

"You—you were the one at the house. The one that kept me." I take a step back, horrified. "You are younger here but it is definitely you!"

No one sees or hears me as I step to the side; I'm not sure what would happen if they went right through me. I slide into the room staying to the side but keeping my real mother Sera and the imposter in my line of sight.

The imposter's face is distorted with a fierce scowl. She is furious, I can see the murderous thoughts that are written across her eyes. She flicks her wrist to the side, and the curtains snap back, the full glass doors behind Sera bang open loudly. The wind picks up as more air is added to the mix.

"How could you, Jade!" Sera screams. She keeps her body between the table and Jade but does not look or give away that the baby is hidden there.

"Don't act like you didn't see it coming," Jade sneers.

"You were like a sister to me," Sera says in reply.

"Family hurts each other the most, don't they?" Jade scoffs back at Sera.

My head turns this way and that, keeping up with their banter. One of the ghostly images passes through me when I don't move out of the way in enough time. I feel a shiver go through me as he moves past. My arm turns cold. I spin around and another creature passes close by my arm going through the middle of the thing I bring my arm up and hold it close to me. The ogre type thing keeps moving around the room as if I had not even been there. "Well that answers one question."

Jade strikes out like a viper with her hand, a high wind rushes in from the open doors. Sera stumbles about not sure of her footing. "The Light doesn't use their powers against one another," Sera calls out.

"They do when it is to fight against those of darkness," she screeches, the wind picks up with her anger.

Sera's eyes glare at Jade. "Don't you dare pretend we are not on the same side. We were getting away from sides, from their war. You know it," she screams.

"You got out." She looks down her nose in disgust. "I still had a job to do." She scoffs.

"You were supposed to follow, supposed to come with us."

Jade cries out. "Awwww, I was supposed to." She grits her teeth. "Don't give me that bullshit!" she yells. "You didn't come back to make sure; you didn't care!"

Sera shrivels back a bit. "We couldn't come back."

"Ahhhh. Yes." Her eyes roam the room. "A child was what kept you, wasn't it? This is why your job is not quite done either, and he will accept your apology for fraternizing with the enemy of a dark one, if you come back with her." Jade looks to Sera, giving her a knowing look.

"He?" she stutters out. "He lives?" She stumbles back as if hit by something.

"Sera." She stares at her baffled. "There are sides for a reason. Our kind should have never mixed in the first place." She gives a sardonic smile. "But now that they have, we must do what is needed in order to keep the balance." She points to the people she has come with off to the sides of her surrounding Sera and the table. "We mustn't let the end of the world come to fruition, or do you not care about this world anymore?" she asks sweetly.

Sera bares her teeth. "Those sides are no longer ours, we left each of them because they cause such strife and heartache look at what they have you doing!" she yells over the wind begging her to see. "Do you not see what we have created here for ourselves, a haven for any and all who are welcome. We work together, and only together can we make things thrive and get past this. You all think we are better than humans in some ways." She tosses her head, and the curls bounce around her face. "That is not so, we follow them and do the same terrible things they do."

Jade punches her hand forward and air rushes at Sera pushing her away from the table, people move out of the way before she collides with the wall. "You are even more ignorant than I thought you were," she yells, walking ever so slowly forward, all while keeping pressure and pressing Sera into the hard wall. The people form a half circle around Jade and Sera.

I shiver as I move through other people to stay near the table. A small cry emits as I lean down close to where the baby was hiding. I crouch down and make shushing noises to hopefully keep her calm in a time like this. I didn't know what Jade and Sera were talking about but I kept listening in case I needed this information for later.

"Go ahead. Ask your rogues to fight the good fight against us then. You will have to go against both of us, the Light users and the Dark users." Sera chokes out a strangle of air, no words are able to be said; she barely is able to gulp down enough breath. "No? I didn't think so, how would you, you went and took a small piece from both sides and you just don't match up do you?"

"You never believe in people." Sera coughs.

"Believe in people. I believe in those who actually do something, cause things to happen. I will tell you exactly what would happen if you asked them to fight for yours. They would cower and hide as they do now. Do you see them here protecting you? Where is your king?" She lets go of the wind and throws her arms out showing only her people surrounding her. "That is a low blow, very cold if you ask me. They abandoned you and yours in your time of need." Jade ticks off her fingers. "Never worry though we will find someone that will give up your vile lover, he can't stay away forever."

The wind calms as Jade turns this way and that. Sera kneels down after being released, catching her breath. A piercing shrill penetrates the quiet lull; I glare at my younger self. "You just had to make noise," I argue.

Jade focuses on the cabinet and smiles. "Let's not forget about your putrid mess of a daughter." She grins as she stomps over to the table.

I scramble back, the viciousness of her face making me want to escape this memory myself.

"You take that back!" Sera bites out through clenched teeth. Throwing all of her weight back and then rocking forward, she crashes into Jade, smashing her own head into hers. The others surround her, but do not move forward to help. Both of them drop to the floor, landing close to the cabinet in a tangle of arms and legs.

Jade glares at Sera, who is moaning and trying to recover from the pain of slamming her head into someone else's. She pushes away from Sera none too gently, but holds her head in pain where she was hit. She moves slowly towards the cabinet stopping every once in a while, to correct her footing. The baby cries out very loud in answer to the commotion, and Jade moves quickly, wanting the baby before Sera moves closer. She tears open up the cabinet; the little one is dead silent and mystified by what is taking place.

"Don't hurt her!" Sera cries.

"She is the cause for all of this, she is going to be the death of us all!" Jade screams back at the top of her lungs. "You know the prophecy as well as I do."

"She is justice. She will not be the monster that you think she will become. As long as that person has a tie to this world there won't be anything to worry over, she won't become the final fate," Sera attempts to defend her point. Tears fall silently from her eyes as she sees Jade's determination and her sneer as she looks at the baby.

"There is too much risk in that plan, and too much riding on this for us to hope the child turns out on the better side, the light side. She has half of the vicious darkness inside of her. What if that is the half that chooses to take lead, chooses to awaken." Jade picks up the baby with no care, and shudders, holding the baby out far from her body. "Ugh I can barely hold on to this thing, how does it not disgust you?"

"You mean the same vicious beast you liked at first as well," Sera rips into her.

My mouth drops with the news of them both liking the same guy.

"Don't act like that same darkness did not attract you as well. How can you call him a monster when you were ready to do the same thing?" She throws out at Jade and to all of those that help Jade.

Jade laughs. "Do you think I actually meant that I liked him? God you are dim witted. That was part of the plan, we wanted him if the darkness would have lost their best soldier, we would have been able to take over everywhere. Though this is just as good is it not?" She bounces the baby without a care. "We don't need your vile lover any more—we have her!" She holds the baby with one hand as she snaps at one of her followers.

"What are you talking about?" Sera edges forward, wanting to take the squalling baby out of her hands.

"Don't give me another reason to finish your pack of rogues off, you deceitful bitch! You are not this stupid!" Jade says with fury.

Sera shuffles to her feet barely and limps toward Jade with her arms fully outstretched. "Don't drop her, just give her to me. Take whatever anger you have on me and not the child, Ivan as well if you need, too. I am the one that took your dreams from you, not Alexia."

"No, she will do well. She has both of you in one little easy to manage package." Jade smiles. "Since you started this process, she will need to be the fuel, her death will come one day but not today." She jiggles the baby into the waiting arms of one of her followers. "Hold this here. She will be the life essence that keeps the light running and strong." She points as if to say *wait here.*

"A life essence spell? What would you need with that? What do you plan on doing with her?" She shakes her hands, trying to keep the anger contained.

"The spell will rectify all that is wrong with you and him, it will make sure this does not happen again, take away all the darkness and we will live in a world that is forever cast in light. No shades of gray or darkness to be seen."

"You cannot have one without the other," Sera yells. "Both need each other."

"With magic you do not need that, there have been other worlds that have done this and have gone on to be wondrous, other worlds have sunk and given into the darkness those worlds are inhabitable now because they did not listen to the right people."

"You will not be able to keep her, we will come for her, you will not build the power for your spell, we will stop you. You will not be able to keep her hidden from us for that long," she yells.

"No, you don't think so," Jade states in a defiant and strong voice, making it echo around the tiny room. She moves quickly and moves her hands inside her skirt, she advances closer to the person that is now holding the baby. A knife appears from her skirts and Jade dangles it dangerously over the baby's form.

The people close in and surround Sera, they move to grab her as a scream rips from her lungs at the sight.

"I can end this the easy way, then, your choice." She pushes the knife closer to the baby, inch by terrifying inch.

I lunge forward trying to stop the scene from continuing. Something about a knife coming at you regardless of this being a memory, it makes me snap into action. My hands simply fade through Jade's and causes a cold shiver to echo through my hands. I try to drive her out of the way and make her move, but all my attempts are futile.

Sera screams in horror and vines burst out from the floor surrounding Jade, the vines curl around the baby and the man holding her lets the baby go, afraid of what the vines will do to him. The vines catch and wrap the baby in a cocoon. The baby is safe in a protective layer of vines, making sure no harm comes to her.

"You are getting on my last nerve Jade. I have put up with you for too long." Sera's hands are outstretched, controlling where the vines go. She urges them closer to her so she is near her baby though she does not uncurl them from protecting her.

Her eyes burn with fury. "You have pushed me for the last time." Her eyes lighten as rage pools into her, more vines slither in from the open doorways.

I peek outside at the jungle of vegetation that can be used. She calls and gathers the energy, pulling more and more vines to her.

"Sera, what are you doing!" A horrific look comes over Jade's face.

I search around the room seeing if anything more than vines come in. Vines litter the floor but I do not see anything else that would worry Jade like she was. "Why are you pulling power like that?"

"You started this!" Sera growls low. "And I will finish this, maybe then you will leave what is mine alone!" Sera's furry rises as static electricity crackles all around the vines that cover the baby in a bubble of protectiveness.

Jade shakes her head in fright. "You do not want to have so many deaths on your head," she croaks, backing up.

"You do not understand what one would do for their child's life and to keep them safe." Sera throws out vines trapping Jade, pulling at her arms and legs, raising her up above all other people in the room. "No matter what others think of her she will always be the best in my eyes." Her eyes shoot over to me. I am close to the baby in the vine ball. The others have begun to run or fight the vines hold them off or let them escape.

My eyes fill with tears hearing her talk about me in such a way, I have never heard anyone speak about me that way before. I wish I could have kept that love with me through this all.

"But you are correct Jade, I do not wish to have blood on my hands. You will never find this land or our people again. I will protect them and my child from you," she says with deep conviction.

Jade's piercing blue eyes zap open and pull the wind in slicing through some of the vines that were holding her and the baby causing it to list to the right toward Jade. She falls to the floor as the wind rips the vegetation loose, she comes closer to the ball of vines. She slashes at them with strong forces of wind, once there is a tear in them, she rips at the rest of the vines and orders the other people to hold Sera captive. They all pile forward the vines easily holding many of them off but there are too many to keep at bay.

Jade rips the last vine free of the baby and grabs her. The baby cries out, her face red and splotchy, too much excitement is going on for this little one.

"Your child's life is in my hands," Jade grits out between clenched teeth. The baby cries harder as Jade's hands tighten on her. She holds her very close to her chest making sure no others can take her from her grasp, watches as some of the others drop from the vines but there are enough that will be able to overtake Sera.

Vines burst out and move everyone out of the way and Sera jumps forward. She rushes forward, grabbing with two fists into Jade's hair. Sera screams as she yanks hard and comes away with two fists full of hair.

"Know this to be true—regardless of what you think you can do; I can do so much worse." She looks down her nose at Jade.

Sera pushes the vines so that she towers over them all out of reach. Electricity pulls up through the vines from outside as lightning strikes multiple times right outside. I see the electricity dance over the vines, feel the static in the air as she gathers more and more power.

"You wouldn't dare!" Jade yells as she grips the child in front of her.

"Test me, Jade, I dare you." She looks pointedly at her and then her daughter. She pulls both fists full of hair close to her. "I bind you Jade from doing harm to my child. If she is harmed in any way, it will take away from your life force, not hers. I call on the Dark King. To swear this allegiance, I accept the blood debt." She yanks a black crystal necklace that is around her neck. She slams it to the ground, and a dark cloud grows out of it.

"Sera, I hear your plea and also accept," a dark voice booms out of the cloud. The cloud spreads upward, as lighting arcs through the entire room hitting everyone in its path.

"What does that mean swearing allegiance?" I ask myself, unsure what any of this means. I scramble away from the lightning not knowing what it would do, but inch closer to the woman that was my mother. "What is happening?" I yell, hoping that he will answer me once more.

The dark cloud spreads out to envelop Sera's lower form and hovers near the little baby in Jade's arms. It touches on the lower extremity but Jade scrambles out of the way and whisks wind through the cloud dispersing it. "You will not take her," she shouts.

"Always question everything," Sera calls out.

My eyes rake over Jade, she is looking at the baby and the cloud before her. I look back at Sera, she is staring straight at me, hand extended down to me.

"Mother? You can see me?" I cry out in question.

"I couldn't always." She rubs her stomach once again and smiles. "Look to the darkness to find your light," she roars out as the dark cloud rushes over her covering her form.

"Where are you, where can I find you?" I hurry up and ask.

"We will meet again one day though I doubt the way you expect." She smiles to herself.

"Tell me what to do! I don't know what is going on!" I glance around the room, noticing the people and things have frozen in place, the memory moving no further. Sorrow bursts from my chest as I crumple to the floor, gathering the blanket that has fallen off from around the baby.

"Trust in Shade, trust in yourself," a tiny voice emits from all around me as the scene disappears into darkness.

I hug my knees and rock back and forth. "I don't know what to do. I am so lost and confused on what all this means." Tears roll down my face and soak the black cotton pants I wear. "He is just a dark menacing figure that kills things that hurt me. How can he help?" I croak out, sobbing into my knees.

"There are other ways to communicate, my little one. Give him a chance, give others a chance where you usually wouldn't," the voice echoes as it fades away.

I fumble around on the ground, scrambling for anything that I can reach. The blanket falls from my grasp for a moment, most things have already disappeared. Something skitters away from me as my fingers roam in the darkness. A little chime sounds from it as it rolls. I crawl over carefully to where I heard it last and pat the ground. It is round with edges and very short. I hold it tight, but without seeing what I am looking at, it is hard to tell what it is.

I hold onto the small object and scramble back for the blanket, or where I thought I had left it. I pat the floor crawling slowly, the wall slams into me. "Ouch." I rub my nose and head and sit down. "Where did that come from?" I can't see anything or hear anything other than my own voice echoing back at me. "How do I get out of this memory? Quintan?"

I hear steps echo on the hard floor, moving closer.

"Quintan," I whisper moving back to the wall I ran into and press up against it, too scared to move. "I want out," I cry, giving a small mewing sound.

Something large and big slams against me and the wall. It wraps something around my throat and pulls upward. My fingers find purchase on cloth, but nothing else that I can grab onto. My fingers scrape through the smooth cloth uselessly. My feet kick out, but do not connect other than with the wall. I push off of the wall to try to make a connection with something.

"Quintan," I squeeze out. My lungs ache for breath. My fingers try to grip onto the cloth.

Air barely squeaks into my lungs as I keep jiggling up and down. I claw at the cloth trying to rip it, it is a slow process and I was losing strength. I kick out my legs, they feel like Jell-O and disconnected from the rest of my body. The fight goes out of me and I lose the ability to move, my eyes flicker shut. I force them open trying to see what has me, but the darkness is absolute, and I can no longer remember if they are open or shut...

Hands claw at my shoulders and haul me up. "Alexia! Wake up." Quintan shakes me roughly and jostles my shoulders.

I come to and breathe in deeply. My hands and arms come up to protect me as I rub at my sore throat. I glare at Quintan, not wanting to trust him. "What did you do? What happened?" I look around, making sure whatever had attacked me did not follow us into the real world.

"I told you it would be an unpleasant return if you did not hurry. It is not me who should be at fault when you did not heed my warning," Quintan says as he backs away with his hands up, not wanting to startle me anymore than I already was.

"What were you doing?" I question, my voice coming out in a whisper, it hurt to speak whatever happened in there felt real enough.

"I had to force you out of the memory by trying to yank you out, but you decided to fight against my pull, you were beginning to win against my already depleted powers. So, I had to physically harm you, just a little, to stop your aggressive behavior towards me so that you could be pulled back into your body."

"It sure doesn't feel like it was only a little bit of pain. I think you did some serious damage." I rub at my neck, still whispering. "You didn't tell me how to get out," I throw back in his face. "This is on you for not showing me how to get out. Are you even trying to help me?" I sneer at him.

"You walked in. You do the same to get out. You walk back out." He keeps his distance, not wanting to anger me anymore. He walks over to his desk and gets a glass and some water from the pitcher he had sitting there.

"I couldn't get out!" I hiss. "It was pitch black, and I tried crawling out, but ran into a wall, and then there was something there with me. Or perhaps that was you when you were choking the life out of me."

"That's absurd. Only you can affect your mind. The spell only blocks you. It isn't a real thing to attack you."

One of my hands is still on my neck, and I look down at my other hand in the chair, Quintan is still turned away from me at the desk. Something is in my fist; I look down and open my fingers one at a time.

Something small with sharp edges bites into my palm. A clear dark crystal lies in my palm, small and delicate. I let it roll in my palm in amazement. I did not have this with me before I went into my mind. I glance up at Quintan's turned back, making sure he does not see what I do. Wherever I went, or whatever I can do, it was not just a memory.

I quickly put the crystal in my pocket and just hold my neck with both hands. "Something rammed into me and choked me," I urge. "If not something else than it, was you."

He turns with the full glass of water outstretched to me. "Choking? I only gripped your shoulders really hard and shook you in the chair, I didn't choke you." He examines the room, giving it a curious look.

I grab the glass of water, the liquid sloshing over the sides as my hands shake. "Yes, choking." I chug some of the water down my dry throat, easing back as it hurts to swallow, only taking small sips instead.

"If you drift into the memory too much, you will disappear into your mind. Maybe that is why you couldn't just walk out like you walked in. What was the memory about? Was it a tough one?" Quintan asks curiously, going back to the water and pouring himself his own glass, leaning on the desk. He still keeps an eye on the room around us.

"It was about my real mother. I am not sure who she was, but she seemed important." I stare at him, gauging his reaction, wanting to look around the room once again, but I knew nothing was there. "I guess you all were right, things were not like it seemed before."

"Did you get a name?" he asks. "A name for your real mother?"

"No, no one said it," I lie, taking a sip to not give anything away. "Jade was there, though. Her name was said, they knew each other. The woman that ended up dead in that house was Jade. She stole me from my real parents. She was younger in the memory but from the pictures I was shown I figured that much out."

Quintan looks at me, his glass of water partially to his mouth ready for another sip, he sets it down and purses his lips.

"What?" I shake my head not wanting to talk much more than I already have, everyone has made me feel like a small child. "I am new to all of this please," I beg. "Please explain what is going on. I didn't even know supernatural creatures existed till the other day. Or at least I don't think I did."

"Hush." His eyes turn cold and angry. "Do not talk with anyone about what you have learned here so far. For now, we will just leave it here and get you settled in. I will set you up with library time to learn more about where you come from." He moves around his desk and picks up a pen, diligently writing notes on a couple of the papers and scratching out a few other things.

I slowly lower the glass down onto the side table next to my chair and start to ease to the side, wanting to get away. My throat throbs in sync with my heartbeat. "Why?" I ask in question. "I thought you wanted me to talk through things and figure out where I came from. Why are you asking me to not talk about this? I need answers from someone. You can't all be bad," I yell in frustration. I squirm in the chair and get to my feet, edging behind the chair. "Why did you guys want me here if you weren't really going to help?"

Quintan moves over to his desk chair, leaning heavily on his left leg, slightly limping.

"Did you get hurt in the memory?" I ask, curious as to why he would hide it.

"No." He rustles through papers on the desk, ignoring my questioning eyes. "I think we will both need some rest for now. I will see you back here before the end of the week."

"What happened to you?" I stay where I am behind the chair as I ask. "Why are you hurt?" I tremble. "Is there something in here with us?" I give into my paranoia and look around the room once more.

"Go get some rest." He gives a gruff nod to the door.

I stare at him for a bit, but he does not back down. "Fine," I say in anger, though my throat twinges in pain and my body fights exhaustion. "You might be right that we need some rest." I rub one of my eyes and back up, not wanting to stay in this room if there was something here.

He nods and keeps writing in my file but keeps an eye on me. "Until we meet again then, I will have you meet with Melissa everyday just to talk and see how you are adjusting to life here she will be the person you go to if you need anything. She will also go over with you in detail of what you can recall from your past along with anything else that you may remember while you are here, you can trust her." He stops writing and eyes me and taps the pen against the paper multiple times before going back to writing. "I will go over what I had witnessed and then get with Melissa to confirm what you guys talk about, then we will talk about the memory and what it means and your future. You will have plenty of time to sort through what you witnessed before you talk with Melissa."

"You just said to talk to no one about it though," I growl, still backing toward the door, I roll my eyes at him. These people made no sense.

"She you will be able to trust, you will understand when you meet her. First though you will need some rest, I can see you're a bit all over the place with your emotions." He ignores my outburst.

"Wouldn't you be?" I growl out.

"I cannot say." He presses a button on a small box that sits on his desk, it makes an awful buzzing sound. "Yes, Doctor Helm. May I help you with something?" a petite voice says shyly from the box where he pushed the button.

"Will you please come in here and help Miss Alexia to her room?" he speaks into the box and pauses in his writing.

"Yes, Doctor Helm," her voice snaps quickly and attentively.

He keeps the button held down. "Also, can you clear the rest of my schedule for the night, I am afraid I won't be much use for that agenda with the way I am feeling now," Quintan states, frowning.

"Yes, of course. I'll be right in to take care of the girl and show her around."

My eyes begin to droop no matter how many times I blink them open. They want to keep closing. I don't know what happened after their talk over the intercom, I sluggishly remember walking through the hallway and being told this and that, but my brain turns off as soon as my face hits the pillow.

CHAPTER 4

I SLOWLY WAKE UP and move around in the bed I am in; the blanket is thin and the bed creaks. I glance out the window that is above the head of my bed and notice that it is dark outside. Yawning I contemplate going back to bed. Off in the distance outside, I can hear the birds chirping in the trees, barely audible through the heavy windowpane.

"That means it is close to morning, right?" I whisper to myself. I do not remember much on my way to this room. Me moving a little more in the bed causes it to squeak multiple times.

I grimace in pain. My throat is dry and still hurts from earlier. I touch it gently as I turn around in the bed facing the door where we entered the room. I search the room for somewhere I can get a drink or use the restroom. The room holds two dressers, three doors on the wall opposite of the window, and two desks.

The other bed is right across from mine against the other wall. A lone form is huddled under the covers. The form breathes in evenly and deeply under there. I move slowly so as not to make the creaks too loud. One of the three doors, the one in the middle, has a window set about eye level in the door.

"That must be where they can see into the room to check on us."

I sit up and set the blankets back away from me, only to have them cover my lower legs and feet. The moon spills in over the room, bringing enough bright light for me to see by, so I don't run into anything. I shudder at the memory that comes to mind and rub my nose in thought. I pull my knees up to my chest out of the warm blankets. The cool night air nips at my fingers and toes. When I lower my bare feet to the ground the temperature of the floor causes me to shiver. My shoes that are sitting next to the bed, reaching over I pull them on quickly, not bothering to tie them. I push up with my arms, getting out of the bed slowly. My eyes squint at each sound the bed makes.

Padding over to the door across from my bed I open it, hoping to find a bathroom. I am disappointed as I stare into the empty abyss of a closet my suitcase is on the floor. My fingers itch toward it, but my throat begs me to continue on. I slide my hands in my pockets unsure of what to do and feel the rock I had hidden there in my pocket.

I sigh and shut the door very quietly then slide across the way to the other door across the other bed. I open it and notice another dark closet, this one filled with clothes. I want to cry in frustration but refrain from doing so since it would just hurt my throat. Barely keeping myself from slamming the door shut in anger, I rub the rock between my fingers instead and shut it normally, it makes a small audible click.

I go to the dresser on my side of the room and open one of the top drawers, I hold the thing up in the light and notice it is like the rock my true mother had held to call to the Dark King. It is dark but almost see through. I slip the black stone into the drawer to keep it hidden, not sure of what it means or could do this would be the safest place for it.

I shuffle back to the middle door and check by jiggling the handle. It rattles a bit, but does not budge. "Drats, locked. How the hell do I go to the restroom?" I whisper.

Gripping on the edge of the window in the door, I hoist myself on tippy toes to see outside.

"Do they make these windows for giants? This is not a normal person sized window."

The hallway is bright and lit, but no people are walking the halls. All the doors are dark and shut like ours is.

I tap on the glass. "Hey, hello!" I say in a scratchy voice, speaking a bit louder. "Let me out, I have to go." I knock a bit louder hoping to get someone's attention.

"Ughhhh. They can't hear you," an exasperated voice explains, her voice filled with sleep and anger.

I gasp in surprise and slam my back against the door, pressing firmly into the wood of the door. "I have to use the restroom," I whisper and fiddle with nervous energy.

Blue solid eyes peek out from the covers and blink at me as they glitter menacingly. She untucks one of her hands from the cozy blankets.

I see her blue arm slide out of the covers and point. "You're blue?" I ask but look where her hand points.

She points at something on my side of the room above my bed in the middle of it. "Press the button. We each have one on our own wall. Let them know that you have to do a thing. They will come get you so that you can do that. Hurry up and either go back to sleep or go do you. I am still tired." She yanks the cover back up over her head and tucks her blue arm back into the cocoon of blankets, ignoring my question.

I stare at the lump of blankets and blink in astonishment, racing across the short distance I hop up onto the bed. It gives a violent squeak in protest patting the wall above the bed I find the small switch. I flip it and notice a red bulb glows and turns on inside a protective plastic case covering. I tap at it trying to discern its purpose, but I am blocked by the plastic case.

"Yes?" a bright voice chirps from the box.

I scowl at the voice and the button. "How are you so perky at this time?" I groan.

There is no answer back, as if they are caught off guard. "I heard that." The pleasantness drops from her voice.

A muffled laugh comes from behind me under the covers.

"I have to use the bathroom... Please," I add softly, trying to make up for my previous comment. I don't know her, and I need to go. "I don't think I can wait much longer or till the morning and the door is locked."

"Okay, someone will be right there," she notifies me promptly, and then the red bulb fades out, and she is no longer there.

I turn around and wait on the bed. A few moments later, I hear shuffling outside the door and rustling of keys fumbling with the lock. I reach back and pat myself on the shoulder where I had last felt the shadow creature settle.

I hoped Shade could hear me. "We need to talk soon." I get up from the bed and whisper on my way to the door, hoping my roommate did not hear me. I do not feel a flutter in answer or see him slithering around in the shadows. "Shade?" I whisper a bit louder.

Was he out scouting out the place? Was he sleeping? Was it really just a spell that came out when I was in pain or needing help? So many questions and not enough answers. I did not want to go back to the mage and wait to get answers, especially if it meant possibly losing my life by being choked. I still believe he had to have done something or knows more than he is letting on.

The door opens letting the light spill in from the outside, sending whoever was in the doorway into shadows. I throw up a hand shading the lights to try to see who it is in the doorway. As I walk through to the better adjusted light, the guard closes the door and locks it back up securely. I bat my eyes against the brilliant light, giving my eyes a moment to adjust. I step back, waiting quietly and finally notice Doug hovering over me, eyeing me with a creepy grin on his face.

"Fuck," I bark in the quiet hall, my voice bouncing back at me. I take large steps away from him, not liking how close he is to me.

Doug's eyes light up as they roam over my form and glance around the empty hallway, looking behind me. He walks off down the walkway. His shoes clack down on the tile smartly, expecting me to follow.

"Are you going to show me the way to the restroom?" I edge forward, but don't want to follow him.

"Possibly." He smiles cruelly over his shoulder.

"I swear, I will pee all over you." I huff and follow him down the way.

Doug shutters and rubs his hands together. "Oooo, what a turn on." He twitches his mustache back and forth.

I fidget back and forth from foot to foot, following behind him very slowly and keeping a healthy distance. "You disgust me."

I am in shock when I pass a sign pointing the way to the restrooms and showers. "You are going to be fun for many years to come." He laughs.

"Hell no," I say with disdain.

He stops near the entrance to the restroom and bows. "My lady."

I keep him in my periphery, but I walk cautiously forward. I open the door and see that it is spacious and has many stalls to occupy the number that is held within these walls. Along with the toilets there are many shower stalls, and a dressing room area along with a row of sinks. I rush in and make sure he closes the door before continuing. It swings shut on silent hinges.

I take care of business as fast as possible, which includes taking a drink from the faucet for my parched throat. I want to go as quick so that Doug doesn't get the big idea to come in here and start something. I am afraid of what he wants to do.

I hug myself, wishing Shade were here with me, either to figure things out or to protect me from Doug. "Stupid gloves," I grumble.

I had noticed that he still had the gloves with him to protect him from any spells that might activate, he took great care to not touch me so far. "Shade are you around?" The mirror reflects my body as I begin pulling at my shirt to see if he is there. It is not easy checking one's whole body for a tattoo especially since he doesn't stay put.

I stand and lean against the sink, trying to think of something more I could do to make Shade appear. I guess I better get back out there before Doug comes in and confronts me. It would be more difficult for someone to come across us or for someone to hear me in here rather than out in the hallway.

I take a deep breath and gulp one more mouth full of water. "Time to face the music," I state. I walk out rapidly and glance at him, noticing his nose is twitching back and forth as if he were scenting something in the air. He looks agitated and nervous at the same time; he scans the corridor once again.

I back up away from him on the other side of the door. He comes at me quickly and grabs both of my biceps, forcing me back into the bathroom, shoving the door out of the way. He traps me with his body between him and the wall. I give a shout of surprise.

He brings his hand up across my body and covers my mouth so I can't scream or shout for help. He traps my hands above my head and squeezes them there with his other hand. The hand that he had covering my mouth he lowers slowly and rests it against my bruised throat gently brushing the sensitive skin there.

"Don't. You won't like what happens if you test me," he whispers against my ear. He shifts his stance and pins my body with his. Each one of my legs are on the outside of his.

I look at him, and then up at the ceiling. A tear rushes down over my left cheek, I squeeze my eyes shut hard wishing he would just go away. A sob is pulled from me without me meaning too, the pressure increases on my throat, his fingers scratch at my neck. I cough in his face. It sounds hoarse.

My shoes scrabble for purchase against the tile wall to release some of the tension he is pressing on me. He squeezes me back against the wall pushing his body into my pelvis and grinds there. He sniffs my neck deeply and keeps pressing on my neck making it harder for me to struggle.

I kick at his outer legs, but it doesn't do anything other than press him into the center of my body. He loosens his hand a bit for me to gasp in a breath, and then tightens his grip once more. I hold the air in my lungs, wanting it to stay there. He inhales once again. I cringe away from his nose, his mustache tickling my neck and repulsing me.

"Stop," I gasp.

"Your fear is intoxicating." He breathes in a deep lung full of air, sniffing a couple of times and holding in the scent. He grins with pure ecstasy as if he is smelling something delicious. His eyes begin to shine and turn red, his nose begins to lengthen and protrude from his face. His teeth buck out and long hairs start to poke through his skin near his nose.

"What?" I gasp in horror; my eyes are glued to his face.

He presses his nose in my hair and neck area, grinding and thrusting against me. The long whiskers press into my skin, making my skin crawl and itch. My mind scrambles to make sense of all of this.

"What are you?" I whisper as he lowers his hand further down my neck, closer to my sternum.

"Rat shifter. I told you I was a rat," he growls. "Do you like?" He nibbles on my neck, rubbing against it.

"I don't know what that is." I neither say yes or no. I wiggle to see how hard he has my hands still pinned. They budge only a smidgen.

"Mmmm, yes, wiggle some more," he chatters. "I can shift into a full rat form or a half and half form like this." His nose fully goes into my hair, his head so close bringing his neck close, his thumb creeps down into my shirt caressing my skin there.

Anger blooms in the pit of my stomach and radiates out to my extremities. "How can a girl suspected of being a murderer, be so filled with delicious fear? You're not dark at all, are you?" He notes.

I am furious at his motives and what he is insinuating. "See you get it! You are the only one to believe me so far, and you don't want to help me at all." My voice turns low.

He laughs. "You have so much to learn. Let me teach you." The hand that was hovering near my throat slides over my small chest and pulls up the edge of my shirt. He hums and then huffs in my ear. "Something else comes forward, fear is but a taste now." He pouts.

I pull my head back and slam forward. He doesn't move. He actually pulls me closer, so I bite down on his neck—hard. He squeaks in pleasure. I continue to keep applying pressure; my teeth clench down. He scrambles away, but I come with him. He lets go of my hands, and I fall on top of him, my arms wrapping around his neck, keeping me close.

The other wall stops him from fully falling down. I latch my legs around him, gripping tightly. Blood pours down my throat as I bite down and wiggle my head back and forth, sliding my teeth through the wet skin, doing the most damage possible.

He pushes at my chest, and I unlatch to try to get a better purchase on another part of his body, my tongue licks my lips as I lunge forward once again. He stops me easily and kicks me against the other wall. I hit it hard and slump down. My breath comes in growling gasps as I glare up at him.

"You bitch!" He takes off one of the gloves and reaches back on his neck and brings his hand back, showing it is covered in blood. He uses the glove stop the bleeding. He looks down on me in horror. "Your eyes. They are pitch black," he says, taken back.

I pick myself up off the floor so he is not standing over me. I bare my teeth and squeeze my hands into fists. Nails bite into my skin, so I loosen them a bit, not able to close them fully. I do not want to take my eyes off of Doug to look down, so I bring a hand forward to hold it in front of my face. My fingers have elongated into claws.

Doug's eyes land on my hands as well and breathes in carefully. "What are you? I thought they said you were a witch?" he says in confusion. "Are you a shifter? Badger?" he questions as he shakes his head back and forth.

"I have no answers for you," I bite out. "Leave me alone." A loud thumping noise beats rapidly. I look at his chest. "Is that your heartbeat?" I ask. The rhythm draws me in, swaying in time with it as I move closer.

He backs away towards the door, retreating. "You can hear that?" He covers his chest as if that would cover up the loud booming that rapidly increases with his movement.

I crouch down, ready to pounce. I smile at him this time and slide one foot forward, ready to make my move. I glare at him, my eyes catching every movement, something in me wanted to fight even though in my head I was screaming that we should be running. I breathe in a deep breath loving the sweet scent that has permeated the room. "What is that deliciousness?" I ask, my mouth watering in answer.

Doug shakes his head and the whiskers, long fingers, mouth, and nose are back to normal size. He is human once more. "They did not state you were a shifter. If I knew that, I would not have activated your animalistic nature." He paws at the door behind him, scrambling for a way out. "He said you were a witch. Why would witches have you?"

"No." I tilt my head to the side, eying him. "You would have made me cower in a different way then." My legs move me forward following him. "You only stopped because you are not the predator anymore, I am." Growling at him, I crouch down scraping my nails on the tile below me, finding purchase to leap before he opens the door. I seethe in a tide of red-hot anger, thinking of nothing else as I surrender myself to this thing that has awoken in me.

"This can't be part of the spell. Where is your shadow creature?" He grabs my arm with the one hand that is still covered. The glove doesn't light up like they did last time. "No, not a spell." He quickly releases my arm and twists away, keeping out of reach.

I slash out with my clawed hand. "I can't wait to bite into your juicy center," I spit out, licking my lips, my tongue catches on very sharp teeth. I touch my tongue to a couple of them and notice they are all pointed. I smile baring my teeth at him.

"What animal are you?" he questions, bringing his nose to the air to scent.

"All the better to eat you with." I laugh out loud.

He gets spooked and turns, opening the door quickly he clips his shoulder as he races through the door and slams it shut in my face before I can launch up at him. A noise fumbles on his side. I walk up to the door and claw at the handle. It doesn't budge. "Locked me in here? You are a coward!" I yell.

"No... You need to calm down..." he stutters. "I will let you sit here for a while and come back with someone to take you back to your room before everyone gets up for the day." His voice shakes.

"No one else will bother you," he says for good measure. "No one that could help you will be able to hear you."

"No, can't have someone find your dirty work," I hiss. "Let me out now!" I bellow and pound on the door in front of me, scraping my claw down the door, leaving deep grooves in it.

"Not until you have time to breathe and think through things. You are more a danger to everyone else with the state you are in now. You don't even know how to control yourself," he squeaks.

The beast inside me riles up, wanting to fight and flee all at the same time. My stomach growls in answer, more importantly it needs substance and his stringy body would do just that.

"I can't wait till I can have another taste," I sing. "Lick that red dripping goodness, letting it cool the heat that you have awoken inside of me." I crouch low, trying to peer under the door. My breath sniffs like his did to me. "I can still smell you, rat." I hear shoes click down the hallway moving quickly away. "Run, run little mouse. I'll be along later," I hiss ramming my shoulder against the heavy wooden door, trying to budge it. I yank on the handle, wanting to tear it directly off the wall and door frame.

Saliva runs out of the corner of my mouth; I wipe it on the side of my shirt. I roar out a cry as I push through the anger and instincts to remember who I am and that I'm not this animal.

"No!" I yell in a guttural voice, not liking how close the walls are. "Let me out of here." I slam my hands at the door once again. I make my way over to the mirrors above the sink gripping onto the sides with my claws and stare at my reflection. "I will not stoop to his level." I say angrily. Staring back at myself, forcing myself to calm down, my arms shake with anger and fear of being stuck in here.

I watch as my eyes return to normal as the fear takes over the anger. My vision dims a little as they return; things are not as crisp or clear as they were. I shudder as my teeth flatten back out. I open my mouth in the mirror and run my tongue along the flat white teeth. Blood still stains them. I fumble with the faucets to turn them on and cup cool water into my hands. I watch as the claws remain, not disappearing like the teeth and eyes, the water overflows running over my sharp talons. I bring my hands up splashing the water on my face and take a sip afterwards from the rushing water.

I hesitate as the claws stay put. "Go away," I whisper to my hands. I sniffle as they do not listen and just sit there not going anywhere. Shaking I try to flick them away. "Stupid," I growl to myself glancing at the door, making sure it does not move.

I find myself getting more and more frustrated as the minutes tick away. I pluck at the claws trying to pull them off and then push down on the sharp points to make them go back in, but nothing I do makes them turn back into human fingers.

I slowly crouch down, leaving the water on, keeping my feet under me. I hug my knees as I let out a small wail. I crouch under the sinks and sit down beneath them sniffling back the tears and try to keep myself from crying and letting it all out. I hold it back inside silently crying and screaming. The blood rushes through my head, and a small moan whisps out, I wipe my eyes. The tears fall freely after that, I let them cover my face as I let go. "What is happening to me?" I bump my back against the wall.

"Shade?" I cry out hopelessly in an anguished growl. "Where are you?" My hands lay beside me unsure what to do with them as I cry into my knees. "Why were you not here to help?" I ask. The sobs rack my body, but I try to pull it back and to calm myself. No answers come to me, though I didn't expect any.

I lean to the left and slowly fall the rest of the way and lie on my side staring at the door from under the sinks. The lights turn off after a bit, I wave my hand to turn them back on. They flicker back to life as the sensor registers movement, I lie there doing that a couple of times the hiccups from my sobs have all but stopped now. I notice to the far right a black little worm-like creature wriggles out of the drain on the floor that is near the first shower. It slithers toward me like some hurt little snake. It pauses near my sneaker. He is small and tiny; his form can be really small or huge and intimidating. I have seen both now. That is good to know.

"Did you not hear me call for you?" I ask, still lying on the cold tiled floor. My mind feels numb as I focus on him crawling over the floor. I watch as my hands melt back to their normal form, but keep my eyes set on Shade's little worm form, lest the stress makes them come back. I wait for his answer as he sits by my shoe.

Shade shakes his lithe form back and forth in a no answer. He curls deeper into the shadows, slithering past my shoe and up my side and sliding around to my arm.

I raise my head up to look down at him. "Why are you small? I know you can be bigger."

He shrinks back into the shadows, calling them as if they were real. He grows to the size of a small cat. He crawls up to me and winds his way over to me. I sit up fully once again.

"Were you hurt?" I pause sliding my hand over his arching back.

He motions his head up and down in answer, yes.

"From the gloves?"

He nods once again.

I take a moment and pull myself back into a sitting position, grabbing his shadow body and hauling him into my lap, patting at the darkness. He feels cool to the touch and smooth, not at all like fur, more like a cool hard marble. He curls into my hands enjoying the pets.

My eyes search his form in question, wondering if that was really what happened or only what he could explain. "I wish there were another way to communicate," I whisper to him.

He nods in agreement but doesn't say or do anything more.

"Where did you go?"

He twirls in my hands, and he settles down sighing and going flat.

"Were you scouting out the place?"

He nods once again.

I take a moment to think of what I could ask him or talk to him about to get further answers. "I need to know what you can and cannot do. I need to know what is going on, and I find it real annoying that I can only talk to you with yes or no answers." I huff.

He shrinks away from my hands, slinking away back towards the drain.

"I'm sorry, wait, don't leave." I reach   out a hand wanting to physically stop him, but I don't want to cause him any more pain than he already was in. "I want to find out some things. I have so many questions."

He stops his forward motion to the drain and just huddles under the sink where shadows collect, grabbing them and pulling them into him.

"Do you feed off of shadows to replenish energy?" I question.

He nods at first, but then shakes his head. As he pulls more shadows into his body, he grows a bit more in size, to that of a medium dog. He twirls once again and pads back over to me and lies down next to me. I brush my fingers over him, being cautious not wanting to scare him away. Or do anything to send him away.

"Shade?"

His head turns up to me.

"Are you a part of me?"

He cocks his head, but does not nod or shake his head, like he is confused.

"I mean, can you see, hear, or read what is in my mind, my thoughts."

He shakes his head no.

"So, you are separate, but a part of me."

He just stares at me, not doing anything since I did not ask a question.

"Are you real or just a spell that will fizzle out?"

He pulls his shadows into that of another form more humanoid and shrugs, not having an answer for me.

I lean my head against his shoulder as he sits next to me. "I am tired of people coming into my life and leaving me with more questions than answers."

He sits there as I am though my body is mostly still his doesn't move at all. There is no breath to him, just stillness.

I go for an easier question. "Did anyone see you while you were on your excursion?"

He shakes his head.

"Well then, I will go over what happened to me after the gloves affected you. Doctor Quintan took me into my head, and I got to see a memory, one of my real mother. She created you, and I found out who those dead people were. Well, at least the woman that took me from my parents, I think I have been asleep all this time, or if not, that was part of the spell to keep my memories locked up."

I lower my head, having more questions than answers.

"Mother told me to trust you though, and you are a key to get more answers, or at least that is what I think she meant." I watch as Shade looks down at his own form and then back up to me. "Shouldn't you know if you are holding a key or have more information then I at least?"

He shrugs once again. I grind my teeth, holding my words in for a moment.

"I am not sure who we can trust or who to even go to get more information. Quintan said he would allow me to use the library, so maybe we can learn something there. I don't know about my roommate, but maybe she will be in better spirits after getting some rest and can help us. Do you know who we can trust?" I look to him, and he stares at the ground. "You have to give me something," I rant.

He pushes his form into a bulbous form taking the silhouette form of Doctor Quintan.

"I think not." I flick my wrist and bat at him with my hand, causing him to fall back.

He looks up at me, hurt.

"Yeah, he helped me get to the memory, but he also caused me pain or were you not there at that time?" I ask, flabbergasted with all this. "Quintan I will be guarded with at the least. He acted really weird after finding out about Jade as well." I give a quick dismissal.

Shade bobs his head in understanding and slinks down in size and climbs up onto my legs and nuzzles my arm before he attaches himself there. He pulls himself into another form that of crossed arrows. And stays on my wrist in plain sight. I run my fingers over the tattoo and try to urge him up my arm into an easier hiding spot. He stays put though.

"Okay, guess you're going to stay there. Why arrows though? Couldn't you be any more cryptic. You could have turned into something to answer one of my questions." I rub at the tattoo getting to my feet and crawl out from under the sinks.

The water is ice cold now that the heat is long gone. I let the water run over the tattoo and my hands, making them go numb.

"Do you feel that?" I coo.

He doesn't move or give an answer, just sits there as two arrows.

A series of knocks bang at the door. "Are you done in there? Are you all, right?" Quintan bellows beyond the door.

"Quintan, is that you? Yes, I am in here." I turn off the water and rush to the door, jumping from foot-to-foot waiting.

"Doug said you had some sort of episode," he says quietly hesitating with the door.

"I bet he did," I growl. "He left me here saying no one would be able to hear me if I called for help."

"He only said that because everyone else is locked in and I and the other guards are in different parts where we would not easily hear if you called out. Is it going to be okay if we open the door? I do have other guards here at the ready in case."

I roll my eyes. "Yes, you will all be just fine." I take a step back. "He's was exaggerating, he caused this you know."

"Hmmm." Is all I hear for a moment and then a click of a lock, and the door pushes in. Quintan and two others stand in the hallway ready to launch at me if needed.

I keep still. "Can I come out now?" I wait. "Last time I lashed out, I got tasered and came here. I would like not to go somewhere worse than this."

He looks around in the bathroom, before landing on me, not seeing anything out of place. "Yes, let's get you back to your room so you can sleep the rest of what you have left of the night. Don't worry about Doug we will be handling him." He motions for me to come forward and backs up into the guard, blocking them from me.

Shade said he trusted Quintan but I still wasn't sure. I would have to wait and see what would come of this.

He walks me back to my room. So much has happened in a small amount of time. The girl in the other bed is passed out on her back and snoring, but that does not stop me from hitting the pillow and falling asleep quickly.

CHAPTER 5

"**W**AKE UP!" A LOUD voice booms in my ear, causing me to startle and flail about, searching for the one that has woken me up so rudely.

"What?!" I shriek and ask in a grumpy mood. After not finding anything to hit, I roll over and face the wall, pulling the blankets up over my head. "Go away," I say, the blanket muffling my voice.

"Oh, someone wants to sleep in now, but at three in the frickin' morning, that's a different story! Guess since this is not an opportune time to bother you, I will not."

No sounds emit for a few minutes. I peek my head outside of the covers. Before I can so much as peek outside the covers, the blue girl from last night grasps at the blankets that are snuggled around me and rips them off, causing me to flip over on to my other side. "Not today, Miss Perfect!"

"Hey!" I sit up, making the bed screech in reply to my movements. I shiver against the cold of the room. "Give those back. It's cold in here!" I demand.

She smiles at that; I finally see her in full light, her whole body or what I could see of it was pure blue in hue. "Cold, nah, this is not cold. Plus, I think it is only fair for causing such a ruckus last night and keeping me awake the whole time."

I glare at her. She stands before me defiantly, keeping a tight hold on the blankets in case I think to grab them back. She is tall and slender. Her left-hand stands poised on her hip, cocked out in annoyance. Her hair is thickly layered in a very choppy manner and short. It's neon blue. Her gaze gives me a bland look with her icy blue eyes. "Bored now." She pouts and drops the blankets on the floor walking back over to her side of the room.

"Who are you? And possibly more importantly what are you?" I question, edging over the bed and grabbing the blanket and pulling it back over me, to combat the chill.

She arches a quizzical brow in my direction, as she turns back. "How rude. My name is Natasha." She smirks. "As for what I am, perhaps I will just show you, since you want to find out so badly."

She waves her arm and suddenly her form changes the light tint of blue of her skin is now a deeper blue; her neon blue hair is now frozen in place in the shape of icicles. Her eyes instead of a piercing sky blue are now a solid blue; the whole eye is of that one color, and where the black pupil would sit in a circle, it is instead in a starburst shape. She holds up a hand and faces her palm upward, cold whisps emit from her palm as ice starts to form in the center of it. She creates an ice sphere and tosses it over to me.

I catch it with the blanket, touching it lightly. It is a dense ball and very cold. "Holy shit." I poke at it with my bare fingertips. "That is very cool." I chuckle.

She smirks. "Impressed, aren't you?" She laughs. "Come on, don't be daft, would it be anything other than cold?" She stares at me.

"Well, umm." I look down at the ice and hesitantly raise my eyes back up. She is still staring at me. "I'm sorry, I am new to all this and what it entails, and I am sorry if I am supposed to know what you are just from that trick, but I don't," I say carefully not wanting to upset her especially if she could just freeze me or throw ice balls at me, let alone what else she could do. "I understand you have powers, and you look really wicked." I give her a compliment, hoping to entice more information from her.

"Flattery will get you everywhere." She smiles, but rolls her eyes when I move closer smiling eagerly at her. She raises her eyes regarding the ceiling and sighs deeply, wings explode from her back. "Might as well get all the surprises out of the way."

"Whoa." I get up and move around her, dropping the ice chunk on the table beside the bed. "Do those just lay down when you aren't using them? Do you have some sort of spell that hides them otherwise?" I fire off rapidly. Her wings are huge compared to her slight frame. "They are beautiful," I whisper, giving her no time to answer my previous questions. I reach out a hand to touch them.

"Hey, watch it!" She flutters them, casting a cold breeze on me as she flies away and turns, keeping them away from my searching hands. "I don't come poking and prodding at you, I would appreciate the same courtesy." She glares at me.

"Sorry." My head falls as I take a step back, putting my hands up in surrender.

"Stop that," she spits. "It's like you are a child!" she yells. "Don't you know you are never supposed to apologize or thank a Fae." She gives a pointed look. "I will let that one pass since you are new here, but strike apologies and thanks from your vocabulary unless you like going into debt with certain Fae. Then, of course, you can be my loyal servant." She gives a mean pass over me and points a finger. "Go ahead, apologize."

I give an audible gulp, but only understand half of what she is saying. "I was held captive or have forgotten most of my life so excuse me for not knowing any of this. Fae—is that what you are, like a fairy? Aren't you supposed to be tiny then?" I pinch my fingers together, showing the appropriate size.

"Fae, not a fairy like you hear about in stories. I am not your fairy godmother, I will not grant you wishes, and be glad I do not freeze you right here on this spot," she grinds out, setting herself down and stomping a slender foot, making her point.

Her wings glitter. Dark blue veins cascade over the icy white expanse of the wings, looking as if lightning hit in the middle of a winter snowstorm. Her lips are black now, as if they have been frost bitten by her cold exterior. Her fingertips are also tipped in blackness. I wonder if her toes match them, socks cover her feet from view. She twitches her fingers back and forth. Her hair clinks and makes chiming noises as the icicles move back and forth with her head movements.

I cock my head, expecting something cold to come after me. I scrunch away and wrap my arms around my middle, trying to trap the heat inside. The shapes of her wings are the shape of a butterflies, except they are rigid and sharp at the end points.

"So, you're like this Fae monster. What does that entail?" I lean back against the edge of her bed.

She scoffs at me and is taken aback.

"Think of me, if you must, like a child. I literally know nothing of this world and the creatures that inhabit it. I was just thrown into all of this literally yesterday," I make the excuse for myself. I stand back up and drop my hands. "I think I am doing pretty well compared to freaking out about everything, which is what I am internally doing but you all seem to think the smallest issue anyone has is a major cause for alarm."

The temperature suddenly drops in the room more so than before and the moisture in the room crystalizes coating the floors and walls in an icy sheen. "I get that you are new and all but before you call anyone a monster you might want to be sure you can take them in a fight or make sure that is what they want to be called," Natasha comments frigidly. She licks her lips, and a black tongue emerges.

"Your tongue is black like your fingers and lips," I say, aghast.

She eyes me, and ice forms from her hand once again this time in the shape of a small spear. "Yeah, what of it? If they were pink like yours, it would have frozen and broken off long ago." She eyes me and plays with the sharp point of the spear, licking it for emphasis. "I am going to need you to stay on one subject and not jump around in this conversation." She points the sharp ice spear at me and takes a bite of it as if it were a lollipop.

I breathe out and see my frosty breath. I wrap my arms back around myself, hugging for warmth. "Okay, I get it, you're the queen of ice. Can we make it less cold in here? You know, some of us like being warm."

"No, I would have never known that." She rolls her eyes again and throws the spear up and down, catching it easily in her hand. "You like stating the obvious a lot."

"Look, I'm sorry, Okay." I whine.

"What did I just tell you, slave! You now owe one debt of my asking." She ticks off one finger. "Hope you do not piss me off anymore." She looks down her nose at me.

"Ughhhh. What am I supposed to say instead of those words then?" I give her an irritated gaze.

"Not my problem. That is for you to figure out, just hope you don't come across any Fae whether they be light or dark, or else you will get more than you bargained for." The temperature warms back up, but the ice does not melt in her hand. It appears as if she pulls the cold closer around her instead of letting it out in the whole room. "If you want to be in debt to my kind, then keep saying those kinds of words." She shrugs. "Hmm, what should I ask of my debt? Or should I hold on to it until later?" She smiles to herself as she thinks.

"Wait." I brush against her fingers that are holding the spear. I bite back a screech of pain.

"Don't touch." She breathes out.

I breathe on my chilled fingers. "I-I—Okay," I say simply. "What I wanted to ask is—you said light and dark Fae? Is that like the light and dark factions, kind of like for witches? Quintan said something about them yesterday." My face scrunches in thought. It feels good to be able to remember the previous day's memories.

"No, witches have their own factions, but they are similar. There are sides taken. Most are divided depending on their base power, though many of the dark factions work with dark Fae, and same with the light and light Fae, though it is frowned upon since we are all tricksters at heart. Fae, though, are from a different world than this one, and there are many other sides other than just light and dark." She smiles. "Fae came here though, since your world is rich in magic and other things that were needed at the time. Most of us had to pick a side based on our powers and what they gravitate towards," she says dismissively. She smiles, showing sharp pointed teeth. "Wanna guess what side I belong to?"

"Let me guess dark?" I say, crossing my arms in front of myself over my chest.

"I wish." She shrugs. "Dark side in this world's context is made up of Spring, Fall, and Dark Fae, the most volatile of us and any of those that belong to those courts. There are Fae that are mixed breeds and have to make a choice and aren't really liked in any of the courts. Winter, Summer, and Light Fae belong to the light side," she says. "Many Fae have decided to come here instead of our own world to get away from the courts politics plus it doesn't help that our world is shrinking substantially."

"Fae, who knew?" I walk around Natasha to grab the comforter off my bed and wrap it around my shoulders. "So, if you are not born to this world, you are given a side? The choice is made for you, dependent upon your gifts?"

She squeezes her fist, and her form begins to diminish and hide the more prominent features, looking more human. The room warms back up and the frigid temperature stops cascading off her. She withdraws the iciness from the floor and walls just leaving a little bit of a wet sheen to everything.

"My expertise is in ice. Fae usually have one of the elements as a base power or a derivative of the elements." She smooths her wings down and shakes her head, breaking the ice from the hair and leaving it full and luscious, the hair returning to normal. She twinges her head to the left and cracks it.

"Is that uncomfortable changing forms?" I ask.

"A bit, but you get used to it after a while. The thing that really doesn't grow on me is keeping my wings down and hidden." She rolls her shoulders.

I nod in understanding. "Is that all there is—Fae and witches? Or what kind of other creatures are there."

"If you can dream it up it probably exists. Wolves, vampires, the snot monster, dragons, all of it." She twists away and flicks her fingers back at me. "Just know each group of 'monster' has their own beliefs and ways of working and you will not come across every one of them." She uses her fingers to quote the monster word rolling her eyes. "Things used to be easier here when there wasn't traveling between worlds, but it is getting harder to distinguish the line with the travel."

"What are you doing here at this place? I know and get why I am here; did you do something wrong?" I edge.

She laughs. "Hell no. Apparently my parents have a problem with my attitude or something like that." She walks over to her closet and ruffles through it, pulling out clothes and discarding them.

"So, you didn't kill anyone?"

She stops what she is doing and gives me a hard look. "No." Her gaze studies me. "Others that are here, yes, but I have not. What are you in for? Since you now know all about me." She places the clothes back in the closet. She closes the door once they are all put away and leans up against the closed door as if guarding it.

"Don't worry your clothes are safe." I shake my head and sit back on my bed, the cover cocooning me in warmth. "I am still not sure what this place really is. I was in a human institution and a spell ended up killing someone, I think and so I was caught and brought here. I was supposed to go to an insane asylum type place." I fidget with the edges of the blanket. "I'm not really sure a lot has happened and I barely understand any of it."

"You killed someone?" She asks in wonder. She looks at me with untrusting eyes. "You don't look like you could kill someone."

"Looks can be deceiving wouldn't you say?" I smile to myself. "That is why I am guessing I was brought here because I don't know if it was me or something just placed on me, I am not even sure what I am. I have been surrounded by witches, so I thought that is just what I am, but no one is sure and has no answers for me. Then last night I had claws. I dunno." I bite at my lips.

"Were you raised a witch? Have you tried doing a spell? Or witch-like things?" She quirks her head to the side.

"I...don't remember." I hang my head in shame. "I have this shadow that follows me." I show my wrist with the arrows crossed. "But they don't know if it is a spell that was put on me or if I created it myself. I have no memory of much of anything other than these last couple of days and what I have been told."

Natasha walks over to me and takes my wrist gingerly in her cool hands. "Don't worry, my body only gets cold when I want it to. Or at least mostly as long as I have my emotions under control." Her fingers rub over the tattoo. "A shadow protector that shows up as a tattoo?" I nod my head. "Does it always take this form or picture?"

"No, it's the first time I have seen it out in the open like he is, and like I said I don't remember anything from the past so not sure if he has been other things."

"It's a he?" I nod once again. "Well, this symbol usually means friendship; can he not communicate with you?" She releases my wrist and gives me a questioning look.

I pull my wrist closer to my eyes to inspect it. "Yeah, his essence feels male maybe I just associate it with a he because he is big and scary. In my memories that are not my memories he is a friend down the street that is a male, so I just continued with that." I shrug. "Friendship you sure?"

"Yep. So, he's not able to speak?"

"No, communication is something we are working on." I roll my eyes. "Sounds like we are in a weird relationship, doesn't it?" I laugh. "He can give yes or no answers by shaking his head but that is about it, I have only talked or seen him two or three times that I remember."

"Have you tried sign language?"

"No, I don't know how to do that."

"There are books on it in the library," she says as an afterthought. "You can at least learn the alphabet and speak to each other that way, that way you can learn more from him. Not sure if it will help but better than nothing.”

"True. Yeah, I have time at the library I think today and will have to check it out as well as everything else, I have to learn." I lie back hitting my bed already wanting to curl up in a ball and sleep away the day.

"No rest for the wicked." She chuckles as she takes the blanket away from me. "I am here if you have questions. I'm not a total bitch only on every day that ends in Y."

"Great!" I throw my hands out to the side raising up back into a sitting position. "Hey, what about people that don't want to be a part of a side either dark or light? What happens to them?"

She throws the blanket to the side and brushes her hands over her jeans, as if there were a speck of dirt or something on them. "Their lives are short and hard lived. No one likes change and no one sides with them much to help." She smiles sadly. "I have heard there are places for them, but they are far and few between, and it is even harder to find people to help them. Rogue's is what they are called and are shunned by all." She swipes her thumb across her neck, showing the image of a beheading, or death. "Or they travel to other worlds if they can make it, hoping for a new life."

"Oh." I sit and contemplate that for a moment. What did that mean for myself? "Do you know where one of these rogue places would be?"

She shrugs. "No clue."

"So, what does being a part of the dark or light Fae consist of? Do you have a leader? Or is there just a main leader of either side?"

"Nothing much. It mostly doesn't change your life unless you come on someone's radar. Which is why I am here, obviously." She gives a flourish with her hand. "That is why my parents were worried about my attitude. My mouth got me into a lot of trouble and was starting to attract notice from others they would rather not deal with."

"Why did you want their attention? Or what was your reasoning?"

"Don't act like you know me from just talking to me for 2.5 seconds. You don't even deserve to know the truth." She points a finger at me.

"Fine, don't tell me. Keep your secrets," I grump. I pick myself off the bed and start to pull the blanket tight, plumping the pillows at the top. "I just thought that we could be friends and learn about each other, and maybe help one another."

"You do not want to be friends with me," Natasha casts back at me.

"How do you know?" I point to myself. "Are you in my head? Don't pretend like you know me after talking to me for 2.5 seconds," I throw back at her.

"I can see it now—girl becomes a bad influence on everyone she meets." She spreads her hands out in front of her as if there was a post in a paper. "I do better with enemies," she says solemnly.

"Have you tried?" I perk up, seeing a crack.

She glares at me. "Fae, for the most part, have longer lives than other things and believe me when I say I have tried many a time."

"How old are you?" I feel like I should get a notebook out and take notes. This was the first person that was giving me more answers than I had questions.

She quirks her head to the side. "What age do I look?" She twirls around for me to see all angles of her.

"25?" I rub my chin not wanting to go too high or too low with the number, she looks around my age.

She bursts out laughing. "Not even close, not even a little bit... I am 249. Think of each century as an age of ten. So, 100's would be my teens and 200's would be my 20's."

"Damn!" The breath gets knocked out of me. "How long do you guys live?"

"Many live for many centuries, others have been around for a very long time and still have a long time to go. Of course, that can be cut short if killed so I don't like to use the word Immortal, because nothing ever is. I will most likely, though my family thinks not if I keep going down the path I am on, see 730 comfortably. After that it becomes questionable."

My jaw unhinges and hangs open in awe. I wipe the little bit of drool coming out of the corner of my mouth. "That is so long to live."

She smiles. "Yep, and not many live that long if they are not Fae." She frowns then.

"Yeah... I get that. Could be hard to make friends when they don't stick around very long."

Natasha chuckles. "See, you're getting the hang of it." She slaps the side of my bicep. I feel a shiver run up my arm as shade slithers closer to where she hit. "Whoa, what was that!" she exclaims, rubbing at her hand.

"I told you that this was a shadow that protects me. You must have hit me a bit harder than he liked."

She eyes my arm. "Is he going to be annoying like every time you get a bump or a bruise he comes out and goes berserk on things?" As I move my sleeve up to see the tattoo there instead, she comes closer to inspect.

"If he's around." I sigh.

"What do you mean?"

"Never mind. No, I don't know that answer. I haven't really gotten to see much of what he does or how he does things. I know he comes out and protects me if I get seriously hurt and he doesn't like it when I am being mishandled," I spit out.

She pats my arm more lightly this time. "All the guards are a handful at best. When do you start testing?" She watches me shrug. "Well, when do you have this library time?"

I shrug once again.

She hangs her head in silence for a moment. "I don't know how we are going to make it as friends. You are so useless." She stares at me with wide eyes, as my stomach lets out a loud growl. "Was that you?"

I bite my lip in embarrassment. "Yeah, I didn't get dinner last night."

Natasha bursts out laughing, doubling over herself and gripping her stomach, heaving breath in between laughs.

"It's not that funny, you would be hungry also."

"Oh, you are going to be so much fun to play with." She twitches her fingers.

"Well, if you are quite done with yourself." I sit down on my bed the coils give a screech as I pull my tennis shoes out from under the bed and slip them on. "Can we go now?" I look at her sock covered feet.

"Yeah, yeah." She waves her fingers at me as she marches over to the bottom of her bed and pulls on some slip-on black shoes.

"Do we have to hit the buttons to get out?" I point to the thing she had me use last night.

"No." She shakes her head and goes to the door, opening it right up. "The doors are only locked at night for everyone's protection supposedly. They unlock at 6 and lock back up at around 10:30."

I nod, putting that fact away for later. I follow where she leads, there are many doors down each side of the hallway some doors stand open others are closed. We quickly make it to the bathroom I used late last night, there is rambunctious laughter and hollering echoing from inside. "Settle down girls." A woman echoes from inside.

"Do you have to?" She nods, stopping beside the door but gives it the stink eye.

I think for a moment but shake my head no. "I'm good."

"I went before I woke you. Let's go." She continues down the hallway.

Soon we come to a main room with many different hallways connecting, a large desk sits in the middle.

"This is one of the main common areas, and where the guards sit."

I look back the way we had come and notice a slight bend in the hallway so you can't see the restrooms from here.

"There are heavy doors that lock in place at night as well for safety." She chuckles at the lady manning the desk right now eyeing us cautiously. "Or for a lockdown situation if they don't feel safe."

There are tables and chairs around the room for meeting or playing games but almost no one is in this room.

"We don't much like it here since the guards are so easily spooked." she whispers. "Or they like to mess with us. We keep our distance it is us versus them."

I pass a couple of hallways and notice plaques next to each set of doors pointing you in the direction of different areas, depending on where you would like to go. Each door had a plaque next to it. The rooms with names written beside it and main rooms explaining what it was used for.

"Our hallway is the furthest from the main areas, we walk through ours and then you can choose any of these halls that head this direction to get to one of the main buildings. If you take one of the other hallways back the way we came, they are just like ours—an extension not an actual throughway."

She keeps walking quickly as more people come out of their rooms, some waving hi others acknowledging us in one-way shape or form. This hallway spills out into a giant mess hall. "You were right." I look to the left and right seeing the halls all pouring into this room.

"Duh, I have been here for a minute of course I know my way around."

I smile. "I thought you would have messed with me." I nudge her shoulder with mine. "Cause we're not friends and all?"

"Stick with me kid and I will be messing you up in so many ways." She smiles as well, but looks up to the ceiling and shakes her head. "If you ever get lost just get to this main way and you can find food at least and the library is off the way back behind us we will go there later." She waves behind her moving towards the food.

"Kid? I'm not a kid!" I yell. "You must be as hungry as I sound."

Natasha floats over to the food line and grabs a tray wielding it like a sword. She rolls her eyes. "This place isn't too busy because hardly anyone wants to be an early riser but since we are super late, it's almost time to close up. It isn't busy either so I will forgive you this time, though there are a lot less options." She examines what is left for food choices.

I look over the thin crowd through the room as I sidle up next to her sticking close by. I eye the questioning food as we pass it. Some if it is noticeable but others are not, I look back at some of the creatures and people that have sat down to eat. Not all are in human form like Natasha.

"What kind of mon... creatures, are they?" I whisper to Natasha and eye her seeing what she chooses.

"You know most of them can hear you even if you whisper." She eyes me then nodding at a particular crowded table. "But that gaggle over there are monsters—stay away."

"Really?" I stare over at the table in wonder as some of the people there stare back with glares.

"No." She laughs and moseys on down the line. "That's for the slip up. Watch it, newbie. But to answer your question, like I said before, you can think it, it probably exists. Many will have a glamor like mine where it hides their true nature. Others will just let it all hang out willy nilly." She sticks her tongue out.

"Why don't you let it all hang out?" I fire back.

"My choice. I don't get much choice in things this is mine to make though. Wait." She taps her pointer finger against her pressed lips. "If you are supposed to be a magic user, shouldn't you be able to control Shade?"

"Shhh." I bump her. "I don't want everyone to know everything."

"Right, right was just thinking about things." She crouches down like we are spies undercover. "Your code name is Muggsy. I will be Wilma, and together, we will blow this popsicle stand wide open and defeat the evil Cheshire." She waggles her eyebrows at me as she picks up a golden, liquid jelly and promptly puts it on her tray, sliding it even further down.

"Okay, you are crazier than I am, Wilma. Our first objective, if we choose to accept, is what is edible for Muggsy? First objective—food. Second—question and answers." I pick up my tray and place it on the sliding bars. going past the golden drink thing. The tray is worn and smooth. "Do they not have anything new in here either? How many washings has this tray been through alone?"

Natasha picks up some more jelly-like substances. There is a whole section of raw meat; I quickly pass that by. "Humans can eat most of this stuff with no harmful side effects. but if you don't want to be adventurous. you should be able to pick something out closer to the end of the line."

"Human food, human food, where are you?" I sing as others that are still in the line glare at me, either waiting to pay for their food or getting in line behind me.

Natasha paws at some shiny cut up, odd looking fruit of some sort. "Down that way." She sticks out her thumb, motioning closer to the drink station closer to the end of the line.

I pick up the tray and move around Natasha effortlessly, leaving her to her own devices and making a bee line for my kind of food. I glance over the human selection of food that looks okay at a glance, but on closer inspection it definitely was not appealing for cafeteria food.

Only a couple of things still remained appetizing when viewed in close proximity. I pick up a chicken and biscuit thing with no gravy. The gravy that I see still in the heating plate is congealed and off-putting. I wrinkle my nose at it, as I catch a whiff, barely holding my stomach together.

"Ugh and this is supposed to be good." I step back.

"That is another reason why it is best to get here first thing in the morning, the longer it sits out the worse it seems to get. When it is fresh, it is pretty decent." Natasha glides up beside me and frowns at the food I am in front of. "That I would agree is not pleasant, not pleasant at all."

I eye her plate, seeing that she has added a couple of other things to her tray. One of the items is purple with polka dots, and it is still wiggling up and down in the bowl it is in. It has plastic wrap over the top.

"What would you consider pleasant? Is your food trying to run away?" I shiver away from her.

She sticks her tongue out at me. "Norms are all the same, no sense of adventure. Better for me, anyway. Keep your eyes off of my yummy deliciousness."

I roll my eyes at her. "Don't worry about that, that is all yours." We get in line for the register. I grab a bottle of water nearby while I look around, worried, and whisper to Natasha, "I don't have any money."

"Don't worry. They give you an allowance. Your name will most likely be on a list."

"An allowance? How do I know how much I can use or get; do I need to check prices?" I turn the biscuit over to see if there is a price somewhere on it.

She pats my tray. "Don't worry you don't have any extras. You will be fine with your sad little breakfast sandwich and water. They should go over that with you later, you just can't use it for extras like too many desserts or other snacks like that." We move forward a step.

"How do we know what we will be doing today? Do you just show me around, is someone going to come looking for me?" My hands clam up as we move closer to the register. Why did I feel like I again did not have enough information, I was tired of feeling inadequate?

"Stop worrying at the register when you give them your name, they will also give you your schedule for the week. They do this because there isn't a set schedule for everyone, they do a weekly schedule, since so many come in and out of this place pretty regularly." She nods to the person at the register.

I inch forward towards the scowling lady. "Name?" she barks abruptly.

I eye her warily and lift my chin defiantly. "Alexia Kremer," I say in a smooth tone.

The grouch of a woman jams her fingers in between the many papers searching through them to find my name. She eyes me and then the paper she stops on, and jerks it out quite suddenly, shoving it in front of my face. I step back a step and retrieve the paper from her outstretched palm.

"Natasha Bragin, reporting for duty." Natasha mimics, as she salutes the lady, a paper is thrown in her face as well, her assistant scribbles down what was taken for breakfast and then we are swept away. The lunch lady glares daggers at Natasha then grumbles at the next people behind us.

"Someone sure hates their job," I whisper quietly to Natasha.

She nods and bursts into giggles. I follow suit. We turn the corner into the seating area and find a place to sit, she touches my elbow. "That is the first time I have heard your name. Why didn't you tell me?"

I think back over our conversation. "No, I must have told it to you."

"No, you were very rude and demanding. I answer all your questions, with you never letting me have my own questions." She leans back in the chair as she sits down and stabs at the fruit pieces that are golden with a fork.

"Why didn't you ask?"

She points at me with her fork. "I am not rude like you."

"Well, you snooze, you lose." I wrinkle my nose at her. "Not like you have feelings anyway, right?" I chide. "Also, you call me rude, you were the one that woke me up, not the other way around."

"Excuse you! Middle of the night payback was inevitable."

"With everything that I don't remember—" I twirl my finger around my head in a crazy motion. "Alexia seems so formal and not me. I am thinking of trying out Lexi."

"Lexi. I like it much more for you. Sounds young and innocent." She plucks at another piece of fruit as I rip into my chicken biscuit.

I unfold the paper that was given to me and read off what it states, nothing stood out to me or made much of any sense. "What does all this mean? How long am I to stay here?" I smooth it over to Natasha. "So, tell me the bad news, Doc." I waggle my eyebrows at her, digging into my sandwich and taking a big bite.

"Well..." She gazes over the paper then undoes her own and sets them side by side for comparison. "The good news is you have an awesome roommate and three meals a day."

"And the rest?" I stop mid bite and wince at the impending doom.

"You have to meet with the horrible Melissa," she says in a low scary voice, and adds for special effect, "Dun, dun, dun."

"Melissa? Who is she and why is she horrible? I thought Quintan said I could trust someone by that name." I ask nibbling at the biscuit slower now after I had gotten past a couple of large bites, the brunt of my hunger diminishing.

"She is a wolf in sheep's clothing, literally."

I shake my head not understanding. "Like a wolf-wolf, like shifts into a wolf?"

"Yes, a person that shifts into a wolf that is what I meant," she murmurs back sarcastically. "But she is, like, the alpha of all alphas, though she may try to trick you at first to see where you rank. Bet you thought I was the top bitch here."

"Nah, you're sweet." I smirk in response.

"Wait till you see this one, she's even worse when she's in heat, but that won't be for a little while, I hear."

"Great, wait in heat? They get like that?"

Natasha nods. "Each animal is different and how it affects them, but yeah."

I grimace and wipe my palms on my pants. "Just my luck, so what is she? A psychologist of some sort? Like we talk about our feelings?" My heart flutters in my chest.

Natasha bursts out laughing and sprays out the fruit she was shoveling in her mouth. She covers it trying to keep it from getting all over the table. "Oh, that is priceless. You will see, just you wait. I myself had to be transferred to someone else when I had her, we did not get along and soon it became a never-ending game. It wasn't good for morale. Never know, maybe you will get along just well."

I give her a dead droll stare. "How did you come to that conclusion?"

"She likes the newbies—easy to mold into her little pawns. Get on her good side, and you can get special privileges."

"You don't think that will work, do you?" I give it some serious thought.

"Probably not. She can smell a lie a mile away."

"Doctor Quintan explained that I should trust her and let her know everything that is going on. He seemed really persistent on this, that I be open with him and her if no one else."

"Do you really trust them? You don't even know if you are going to get out of here one day, right?" She pouts and stabs the next thing on her plate, which are the little tentacle moving things. "Will they let any of us leave without the approval of the ones that put us in here? He's a weird one. I have never dealt with him before, so I'm not sure. I can't really say one way or another."

"I guess time will tell, when we are done you will show me where to meet with Melissa, won't you?"

"I guess someone has to do it, don't they? She sighs very loudly and rolls her eyes to the side. "Fine I guess, you can be my good deed for the day or something to that effect." She starts to eat slower, taking longer than necessary, to stall for time.

"You know there are times next to these appointments."

"Yeah, those are just suggested times." She motions my paper back over to my side.

"Somehow I think not."

"The other good news is we have the library time around the same time so I can help you find some things and help you get some answers."

I nod and finish the rest of my sandwich along with the water, waiting for her to be done so we can head out.

CHAPTER 6

"THANKS, I WILL SEE you later on then." I laugh at Natasha as I watch her twitch away, she waves her fingers at me. "Good luck!" she yells back.

I shake my head looking back at her as she moves away from me. I fold up the paper that the god-awful lunch lady gave to me and tuck it into my bra strap, not having pockets. My hands needed to be free when going up against this Melissa. I don't know exactly what is going to happen, but I want to be prepared for anything.

I take a deep breath and open up the door hesitating in the doorway. I poke my head in, seeing a bland room with waiting chairs and in the center near the back of the room is a large round desk, with a huge creature curled up behind it. I poke my head back before it can see me and make an audible gulp. I breathe in deeply and school myself and my features to meet whoever this was head on. This creature didn't look like an alpha wolf, more like a dragon or a dinosaur. I walk through the doorway and come up to the desk, facing this thing. I wasn't sure what to call it.

"Excuse me," I say in a small voice, the thing looks over at me and groans. "Are you Melissa, or is she around here somewhere?" I place my hands on the counter lightly.

The beast looks down and eyes me warily. I make a note of the purple hue that flows down its whole body. It has four long arms and two hooves that it sits back on very powerful haunches. It also has a tail that is curled up and split in two. It goes over the back part of the circle desk, its tail ends in a pinkish hue instead of the purple.

My eyes go wide as I take in the whole sight of this new creature that I have never even heard of let alone seen. I cough and think about whether I should attempt any more conversation with the creature or to even ask what it is.

"If I may ask, what are you?"

The thing stares at me and doesn't say a word. I fidget nervously.

"Well, you see, I am new to all this, and I just have never seen anything like you and am not sure what you are or what any of this world is."

The thing turns fully in my direction now, and I see the creature face on. She doesn't have normal eyes; there are six of them, not just two. Where a nose would normally be, there are just two slits. It groans once more, but does not say much else.

I look around the room, hoping for something. "Do you not speak?" I give it a questioning look. The thing's eyes are pink and solid in color, except the eyes that are almost on its neck those appear almost like a cat's eyes, but still pink in color.

The thing rises up on its haunches, placing its four elongated hands on the desk, heaving all its weight on its haunches and hooved like feet. The desk groans at the extra weight. It elongates its neck and because of that I can see down its long stomach, though it is large the muscles are well defined.

The thing groans as it turns away from me, rifling through papers and a drawer in the back. The spikes on its back look like a dinosaur, but they are shiny, almost glittery, and a deep violet. My fingers itch to touch them and see if they are smooth or rough in texture.

I freeze in place, trying not to cower under the lip of the desk. Instead, I take a step back not standing so close. The slits in its nose expand as the creature takes a whiff of the air and scents me. I stand, still hoping not to endanger myself any further, not knowing what to do, barely keeping my hands down wanting to smell myself, making sure I didn't smell bad.

"Ummm... I am here for my appointment to see Melissa. I am guessing that is not you." My fingers shake and itch to feel the doorknob below them so that I can leave this place. I did not want to get eaten on my first day.

A low groan comes out of the thing again as it moves its slender rail thin fingers over a ledger. With a feathered pen in hand, it scratches against the book that is large and ominous. The book takes up most of the left side of the desk. It peers at me bringing its elongated neck forward, making its face come closer to mine, looking at me expecting me to say something. I fidget nervously at its intense stare and then back to the door contemplating escaping and running away.

It moans again slowly. "Name?" a low growl flits through my mind, speaking to me.

I pause to glance around, like someone might get behind me to whisper in my ear. There is no one else in the room other than me and the thing in front of me.

I glance at it and then back to the door, still contemplating. I face back to her and breathe in deeply before moving forward. "Did you just speak in my head?" I ask quietly. "Because if you didn't, you are about to see a person-shaped hole in the middle of that door." I point behind me.

It nods in my direction, shaking its body in time with the motions of its head. "Thissss issss how I communicate." It hisses its S's. "Ssss-sometimes it takesssss me a while to find the right frequenccccccy, to talk to ssssomeone. That issss why it wassss quiet for sssso long. I wassss trying to find your frequenccccy to communicate, I hope I did not worry you too much." A soft feminine voice whispers through my mind.

A peaceful sound emanates through my mind as she speaks to me. "That is amazing." I squeak out, feeling much calmer. "Are you a girl? What should I call you? What are you?" I blurt out, I can no longer hold my questions back, I find it too interesting.

She eyes me warily and groans, but no words follow till a minute after. "Name?"

My nervous energy comes back as I fidget with the bottom of my shirt. I look down. "Alexia?" I bite at my lip worried if I had taken the questions too far.

"Are you asking me what your name is or are you telling it to me, youngling?" The words flit through my mind clear and sure unlike the last couple of times.

"Telling you I suppose, can you not physically speak then?" I move forward towards the desk and have to lean my head back a bit to see up to her head.

"This is how I communicate, young one." A definite feminine tone scrambles into my brain. "Most of my kind have to give up something they value in order to learn the things they really want to know. I gave up my physical voice that was known for its beauty to be able to retain the knowledge that I am given and strive to learn everything that there is to know. Through the knowledge I gained, it has given me a new way to communicate to others, not needing the physical one I missed so," she says tenderly, showing me pictures of her tribe and what it took on her journey to overcome the obstacles put in her way to achieve her dreams. "Along the way, I have learned a few other tricks, making it well worth it in the end."

"Oh, wow." My mouth is left hanging open as I learn all of this in a few moments. "Could I do something like that? What I wouldn't give to know some things."

"No little one that is for only my kind." She moves back and sits back. "I will answer your questions because your mind is filled with many dark holes, and you need someone to finally be able to fill some of those."

I nod eagerly, happy to find someone that can give me some answers even if they are not to my memory necessarily.

She waits patiently for me to gather my thoughts to ask the questions I wanted to know.

"Oh. You're waiting for me to ask them again?"

She doesn't say anything more and waits once more. I look back and forth before I peer at each of her eyes.

"What is your... kind... if I may ask? I am working on trying to get the wording down and not offend," I rush on hoping she took better than if I had said monster.

A laugh flitters through my mind. "No worries, dearie, some say that my kind are descendants of dragons, some say dinosaurs, and still others think different species from another world all together like an alien. Those of my kind and tribe have come up with a name for others to call us which is, Teager." She brings her head down to my eye level, so I don't have to strain my neck, looking up. "We know very little magic and are able to make some miraculous things happen. My sister though her coloring is opposite of mine pink to my purple, she works in the library she will be able to help you if you need it. I have let her know to keep an eye out for you."

I stutter, "Thank you. You didn't have to do that."

"I know I didn't, but I needed to do it all the same." She sniffs the room once again, her nose reaching toward the tall ceilings. "Melissa will see you now, lost one." Her head skitters to the right showing me the door that is set into the wall there beside her.

I study the door and hesitate, wanting to speak to this pleasant creature rather than face off with a mad woman that will most likely not want to help me. "Wait, what is your name or what do I call you?"

"Tallia. Go on now, do not keep her waiting. We will talk again. If not, my sister will give you a message." She butts the back of my arm with her head, pushing me forward.

I nod my head as my mood spirals down, not interested in the least to go in and meet with Melissa at all. I grumble under my breath, "I would have much rather had more time with the Teager instead of doing this, at least I may have learned something more than I would going into this meeting." I perk up and look back at Tallia before heading in. "Maybe I could talk with her after my session," I comment to myself.

"Never fear, you will make it through this, and we will have plenty of time to talk if not after then you definitely will have time with my sister." She extends one of her clawed hands out and waves as I motion through the door.

I nod now smiling slightly as I move forward into the room. "Thank you," I whisper, and wave goodbye.

As I go through the door, I notice everything neat and in a certain place. Everything was very bland and plain. They were all in the colors of black, white, or silver. No color lived here. It was all very modern looking and was not well lived in unlike Doctor Quintan's office. "I am guessing we will not be discussing feelings today," I mutter.

"Miss Kremer?" a sturdy voice emits.

I bring my eyes to rest on a fashionably dressed business woman in a normal black skirt suit, which fits her exceptionally well. "Yes?"

She walks over to me in high heels that seem really dangerous to be strutting in.

"Are those expensive." I stare down at the killer heels. My eyes don't want to raise up.

She looks down at the shoes and then holds a handout for me to shake. "I'm Melissa; yes, they were quite expensive but well worth it." She smiles. "We will be going over something that you have learned from last night, and anything else that could possibly help, maybe memories were jogged in the aftermath." My eyes raise slightly. She bares her teeth in her smile. "Feelings may not be the basic concept of what I am trying to get at, but they will be there."

I shake her hand politely and grimace at the strength of her grip on mine, as if testing me to see where I stand up against her. Her straight, blonde hair is pulled back into a tight chignon, making her appear classy and elegant, but she still portrays the bitter bite of do not fuck with me.

"Please take a seat." She motions to the couch as she releases my hand.

The couch is placed near a plush, leather chair. It is facing the couch where she wants me to sit. I regard the inspirational photo that sits behind the couch. It reads in big, bold letters *Dedication*, and in smaller writing beneath it, *it is the effort of many that create the ripples that can move mountains*. The picture includes a lake that is surrounded by mountains and the day is clear as it brings clarity and peace to the one viewing the picture.

"Are you moving mountains here?" I cock my head to the side, not moving forward to the couch. "Or are you a wolf in sheep's clothing?" I ask, wanting to know if Natasha is right about everything or if I should trust Doctor Quintan and reveal to her what happened yesterday.

She gives me a double take and squints her eyes at me not understanding where that came from. "Excuse me," she whispers.

"I think you heard me." I stand my ground and face her head on while looking her dead in the eyes. If she is the alpha of all alpha's, her world is not mine, and I'm not going to be cowed into something. She set me on edge and she knew it.

Her head raises a centimeter to be above mine and looks down at me. "Who dropped you off here? Or did you find the place on your own?" She sniffs the air for a moment as she lets the uncomfortable sounds resonate between us. "I read in your file that you were rooming with Natasha. Is that who dropped you off or at least talked to you about me?"

I nod.

"Of course, she did." She sighs deeply and drops her gaze. "She likes to ruin my shot with the new people before I even get to them. I am not the bad one here, neither is Natasha." She backs up. "She just likes to play these games that she doesn't need to."

"I guess it is not fair for me to judge you. I don't even know you let alone any of what this means to be Fae or wolf or witch even." I shrug and plop down on the couch, which is not as plush as it looks. Melissa sits in the chair across from her, sinking into her chair a lot plushier than the sofa by far. "One quick question, though, before we begin, please," I insist. I need to make up my mind about things on my own. I will use the knowledge given to me by others to help come to a conclusion, but I won't just hate her because Natasha does.

"Go on. Ask your question." She motions for me to continue.

"The quote above me." I point behind me at the picture. "Does it have a deeper meaning?"

Melissa glides a pen over to her notebook to take notes in. "Of course, it does, sweetie. Don't all quotes have some deeper meaning?" she asks.

"I don't know, I guess I never really gave it thought before." I fall back against the back, not liking the answer given.

"I have noticed it is not always about the quote or the exact meaning when it was written, but more about how the viewer interprets the words. How they adapt and change it to fit their needs," she goes on. "Quintan wrote down here that we had helped you to view a memory, is that correct?" Jumping right into things then.

"Yeah, that is right." I push myself to the edge of the couch, not able to really sink down in the plushness, so I would rather be on the edge of the uncomfortable thing. I rub my hands together and notice Melissa watching me move. I put them under my thighs, stopping the nervous movement. "You're a wolf shifter though, correct?" I fling my own question out.

"This session isn't really about me now, is it?" she bites back.

"No, but it should be about what I do not know about this world and the creatures it inhabits. I don't want to accidentally get killed or worse for saying the wrong thing." I throw logic at her; perhaps that will get me more answers.

"Point taken."

"You ask and get an answer and I get the same in return."

"Are you trying to make a deal with me?" She chuckles.

I roll my eyes. "It seems like the only thing that will work if I want answers to not take forever by researching."

She thinks for a moment, pursing her lips. "Fair enough." She nods. "Though it is up to my discretion whether or not to answer it fully or not."

"Same." I glare back at her; two can play this game. Natasha was not the only one that played games, Melissa also liked them as well.

Her eyes return to her notebook. "Why don't you start at the beginning of the memory that Quintan helped you see, and then walk me through it? I will stop you if I have any questions about anything."

"One big question deserves a couple of questions of mine answered."

"Nope this is not how that game is going to be played." She gives me a blank stare.

I just stare at her and fidget in the silence. Why did the silence seem like a physical thing, I already itched to say something, she was going to win this damn it? "Ughh," I blurt and go over the memory in as little detail as possible. "Why would Doctor Quintan tell me to trust you?" I leave her with a question.

"He trusts me, easy as that," she says with finality. "That memory—let's go over it. You said you saw your mother. What was her name? Was she the lady that was murdered, which brought you to us?"

I smile now. "Is that two or three questions?" I bat back at her. "What can a wolf do to help me work through my memory?"

She waits to see if I will answer first. "He sends me tasty morsels to eat, I am good with getting one past fear usually by facing it." Her eyes glow golden as she bites out the words to me.

My hands stop fidgeting, I stop bouncing my legs up and down and freeze altogether. "Is that your wolf?"

"Answers. Was she the same lady?" she all but growls.

"No, Jade came in later in the memory. Did I leave that part out?" I say innocently.

"Perhaps you are more like Natasha than anyone would like," she hedges. "So, you, your mother and your father were in front of a big grand place? What was happening? Was there a celebration?"

"I don't know." I shrug and answer honestly.

"What happened next?"

I shake my head. "First, why does Quintan have such high hopes for you to be able to crack me?"

"I know how to get at fear and can unbind it and move you past things. Now, what happened next?" She grows impatient.

"How could you? The only thing you could do is physical pain and that won't help me move past things?" I ask, clearly confused about the situation.

"What happened next?" She goes deathly quiet.

"Jade came in with her goons and fought over me. I was given a gift before I was taken and a curse I am guessing was cast on Jade, it was really confusing." I shrug, giving her more so that maybe she would do the same with her answers. "Now what can you do that would move me past this?"

"Be careful what you wish for," she snaps.

"What are you, a fortune cookie, or are you here to help me?"

"Doug said you were feisty." She smiles, her mouth looking more elongated and her teeth sharp. "Yes, sometimes I am like a fortune cookie."

I go still once again, and my breaths come in short bursts. A lock clicks into place behind me, and I stare at the door. "Did that just lock?"

"I don't think I need to give you any answers until you answer some more of my questions." She breathes in deeply, sniffing the air and holding the smell inside her. She closes her eyes enjoying what she smells. "So good." Her eyes stay a bright golden. "I see it, I feel it." She gets up and stretches, kicking off her pumps to the side. "My wolf likes coming to the surface."

"Why do you need to let your wolf come closer to the surface?" I try not to move too fast, keeping my advancement slow and calm as much as possible.

"To get at those answers, of course." Her face elongates and fur sprouts out of her skin. Her limbs shrink as her body begins to change.

I pick up my feet and jump to the top of the couch hoping that would help. "What are you doing?" I sit on the back of the couch fully keeping my legs up.

She growls at me and falls to all fours, padding out of the dress she was wearing, shaking her fur out. She looks at me and sniffs the air.

I don't meet her eyes this time and let the fear envelop me that I try to hide. "You don't want to do that." My teeth chatter, but I look down at the tattoo, hopeful and worried at the same time.

She yips at me and climbs up on the couch as if saying *yes, yes, I do*. I kick out my legs and keep them up blocking her. I climb over to the side and she easily keeps up, my hand reaches for the couch and finds empty air, I fall off the side not paying attention. I scramble up and rush to the door trying to open it. "Be unlocked, be unlocked," I chant over and over again.

She lets out a growl and launches at me. I smash into the door and twist around before landing on the ground. I get an arm between us and protect my face and head. "Stop, you don't want to do this." I cry out.

She does another growl and I feel teeth pierce into my arm. I open my eyes wide as I see her large mouth around my arm, crushing it. "Shade?" I yell, hoping he can hear me. Is he choosing not to help because of fear of the gloves?

She twists her head this way and that as if wanting deeper into my flesh with her teeth, I scream out as it shreds my skin. I watch as Shade changes into a snake and flows down my arm, not lifting off my skin. He comes to a stop where her teeth meet my skin. He pulls up a corner of himself and raises his head, he attacks with a viper-like strike into her muzzle and easily peels off of me as the wolf rears back unlatching from my arm. Shade wraps around her muzzle encircling it, effectively muzzling her.

My heart beats out of control and tears run down my face. I sit with my back against the door to catch my breath as I see the wolf wrestle with shade trying to scratch at it with her paws. He sticks to her like glue.

"Thanks," I breathe out and hiccup, gulping in air. I try to calm myself enough to hold my breath to stop the hiccups. "Though why did you wait? Why didn't you help out sooner?" I wonder aloud, not expecting an answer.

I grab at my arm; there are little holes from her teeth. Some are ripped and blood starts to pucker up from the wounds. I hiss in pain and hold my arm to my shirt. I look up from my arm keeping one eye on the wolf. She backs up into a light and a side table sending them careening as she backs into them trying to get Shade off of her snout.

"Keep on her, Shade," I growl, moving forward away from the door and towards the desk, hoping she has some gauze or something to wrap my arm up.

I look in the drawers and just find papers there, there is a locked drawer, but I don't see a key laying around. I slam the last drawer shut not seeing anything that I could use, my eyes land on a slip of a dress that hangs on a rack next to her desk.

"That could work," I say to myself. I move around the desk toward the black dress, keeping my eyes on the wolf and Shade. She has stopped pawing at Shade and settled down on the floor, closing her eyes.

"What is she doing?" I question as I reach over to pick up the dress. I try not to jostle my arm too much.

I hear a snick of a door and shoes coming across the carpet quickly. I turn to see who it is and am grabbed from behind. Hands encircle my head, and a purple haze descends upon me.

"Quintan!" I scream.

Why would he do this? Isn't he trying to help me? I kick, but am thrusted headfirst into a wall and darkness embraces me.

"Don't fight me," I hear Quintan call, as if he were very far away down a long tunnel. A large crash echoes around him.

"Alexia," a voice hollers out from the purple mist. A sharp pain echoes through me.

"Ugh," I groan. "What the hell happened?" I ask not seeing who called my name.

Another shout goes out. "Alexia."

"Quintan, is that you? Why did you do this?" I sit up and rub at my temples. "That really hurt."

"Alexia," his voice grounds out, more incessantly.

"What?" I whine, finally looking around to see where we have landed.

I sit on a chair on top of a rock. Thunder and lightning are going on in the background and there are lit fires throughout the crowd. They are surrounding me but there are no individual people that I see, just a mass of black shadows making up a crowd.

"Are we in my mind again?" I yell, still not seeing where Quintan ended up.

"Yes, we are in your mind, once again." He chokes off.

"What is going on?" I search for where his voice came from down below against the rocks that hold up the seat. I see a group surrounding him. I peer down, but cannot see much from this distance. I carefully rise and make my way down the rock formation. "You better be in trouble," I groan. "How can I still be sore and in pain in my own mind?"

I peer down over them as I get closer and see him surrounded by shadows. One is holding him against the rocks, choking him, cutting off his airway. He peers up at me, gasping for air. His face turns red. "Hey, stop that," I call out.

I'm not going to reach him in time. I look down once more judging the distance between me and them. This is in my mind; I could do what I wanted and needed, right? Right?

I let go before I give myself another chance to doubt myself. I fall back away from the rocks, scrunching into myself and ready my legs to take the brunt of the pain, I hit with a jarring thud and tumble forward into Quintan and the circle of shadows. I stumble to a standing position.

"Hey," I yell out at the still shadowed crowd. "I said let him go." I throw back my hair away from my face and shoot daggers at them.

They back up once I come forward. Shrinking back away from my light, I look to Quintan and shove him myself. "What the hell!" The crowd pushes in around us, circling him.

Quintan drops to his knees, coughing, and tries to breathe in deep breaths. He gasps out, "You don't understand." He holds a hand up asking us to wait for him to explain.

I back up and the crowd follows my movement. My eyes keep trained on them unsure of what they could or would do. "This isn't like the last time we were in here. It was dark before and full of tunnels." There are rocks and pitfalls all around and all of us seem to be teetering on the precipice. "Are you sure this is my mind and not yours?"

He glares at me and then points to the things behind me. I look behind me and they back up another step. "They," he gasps again, "feed off what you are feeling or wanting." He coughs and falls back from his knees onto his butt and leans against the cliff. "The reason why everything is different from the last time is because of Melissa."

He utters Melissa's name, and the darkness of the crowd pushes back in on both of us. "She bit me." I say darkly, not moving out of their way for them to get at Quintan but not stopping them either.

"She had to." He holds out a hand not wanting them to come any closer. "Wait, you have to understand." He urges me. I raise an eyebrow and they all halt at once. "Yes, she is a wolf shifter, but she also has an extra power most do not. She has been an alpha for a long time, and maybe she will tell you her story someday, but for now, all you need to know is her teeth—or more importantly her bite—can destroy spells." He doesn't say more, letting that settle.

I hesitate. "We didn't know if there was a spell on me though not for sure."

"You did not at the time, but I knew once I came into your mind last time. I could easily see that it was a spell at work. Your mind would not restrict you from memories like that, it would place barriers or monsters deterring you but this is your mind you should be able to go wherever you like if you would really want to. Some other spell was keeping you and you alone out, I could have passed the barrier easily the other time but I had to hold it open so you could have a chance to look at it."

"So, you sent me to Melissa to bite through the spell, so I could what? Access my memories now. Why couldn't you have warned me then?" I ask.

"It is a two-step part. Melissa can call on her wolf, but she finds it easier to bite through things when her wolf has proper motivation." His face falls uneasy. "She needed that fear to feed her wolf, I don't always approve of her methods but they do get the job done." He nods. "Since she does good and gets results the group lets her get away with some things that shouldn't always happen," he says dejectedly.

"Hence why Natasha warned me instead." I think over my thoughts, searching for memories. "Well, whatever Melissa did," I spit out, "didn't work. I don't remember anything from before." I cross my arms over my chest, the group getting restless and pressing in on the sides.

"Natasha shouldn't have said anything, she doesn't understand how this is needed even if she doesn't agree," he says cryptically. "The memories will start to come in little spurts, they will unlock over time. We will do more sessions and work more now that you will be able to reach them without me having to hold each one at bay while you view." He nods.

"What do you mean about Natasha?" I hang on. "I trust her a lot more than I trust any of you."

"Her story is her own to tell and doctor patient confidentiality. Though she likes to think she is at the center of everything she isn't, and sometimes that is on purpose." His eyes roam around the group not being able to bite off his words.

I glare back at him and flick a loose piece of hair back over my shoulder. "Great more waiting." I huff out.

"We will have to do something so your mind doesn't attack me each time I try to help you. We won't always land close together, when we get thrown into your mind. Yours likes to tear us apart."

"Do you think maybe it is because I don't trust you, and can't even begin to trust you?" I look at him pointedly. "You barely tell me anything you hide more than you answer."

"Could be." He takes a moment and raises off the ground having caught his breath and starts to calm down. "It could be partially that and partially because of what you have been through." He shrugs. "What do you say about getting out of here? Right now, we do not need to go exploring, it was just to make sure that the spell had time to dissipate. That is why your layout in your mind has changed from tunnels and hidden chambers to this open chaos and pits." He hedges.

"Does that worry you?" I peer over at the closest pit.

"Yes," he says.

"Go on." I stand there glaring and waiting, not going to move until he starts talking.

He groans. "Your mind is literally on the edge. It could go either way, into chaos and darkness, or you could start to build again anew. It is up to you and what your next steps are." He looks at me, leaving the choice in my hands.

"In order to grow from here and not fall into a pit, so to speak, I have to learn about my past, right?" I ask.

"Essentially, yes. It isn't as cut and dry, but for the most part, yes. Sometimes it is okay to fall back into a pit and skid backwards in order to move forward," he states.

"My mind is whatever I make it."

He nods even though it wasn't really a question. "Want to get out of here now?"

The crowd has eased back now and are not pressing in anymore.

I nod. "Yeah, I will try not to fight you this time." I come forward and hold out my hands to his. He takes them and purple smoke emits from him as he closes his eyes. I close mine as well, so I don't get motion sickness, and it just seemed like a good way to transition back to my body.

"There we go," Quintan's rough voice says to me his hands still on my head, when he came in from the door.

I open my eyes and look around the room it is a bit darker than when I first came in, and things are knocked over I see a naked Melissa and a dark black pool on the ground next to the couch. The dress only partially wrapped around my wounded arm.

Rolling it the rest of the way around, I run over to the dark pool and touch it with my toe. "What did you do?" I eye Melissa.

She snores softly. The black ink-like puddle just slides over my shoe and doesn't move. I skim my shoe back over it. The puddle goes back to the original size.

"Are they sleeping?"

"I didn't want Shade to attack me as I was checking on your mind, and Melissa didn't need to fight it until we came back, so I knocked both of them out with a sleeping potion that I made."

I step back on a piece of a broken bottle and hear it crunch.

"Careful." Quintan motions me away from the broken glass.

I see Melissa's pantsuit and bend down, picking up the pieces and draping it over her. "She won't get cold, will she?" I worry. I frown, upset with how things happened.

"No, she is hot blooded in more ways than one." He chuckles.

I nod. "Why isn't he back in tattoo form yet? Isn't that his hibernating form?"

Quintan picks up the glass and places them gingerly into the trash can. He steps around the area. "In case there are smaller shards that can't be seen." He grabs the can and sets it in the middle of the area. "I will have to get someone in here to clean that up properly." He walks over to Shade's puddle and kneels down with effort, poking at the pool of darkness. "It acts like a physical object, but is not." Quintan tries to pick it up, but the shadows act more like a liquid and pour through his fingers. "We will have to test his limits as well as yours. I am wondering if it is because I knocked him out before he could change into its other form and attach to you."

"Well, wake them up," I urge

"They should both really sleep the potion out of their system." Quintan struggles to stand from his knee and walks back over to the door. He opens and calls out, "Tallia, can you please get someone to help in here? We have Melissa sleeping off a spell and an inky puddle that belongs to Alexia. We will need a jar or pale of some sort, please. Also, schedule some time for Alexia to meet with me tomorrow."

A groan emits back as Tallia answers. She does not project the answer out to me, so I just have to assume she says she will get on it. I stand there not knowing what to do, but don't want to seem like I am in the way.

"What do you need help with? What can I do?"

Quintan gazes at me then back to Tallia and then to the sleeping forms on the ground. He looks upward for a moment. "Could you please wait out here with Tallia? I don't want you going too far. You need to keep Shade close to you. Tallia will also print you off some directions for tomorrow so you know your schedule." He nods in Tallia's direction, keeping the door open.

"But I can help," I call, taking a step back. "Don't I have my schedule for the week?" I wave the paper, pulling it out from under my bra strap.

"Not with this. You would be in the way. We have had a lot happen for one day. Let the professionals deal with this now." He motions for me to come forward and go into the waiting room. "Your schedule has changed some since this morning."

I press my lips together in anger.

Quintan brushes against the front of his button-down shirt where his pocket is, searching. "I could always use one of the sleep potions on you if needed," he threatens.

I glare at him, but do not want to test if he actually has one more or not. I stomp my way through the door and hear the door shut softly behind me. The lock turns in place so I can't come back in.

I grumble to myself as I storm into the waiting room and sit in one of the chairs closest to the desk that Tallia is behind. "I could have helped."

Tallia quirks her head and studies me as she clicks something on the computer. "Perhaps. But with what you have been through recently, do understand Quintans point that you need to rest and recharge. You still have a lot to go through, little one. Enjoy the calm times as you have them and learn from them. Soon, you may not have them like you do now," she states.

Though she has logic on her side, and she is correct, it still makes me angry. I lean back in the chair and huff out a sigh. I watch as Tallia walks around the desk and moves papers and things around. A few moments after two guards run in and rush to the door. They stop to unlock the door then enter, shutting it closed again before I could move an inch.

"They didn't have a pail or anything for Shade," I comment.

"They will most likely use something that is already in the room or call for me to have someone get it." She bustles back behind the desk her long tail keeps sticking out in the waiting room sort of in front of the desk.

"Are they doing tests on Shade now while they can?" I ask.

Tallia groans but does not comment. She taps at her computer and I go back to sifting through my thoughts trying to force a lost memory forward. There was nothing else I could think to do, since I had to wait till, they were done.

Something whirs up and makes a lot of commotion behind the desk. I peer over the desk and notice Tallia has turned to a printer. "Come here, little one."

I get up from the chair sluggishly and walk slowly up to the desk, not feeling like helping with anything. Tallia's tails lay in front of the desk a bit. I do not want to step on them, but they are in between me and the desk. She was holding a paper out to me to grab.

"Umm," I stall.

"Come on now," she urges and her voice becomes stricter.

I keep an eye on the two pink tails they are laying still on the floor. I gently place a shoe in between the two of them and balance there for a moment, holding my breath so as not to fall. "Don't move," I whisper as I pull my leg up to maneuver over the second part.

"Huh?" Tallia calls out and moves her tail up a bit catching the edge of my shoe.

It sends me forward, careening into the desk. My stomach hits the edge hard before I catch myself. I fall to the floor hard on my knees, the air knocked out of me.

"Oh, sorry dear," she calls out, brushing her tail back and tucking it behind the desk. "I didn't notice I left that out. Sometimes being this big around smaller creatures can be tough."

"I am sorry if I hurt you." I feel bad now for giving her such a hard time earlier.

"Oh no, dearie, that was my fault. It usually is just me or other creatures that are used to being light on their feet. I should have paid better attention."

"Stop being silly. I could have asked you to move it." I wave the paper that she had held now lay discarded on the desk forgotten about. "What's this?" I look up from the ground and after learning how to rebreathe I ease back up.

"That is your schedule for tomorrow, usually the schedule that we come out with at the beginning of the week is for all week, but we had to tweak it a little so that Quintan could get some time in, yours will most likely change a little bit here and there since you are so new."

I nod and glance at the paper, seeing a lot of time with Quintan on here. "He sure wants to get in my head and figure things out." I say. The door opens an inch, and a trash can is set outside the door. I move over to it just to check out what is in it. I see the darkness of Shade. His shadows fill the can halfway full. 'Well, that is just rude." I say to the door.

"Is that your shadow creature?" Tallia asks.

"It is." I grab the can and lift it up, using my knees. "Gosh, he is heavy for a shadow." I strain as I move closer to Tallia, setting him down carefully. "Wait, how did you know I had a shadow creature?" Shade rises slowly and sluggishly out of the can, a skinny snake that lists to the right and then the left side when he tries too over-correct himself. "Is he drunk?"

"He must be coming out of the sleeping potion, and that is why they put him out here. I could sense him on you when you came through the door. I sense magic in all forms, he would have put up a big fight in there if you were not around." Tallia nods and twirls her fingers through his darkness.

I hold his head up so that he is more stable. "How do you know that? He can't talk."

"Oh, I see it in his mind." She thumps her tail in answer.

"You can talk with him?" I ask incredulously. "Wait, he has a mind? It isn't just purely a spell?" I ask, even more confused.

"It is a spell, let me make that quite clear, but it has the capabilities to be more than that." She presses on, "All magic does. Magic is believing in something enough that makes unbelievable things happen."

Shade rises up and shakes his head and moves between Tallia and I. "What are you doing, Shade?" I ask.

A tinkling of laughter comes from Tallia. "Little one, I am not going to hurt her; you can count on that." She pats its head and moves back a few steps.

"He thought you were going to hurt me?" I ask looking from Tallia to Shade.

"No, not really, but he doesn't like me knowing of him and how he works. He is okay with the others because they do not know the extent of his power or yours, but I, on the other hand, can sense that and he knows."

I place my arm around him holding him to me hoping he didn't try to strike out at Tallia. "I am supposed to have control over him, how am I supposed to have that if I don't even know what he is thinking or saying." I give a sad frown, but Shade is having a hard time and not concentrating on me. "Can you help me Tallia, can you tell me all you know?"

Her eyes focus on Shade's head for a moment and then back to me. "Sadly, no little one, this is not my story to get involved with." I am about to say something, but she interrupts my thought. "Hush now there are reasons why I should not interfere, you will find them out on your own. But I will help out in one way to help you get there quicker than you would."

I nod not wanting to interrupt her and where she is going with this, I would take any help I could get. She doesn't go on, so I ask. "What is it?"

She swishes her tail back and forth a moment and then comes back to me. "Okay, everything is set, when you go to the library later on today you will have a surprise there for you that will help you with Shade and your communication issue."

"Natasha came up with the idea to try to learn sign language to figure things out."

She nods. "That will work as well, but this will help a bit quicker I would still rely on learning the sign language because the spell my sister will help with you will have to be touching in order to hear each other, but when you are needing to be apart or are apart, I have a feeling you will still need to communicate and know what the other is thinking."

"Okay," I say hesitantly.

Tallia looks down quickly. "Oh, hush now, soulless one. Your secrets are your own." Her tongue flicks out at Shade as she curls her tail back behind her.

"He has secrets?" I look at him again rethinking my take on the whole situation. I whisper to Tallia. "Is he more like a dog or pet, or more like a person."

Tallia thinks on this for a moment; her tongue flicks out once more. "Think of him more like a person if you must but he does not have a soul and is controlled mostly by the spell in place."

"Would he disappear without the spell?"

Tallia shrugs her dragon-like shoulders. "Who knows. Magic is a wonderous thing sometimes." She tuts.

Shade shrinks down back into the bucket no longer wanting to partake in this conversation since she wouldn't give up the information on him, he was content with the situation.

I fold up the piece of paper that shows tomorrow's schedule. "I guess I better go. I have library time later. I will catch up with your sister then." I eye Tallia and then look down at Shade. "Can you please transform back into a tattoo so I can easily carry you instead of this obnoxious plastic bin?" I question.

Its ink-like texture shivers and then diminishes and grows foggy and almost see through. It lifts up out of the can and hovers over it going very slowly. "That spell sure did a doozy on you." I comment. He flits in front of me jerking and trying to form into something. It loses strength and falls a bit before catching himself. I lift my arm up in case he were to fall again. "Just rest it doesn't matter." Shade stops moving and comes to a rest on my arm laying across it in just an inky splat, he slithers up my arm moving to my back to rest there comfortably.

Tallia looks to the door behind me. "Go on, you do not need to be here any longer, go on and meet my sister, she is the nice one." She flicks out her tongue once again.

I stick the paper under my bra strap on top of my shoulder and move forward quickly, placing my hand on one of the Teager's claws.

"No, thank you!" I caress her claw and slip away as the doorknob begins to rattle.

Chapter 7

Surprisingly, I have no issues finding my way back to the cafeteria. I look at the clock noticing the time is still early in the day. I glance around the room. It is dim, but not dark, many are just hanging out and doing their thing. The food area is where it is darker since it is in between eating periods though there are still certain foods for purchase if one was feeling peckish.

"What should I do?" I question. I slide out the paper with the new schedule on it and unfold it slowly. I don't see much of anything on it till later in the evening. I take a seat at one of the many empty tables.

"I guess I will wait for Natasha..." I sigh and groan, laying my chin on my crossed arms. I twirl the paper in front of me. "I could always walk around and see what there is to do around here," I mumble to myself.

Shade slides up my shoulder and down my arm and wriggles my fingers, nudging them. Hearing my questions must have brought him about. I thump my fingers against the shadows on my fingers.

"Later, you need to rest. You need to recuperate your strength." He tightens sluggishly around my fingers. "Can you talk or communicate at all?" I nudge him trying to push him back up my arm under the sleeve so no one sees properly what is on my fingers.

I look around keeping an eye on the people that are lingering and sitting at the other tables. They don't pay any mind and are not looking at me.

Shade slowly glides up my upper arm but no words come to mind like they did with Tallia. "You can't just motion like a yes, or no even." I roll my eyes and grab the paper that sits in front of me. Folding it back up into a small sloppy square. I place it again under the sports bra strap, not wanting it on hand. I pull out the other paper, the one that is now obsolete and crumple it into a ball, getting up slowly. I throw it away before coming back to the same table to sit back down.

"I wonder what her sister will have for us to help with communicating." I grumble, Shade flutters on my shoulder in comfort. I shrug in discomfort.

"Whatever. You don't need to talk to find us a way out of here because sooner or later we will need to leave regardless, we both can agree on that at least." I feel a light pressure against my mind but no actual words that come through just more of a feeling of agreement.

"Yeah, yeah. Later," I whisper back, roughly both with my words and in my mind. Letting him know that I was still upset. "I'm going to need something to keep me hidden or learn enough to get me up to speed in this world to survive. I need to learn to control either this creature or my own powers." I shake my head. "Or at least know more about the people or creatures I now know. I could also look at finding a medical kit or something instead of the make shift bandage of a dress."

"Are you speaking to someone in particular or just yourself?" someone states, a hand brushing my shoulder.

I turn to see a guy waiting for my answer. "Who are you?" I ask, giving him a strange look.

"Who am I? Didn't Nat tell you?" He waits a moment. "I am sure she did." He nods in agreement and continues coming around on the other side and sitting across from me.

"Who?" I question once again getting more and more upset.

"Nat." He sees my confusion. "Natasha, I already stated that." He looks at me expectantly.

"Okay." I say slowly. "Yeah, I know a Natasha, but she never said anything about you so who are you?" I ask once again.

"It's Jack." He nods. "Jack!" He shoves his hand in front of my face to shake.

I shake it reluctantly.

"Good, good." He smiles. "Natasha needs more light in her life." He nods looking past me.

I glance around wondering what he is seeing that is behind me. "What are you...." I peer back at him shyly wondering what he is and what his powers are or what he can see that I could not. "What do you mean?"

"Lunch." He yells loudly. His mop of brown hair flicks into his eyes, he swipes it to the left.

I notice others look over at him but go back to what they are doing as if this happens all the time. More people pour into the room in preparation of the food coming out for lunch.

"Looks like you are just in time for it to start, you better go line up." I usher him to leave.

He nods and stands up. "Oh, right." He hesitates and sits back down slowly. "She wanted me to let you know that she is going to be late. Prolly won't get here till way after lunch is done." He picks at his fingernails, not realizing what is going on around him.

"Okay," I say slowly, not sure what to say to not set him off. Since he is not moving to leave, I get up.

"Hey, where are you going?" He questions loudly.

I stop halfway up. "I am going to go get in line for some lunch, which is what I thought you were going to do originally."

"No... no you can't!" He stresses and reaches out for my arm, grabbing at it.

I back up and pull my hand and arm away from him, not wanting him to touch me to set off my powers or Shade. I fully stand up compared to my half crouch and edge away from him.

"Why not?" I rage. "You were just talking about lunch. Why can I not go get some while everyone else is lining up?"

He scoots closer leaning over the table urging me to come back to the table. "They will get you that way," he whispers out harshly.

"What are you talking about?" I look around once again and stare longingly at the growing line. I sigh loudly, but end up settling back down at the table. "What are you? What do you do?" I motion with my hand for him to continue. Perhaps he could connect some more pieces that I was missing like Natasha did.

He sits back against the chair and chews on one of his fingernails. His left leg bounces and he cannot sit still. "You can't let them know what you are thinking. You can't let them see the thoughts that you plan to escape," he says in a hushed tone.

I glare at him and sit back as far as I could without moving my chair. "What do you mean? I'm not thinking about leaving," I whisper in a low growl.

He shakes his head and hits it with his fists. He moves forward and puts his elbows on the table, knocking his fists against his head. "She doesn't know. Doesn't see." He stops hitting his head and instead rubs it with his fists, and then pulls at the dreads of his short brown hair.

I back up a little, worried where this is going or if he is just really insane. "What have they done to you? Are you okay?" I say in a calming voice.

"Do you think I have always been this way?" he asks instead.

"I'm not sure..." I state calmly. "I am not sure what you are wanting from me, or want me to say."

"Jack, my name's Jack," he states and sits up straight looking at me with a smile.

I look at him for a moment, wait a moment then say slowly. "Hi, Jack."

He notices confusion written on my face. "We did that part already, didn't we?" He asks and rubs the back of his neck. He glances at the line forming by the food, but glances back at me and stays seated. He rubs his hand on his shirt and sticks his hand out for me to shake.

I eye his long thin fingers; the finger nails are raggedy and look like they have been chewed down to the nub. "I am very confused about what is happening?" I don't move forward to shake his hand. "I know you are Jack."

"Right, Nat must have told you. She is good peeps." He takes his hand back and knocks his fingers on the table.

"No, we just discussed this. She did not tell me anything about you. But you sure seem to know a lot about me," I spit out, growling in irritation.

He nods his head in agreement and withdraws into himself. "That's beside the point. Nat says you are right, so I help. Nat don't know this, but maybe you help as well. I see you for you. You, see?"

"No, I don't see. Do you have some power where you talk in riddles?" I question, not understanding his line of thinking.

"Why do you ask that? Are you a mind reader?"

"Nothing forget it." I rub my own temples, trying to keep up with his chaotic thinking. I gaze around and notice the lunch line dwindling. "Well, we better go get in line for lunch," I suggest.

"We need you safe. Some way to get you out of here undetected. Though many have tried and there is no known way to get out of here without incurring others' wrath," he goes on, ignoring my lunch talk.

I lean forward more interested in his ramblings. "I'm not sure why you keep fixating on me leaving, but what were you thinking if someone were wanting to do just that?"

"Well, it is what you need to do is it not? What you will do? What you have done?" His eyes dance around seeming very confused. "When are we?" he asks, glancing at the clock. He shakes his head. "Stupid, stupid!" he yells. "For once in your life, be clear. This is important." His right-hand pounds at the table, but he takes his left hand and rubs down the back of his hand trying to calm himself down. "There is no way through, there is no way through," he repeats over and over to himself.

"I didn't see any fences around here keeping us in. Seeing as this place is crawling with paranormal and weird things that they can do it shouldn't be hard at all to escape and get out of here right? Do you have any ideas of how to get out of this building though?" I urge and push him forward into the line of thinking that I am needing.

He laughs and chuckles.

"Jack?" I ask.

His head comes up. He still is laughing, but tries to talk through it. "No, getting out of the building is the easy part, silly. On the outside, there is a barrier surrounding this place." He puts two fingers on the table and moves his fingers to signify a person walking. "When you hit the barrier, BAM!" he says loudly and smacks his hands together for emphasis. He throws his one hand up that he was signifying as a person and throws it on the table landing still. "It encircles this place and is keyed to keep people like us from getting out." He brings his arms back in and crosses them in front of him.

"There has to be some people in here that have powers that can take care of that," I say looking around trying to guess which people would have them. "That seems dangerous to have something that could kill a person."

Jack shakes a finger at me accusingly. "Nice try, witchy." He shakes his head. "Round and round it goes like a carousel. Where it stops, nobody knows!"

"What is that supposed to mean? You said bam and showed someone landing still that means like they are dead right?" I grow exasperated.

He shakes his head "You loop." He looks at me and draws circles on the table with his finger. "Till you puke." He laughs out. "Or pass out."

"You mean you go in one side of the barrier and you come out of another part of the barrier on a different side."

He nods his head very excitedly. "Yep, by golly I think she's got it."

"Jack!" The stern looking lady from breakfast stands out from behind her cash register. "Come on, come and get something, stop badgering people with your gibberish," she urges him over.

I glance between the two of them.

"Did we not do that yet?" He glances at the clock once again and shakes his head. "Must not have." He gives a sheepish grin and nods. "I'm sorry."

"No, that is okay, I'm not very hungry."

I watch as the lady walks up to our table and eyes Jack. He slides out of the chair and edges past her and runs the rest of the way to the food to look at what is there. She watches him go and turns back to me. "Jack is not bothering you too much. is he?" She glances back, her expression is worried but breathes a sigh of relief as she sees him talking to himself and deciding between the foods.

"No, not really bothering, more just saying confusing things," I say in general.

"Unfortunately, he sees many possibilities and they all blend together. Sometimes he doesn't see the present, he sees the past or possible futures. So, time is hard for him, and he has to be reminded to eat since he is not always sure when the last time was." She nods and glances back, keeping an eye on him. "He is pretty lucid right now, but there are worse times." She frowns. "It's hard to keep track of when he is talking since, he might be talking about a future conversation, or a past one. He could be talking just at the present as well. I wouldn't put too much stock in what he is saying. Most barely understand him. He usually keeps to himself other than Natasha. She enjoys the chaos of it." She frowns deeper.

"Yeah, I can understand that. It was very hard to understand him and keep him on a topic and not get lost." I nod with her, keeping an eye on Jack.

"Don't be like Natasha and use him for his chaos. That girl thrives on darkness." She gives a pointed look.

I glare at her. "First, you don't know me like that, and second, Natasha may be chaotic but she isn't mean about it. Like Jack she is just harder to understand than most," I ground out. "I myself am different, and coming from what I thought was normal, I can understand why you all think we are just a menace to society. You forget though usually we go through something that makes us this way so please try to understand where we come from before you judge us so harshly," I seethe.

She scowls at me. "What did he say to you?"

"Like you said, you can barely understand him. I didn't get much from him other than his name." I smile at her scowl.

"Are you sure?" She squints her eyes at me, looking me over.

"Well, no, now that you think of it, I am not sure." I tap my finger against my lips in contemplation. "I may not be remembering correctly or maybe I didn't understand him right. Who knows?" I shrug.

She nods as if she understands, she stares at me going very slowly over my form as if looking for something that is hidden. "Well, you let me know if he bothers you again. So far, he hasn't harmed anyone but he has threatened," she warns.

"I will let you know," I agree as I watch her walk back over to the kitchen area, cleaning up after the lunch rush.

I get lost in my thoughts as I think over what Jack had said before he ran off. I watch him get distracted and leave soon after he picks a few items from the line. He didn't come back over to chat; I would have to find him later when someone wasn't watching to maybe find out more information. He was the first one other than Natasha to talk about this place in such a way. I needed more information like he had but maybe not as confusing. I think over my conversation with Jack trying to remember and piece together all the facts and information about this place that I could get. Anything that may help me get free of this place in the future.

"Hey!"

A hand lands on my shoulder startling me completely, I glance back and see Natasha standing over me waiting for me to yell something back at her. "Hey, how's it going? I met Jack!" I blurt before she can say much else.

"Seriously, if I'm not killing myself in this place, then it's a grand day indeed," she states way too eagerly. "Ahhhh, so you met Jackie boy. I see you got my message from him about being late. So how was Melissa's sesh?" she fires right back.

"Well," I hedge. "I can see why you would dislike her so."

I glance at the clock, noticing how much time has passed while I sit here and contemplate everything Jack went over. Lunch had definitely ended, though hunger did not claw at me. I grab the paper under my bra strap and unfold it once again and slide it over to her for her to take a look. "Soon, I will have to go see someone to help me learn some fighting or unlock my potential abilities and powers. Or once we know for sure how they work and how to control them. Also, your friend Jack seriously has a screw loose somewhere, just saying. The lunch lady came over here and explained he sees past, present, and future so I get that it is hard but don't they work with him."

She sits back in the seat and bounces her foot and leg, worried. She takes a look at the paper and purses her lips in contemplation. "They gave you a new schedule so soon? Something must have happened," she voices in a surprising manner. "I thought you were a witch or had a spell put on you?" she questions.

I bite at my lip and she sets the paper back down and continues to look at me.

"Jack is one of the saner ones. You should see the others of his kind." She eyes me. "Your turn."

I break eye contact and fidget with a loose string on the hem of my shirt. I shrug. "I don't know anymore. They know about the shadow creature I carry with me. The guard though that came to get me from our room, well he is a rat shifter, he triggered something in me."

Natasha nods. "He is a sleaze ball, that one! What did he do to you?" she says more gently now. "I could always freeze something off." She grins as blue ice sparks cascade off of her fingers.

I rub my lower arm, not wanting to relive last night again. "Something about him felt off to me. I could just see it in his beady little eyes of his that he wanted to do something bad to me or with me. His words weren't much better." I shudder. "I was angry and confused about a lot of things and mostly at him. He had a hold of me up against the hard concrete wall. I was filled with terror, but more importantly, I think he liked that I was afraid. Rage inside me grew and it was just like a dam bursting inside me. I was no longer able to hold it back. Part of me changed, I think." I shake my head and raise my hand to my head to run my fingers through my hair. "I'm not sure anymore. I didn't tell them, but I knew he had to say something."

"Why didn't you say something to me this morning or geez to one of them?" She glares outside the cafeteria, looking as if she wants to go find him and make him pay.

"I'm not sure of what I am exactly, but Doug told me I might be a badger. He could smell it on me, I guess. He got worried and scared of my new form as things progressed." I chuckle a little bit at that. "Guess he is not used to a woman standing up to him and being able to take care of shit," I blurt, needing to tell someone the full truth. Either she liked me regardless of what I am or she didn't. I didn't need that sort of person in my life if they were not all in. "Plus, Quintan said they would look into it and he would take care of things."

"Hold up! Wait a second! Huh?" Her eyes open up wide with all of the onslaught of information that I unloaded onto her. Her voice gets higher pitched with each statement.

"Yeah," I say sheepishly, sliding down in my seat. "I think that is what happened to my 'parents' as well. They angered me or did something to me that unlocked this rage inside me. Which landed me in this place. I don't really remember that part yet though Melissa did something that should correct that apparently." I caress the black dress I still had wrapped around my arm. "I should probably get this bandaged. Quintan said memories should start coming back to me now. All I know is after last night they had to do something so wrong or bad to me in order to trigger that part of me to make me shift or do whatever I did." My hands shake as I fiddle with the makeshift bandage I had all but forgotten about it. "I craved something last night and I think I have had that craving before. I think I quenched that craving before," I say very slowly as I come across the realization.

Natasha stickers her forefinger against my lips. "Shhhhh... just for a second. You're losing me and rambling. Let me get this straight." Her eyes ping pong from left to right rapidly as she pulls on her hair. She holds up a finger as she slides out of the chair and races away towards the kitchen, she comes back a few moments later with a box in hand. "You're a shifter that you think is a badger possibly, and maybe a witch or someone put a spell on you, is that right?" She doesn't wait for an answer before continuing on. She opens the box up and takes out wrapping and scissors along with tape. "And the other part of the story about your parents I don't understand what you mean or what that is about we haven't really discussed them until now."

"It's a long story," I emphasize, I start unwinding the dress from the wound.

She looks at the clock once more. "Okay, summarize it for me. Give me the three-dollar tour. We can always circle back to it later on if needed." She moves the dress away as she grabs some ointment to slather on the mild bite. "Melissa did this? Is that her dress!"

I nod in answer.

"Can I keep the dress? I would love to torment her with this!" She pulls it over to her before I can nod. "The bite isn't very deep. I have heard she had a special bite. Never knew what it was though. Interesting, very interesting. Okay you were talking go on."

I nod, averting my eyes from the wound as she begins to doctor it, some darker part of me drawn to it. "Okay, I will basically tell you what I told Melissa. Apparently, my mother's friend—they were like sisters, maybe they were sisters but look nothing alike I don't know that part is still confusing. She stole me away from my parents when I was just a baby. I don't understand why they would want me." I stop and study her for a moment. "What would happen if I were a shifter and a witch mixed together?"

"Over the years, that has occurred and will continue to do so as we keep interacting with other worlds. The part that is frowned upon is the different sides."

I cry, not wanting to lose Natasha since she is the only one nice enough to help me so far. "I'm not even sure what side I belong to. I haven't really done anything that proves I am a witch other than having this shadow creature with me which could have just been placed on me. They at first thought I was one because that is what Jade was, she is the one that stole me away. I also don't really understand how everything works. Do you automatically get things passed down from your parents or is it a tossup?" I say sullenly, trying to figure out what I have seen in my memory, but not having enough answers to create a conclusion.

"This Jade is the same family member as your fake parents, right?"

"Yeah," I say.

"What about your real, biological parents? What do you know about them for sure? Not based on the one that took you," she questions as she wraps the cloth around my arm, tightening it and cutting off tape to hold it in place.

"I don't really know them, never knew them. She took me from them at a young age. I was told by the human authorities that they were my parents." I rub at my temples. "I still don't know much from that time, they said it would come back over time and that I would start to remember what really happened to me." I mumble. "But it's not working fast enough." I stutter.

"Have you tried looking them up and researching to see if they are still alive or not? Or did she off her own friend?"

My eyes go wide. "I never even thought of that before. What if they didn't kill my real parents? But don't they have to be dead since I was never rescued? Do they even want me back if they were alive, maybe they were like good riddance?" I think through all the possibilities, my mind racing a mile a minute.

"I don't know but we could check," Natasha points out. "Never hurts to be in the know."

"I wouldn't even know where to start, if they are alive that is. I barely know what either of them looked like and I have nothing else to really go on location wise," I stutter. "I don't even know their full names. Just Sera and Ivan."

"Hmmm." She hums to herself.

"What, did you think of something?" I ask excitedly.

She glances at the clock and glances over her shoulder. "I gotta get going, I'll see you later at the library." She gets up suddenly.

"Wait." I reach for her hand; it slides out before I can fully grasp on to her. "Where are you going, what did you think of? Slippery little devil." I say as her hand slides through mine.

"Nothing yet," she says over her shoulder as she scoots away but smiles at me. "I like that as a nickname though."

"Wait, do you know my parents!" I glance at the clock, noticing it is getting closer to when I need to go to the defense class. "Can you just tell me what you thought of?" I ask in a small voice. "Do you hate me for not telling you everything off the back, or because of what I am possibly?" My voice dims down as I get more and more depressed. "It's okay if you do." I state hoping to not sound too desperate.

Natasha stops and freezes for a moment then turns back toward me, smiling at me gently with a half-smile. She walks back and towers over my sitting form and places her hands over my own. "Trust me hun. When we have library time, I should have something ready for you that we can try. I am not trying to ditch you or anything I just have to get some supplies and things for later and I have to get going if I am going to get my hands on it today, I also have a meeting with one of the old ones so I gotta hurry if I am going to make everything work in a timely fashion." She bounces a bit before backing away.

"Oh okay." I smile back tentatively and say in a brighter voice. "Awesome, that sounds great." I wave as she hesitates a moment making sure I was okay before turning to leave.

I frown in puzzlement at what she could be up to and if she really is afraid of me or for me. But what did I know, maybe she really was going to help me and figure things out? If not, there were other ways to get information. I needed to find that library Tallia was talking about earlier but first I had to get to this self-defense or fighting class.

CHAPTER 8

I STAND UP AND stretch my limbs. I could always look around if I find the place right away and see what kind of secrets are hidden here or it may take me forever to just find this next place. "No time like the present. I thought Natasha was going to help me find this place," I call out to myself as my arms pop and my back cracks, working out the kinks.

My stomach gurgles and knots up in worry and confusion at what is all going on and the different lies or half-baked truths that I have to work through.

I grab the paper off the table before leaving and follow the directions that are printed out on it that Tallia had printed out for me. They were easy to follow and figure out where to go. "I hope I get more time with either Tallia or other Teager's like her, I think I could learn a lot from them. Tallia could help me the most since I couldn't hide much from her anyway, she was able to rustle through my mind," I whisper to myself, not thinking I could talk to anyone else about these thoughts rumbling through my head. "She seemed to know things about me, or my past. If anyone could help me, I bet it would be her or her sister. Maybe she could even help Jack, but why wouldn't they have helped him already," I keep chatting to myself.

As I walk further down the hall, I come upon the room where I am supposed to meet with my new trainer. I expected to see some sort of office but am instead greeted with a room full of mats and sparring equipment.

"This is a legitimate fighting room!" I say surprised as I go through the glass door. A sign is standing right inside the room and it reads training studio. "Well, at least I know I am in the right spot." I look at the sign once more and then back at the paper and fold it back up.

I play with the edges of the paper as I spin around the wide room in awe. I notice some real weapons that are on the far side of the room. Most are on the wall stacked neatly. Others were on tables spread out evenly. There were also stacks of fighting pads which are closer to where I stand. There are also practice dummies in the center of the room.

I step on one of the mats, the weapons begging for my touch. "How will learning to fight help me control this thing inside me, wouldn't that just help give it better weapons?" I question myself.

Something on the back wall calls out to me and I walk slowly over to the knives as if they are drawing me forward and speaking to me. I hear whispers become louder and louder as I grow closer.

"Hey, are you my five o'clock?" a very male voice grumbles at me from the side.

"For training or something like that?" I stutter. I have frozen mid step, my eyes trained on the weapons. I struggle to pull my eyes away from the wall.

"What are you doing?" he asks.

I argue with myself internally a bit before finally turning towards him, forcing myself away. His hair is wavy and brown and comes down to his shoulders. It bounces as he shifts his head slightly to the side in a questioning look.

"Nothing, yes, I am here to learn," I say more sternly and confi-dently.

His eyes shift behind me and then back staring straight at my eyes. "Are you ready to learn how to unlock some of your abilities and when to use them? Melissa told me we have a long way to go." He smiles, causing two dimples to poke from his cheeks, making him seem even more rugged and a tad handsome.

"Sure." My heart flutters at his attention and how his accent is thick and low, like a lullaby to my ears.

He walks over to me, sure of his footing across the mats that are set up on the floor. He passes by me to a door that is to the right of me. There on the door is a folder holder. There are many folders waiting there. He flips through the colored tabs and stops on one, studying it closely, then pulls it out.

"Alexia Kremer, correct?" He searches through the papers in the file, glancing up at me waiting for an answer before continuing.

"Yes!" I squeak out barely, still watching his wavy hair and the light brown curls blow into his eyes in the cool air conditioning. His hazel eyes flick to me, then he looks down at the paperwork in the file.

I cross the floor to get to his side so I don't yell and perhaps to gain a peek at the papers that are in the file. "Yes, that is me," I say stronger this time.

"That is peculiar," he states as he flips back and forth between two papers.

"What is?" I ask.

"It does not say here what you are for sure. It's guesses from a couple of people, but not for sure. Do you not know?" His square jaw firmly contracts, upset.

I shrug my shoulders. "Your guess is as good as mine." I try to see over his shoulder to what is hidden in my file. "Doug triggered something last night. There were claws, fangs, and black eyes, but I am not sure what that means. Doug said something about a badger, but I was a bit preoccupied you could say." I smile. Something about him was calling to me. "But nothing I saw would lead me to believe it was a badger. There are lots of animals with claws, sharp teeth and black eyes," I say in disgust at having to be reminded of what started this whole thing. I step closer and brush my shoulder with his.

He snaps the folder close; his bright eyes hold my gaze.

They pull me in as I lean into his body. Something deep down was answering something I saw there.

He turns around slightly, but he keeps me in his line of vision and away from his back. He puts my folder back in the holder.

"What's wrong? Are you afraid that I will attack like last night?" I ask, skeptical. My body sways, and I want to follow and keep close to him.

"No not fearful, but cautious yes. I am trying to watch for signals that your animal may be sending me without you fully aware."

"Like the animal would take over?" I fire back at him.

"It could," he states. He slaps his palm across his thigh. "You said Doug triggered you. Have you been around any other shifter males? What did he do exactly to trigger you?"

"I would advise not having him trigger me again. It was anger and fear, that's all you need to know," I state, biting my lower lip and finally looking away from him. I rub at my arm covered in gauze and step away from him.

Blaise takes a step forward and raises my head up with his fingers under my chin. "Believe me, I don't want to do that if at all possible. It's up to you if we have to go that drastic. I will be here regardless so nothing can happen without my say if you want to go that way," he tries to reassure.

My gaze is captured by him once again and I melt into him. "I don't even know your name?"

"Oh, I thought you had it there on your paper." He smiles.

I look down at my hand, still holding the dumb wrinkled paper. I just shake my head and look back at him.

"It's Blaise," he all but whispers. His thumb caresses the side of my chin as he releases the pressure.

I stare at him as his hand slides down my neck and freezes. My stomach flips as his warm fingers. I barely breathe let alone move. "Nice to meet you, Blaise," I whisper.

He nods. He stares back at me, not breaking my line of sight. His eyes are hypnotizing to look at, as if they are pulling me in, and all I have to do was ask and he would take care of me and anything I wanted. I shake my head trying to dislodge whatever had a hold on me.

He takes his hand away. "You're staring."

"What are you?" I wonder. Did I say that aloud?

"You might not want to go staring at shifters specifically," he bites out. "In the shifter life, it can be viewed as a challenge or something more enticing."

I glance away. "Well, how should I know? I am new to all of this," my hands curl into fists. Whatever held me in trance broke for the time as my anger unfurled. "All of this is new to me. There are rules that I am not following and ones I don't even know exist. I myself am useless and cannot seem to do anything right," I unload.

He chuckles. "A part of you doesn't believe that you are useless." He steps back, giving me room. "But that is what these training sessions and classes are for—for you to learn what and, more importantly, who you are. Most shifters are raised with packs to keep in control. There are few out there that can be on their own and comfortable being by themselves. Though most can't function like that and need the structure," he states as he leans against the wall behind him.

"Like yourself?" I ask.

He nods. My anger cools back down and something stirs the air between us. I slide closer my body moving before my mind catches up with what I am doing.

"I really would like to know these sorts of things so I don't just start a fight over a look." I stare, but lower my eyes, though it gets harder and harder as his eyes draw me in. I step closer and my arm bumps his.

He hesitates and sniffs the air. He nods to himself. "Yes, that will be the first step in learning all you can on all different pack dynamics. Some are more randy than others but there is always a basic pecking order." He takes another step back.

I give him a curious look as I step forward. "Why do you not have a pack or a family?" I ask.

"Sssstop," he hisses.

I shudder and freeze where I stand. "And what kind of shifter are you?" I all but purr.

He grumbles and walks back to the door. He rips the folder back out of the holder. He flips through the pages furiously and mumbles to himself. "How old are you?"

"23."

"And you don't remember much beyond these last few days, right?"

"Right."

"You are literally running on instincts," he says as if in answer to some questions. "We might need to bring in Doug." He stares at me for a moment.

I notice his pupils widen. "Why can't we just do this without him?" I question, backing up, making sure the wall is the only thing behind me. "What's wrong with my instincts?"

"Because I don't think you have the same... type of instincts towards me." He states.

Blaise flips through the papers once again, he sniffs the air.

I pick at my fingernails. "I'll try. I promise. Can we just try without him first?"

His eyes roam over me in a hopeful manner, placing the file slowly back in the plastic holder. "Perhaps we can try something else. They did not tell me you were new to everything. It might be best that you first do some reading on shifters before we get into too much. We will have to see and perhaps gain trust and understanding between us two that way."

"Can I ask a question about you and you answer?"

"Go ahead." His mouth hangs open a bit but leans against the wall a bit further down the wall from me.

"What type of shifter are you? Since you have an inkling or will be learning what type of shifter, I am I should know what kind you are?" I rush forward.

"You don't want it to be a surprise?" He smiles wide.

"I have had enough mystery for a lifetime, thank you," I say in a tired voice.

"Fair enough." he says with a sly smile but doesn't go further.

I give him a once over and stand up straight and stare. My back is rigid and tense. "I think I deserve to know who and what is teaching me. I may not know what I am doing exactly, but I know enough to be dangerous and am being quite nice I think for what I have been through," I bite out.

His eyes open wide with surprise at the sound of my fierceness. "So, you think you have it all figured out then?" He gives a chuckle.

"No, I didn't say that. Stop mincing my words like that," I grumble.

"Then say what you mean." He urges me forward.

"I do want to know everything and anything possible. I know I have a lot to learn, but it does not mean I also have to put up with being looked down upon or belittled. Just because I was dealt a different hand than you does not make me different or needing to be treated with kid gloves. I am a woman that may have been through things that I don't even know how to figure out yet and am not sure how it will affect me in the future. But I can feel when someone is treating me as less than and I do not deserve that kind of treatment," I growl with increasing anger and huff a breath at him. "I don't want to believe everyone is a rat physically or mentally like Doug, but it seems like every person I meet falls into a category like him. Other than the people that are in here like me, I have not found any others that I feel like I can trust." I give him a once over. "Answer this honestly—is this a place people come to get better?" I ask, really wanting to know that answer more so than anything or if it was just a cage to keep their problems locked up.

"For those who want the help," he says cryptically.

I frown at his answer. "How very safe of a response you give," I say in disappointment. "All I know is that you don't have the same slimy feel as Doug does, but you are sly all your own, aren't you?"

I sniff the air like he did and try to see if I pick up anything like the other shifters did.

"What do you smell?" he questions.

"Nothing, just normal smells," I answer, though my body flushes in excitement.

"Listen to her, the thing deep inside of you, your animal." He grins in response, eying me as he walks forward. He passes me on his way to the mats, moving closer to the door that I came in through earlier. "I'm a snake charmer, by the way," he says calmly. "Sly would be one of the words I would describe my animal." He nods.

I cock my head in confusion. "Do you charm snakes or turn into one?" I ask genuinely interested as I follow him over to the same mat where he is now standing, I stand across from him but far enough away to not impede on his personal space.

"Or something." He turns his back to me giving me a supple view of his powerful back and his firm shoulders. He pivots and turns circling around me as he pulls his long sleeve shirt over his body a black tank top sits comfortably on him.

My eyes feel pulled to him once again, this time for a completely different reason. Something stirs and flutters in my stomach.

He turns once again, circling up my other side and steps away toward some chairs and props his shirt over the back of the chair.

I lick my lips and my heart rate increases. I feel the thud in my chest. I swallow slowly trying not to gulp or leave my mouth on the floor. His biceps bunch together as he clenches his fists; they are well toned but not overly muscular. He looks like he would be quick and agile, but enough muscle to take care of business if needed.

He glances back at me since I say nothing more. I glance away quickly, but feel my face getting hot. I press my hands to my cheeks and turn back to the weapons that are behind me, trying to avoid him seeing me blush.

"So do you usually start with weapons or more hand based till we work up to it?" I ask, clearing my throat at the end of my sentence, noticing my throat is becoming parched and is lower.

I keep my focus on the weapons once again the whispering begins again. My hands caress my cheeks to make sure the heat is not continuing to radiate there. I hear a more urgent whisper behind me but cannot find a way to turn away. My eyes bounce over each weapon trying to discern which one the whispering is coming from but I can't tell, only that it wants me to come closer. I take a step forward and another sound shifts closer this time.

"What?" I whisper out.

Something hits my legs and knocks my feet out from underneath me. I go down hard and slam into the blue mat. I flip over to look at what brought me down and see Blaise crouching down with his leg out stretched.

"What the hell!" I yell.

He smiles, but his eyes are on the wall behind me. "You weren't ready? Hand to hand is where we will begin."

I purse my lips and glare daggers at him. "No, why would I have been ready?"

"Does an attacker ever wait for their victim to be ready for an attack? No, I think not."

I mock him silently as I pick myself back up slowly. "That will teach me," I gasp out, my lungs try to catch up with what was knocked out of me.

Blaise also rises up from his crouch, staying on the balls of his feet. "Oh, is that so?" He smiles. "I think you have a lot to learn."

I growl as something dark inside me slithers forward. "I may not be trained and tough, but I'm not a weakling either."

"Show me?" He motions with his hand for me to come forward.

"Be careful what you wish for." I crack my knuckles as I walk around him. I fling my fist out to connect with his shoulder.

Blaise slides to the right, and grabs my wrist holding it there in front of his face to inspect. "Good form, but untuck your thumb from your fingers. If you connect hard enough, you can dislocate your thumb or even break it." He blows a light breeze over my fist.

I hold my breath. "Okay." I move my thumb out and set it outside of my fist. "Like this," a whisper of fur and warmth brush up against my side.

"Yesss," he hisses. He relaxes his hold on my wrist and slides his hand away.

A shiver runs up my spine. I shake my head to try to clear it. My arm goes weak falling down to my side. "What is going on?" I growl out. One minute I want to take a bite out of him and the other just nibble a trail down...

"Perhaps instead of fighting, we first need to get you a couple of books for you to go over," he whispers, circling behind me.

My eyes swivel over to him. I roll my head to the side as he interrupts my thoughts. "Why can't you just go over it with me?" I utter back.

"Are you sure you have never been around a male shifter before? Other than Doug?" He snickers. "He doesn't count. And I mean a man, not a boy," he clarifies.

I can feel his form towering over me, the heat of him fiery and intense. I can feel it beating at my side as he moves closer to me.

His words grate on me in an annoying yet delicious way.

"No, why? At least I don't remember a time," I fire back, squinting my eyes.

I keep my body light. I pay attention ready for him to pounce. I feel a warm breath on the back of my neck, his face inches from my skin. Another shudder goes through me. I groan and quickly flip on him and pounce before he can do anything else.

"Why don't you explain it to me?" I say close to his face as he catches me before we hit the mat.

Blaise yanks me up close to his body and spins me around facing me towards the wall pinning me. His arms come up wrapping around mine as he forces them above my head and puts both of my wrists in one palm. I snap my head back, trying to hit him, but he grabs me with his other hand against my neck and pushes me closer to the wall with his body. He traps my body there, his heat enveloping me.

"What would you like me to show you, little minx?" he whispers into my ear.

I close my eyes as another shudder works its way down my body. Him being so close this time, he will have felt it as well. I feel his hands tighten on my wrists.

I growl as I try to wriggle out. "You think you can teach me something?"

His fingers rub slow circles on the back of my neck as his feet kick my legs wider.

I whimper and bite my lip, not wanting to utter anything else. I try tugging my body away from him, but he has made sure I have hardly any wiggle room.

His fingers stop rubbing at my neck. He slides that free hand down, encircling my waist, pulling me against the hard length of his front. The fire in him ignites the flame in me. My eyes hyper focus and clear as they did the other night. I feel claws rake my skin from the inside.

"Are you sure we couldn't teach each other?"

My head falls back against his chest leaning more into him as I breathe heavier.

His arm tightens around my waist and hisses a shaky breath.

I slide my head to the side trying to glance at him and see why he is hissing. "What are you doing?" I growl once again, my voice coming out low and rough.

Teeth nibble into the side of my neck, not hard, but there is pressure. I freeze, not knowing exactly what to do. His fingers draw gentle circles on my stomach.

I lean more of myself into him and my breath comes out in pants.

He slides us to the left a bit where a full-length mirror stares at us. He places my fisted hands on the cool mirror surface. His hand caging my wrists never leave my hands.

"Look," he says his teeth graze my neck, and a cool tongue sweeps away the hurt of the bite.

I look to his face in the mirror and see his eyes. They are slit like a snakes, the pupils are thin and straight like. He notices me looking at him and stops what he is doing to open his mouth wide before two pricks of teeth flash out further and pushes them against my skin, not breaking skin. He then scrapes them against me.

A noise groans out of my throat as his lower hand hedges down my stomach brushing the top of my pants. A purr emits from my throat it causes me to cough shortly after. Not used to the feeling a purr makes in the back of my throat. My eyes roam down as I glare at myself. giving a hard look. I notice my eyes have gone fully dark and are liquid black.

"What are you doing to me?" I groan out pressing back into him, feeling that I am not the only one to be affected by what is going on here. "What is this?" I growl out.

He pulls his teeth back enough to talk, but continues to kiss down my neck. "Your animal will at times ride you in ways you do not even understand." His lips brush against the sensitive skin there and makes me go more limp. "I think we can safely say Doug was correct, you are a badger shifter," he utters. He rubs his face against my neck and face. "Your animal brushes against the surface—can you feel her?"

I see red at the mention of that name, and claws rake down inside me with acute pain. I rear back forcing him to take all of my weight. I kick back on the wall and push into him. I kick out again, trying to flip over him, he lets go of my wrists to wrap tighter around my middle. Both of us fall to the mat in a bundle of limbs. I scramble to my feet. He raises up slower than I.

"Why did you have to say his name? You think you know me and everything I stand for?" I howl. My fingers burst into claws. A scream rips out of me as I flex the claws in pain.

"What did he do to you?" Blaise eyes the open door to the room, and then his closed door for his office.

I pounce on him before he can even think about making a grab for me.

He bends his knees and readies to catch me out of the air. I wrap my legs around his torso and grip him. He lets my weight pull us down onto the mat, but rolls until he can get his legs back underneath him.

I slash out at him. He hisses in pain as I connect with a shoulder. He grapples with my arms as my lower body clings to his torso. He grunts as he muscles his way over to his office and kicks open his office door. He slams the door closed.

I scream out in anger as he pushes me off of him. My feet hit the floor hard, this area is only carpeted with no soft mats like there is out in the main room. He slips through his office door, closing me in. I hear a loud bang as the other door shuts.

"You better not be running away, coward!" I growl and bang on the door, my claws fully extended. I press them against the wood making indents. I like the feel of the wood against them so I press harder, rattling the door. "Let me out," I press on.

"You need to breathe through this and come back down," he urges. "What set her off? What made her come out? Think through it."

I glare at the door as I seethe. I look around at the tiny room and notice papers on a desk with a computer and a chair. The office is very bare. I grab at the papers and throw them around, not stopping to read them. I grab the wires behind the computer and yank hard, causing as much damage as possible, ripping and tearing at everything that I can grab on to. "I am done with waiting. I am done with all of you."

A loud bang echoes behind me. I twist my head and see Blaise storming through the door slamming it back in place.

"Stop that!" he bellows out and pushes me out of the way. "I can't help you if you don't tell me what Doug did. I know it was him that sets your inner animal off."

I stumble out of the way and scream back at him, reaching out to slash at his back. He jumps out of reach before I can slash through him again. He turns and rushes at me, grabbing my wrists, keeping my claws away from him. A snake-like tongue flicks out near my cheek. I bite at it. My teeth clamp down, but I don't feel anything between them as they snap shut. He spins me, forcing me up against the wall. My head whips around to keep him in my sight.

"What are you doing?" I ask out, fear coating my tongue. My mind pulls back to the night before. How does he keep pinning me so easily?

He unbuckles his belt and pulls it out of the loops of his pants. He loops it over a low hanging metal pipe and maneuvers it around my hands, locking it in place where my hands do not have much movement.

"Only what you deserve," he hisses back. His tongue flicks out again. "Don't insult me. I am not him. I'm not Doug." He looks me in the eyes.

The anger rises in me. "Are you just going to leave me here?" I question. I glare at him, raising my chin.

He grabs my hips, keeping me in place. "Do you have another suggestion. You don't want me here?" His breath flutters over the side of my neck. He is so close to me.

My neck relaxes to the side and my eyes fall close. I lean back, pushing up against the wall into him. His thickness is hard and full, pressing against me. None of this has calmed him down. I pull down hard on the restraints, but they hold secure. "Don't leave," I whisper. "...me." The last part is barely audible.

His thumbs draw small circles on my side where he holds me in place. My breath hitches in anticipation. My eyes flutter open and close, having a hard time deciding between fear and arousal. "I am supposed to help you, but not in this way." His tongue flicks out once more against my neck, unable to keep from me. "But sssomething of you callss to ssomething in me," he hisses.

His left-hand toys with the waistband of my pants, dipping under the cloth there. I bite my lip hard, not knowing if I would scream in frustration of him not going where I needed him or yell at him to stop. "Look at me, little minx." His other hand squeezes my side.

My eyes raise up to his. His hand moves a bit lower. He is so close to me; his scent surrounds me. My mind keeps flipping between dark thoughts or ravenous thoughts.

I push myself more into him. "Aren't you worried?"

"Worried? Only if this is not truly what you want." His free hand raises up. He grips my chin and brushes his thumb against my lower lip. His other hand travels down lower brushing my curls as he dips one finger parting my lower lips, a moan bursts out of me as I melt into him. His thumb dips into my mouth and I nibble at the pad.

His hand below continues to work and tease. "Is this what you had in mind, little minx?" he whispers, his head bent down to my ear.

He removes his thumb and kisses me lightly at first, but as I meet him with eagerness. I feel my animal shift inside me, but in a different way. Instead of claws and teeth, the warmth of fur rubs. She wants to be caressed; I want to feel this.

His free hand slides over my neck. He feels the quick pulsing beat as his hand moves further down. He encircles my nipple and lightly pinches it as he slips another finger inside me, caressing me just at my entrance. "Little minx?"

"Yes." I sigh and give a little whine. I press harder up against him, but my hands stay restrained up above no matter how hard I tug on them.

"You are so wet," he whispers into my ear as he slips another finger inside me and grinds the palm of his hand against my clit.

I buck at his hand wanting, and needing more.

"Will you let me taste you?" He nibbles at my neck, but does not press too hard with his sharp teeth. They only graze my skin, heightening the sensation.

"Unchain me first."

He massages my breast as he removes his other hand from my pants. "This is better." He smiles against my neck as he continues to nuzzle, his tongue flicks out.

"Please," I mumble out. I rub my body against his as much as the belt will allow me to.

"Please, what?" he whispers as both his hands roam over my sides and breast, teasing and tantalizing the sensitive skin.

"Yes... Taste me," I whisper, leaning my head against the wall.

He grins before his face closes into mine and kisses me deeply.

I match his fervor and push against him, wanting him closer, needing this.

His hands work their way down my body. He stops the bruising kiss and kneels before me. He slides my pants and underwear down my legs removing them from my lower half. I keep my eyes trained on his movements, the wall keeping me up right and the tightness of the belt on my hands.

My legs shake. Whether in fear or excitement, I'm still unsure.

He lifts one of my legs and places it over his shoulder. I put more pressure on my upper back against the wall as he urges the other leg to lift on to his other shoulder. I pull tight on my arms trying to take some of the weight and balance there. He stands up with me on his shoulders and uses the wall to help guide me upwards. My arms loosen, and I grab onto the pipe that the belt is tied to.

I breathe in sharply. "What are you doing?" I ask looking at the ground that is much further away now, my legs tighten against his face.

He rubs his cheeks against my thighs that are surrounding his head. "Relax, little minx." He runs his teeth gently down my inner thigh.

I look down at his head, watching and waiting. My legs slowly unclench and relax. He kisses his way up my thigh all the way to my clit and then starts to suck and lick his way down as he sticks his tongue deep inside, as much as he can.

I gasp and arch back, pushing my lower hips more into his face for better access. His hands come up to grip my ass, helping me connect better with his mouth. He laps and sucks at the front as he pushes a finger inside.

I moan in ecstasy as my hips rotate, wanting more to ride. He grinds his face more into me as my hips buck forward. I scream out as I come, my legs locking him to my body and squeezing around him. He removes his finger and hands, his tongue replacing them as he laps up my juices. My breath comes in and out in gasps as I look down at him. I notice my hands are back to normal, they must have changed back sometime during everything. My body twitches as his tongue runs through my sensitive lips. My body pushes down wanting more.

"Blaise?" I ask, the fire ratcheting back up just as strong.

He slowly moves one of my legs off of his shoulder to ease it down around his chest. He undoes the other leg from his shoulder, having me slowly slide down his body. He kisses and nibbles his way up my body as I slide down his. He settles my legs around his hips as he draws circles with his hands on my hips and butt. He stares into my eyes, not dropping my gaze.

I keep my eyes on him. I wrap my legs tighter so as to let him know I am not allowing him to leave. He slips a hand between us to nestle against me, rubbing my clit once again. A moan slips out of me before I can stop it.

His pants drop down quickly, and I feel something thick and hard spring up against my inner thighs.

"What do you need?" He stares at me as his one hand maneuvers his hot, throbbing cock to rub at my center.

I flex my hands and arms and grab onto the belt and lift myself up a little bit away so I can move my hips to impale myself onto him. He moves with me, just keeping up the light touch and the questioning rub up and down my clit and lips.

I snap my teeth at him and glare daggers into him. "You," I breathe out.

One side of his mouth lifts up into a half smile as he slowly inches inside. He wraps both hands around my legs and ass to hold me as he lowers me down on top of him inch by delicious inch. I sigh and close my eyes letting my head fall back a bit.

He stops suddenly, not moving.

My head comes up quickly. I glance around trying to see what has caused him to stop. "What are you doing?" I look at him. I wiggle around trying to complete the action.

He hisses and holds me firmly against the wall. "Why didn't you say something?"

I hold his slit eyes in my gaze and scrunch my face in confusion. "Say what?" I ground out, anger starting to creep back up my body. The fire is too much. I need to shake this thirst one way or another. "If you do not move, you will become prey instead," I grit out as sharp nails caress my insides again fluctuating between claws and fur.

He looks at my face intently. I just stare back, waiting. He moves his arm slowly up my back and unloops my hands and unbuckles the belt letting my arms loose. They fall to my side. I shake them out and make fists with my hands to get the blood to flow quicker. He lets go of my legs and steps back from the wall. I tighten my legs around him and grab at his shoulders, my fingers grip his shoulders keeping me where I am, the tip of him toying with me.

"Have you not been with someone before?" he questions, cautiously. He hitches me further up his stomach, pulling himself out of me.

I look at him and then try to think through the red-hot haze that seems to have me. My animal was calling for heat in one form or another. Either from the blood of my prey or one from a lover. "You know my file. You know I may not have. I don't have those answers, since I don't remember much."

His animal fades from his eyes, his pupils going back to his human sized ones.

The heat cools from him, as if this was something he could switch off or turn away from.

"Oh, no you don't!" I growl.

I feel the points of my teeth against my tongue. I curl my one hand around his neck and into his hair. My fingers tangle in his curls and force his head back. I open my mouth and strike at the side of his neck, biting into his skin. I warned him if he did not finish this, something would consider him prey.

My teeth slice into him easily, and blood blooms on my taste buds. I lap greedily at the blood that coats my tongue. Rough skin puckers up against my tongue. I open my eyes and see diamond spotted scales erupt along his neck and back, disappearing under the tank top. He breathes in and hisses between clenched teeth.

Blaise stumbles back and sits down with a loud thud against the chair. I unwrap my legs from behind him as he does this and sit on him so as not to lose connection.

"Fine, Alexia, you want this, you are in control then. But you make the decision. I only know of what you told me and little else." He eases back, his hands skim up my legs and rubs at my sides. "But go slow," he warns.

My eyes squeeze shut as I lower myself onto him. His hands slide to my bottom and spread my lips for easier access. I retract my teeth from his neck, but continue to nibble and suck there. I ease all the way down, feeling him connect solidly. I start to pull back up and a sharp pain echoes through me. His hands slide back up to my hips and hold me down on him, keeping me there.

"Slow. Wait, just a moment." He breathes in deeply. His hands unclench from my sides and he bunches the shirt and bra up and over my shoulders. I sit back as I feel them pushed up and over my head.

I gasp as I feel more of him fill me and my lower parts press and squeeze around him. I move my hips around in circles and feel my lower muscles constrict around him.

"If you keep doing that…" He grits out. "This will not last long." He breathes slowly out between clenched teeth. He rubs his hands and thumbs over my taught nipples. I shudder at the sensation.

A moan escapes me. My body thrums with excitement, swaying closer to his hands, and I wiggle my hips around, but do not move otherwise. My fingers dance over his arms and caress his shoulders, the scales covering his whole top part. I pull him in closer to me.

He hums in approval. His hands slide to my back as he pushes me forward. He kisses me deeply as he holds me close rocking into me.

"More?" I urge and ask at the same time. I don't wait for his answer as I start to move ever so slowly up and down. A sharp twinge has me hissing, tears prick from my eyes.

"Look at me." He murmurs. I urge down slowly on him and feel him fill me to the brink again. I purr, but a slash of pain causes a tear to fall down my cheek. He grips my chin and pulls my face down urging me to meet his eyes. "Stay with me," he whispers.

I look down, not being able to look anywhere else, his voice calls to me. His thin irises stare back into me further than just my physical form.

"Is this too much?" He waits holding my gaze, never letting me move away from him.

"I don't know," I whisper out, and a small whimper escapes at the end. "She doesn't want you as prey," I whisper, talking about my animal for the first time.

"If you want to stop, you can. You have the power here. Don't think with only the animal part of you. What do you want? I took the edge from you earlier." He gives a sly grin. "Think through her needs and yours." He bares his neck showing off the bite mark. "Take what you need, and only give what you can," he urges. His hands brush against my sensitive nipples, making the lower parts of me twinge and clench.

I gasp as heat races through me in answer to his touch. He flicks and pinches my nipples, causing the heat to burn brighter. I start to move slowly up and down, holding his eyes in mine as he toys with me. He stares at me, letting me find my rhythm. My hand slide over his shoulders and grip in his soft hair. He takes one of my hands as I start to move to a faster beat and guides my fingers to his mouth. He nibbles on the pads there, and a tongue flicks out to tickle them.

"Feel ussss," he hisses as he guides that same hand down my body to where we are connected.

My fingers dance through my folds and feel the wetness he is cre-ating. His large cock rubs against my fingers as I continue to move. My eyes close as I use my sense of touch to see what is happening. He guides my fingers and rubs them against my clit with a vibrating sensation as we continue to climb faster and harder.

I cry out as I slam down on him. My head strikes forward, my mouth and teeth latching on to where he is still bleeding from before. He moves my hand to the side and pulls me closer to him. He grinds against me, fully seated on him. His arms wrap around me as he pushes me down on him. He also forces me closer to his chest.

I suck on and lick at the bite teasing. Blood trickles down, but I lap at it. My fingers work their way under his tank top and caress his back. As I lick the trickles of red that run out of him, I feel my fingernails grow longer as they start to scratch his back more forcefully.

I hear movement as a drawer is opened up. He rummages through the drawer. My ears focus on that, but I quickly ignore it as I splay my hands across his back, feeling the muscles bunching there. I twist my hips and feel him still hard and filled deep inside me.

I moan and rumble against his chest, licking my way down to his own nipples, flicking my tongue against it. Cold liquid flows down my back and over my backside his hands quickly warm it up spreading it further around. He pulls me up off of him and sets me standing beside him.

He stands up and turns me to face away from him and bends me over his desk. "You are a feisty one, do you need more?" He rubs the length of his cock over my ass.

My fingers bunch in the papers that were thrown there, and I look back at him over my shoulder. My eyes wide watching him to see how he would handle me.

His fingers dig into my skin. He pulls me to him, grinding his cock against me. The tips of his fingers massage and move near the opening of my ass. He moves in slow circles, the liquid he poured before makes everything slippery and hot. I gasp out as I wiggle toward his fingers, and push back, wanting his cock back inside me.

I look up at his down turned face and bite out, "More."

He rubs at the entrance to my ass, antagonizing me. He takes his cock in hand and pushes at my entrance there but slides down into my heat, still toying his fingers with my ass as he pushes himself in. I gasp at how much more he fills me in this position, I can't stop myself from rubbing up and down on his shaft, though his fingers cause me to pause.

"Come away from the ledge, and I will give you what you want, my minx." He pushes a bit of his finger in as I push back on him, and as I move away, he pulls the bit of finger back out he continues that as I continue to move. I breathe out slowly, not understanding how this could feel so good. "There you are," he says as his eyes stare into mine.

Though I can't see them, my eyes must have changed back to human eyes. I notice my nails return to their normal size.

"Your animal is showing." I gasp as he pushes forward into me before I come back. I hitch in a breath as he pulls out slowly.

His tongue flicks out again in the air, and he wrinkles his nose. He pushes both the head of his cock and his thumb in at the same time. I gasp and push back onto him more fully. He spreads my legs out with his so I sit comfortably against him. He rears back, taking his full length out of me before pushing back in his thumb going at the same tempo, his other fingers massaging the skin between the two regions.

"I was not telling you to put your animal away."

I gasp and scream out each time he pushes fully into me. My arms scramble out and push me up and back meeting him there, the friction building as the tempo moves faster and faster. This time I can see the edge and feel me moving towards it.

"Blaise!" I scream. I want him there with me. I slam back into him as he pumps three more hard thrusts before he utters a growl and pulls the top of my body up to his chest. His cock jumps inside me and I feel hot liquid run down my inner thigh. He rubs the front of his chest against the back of me, pinning my lower half to the desk so I can't move until he is finished.

His right hand comes up and pushes my hair away from my neck. He nibbles at the nape of my neck, his teeth scrape. He wraps that same arm around me and my chest, holding me tight. I am limp in his arms, trying to catch my breath and my voice after that. It was nice to feel that he had me when I was so sure if he let go, I would fall to the floor in a heap.

"So, I am guessing you can, in fact, change into a snake?" I huff out.

I feel his mouth turn up at the back of my neck. "Yes, I can, but a snake charmer can do so much more than just shift into a snake." He chuckles.

"Well, you charmed me right out of my pants, I see." I look around at my clothes strewn about the room.

He releases his hold and glances down at the damage done. "That was not what I intended." He rustles the one drawer closed and opens another.

Below it there are water bottles lined in rows neatly. He takes out one and grabs a towel that is at the end of the other desk. He opens the bottle and pours it over the cloth dampening it. He kneels down before me, I turn to see what he is doing.

He glides it up my inner leg, cleaning himself from me. I widen my stance so he can reach the rest of me. He wipes himself from me and I watch as the cloth comes away with red spots.

"What is that?" I ask worried, worried there was more damage done then to the room.

"It was your first time. Sometimes that can happen," he states calmly, keeping his focus on cleaning up. "It's why I stopped part of the way through and made sure this is something you want."

"Oh," I say, I feel a twinge of anger at not knowing that, but the fire does not build. I lean on to the table, not trusting my legs fully. He pulls up his pants the rest of the way and tucks himself inside. He walks over to where he had tossed my clothes and picks them up one by one. He comes back and kneels in front of me again with my panties and pants waiting for me to lift my leg. I watch cautiously as he dresses me.

"What does a snake charmer do? Is this normal?" I ask, not wanting to ask something dumb again but not sure what to do next or how we continue from here. Something still inside me called to him. Did he feel the same?

"No." He laughs. "Nothing about that was normal," He bites back. "You are correct, I am a snake shifter, but I have some power in charming people, you could say."

"So, you charmed me?" I ask in confusion. I felt better with my pants on and not being as vulnerable. I grab my bra and shirt from his hand as he rises. I quickly pull them on, feeling as if I needed something to cover and defend me.

"No, the only time you may have felt the pull was when you tasted my blood."

I flinch back. He pulls his hands away from me, not wanting to cause further tension.

"You needed that pull. You needed my help." Seeing my confusion, he continues, "Your anger or rage started to take over. It was either let you go to harm who and what you could before you tired, try to take you down before you harmed others, or distract you. The blood ignited the animal's strength in you and she was pleased with the distraction. I did not ever think it would go this far for your sake and mine." He touches the bite lightly before he cringes away. "Each step was your choice, as well as mine."

I stare at the mark that I left on him. "I didn't mean to do that. But once I had a taste, I needed more and it urged me to continue." I try to move my mouth, but no words would continue to work their way up my throat.

He hushes as he comes forward and envelops me in warm arms, turning me to hold me close, my face against his warm chest. "Don't worry about it. It doesn't bother me. It will heal soon enough," he presses. The scales have smoothed to normal skin once again.

My arms encircle him, holding him back. "I don't think this was what you were supposed to teach me," I mumble into his chest.

He laughs out loud. "Yeah, believe me, this is not something I teach, minx." He nudges me out of his arms. He brushes a hand through his hair. He slides past me continuing to clean up the damage we did during and before the incident.

"Minx? My name is Alexia or Lexi," I say, looking at the door and then back at him.

"What?" he asks, looking back at me, stopping what he was doing. "I know your name." He smiles.

"Then why minx?" I frown.

"It is what you are. Feisty, temper, and trouble. Sounds like minx suits you."

I smile, liking the way he described me and liking the pet name. "If that is the way things are going to go, perhaps I need to think of a name for you, Mr. Snake."

He cocks his head as if listening for something. He shrugs. "It should be about dinner time. Go ahead and get something we will pick up at another time. I will reschedule you on a different day." He changes the subject and dismisses me.

"We're not going to talk about this?"

His eyes go to the door and then return to me. "No. Not right now."

I turn away and move towards the door not knowing what had happened or what to even say, so I decide to go not wanting to say the wrong thing or break down and cry. I really needed my anger now more so than ever but that fire I usually felt did not seem to be there.

I open the door and run into Doctor Melissa standing there in front of me.

"Hey, Alexia," she says happily at first, her face falls slowly as she takes in the state of the office and Blaise. She quickly moves around me stomping in her pumps and keeps me at her back. "What did you do?" she yells accusingly.

"None of your damn business," he yells back as he turns fully to see Melissa.

I stand in the doorway not knowing exactly what to do or say.

Melissa takes a deep sniff, her golden eyes dart to me and my face staring at me searching. Her head whips back to his. "What happened?" She seethes.

He glances at me and then back at her.

She slowly breathes out and turns toward me as she faces me. "Are you okay?"

I nod not trusting my voice.

"Good, go ahead and get out of here I will follow up tomorrow." She nods for me to leave. I hesitate looking to Blaise. He nods so I turn and head towards the door. The door clicks behind me as I hear rumbles erupt through the door. I stop and stand for a moment in the fighting room, then look at the dark room and the door to the hallway is still closed. "What they don't know won't hurt them," I whisper as I tiptoe back to the office door to listen to their conversation.

"She marked you? Why? How? Does she know what that could mean? How could you do this?" Melissa barks in frustration.

"Of course, she doesn't know what it means," he growls. "And you're not going to tell her."

"Good going, snake charmer. Is this how you go about doing things? Do you do this with all the people you teach?" She scoffs in irritation. "No wonder you are part of the dark side!"

A loud bang happens and the wall vibrates a bit as if someone has been thrown and pinned against the wall. I glare at the door, wanting to know what happened but also wanting to continue to know information. I wait and continue to listen.

"Don't pretend you know anything about me, and last I checked you are part of the dark side as well." Blaise hisses.

Another thud happens. "Don't think you can charm me, snake. I am not into cold blooded things. You were chosen to do this job because you would not pick up on pheromones like other warm-blooded creatures and you are cold hearted or at least that is what it said in your own file." She throws back at him.

"Would you like a demonstration on how cold I can be?" he says coolly.

"Then why did you let her mark you, I didn't see that you marked her but there are other places that you could have done it. Is that their game for you and her?"

"Believe me I know what it is like to be stuck and in a cage, unlike her I knew what I was. She does not, she does not know yet what she is capable of. Her strength comes out in ways she is not always ready for. I did the best I could with what I had and what she needed."

"I thought all you snake people didn't have feelings let alone sides. You are hired for one thing and one thing only." Melissa growls out her voice becoming gravelly. "If she learns who you belong to and her animal has a hold on you with that mark, she will not let you go freely."

"I know," he says quietly.

"You are part of the darkness. Why didn't you bring out her darkness and be done with their game," she says.

"And take away her choice? Push something onto her that she herself doesn't even understand. No wonder she lashes out at the simplest of things. I would, too." The wall moves again as something hits it again.

I growl deep and low in my throat not sure who is doing harm to who. The growl grows and gets louder at them talking about me and not giving me the knowledge, I needed to know. Blaise seemed to know a hell of a lot more than he originally stated. My hands shook with anger, the library time would help me figure some things out but what could help me figure out my blank past, this world that is not mine.

A song whispers behind me lulling me to the back of the room. The melody continues to flow around me. I turn away from the arguing and am drawn to the wall of weapons behind me. I move slowly across the floor, trying to hear which weapon that wonderful sound was coming from. I hum along with the melody and my body sways from side to side coming closer and closer. I slide to the far right hearing the sound better there. The whispers intensify but I can't make out the words that are echoing around me. The haunting melody is what brings me closer. I stop in front of the wall but it is hard to tell which one this tune is coming from.

My hand reaches out and brushes against the cool metal of the weapons and sharp edges. The whispers begin to chant louder and the melody begins to dim away. I reach up high, my eyes latch on to one long looking dagger the metal point is wavy looking but still looks deadly sharp. My fingers brush the hilt and the whispers die down and the song is crystal clear. I put my other hand on the wall for balance and raise up on my tiptoes to reach it fully. I push the dagger up and over the metal holders and pull it into my hand. I scream out as a flash of darkness consumes me.

My mind flashes back to the night I was found, the darkest night I remember where I was surrounded by blood and bodies. I close my eyes not wanting to see the horrible mess once again. A squeaking sound causes me to reopen my eyes. The blood and gore are gone. I look around and I see a lone light bulb sway above me through the stale stagnant air. I glance around and see the light touch on some stairs, everything else is concrete and cold, a big metal ring sits in the middle of the room and a rustic looking chain is attached.

The chains are loose and are not connected to anyone or me. I focus on getting out of this room. The bulb sways back towards the stairs showing a door at the top of them. I move over to the stairs and slowly ascend them. The wood gives out a groan as I put my full weight on the step. I hesitate to continue but only hear whispering and chanting above me. The light seems to sway in time with their chant.

I make my way up and reach the door as I reach my hand out to grab at the door knob, I notice the claws that I have in my half monster half human form. Anger pulses in me as darkness starts to spread down my arm and envelop my clawed hand accentuating it even more. Making them larger and sharper looking. Darkness comes off of my form and also envelops the door; it swings open without any noise. Once I pass through the doorway the darkness bounces back to my form covering me, protecting me. I peer down the dark hallway, a bright light emits out of a large room at the end of the hallway. I slowly make my way down to the room. I peek around the edge of the wall noticing a room with many places to sit, there are many people some sitting others standing and still others dancing along with the sway of the chanting. Their words were not able to be heard clearly, I could not understand what they were trying to say. It sounded like a different language altogether.

"Alexia?" A man's voice whispers, I could make out that but could still not make out the chanting whispers.

I blink and my mind flashes once again to that same night but later on. I see bodies sprawling out in several pieces around the room. The lights were no longer bright, most were broken and others splattered in red. Most of the room is shrouded in darkness.

"Little minx," Blaise hisses and repeats, this time louder. A shudder races down my back as something tugs at me.

"What?" I growl back, yet I keep my focus on the memory. I send my darkness down and out around me to grip on to the memory hoping to keep me here. I needed to know more. I needed to know and see what happened here, how this started, why this started. I needed to know what everyone was keeping from me.

"I need you to let go of the dagger," he says right behind me his heat caressing me. I could not see him yet but I could feel him there breathing on my neck. The darkness did not cover right behind me, though it did creep that way I did not push it faster.

"Dagger?" I ask in confusion. I bring up both of my hands and feel the blood drip down my dark covered claws.

A low rumble interrupts the scene before me but it is too low to hear properly.

"The dagger you are holding is a truth dagger. You are most likely seeing something you want the truth of." He rumbles behind me. I feel the warmth of his chest behind me. I reel in the darkness as his warmth envelopes me.

"Truth." I echo. "I need the truth." I state.

"We will get to the truth but not this way." He caresses. "Sweetie your shadow creature is there with you wherever you are but you are not physically there. You will harm those around you to get to the truth."

I growl out, shadows begin to climb once more pouring out of me. "First off, I am not your sweetie anything!" I shout out. "And second you must be lying because you are not being harmed." I shove him out of my mind and enunciate every harsh word carefully and clearly. My mind is reeling in madness and can barely think through the anger swallowing me whole. He was just using me, he wasn't there to help me, none of them were. It didn't matter what he said previously he wanted me killed or caged like everyone else. "You all want to force me to do things I am not ready for, for your own gain." I scream out. A wind stirs up swirling around me in the room and memory begins to fade and darkness starts to surround me along with the wind.

This has become all too much. The rage choruses through me. "You are all unworthy to pass judgment on me." My voice booms out. My fist grips tight against something and I angle my fist up and a silver light glints in the darkness. I raise the dagger I held in my hands; it whispers to me once again but this time I can understand what it is trying to say.

"Use us and we will grant the truth." It keeps whispering over and over again.

"Now I pass judgment on all of you, and you will not escape my truthful sight!" I call out. My hand tightens on the hilt and new whispers call out.

"Blood! Blood! Seals the deal." It sings out in that ghostly melody.

I slice it across my palm and scream out as power rips from me. The darkness changes to hues of blue colors causing the darkness to retreat a bit. The darkness fades and I am back in the present, the knife held firm in my hand as my blood drips from it. Melissa looks at Blaise and he shares a look with her.

"Stop hiding things and start telling the truth." I scream out stretching out my hand that is sliced. Dark tendrils snake down my arm and caress over the cut, they fly out at the two as I turn and face both of them.

The darkness flies at them and splatters against them squirming this way and that, trying to find purchase. Melissa growls and scratches at it hoping to remove it. Blaise looks at me and just stands there staring. "The truth is what you will have," he says calmly.

Melissa runs by me to the door hoping to get away from the spell. I let her go but call the darkness back it has already deposited the blood into her, the spell sealed. "Truths will be revealed." I laugh. "She cannot run away from the truth and those who seek it."

"There is more to that knife than you know. Weapons of power should be treated with respect."

I stare back at Blaise, "What are you hiding?" I cock my head to one side, holding the dagger firmly in my hand.

He lets his hands fall to his sides, palms up and looks to the ceiling. As he relaxes scales and color wrap around him, His clothes stretch and break as his body morphs into his snake form. His lower body turns into one long form ending in a point like a snake's tail his chest and head flare into a hood surrounding his shoulders and above but is more muscular and in the shape of a human male chest. His tongue flicks out as he hisses at me in warning. He thrashes his tail as it curls around his form, His chest and upper body stands up straight. The darkness that was trying to find purchase slips easily off of his scales. The spell not finding purchase. Two fangs elongate from his upper mouth as his jaw unhinges making an even louder hiss. His fingers elongate into thin needle like claws, green liquid oozes out of the tips of them onto the matts below.

"Is this what you want to know, to see?" He hisses out. His gaze never leaves mine.

I look into his slit eyes and search them; I could still see Blaise even in this creature. His eyes pull me in causing a breath to hitch out of me. The darkness pulls back away from him coming back to me. He sways back and forth his form coming closer to me but never moving from eye sight. As he moves forward, he slithers around me slowly, I move with him in a circle. I feel something at my ankle but do not look down. He holds my gaze as his tongue flicks out tasting my cheek.

"Minx? Is this what you wanted to see?" He asks his words coming out barely above a whisper.

Sweat breaks out on my hands and forehead, my hand on the dagger slips and it falls from my grip, hitting the floor with a dull thud. A tear escapes my eye as I feel him tighten around me. "Are you going to hurt me?" I whisper just as lowly.

"Do you want me to?" He gives a devilish grin. His tongue flicks out once more and catches the stray tear that fell down my cheek. A hum comes out of him as if he enjoys the taste.

"Stop!" A voice booms behind me.

My eyes try to move away from Blaise but he holds me there entrapped. My legs are held tight by his tail and lower body. "Breathe," Blaise whispers across the small gap between us.

A breath blows out quietly.

"In," he urges. He waits a moment. "Now out... Good, in once again."

I breathe in and out as he continues to tell me to, not being able to deny him or his wants.

His hand comes up and I see him motion Quintan on the outside of my periphery. "That's good, keep breathing in and out," he says in a smooth voice.

Quintan's voice echoes behind me but his voice seems further away than Blaise's. "Don't fight this; we will help you figure out what is going on and why things like this keep happening." A purple haze starts to mist up from the floor.

"No," I whisper, trying to force Blaise to see the fear.

"We tried things your way, now another. I will keep you safe." He slithers back and forth making me follow his eyes, pulling me further in.

I try to struggle to strike out, to even scream nothing comes from me other than me standing and staring at Blaise.

"Melissa came and got me in the nick of time, I think," Quintan calls out as his purple haze starts to make its way up my body, his hands coming to rest on the sides of my head. My head falls back as my gaze breaks from Blaise. His purple clouds pull me in and my eyes fall shut.

"Lay her down gently," I barely hear Quintan say, as his purple haze envelops me and I swim down deeper into the purple sea.

Not again... I think to myself as I drift off.

CHAPTER 9

I LIE SUSPENDED IN a blue cloud, floating in a sky of blissfulness that is colored in pinks, purples, and blues. There is no cave system in sight, just these fluffy clouds. Not even the mage was anywhere to be seen unlike the last time he helped me with my memories or sent me to sleep. I look down at my hands and feel my teeth that are back to normal and no longer animal like or shadow covered.

"Shade?" I whisper quietly, needing him here with me. I hope he is more healed now. I was getting tired of not being protected as the spell was supposed to work.

A dark form emerges from the hues of blue, something seems odd about the way it moves and a weird purple glow emits from the center.

I roll my eyes, "Quintan, is that you?" I bark out. His form comes closer and begins to materialize into Quintan's form as he comes closer.

"Alexia, why yes, it is me, are you yourself again?" He wheezes a bit as he makes his way over sluggishly, leaning to one side. I rise up from my position, it looks like we are in the clouds but the ground looks solid enough. I give him a once over as he hobbles closer.

"I was always myself. What is wrong with you?" I cross my arms in front of myself.

"You grew so angry, I had to knock you out once again to figure out what triggered you to attack." He huffs out. "Though the snake charmed you partially you did not make it easy for me to put you out when you were in that state."

"I was fine." I ground out. A shuddering sound echoes far away.

Quintan gasps and looks around waiting and searching around us. "I do not say this to upset you, please know that, Alexia. Blaise had to help keep you calm. His is a gift and why we need him here helping. He can step in and control a situation if it gets out of hand."

"You could have gone about it a different way." I pause. "Or you know, try asking?" I say in a snide tone.

"The dagger would not let you calm down, it wanted blood, more importantly it wanted to be used," he states calmly, still looking around at the clouds as they roll by.

"Right," I echo, looking down at my palm at the slice that was there but not there. I flex my palm feeling the sting of it regardless. "What was that dagger anyway?"

"A relic and ancient athame that was imbued with powers to get at the truth, it can also be used in certain spells to make them stronger." He continues. "Though it should have been kept locked away behind some sort of protective barrier."

I think back over the last few moments before everything became hectic and I lost control. "It sang to me, called to me." I hum a few bars at the end.

Quintan turns fully to me. "It did?" he says in confusion. "What did it say?"

"I couldn't hear it fully, I don't know." I fall back against the cloud using it as a wall as I feel defeated. "The whispering never grew clearer just the song." I hum once again.

He shakes his head no. "I don't know what a song would have to do with a dagger." He replies.

"If it does tell the truth I should have cut you all with it when I had the chance, especially Blaise." I growl out, angry at everything that kept happening. "Then maybe you all wouldn't lie to me or hide things."

"Don't be upset with him, he was doing what he had to, if there was another way, he would have done it." Quintan, urges trying to reassure me.

Another loud rumble echoes in the distance almost like thunder. I look up at the sky same as Quintan and he slowly looks over at me, I notice him and glare. "What?"

Another crash echoes around us. "This place is attuned to you; your anger will push this place to extremes or if you want answers we can keep talking." He replies sitting down on a puff of the cloud relaxing one of his legs away, not putting much pressure on it.

"You weren't hit with the truth spell." I respond.

"And yet that does not keep me from telling you the truth now does it," he says in a sarcastic manner.

I mimic him silently. "Fine!" I say, breathing out a harsh breath. "Why aren't we in the cave system with all the glowing symbols or in the chaos pit like earlier?" I walk in a circle on my cloud trying to peer over the cloudy air below.

"This could be one of many things that happened but I have two likely scenarios." He explains.

I wait for him to continue but he just rubs his leg. "And they are?" I throw out my arms in frustration.

"As our minds grow and subconscious grows our thoughts change and how we perceive things change. Though in such a short time span I don't think that is it. We have not got to the root of your anger and your memories so I do not think this is the most viable option." He states critically. He takes off his glasses and pinches his nose in thought.

"And the other more viable option is?" I spit out, not wanting to wait any longer for him to go over every aspect of my life.

He glares at me but then looks off into the distance, massaging his leg. "Your magic flared out at the end, sending us into this, this stasis plane of existence. You wouldn't let me fully into your mind since you were in overdrive with panic, even though Blaise had his eyes on you a part of you rebelled." His arms fling out around him. "So, we are stuck here until I could find you and help. If that is what this is then we now know you can tap into magic and get us back to your memories where we should have ended up to begin with."

"Again, you could have asked instead of forcing me into this, I am getting very tired of you all just doing whatever you feel is right." I ground out. Lightning, lights the sky as a low rumble rolls in. "Also, you said this place feeds off of my emotions if we are not in my mind how does this stasis plane feed off of me."

"Think of it as a realm where dreams and nightmares come together. This place feeds off of every and all emotion so it is a place of light if one is having great thoughts, or it can be one of darkness." He leans back, relaxing into his cloud, not causing it to dent or buckle.

I try to look below his cloud but can't see that far underneath. "Why do you not want me to get angry then, it just sounds like it will get a little dark here." I question, looking at the darker clouds that seem to be rolling in, the dark blues becoming deeper and darker. "You must have a strong cloud there." I fling out smile full of teeth.

"I know you are hurting; I see it, I feel it." He stares over at me. "Do you want to deal with stuff that only people dream about in their nightmares?"

I quickly look away, not liking how much he can see. "No, I guess not." I stomp on the cloud and press against the cloud, even though it looks soft it is not and is not buckling under any pressure I push on it. "How do we get out of here then? I obviously can't control the magic or have any say over what I am doing." I again roll my eyes mostly at myself, only a little at Quintan.

"Your magic is unpracticed, chaotic, and unpredictable. You have no discipline yet in order to use it. I am hoping I can pull some of your magic from you into me and use that to force us finally into your mind. All I need from you is to come closer and place your hands in mine."

I glance over the edge of my cloud and over to his. Though they are not far apart I still would not jump across not knowing how far down this hellscape went. "One problem." I gulp. "How do I get over there?"

"You brought me closer thinking of me at first. You keep us apart." He states.

"Why does this have to be something I am doing? Why can't you be inadvertently doing something?" I call out. Thunder crashes growing closer.

"Whose emotions are higher here."

"Ugh." I screech out.

"Think back to before your fight happened with Blaise and Melissa, what happened exactly. What caused your rage to trigger and consume you so easily." He moves his arms in a breaststroke trying to force his cloud closer to mine, to no avail.

I burst out in laughter seeing him trying to swim his cloud up to mine. "Didn't you just say that would not work?" I chuckle.

He shrugs. "I had to try."

I look at him warily. "Do you even know what you are doing? Why can't we just go back the way we came in? Why do we have to go into my mind at all? Why can't we just go back to our bodies and start fresh?" I question backing away from the edge of the cloud moving further away from him.

He shakes his head at me. "I do know some things; the mind is a very delicate situation and so is mind magic. It is more of an art than a science." He recites as if reading from a book.

I give a bored look and yawn at him in a loud obnoxious way.

He huffs and pushes himself into a higher sitting position. "As soon as you would enter your body the anger would take over once again and your magic would release everything and try to help you get away causing harm to the two of us and probably many more. You could cause a lot of destruction and many deaths of innocent people." He stops noticing me about to call out something. "And before you say once more that we could ask you to step down and calm yourself, if you recall we did do that and you or some part of you decided to ignore that and start attacking. If you did not stop, the power you hold could ignite a spell that is so powerful and could be the start of a death spell for you, much like your mother's last curse."

I stop and stutter as I reel over that information. "Melissa told you!" I yell out. "Is there anything that is not sacred, do you all conspire against the inmates, because that is what we are is it not!" I yell out.

"We are here to help you so yes at times we must compare notes and share with each other things that are told in confidence to help you find your breakthroughs." He states, struggling to rise to his feet, wanting to be on equal footing. "I explained that to you last night before you left my office."

A lot had happened between then and now, I had forgotten he explained he would talk to Melissa to compare notes. "Why should I trust you?" I back up another step.

"We are all here to help you, why not trust us? I have not caused you harm, only helped protect you and the people in my care." His face falls. "We are not the evil ones you want us to be."

"Like you guys understand what I am going through let alone feeling?" I scoff out. "Because if you did, how could you possibly not understand what I am going through. Better yet why not take it one step further and just do to me what those people who took me did, use me and keep me locked away. Didn't turn out too well for them, did it?" I scream out, throwing my hands out as I reach out towards the sky lightning spreads around us arching out from where I stand.

He says quietly, "We did think about it. I'm not going to lie, but like you said see where that got the others. We wanted to give you this chance to grow and learn, but know we are doing our best in situations such as this. There are worse people and worse ways." He gives me a knowing look. "There are others like the rat shifter and your aunt." He croaks out.

"Aunt? I wasn't sure if she was my aunt or just a friend. How do you know she was my aunt?"

"If you are who I think you are from what I could gather so far. Then there are a great many questions that you will have and none of us have the answers to. Jade had a half-sister named Sera and you might be the missing link that so many have been searching for." He bites his lip "I am unsure of how much more to say; but know this that we will get answers both you and I, together."

I let my hands fall to my side and my face fell in defeat. I turn away from him and think over things, I try to see the extremes from their point of view. "What do you want me to do? Let's just get this over with." I say in a low voice. The thunder rumbles but further in the distance then just a moment ago.

"Think back to when you first felt that tinge of anger. What happened with you, Blaise, and Melissa? Why did you grab the dagger?" As the questions sink in the clouds move closer together but do not touch yet.

"It started with the dagger." I look around me. "Shouldn't I be lying down on a couch or something."

Quintan gives me a droll stare. "Just keep thinking back and answer the questions. Walk me through what happened. Why did you pick up the dagger?"

I think back over things. "The dagger called to me." I say in a simple tone trying to think of why it had called to me.

"What were you doing before that?"

My cheeks warm at what I picture doing with Blaise before I picked up the dagger. "Umm." I stutter out not thinking he needed that information.

"Was Melissa there? She came and got me." He continues seeing me having a hard time continuing forward.

"Yeah, Blaise and her were having an argument. The walls were shaking as if someone was being thrown against them." My face scrunches in thought.

"Did that upset you?" He asks and waits patiently.

"No, not at first." I say very quietly.

"Could you hear the melody or the whispers come from the dagger at that point?"

"No not at that time, but I did hear them before I met Blaise, they called out to me whispering me closer but then I got distracted when

Blaise saw me and called me over. So, they might have been talking to me but I did not hear them or pay attention to it enough to notice." I argue, not quite remembering when I did hear it start.

"When they were arguing, what were you thinking about, what were you feeling?" He pushes once again.

"Upset because once again I was not being told information that I feel I should have." I call out accusingly.

"And what about what Melissa was doing, did she throw Blaise against the wall?"

"I don't know that for sure." I stutter out.

"What about the mark on Blaise's neck?" He questions.

I bite at my fingernail and turn away from him. "I don't see how that is pertinent to why things keep triggering the darkness to seep out of me." I call out.

He stops and stares at me making up his mind on something. "To mark someone is either a very intimate and reciprocated act or one to use as a power move showing they are stronger and more powerful than the other. What were you feeling when the mark was created? When you created it?" He asks extending his hand to me.

I turn around looking at him and his hand, both him and his cloud still a bit out of reach. "We were having sex, all right!" I belt out. "Is that what you want to know?" I puff out. Quintan stays quiet letting me think through things. "I felt too much in the moment but I was in control. He gave me the power and told me to give or take what I needed. I felt...." I blink and look around. "Safe, needed, hungry?" I go through naming them as they came to me.

He nods in understanding. "And when someone threatens that safety what do people usually do?" He waits for me to come to the answer.

"Lash out? Fight back." I cringe. "After I heard the second louder thump in the wall, I figured it was his form hitting the wall instead of hers. That is when the whispers started."

"Then what happened?" He continues walking me through, the clouds moving closer as we come closer to the truth but he didn't move to mine or urge me on to his until we got to the center of the truth.

"Then I was pulled closer to the wall wanting to know where the whispering let alone the song was coming from. I reached my hand over the blades and found the one that was the loudest. As my fingers skimmed over it, I knew I needed to hold it. I removed it from the wall and when it was fully in my hand, darkness washed over me and I screamed." I step back recalling.

"Where did you go?" He asks eager to know the answer. "What did you see?"

"It was a flashback to... to the blood and gore where I was found, then it even flashed to before that where I was kept in a basement. I could hear the same whispering sound, though I don't think it was saying the same thing." I shake my head trying to keep away from there, not wanting to revisit it all again.

"Was it just the whispering that triggered the memory?" He hobbles forward as our clouds come closer together. "What led to the pain what brought you there?"

"I don't want to go back there." My voice shakes. The cloud shudders and moves away once again.

"We are just talking for right now. We may end up going there but it's just a memory." He reminds me.

"It could have been the darkness of the room, the thumping, and whispering all together. I felt small and insignificant that I didn't even deserve to know what is going on. You all treat me like I can't control myself." I shrug my shoulders and huff out as my cloud bumps into his and sticks to it. I hold my anger in check as I cross over to Quintan's cloud. "You all thought this was for the best." I growl out, the anger unfolds from a dark place within.

Lightning, lights up the sky as the dark blue of the clouds collide into one large cloud. They clash together turning into a large black cloud, the blues and purples have dulled away as the thunder and lightning comes over us.

Quintan looks around. "What are you doing?"

"You want chaos! I say bring it on, if it's worrying you maybe you all should be worried and more careful with how you think I am going to react!" I snap back.

He grabs my hands into his and starts to mutter something in a different language. I whip my head back to his and try to dislodge them from his.

I yank and pull. "Let go."

"If you are going to go rounds, make sure you hold all the power." He fires back at me not unclenching his pudgy hands.

The colors start to blend together into a grayish dull color. The wind picks up causing the clouds to whip into that of high-speed winds. They whip my hair around this way and that. The clouds start to move in a circle funneling downward, I try to snatch my hands away and edge my shoulder and hip into his, at the same time pulling my arms away. He follows forward not budging, Quintan has a tight hold.

"Quintan!" I yell above the high-pressured winds. The funnel goes further down growing into a tornado, the lightning gets pulled down into the middle of it, flashing throughout and the light shows a vortex has formed. For now, we sit above the tornado but the wind starts to suck at us and our large cloud start to go round and round with some of the others. "If you don't stop, we will go into the center of this thing! Is that what you want?" I yell over the loud thunder and horrendous winds.

"What's to say that is not exactly what I am wanting to happen?" He smirks as he continues to mumble under his breath in another language.

The world sways as we head down being pulled into the middle of this terrible storm. We spin faster and faster as we get closer, it pulls us under and eventually dumps us down on the ground. Our hands still clutch each other. My hair has been pulled out of the ponytail that I had it in.

Lighting strikes the ground beside us and a booming thunder clap echoes around us. I crouch down not knowing which way is up or where to head to for cover.

He continues mumbling, though I can't hear the words whispering out any more.

The twister spirals back into itself and pulls back, receding out of sight as quickly as it came. My mouth waters and my stomach bucks. I bend over not being able to stop what happens next.

I mumble something intelligible, Quintans hands spring away from mine, as he lets me bend fully over. I unload what little is still in my stomach from breakfast. The contents splash on a hard floor and I rub my blurry eyes as I get my stomach under control and take a look around.

"Where are we now?" I ask, trying to find my bearings. I place the back of my cold hand against my warm forehead.

"I'm not sure." He squints his eyes trying to see things clearly, there was only a little light that is glowing over our heads by a single light bulb.

I glance up as it sways this way and that. "Are we back to the memory I was avoiding?" My back slams against a cold hard wall as my breath wheezes in and out in fast bursts.

"I don't think so." He hesitates. "But I do think it is a different memory of yours."

"One I have forgotten?" I whisper back vehemently, looking around, I notice a ring in the middle of the floor. As I search around, I notice the steps from the memory I had before. "Are you sure this looks like the memory I just had?" My teeth chatter.

"Are you sure, I don't hear any whispering or music? You said there was chanting or whispering right?" He tries to knock me out of my fear.

I make myself stand still and hold my breath. I don't hear any chanting or noises up above. "Okay maybe you're right." I breathe out slowly. I walk towards the stairs. "Are we like a third party seeing the vision but not a part of it? Or am I in the body of my past self?" I question trying to look at my body and notice any differences, nothing seemed off or different.

He looks me up and down. "You don't look any different so we should just be a third-party entity to your memory like it was last time."

"It seems like when you take me to these things, I am just watching the memory. But when I remember myself or am pulled into the memory then I have to relive it. Why does this happen? Why can't I be pulled in to remember my time from then?" I whine.

"Would you really want to? Think about it. I try to bring you outside of the torrent of emotions if you were trapped in your past body with no way out and no way to change things. It causes worse things if you can't go outside the box and look at it from a different way, your mind could break," he says with a frown. "My power gives us the option to view the memory in a different way so you don't have to live through that trauma again. Though you still feel your own feelings and thoughts you are not fighting against things you felt then."

I glance away from him not fully trusting him but kind of glad he was there regardless. "Shouldn't you know all this stuff? Can't you tell where we are exactly like before?" I throw out.

"Again, magic is an art form not a science. And just because it in theory should be one way does not make it so. The spell I chanted should have traversed us over into your memories but with your anger and that other place feeding off of it, we could have blown into your memories or someone else's. You said this looks familiar." He glances around the empty space noticing the hard cement floor and stairs as well.

I head towards the stairs wanting out of this dark and dingy room, not wanting to stay here stuck. I place a foot on the wooden stairs and it emits a loud creak. A loud thump pulls my attention back into the room. I look around and notice a door directly behind us. I glance at Quintan who is also looking at the door. "What was that?" I look back up the stairs contemplating escaping whatever would show behind that door, but which place would be scarier which one would I not want to view more. The horror that could be upstairs or what is thumping in a slow manner behind the door.

Quintan cocks his head to the side. "I'm not sure. Why don't you check it out?" His form fades back out to his hazy purple form like it was when we first did this. His form floats behind me like a huge specter ghost who is too scared to haunt an already haunted basement.

"Sure, make me do everything for you." I throw my hands up in the air. I don't take steps forward, shying away from the door. "And if I don't want to?" I ask, eyeing the basement door up above us.

"You have to face things; how else do you expect to get answers? You said you wanted answers earlier, did you mean just when it is convenient to you." He throws back into my face.

The air becomes heavy as I look at the door. Quintan ghosts behind me trying to urge me forward. I huff out knowing he is right but not wanting to deal with this right now.

I toe the door, contemplating my life choices at this very moment. My fingers reach out and touch the door knob. It feels ice cold beneath my sweaty palm. I turn the knob and hear a small click. I pull it open slowly, the door itself is very heavy and steel enforced. "I am surprised we heard anything through this door." I say in surprise. The thumping continues even louder as I open the door. Though the door is heavy and takes a moment to fully swing open it does not make too much noise.

I scrutinize the room before me. It has a little bit lighter but that is mostly because the room is very tiny and the light has nowhere else to go but it lights up the entire space. The room is only long enough to lie down lengthwise and only goes back about the same amount.

The light switch that is in the on position is placed on the outside of the room making me think that whoever lives in this room spends much of their time in the dark. I look down and gasp as I see a girl curled up in a ball in the corner farthest from the door. Her hair covers most of her face and even her body, keeping her shrouded in mystery. Her hair is matted and knotted up in many tangles and very dark. She looks very young and little but that could be due to the mistreatment and lack of nourishment.

She knocks her head and body against the wall almost keeping a beat. I stretch my neck out to the side and rub the back of my head as I watch her continue.

"Is that you?" Quintan comes out from behind me as we both look at the pathetic form before me.

"It's my memory, so it has to be right?" I ask not wanting to hear his answer.

He looks at me and the horror he sees there makes him not continue with explaining how it has to be me.

A loud creaking sound happens behind us echoing down the way. Multiple feet hit the wooden stairs, descending down to us. I stare straight ahead not wanting to look behind me. I walk into the room sliding to the side to stay out of the way. I peek out around the wall of the room and see who is coming down the creaky stairs to this dreadfully cold place.

Voices echo in the small place bouncing around. "Jade every day we keep her alive we risk another day of her getting free." A man bellows back at someone behind him, his face is turned over his shoulder so I cannot see him clearly yet.

I look back at the girl that is in the room with me and see her pull up her knees to her chest and she brings her arms around them holding them close to her. She shudders but stops rocking and hitting her head against the wall though red blood splatters against the wall so the evidence can't be hidden.

"Tom you're not the one with the curse put on them, would you really want me to end my life for the better of it all?" She angrily asks, her hair is frizzy and very messy, she walks around him as they come to the final step and into the basement. Jade's pale face comes into the light and her sickly pallor shines there. She did not look as well as she did back when I was a baby.

"Is that Jade? As I stated before after Melissa told me that you had thought she was not your real mother I did some research. I reviewed the humans documents and found out who actually had you." Quintan asks, whispering not wanting to interrupt the conversation that was taking place in case they said something important.

I nod, but don't utter anything in context, keeping an eye on them. "I knew they were blood thirsty but killing someone innocent," I growl.

"No, of course not, I do not wish to lose you. They have taken too much from us already." Tom grabs her and hugs her close, brushing his knuckles over her cheek looking deep into her eyes. "We haven't found a counter spell for the one binding you and Alexia together. I won't let them take you away from me, darling."

"Don't say that things name in my presence!" Jade screams, stomping away from him.

My face scrunches in confusion at first and then I remember the memory where she had taken me from my family. My mother near the end of the remembrance in order to keep me safe, she bound me to Jade till I developed some powers to help me escape from her. My head whips back around to the form trying to bury herself into the wall in the corner. "I don't even see myself in that thing." I reject the form before me. "She is a broken shell of a person. I feel I am not that," I call back to Quintan. My shaky hand slowly slides up over my open mouth in surprise. "How could I have forgotten all of this? Am I even this person?" I point out.

"You know that is you, and is a part of you. Not the whole part but an important part of what has been done or what you have been put through to get you here, unfortunately since you don't remember going through most of it you have to deal with somethings without knowledge, but your body does not forget as easily as your mind. No matter what, you do not forget the scars," he says, sadness tinges his words.

The cold whips through me. I bring my arms around my center, my teeth chatter as I rub at my arms trying to warm my insides. "How did I endure all of this, for so long." I cough out. My form shivers as I continue to listen to what Jade and Tom are discussing. "Jade must really hate me in order to put herself through so much just to get at me and my family."

"I am curious how they made you forget all of this." Quintan says in astonishment, keeping a close eye on everyone.

I shush him, wanting him to be quiet so I could hear what they were saying outside the room we were currently in. Quintan's form floats up near the ceiling to have a better view and to make room for the growing crowd.

"You know death curses are nigh impossible to break." Tom holds on to Jade's fingers, keeping her with him.

She lets her fingers rest in his clutches. "Nearly impossible, but not improbable. I just need a little more time. I mean it hasn't gotten any powers as of yet who's to say it will even get any at all. Perhaps mixing the blood causes that sort of thing that must be why it is frowned upon. It weakens the blood. They usually have a defect of some sort. Perhaps this is her punishment and must now live in a land with no power or magic, maybe that is its curse," she says boisterously puffing up with pride.

I turn rigid as ice, furious at this woman who doesn't even know me only judges me by who my parents are and how I came into this world. "How dare you judge me for just living and being, I can't help or choose how I came into this world." I throw back at her, even though my words are not heard by her. I look back over at Quintan to see how he is taking the news, since he didn't know too much of my past other than what I have given. Hell, I didn't quite understand what I did know.

"You are a hybrid?" Quintan asks, he is floating beside the younger version of me looking down at her, trying to study her.

"Yes." I say simply, I turn away not wanting to see his judgment either. If he had anything to say he could just talk to my back since I was done seeing disappointment when others found out.

"Who were your parents?" Quintan asks and floats closer to the corner I am huddled into.

"Unfortunately, since its parents were a badger shifter and a strong witch, along with them being in charge of a rogue group. Who I might add is still looking for it. Makes it harder to cloak us and keep us hidden." Tom says in answer both to Jade and Quintan.

"Answer enough?" I ask Quintan.

He blinks in surprise and just nods once before cocking his head to the side.

Jade and Tom move forward dancing together as their hands are interlaced together. They stop outside the open door, inspecting it. "Did you forget to close the door again?" Jade gives him a side eye.

Tom lets go of Jade's hand and feels around the door's edge and even looks into the room. "I don't think so? And I only did it once or twice. It's not like she can get out of this basement. We keep the upper door locked as well and there are no windows." He states.

I edge back into the corner not wanting to interfere with their movements or anything.

"Was the door open partially when we entered the memory or did, I cause it to happen?" I think to myself out loud.

"Or your powers started to develop at that time and she, I mean you opened it." He looks pointedly at the shivering form on the floor.

"And I just perceived it this way?" I ask.

He shrugs. "They noticed the door open in your dream so either they left it open."

I interrupt. "But when I turned the handle, I heard it click that it opened like it was shut before and then the door was very heavy so I pulled it open slowly." I glare at the door, remembering the heft.

"You may have thought that but opening the door really was your past self-finding a way to force it open." He said with a matter-of-fact tone.

"When was the last time you came down here?" Jade questions. "Was it to feed it?"

Tom glares at Jade, but bites at his lower lip. "I did not feed it." He stutters a bit.

"Sure, looks like it's been fed." She kicks the tray that was next to the door.

"I had the cook bring it down." He glares at Jade. "Before you go working yourself up, this is not the first time I have asked him to take it down here. We can trust him to keep his mouth shut. He has been here forever and knows what we stand for plus he knows about the girl anyway, has had to." He fires right back, leaning against the door he folds his arms in front of his chest.

"We will have to talk to him about this if it gets away or out, that will be the end of us no matter what!" Jade says breathlessly. I lean in to hear them better as they whisper back and forth.

Tom pushes up from the door and walks past Jade going into the room checking the corners making sure no one is trying to pull something over him. His eyes roam over me but doesn't see anything there. I breathe out a held breath. "At least we know that they can't see us for sure."

"Were you worried?" Quintan chuckles.

I glare up at him. "Well, yeah, things tend to change around me at a moment's notice without any real reason why." I cross my arms in front of my chest and lean against the wall.

"I know what happens if they get her, more specifically if the rogue group gets her. They will have their hope." He grimaces moving to the side to the left so Jade can see into the room.

Jade stops at the door jamb and refuses to step more into the room. "The hope for some stupid prophecy that may or may not be real." She mutters out.

"So far, the witches have sided with us so if she does get out, they know to bring her back here. They don't want the end of days to come any sooner than it has to if we can avoid conflict all together. They will keep letting us avoid it as much as we can, though they prefer just disposing of her all together."

Jade sneers and glares at the thing in the corner. "I know and if I wasn't so well liked by the council and helping them gain their precious knowledge and power then perhaps it would be all over for us but for now, they will let it go." She curls her hands into a ball and makes a fist but keeps it down beside her leg.

"It's a good thing the prophecy is vague and doesn't explain how she will bring about the end of the world either by her death or her being alive." He smirks.

"Yeah, that is true." She shakes out her fist and runs a hand over the top of her frizzy hair. Her straight blonde hair is loose and down around her shoulders. Her movements become rigid and more frantic as they spend time down here. "But if she escapes, they might not be so nice or even care anymore and just take care of the problem regardless of the circumstances."

"Right, I didn't think of it like that." Tom adds absentmindedly.

"And then if a rogue does find her, more importantly if they find her and know what to do with her or how important she is then what." She goes into further defense.

Tom notices her jerky movements and her far off stare. He moves closer wrapping her up in his arms giving her comfort.

"Ugh just gag me." I call out moving so my back is towards them so I do not have to watch this.

He shushes and calms Jade down, kissing her gently. "It will be all right, my love," he says calmly.

"I know it just upsets me so and even more when I come down here." Jade pats his cheek and then his shoulder.

"My love I can handle this, if you do not wish to be down here."

"No, I must," she states. "As long as we keep giving her the spelled serum so that even if she does get out, she won't get far or even know where to go if at all. What we have here is a blank slate." She smiles cruelly over my young form.

"She is so pathetic for someone that doesn't even know what we are doing to them let alone their past." He laughs.

The thing in the corner starts to mumble and whine as she moves back and forth, thumping her back against the wall once again. Her head doesn't connect like she was doing before but she does scratch her ragged nails over the cuff that is linked to her ankles, yanking and pulling on the links of the chain that is connected to the loop on the cement floor. They don't budge, but her finger nails do as they break and bend as she scrabbles for purchase on the metal.

I look around the room expecting to see Shade and his form fall off of her and start to fight for her. "Where is he?" I question, I look up at Quintan's purple gelatinous apparition, He looks between the two of us trying to keep us both in his line of sight.

"Where is who?" Quintan asks.

"Remember to take care of its little spell that is on it that protects it constantly." Jade rubs at her wrist on her right hand. "Before it tries to attack me this time." She calls out.

Quintan nods as Jade explains, "Shade right."

Tom grumbles but nods to her as he continues forward. "Yeah, well you try to find the shadow creature easily with her wiggling and moving." Tom calls out. "It would be better if you helped her stay in place or even came over here to help." He waited.

"It seems like no matter how many times we give her the spell to forget she still comes back with a vengeance and hates us even more than previous times." Jade edges back out of the doorway and rubs her bare arms. "I've given her everything possible and she still does not cooperate."

"She is a born defect; darling do not blame yourself for her issues." He tries to console Jade.

"Or it could be the way that you are treating the past me or you know stealing me away from my actual family!" I yell out at the memory, furious at what I am witnessing. "How can you just sit here and watch this and not be angry?" I call out in accusation to Quintan.

"We can't do anything here. All we can do is witness and learn." He gives a sad look.

"Maybe someone should do something about it." I rage.

Jade stops and freezes at the same time Tom jumps back into a corner away from me and my past self. Tom places his back to the wall searching the tiny room, his face pales. "Hello?"

At the same time Jade asks, "What was that?" She pokes her head into the room, but holds onto the door ready to shut it at any moment. She looks back to the stairs that go up out of the basement but shakes her head as she closes the door a bit making the opening only wide enough for her body so nothing can escape.

"What did you hear?" Tom asks, pulling at his ear as he continues to look around the room.

She shakes her head. "Not sure exactly."

My face looks back and forth between Jade and Tom as their conversation continues.

"It sounded like a high-pitched whistle or screech. Perhaps the cook is making tea?" Tom asks, trying to volunteer an answer that makes sense.

Jade looks back at the basement door, waiting to see if they hear the same sound as before. "Sure...That could be it." She takes her hand away from the door and bites on her thumb nail as she stands there in the doorway, still blocking.

"Did they hear me?" I look around and down at myself, I eye Jade and Tom wearily. "This is a memory is it not? Is it possible this is the actual past?" I whisper very quietly but harshly in Quintan's direction.

Quintan floats over to me and places a cold hand on my shoulder. "Calm down, that takes more power or objects to cause that to happen. Would I be in this form also if we were in the past?" He opens his hands to show me his portly ghostly purple figure.

"I guess you're right." I bite back a thought from escaping. "I guess I was afraid for nothing." I rub my arms. "It's not like I can really affect anything here." I walk up to my past self and kick at the chain she still has in her grubby little hands.

The chain spills out of her hands as if she felt the chain be moved by my shoe. I throw myself backwards again going to the far wall away from everyone.

My past self-screeches in horror, Jade and Tom who were not looking in that moment glare at my younger form in the corner.

"What is wrong with it?" Jade looks at her and then back up the stairs. "Though this entire room is soundproof, hasn't it learned that making noise like that will do nothing."

Quintan comes to stand near me away from everyone as well.

"What do we do?" I whisper to him.

"If we are in the past. Which I do not know how that is possible with me being in this form." He looks at me pointedly, holding a finger up to quiet me. "As long as we don't shout too loud." He gives me a look. I shake my head and glare at him. "Bump or move anything then they shouldn't be able to pick up on us being here. We are on a different plane, one that they can't see."

"What do you mean a different plane?" I ask. "Also why are you not like me?" I spread my hands over my solid form.

"Magic is tricky especially for you, when emotion is put into it and is unbridled and untrained wonderful and terrible things can happen." He grimaces. "Your magic mixing with mine must have twisted what I asked of it. Be careful while you are here." He pats my shoulder.

I shove his hand off of my shoulder. "What's it matter to you? It's not like I can free myself or change things. I can't even do anything properly being a half breed and all. I can't shift properly; I can't call up magic properly, none of it." I say bitterly, giving him eyes that burn him with searing hatred. I turn away and say softly. "What does it matter you're not here to help me anyway."

He whispers back just as quietly, "You have no idea." He backs away, giving me some space trying to ease the tangible tension.

"Let's hurry up and get out of here," Jade urges. "I hate being near it, it causes pain each time and the proximity causes it to intensify." She calls out to Tom. "We should really see if the cook can give it a good washing. It is starting to smell down here." She waves a hand in front of her nose.

Tom's eyes sparkle. "But the pain we cause her is the best part." He grins, placing a hand on her dirty leg, and yanks her over the cold ground closer to him. "You like seeing the pain I cause this thing don't you, my love," he says, staring at Jade.

She smirks at that and shivers. "It's the only pleasure this gives me." She pants.

He lets the girl wriggle away from him as he slides back over to Jade in the doorway and brushes the hair from her shoulder. He stands in front of her and kisses her shoulder as he pulls her into the room closer to my past self. His hand caresses across her breasts slightly.

She laughs and twitches her fingers at him. A flutter of wind caresses his hair blowing it back. She turns toward my past self and an icy glint turns her stare hard. She spreads her fingers wide and a harsh cold air plasters my little form against the floor. I watch my past self-try to find hand holds against the smooth floor, she tries to find purchase to scrabble away from these predators.

"No, no, no, no." A small wail emits from both me and my past self.

A tear escapes my eye as my hand covers my open mouth. "I... we didn't do anything." I mumble behind my hand.

Hoarse screeching emits from the small form.

Jade raises her hands, increasing the winds vigorously, the winds whip at my hair and grab at me pulling me in. I watch in absolute horror as she pulls her over the rough concrete floor to be in the center of the room. She uses the wind to position her where needed.

The small girl tries to pull down the thin hole covered shirt so it doesn't blow off, also trying to keep her skin from scraping across the floor and shredding.

I see when she twists this way and that Shade is settled low on her back, it looks like he is trying to peel off but the wind bats at him and keeps him there. Jade smiles as she sees him there and pushes her winds harder. "Help flip her on to her front. It is there." Jade calls out.

Tom glides behind her before moving past her brushing her lower back as he passes and careful to avoid the blasting wind, he flips her over so she lies on her stomach.

"Got it!" Jade calls out sending a sharp wind arrowing at the small spot of Shade. Jade smiles, focusing all of her power on that one spot.

He laughs and moves my past self's arms and rests his knees on top of them pushing his weight down on her arms keeping them pinned there.

She lets out another scream of pain, but does not struggle to free herself.

He takes out a bottle from his pants pocket and shakes it gently. "Tis time. Open up."

She stares at him, not moving. She shakes her head a bit.

"You know you need the sleeping pills before we give you the magic shot. Soon it will not matter, we must get our fun out while we can," he says cryptically.

"Fight!" I yell.

"What are you doing?" Quintan seethes.

"I am not watching this." My fear and anger rise as one. "Neither should you."

My younger self whips her head back and forth shaking her head. I bend down close to her avoiding both Tom and Jade. "Let me help you, Lexi," I call my younger self. I touch her arm hoping she could feel me beside her.

She looks at Tom and then back at Jade. She tries to kick her feet out but the big chain prevents much movement.

I move towards the chains and look closer at the ankle cuffs. "Quintan, how can we remove these?"

"I am sorry, Alexia," he says sadly.

"What do you mean you're sorry," I burst at him. "Tell me how to remove these."

Tom forces Lexi's jaw wide open with his hands, I hear a crack as he forces her jaw open too wide.

I growl.

Tom quickly drops the pills in her mouth and slams her mouth close with his hands. He rolls around forcing her into a head lock of sorts and placing his hand over her mouth.

"Now." He gasps out.

"Oh, you know how it turns me on when you are forceful." She gives a wicked laugh as she takes her other hand, the one not concentrating on Lexi's back and she yanks towards herself. As she pulls her hand back the little one on the ground mumbles behind Tom's hand fighting, Jade had a hold of something.

A low rumble rolls in the pit of my stomach as I move back to the top part of my younger self.

Lexi starts to struggle her fingers trying to reach up and grasp at her neck and Tom's hand. Tom's other hand travels down her neck. "Just swallow and you can have it back."

"Have what back?" I call out.

"Don't you want that sweet air?" He whispers as tears run down her face.

"She is stealing my air!" I screech out trying to be loud and obnoxious, so they would stop. I pull back visibly shaking. "And you wonder why I am not okay with all of you." I throw at Quintan.

"Are you trying to get them to notice us?" Quintan asks. He moves over behind Jade. "She must be doing it so you will swallow the pills, this is how they kept you and tortured you. This is how they keep you from remembering." He nods.

"Tell me how to stop this. Why can't they hear my loud yelling and shrieks now and they could before?"

He shakes his head.

"Tell me." I yell once again.

"It means we are at a spot in time that can't be changed or messed with. Other times small things can happen or certain things can be altered, but there are points in time that can't be changed unless you know the small things to change to avoid it." He states. "I am not a time master; I can only tell you the basics."

"I just need them to stop," I sob.

"Alexia," he says in a soft voice. "This is all in the past... it has already happened... you live; this does eventually stop." He floats closer to me trying to give me comfort without crowding me.

I growl and sob, stepping away from him. "Are you with them, are you like them?" I needed to know the answer. "Do I have to worry about you killing me or turning me over to someone when we get back?" I ask in turn.

I hear a gulp distracting me from my questions as my younger form slumps with no fight. Quintan's lips purse but he stays silent. I focus on my younger form. "I will get answers later." I grumble to myself.

"Done, let her go," Tom calls to Jade.

I glance at Jade and notice her keep her hand held back a moment longer but stumbles and jerks forward her magic failing her. She puffs out a held breath and breathes in deeply. "Dammit."

"You know the curse is tied to her, why do you test it each and every time?"

Jade glares at Tom, noticing his hand still caressing her throat. "Why are you still touching that lesser thing!" she screeches.

Tom stops his fingers and edges away from her; she falls limply out of his arms, her eyes flutter and struggle to stay open. She moves her arm up uselessly as the drugs take effect. "I was only thinking of you, it is always you." He rushes to her side.

"Is he ready?" Jade asks. Her eyes slide back towards the basement door.

"Come on down!" he calls. "Can we trust him?" he whispers.

She gives a silent nod. "She will be out soon." She turns her back to the room and faces the stairs. She sways on her feet and Tom helps her at her elbow, helping her forward. "You overdid it didn't you?" Tom whispers.

I follow them out needing to hear better.

"That's silly Tom." She bats at his hand and her steps are surer and firmer as she climbs the stairs

Tom pauses at the bottom of the steps and holds his hand out for a shake, a dark gray form stands tall and a large palm envelops his much smaller one.

I look back at Quintan expecting something from him. I see horror written across his face. "What are you worried about?" I whisper.

The man that is shaking Tom's hand is heavily robed in dark cloaks. As he looks around the room his eyes glow and are copper in color almost a reddish hue. Sound and warmth leave as his presence takes up more space.

"Your kind sure does know how to suck magic out of things and keep it in doesn't it?" He breaks the silence with a joke.

The creature stares down at Tom and just stares at him, not moving an inch.

"He is very tall and burly." I blurt out. I cock my head. "He is also very lonely I think."

"What do you mean? They can't be lonely!" Quintan squeaks.

"Why not?" I ask genuinely curious.

He just shakes his head. "You have a lot to learn." Is all he says. "Hush now."

"You are sure you can keep her out until we can find a way to break the curse and then we can end her sorry excuse for a life?" Tom asks as he releases the man's hand chuckling to himself, nervous.

Jade has made it to the top of the stairs, light falls over her form but does not descend the stairs. "Of course, he can. They are for hire and we paid the fee." She states.

The tall creature grunts and nods his head once as he moves further into the room getting closer and closer to Lexi, I move out of the way as he gets closer.

"Okay. Let us know once it is done." He jogs up the stairs and they both shut the door leaving this thing down here with my past self.

I walk slowly behind the creature and once he is fully in the room I slide to the right, his form takes up most of the small area making this room feel even smaller.

Lexi moves her mouth open and close as if she is trying to scream or say something. She shakes as she moves her head back and forth. Tears stream down and over her cheeks. Her movements start to slow down and begin to be choppy as she flips on to her back, her eyes glaze over as the light begins to fade out of them. Her lashes close and they don't budge or flicker open and her arms crumple down onto her as she passes out, the drugs fully kicking in.

His eyes warm up to the color of honey as their glow intensifies. They stare at her and the room, unblinking. He leans down and kneels next to her; his rough huge hands envelop her cheek, his thumb brushes over it as he lowers her face to the side gently.

"Hey!" I yell at his side into his face.

Quintan gives a sigh. "What are you doing?"

"Maybe if I yell loud enough, I can get his attention and do something about all of this." I stomp. "Maybe I can do what I did earlier." I kick at the chain hoping the slight movement catches his eye. "Stop that, help her... I mean me." I squeak out.

His gaze flickers to me briefly, but then goes back to searching for something in his robe.

"I wouldn't do that." Quintan hesitates, saying much more above a whisper he backs away, not coming into the room standing as far from it as he can and still see us easily. "You don't know about their kind."

I shake my head. "I think he heard me! Plus, what does it matter, you don't care." I throw back at him.

"They are death dealers," he hisses through his teeth still trying to be as quiet as possible.

"And that means what? He eats death for breakfast?" My hand comes to rest on the large creature before me.

It growls.

I take my hand back startled. "Did he feel that?" I ask in a high-pitched whisper.

"Death dealers see all planes of existence and can interact with it if they so choose. They are ones that can change things, they are who you pay to help you fix past mistakes," he says with dread. "They can also interact with different worlds that coexist with ours, they deal with the weird and strange and can make almost anything happen." Quintan backs up some more. "And even if this was just a memory, if you bother him too much we could be in some trouble. They are loners at heart and definitely do not like to be touched." He chatters on uselessly.

"How so?" I ask in shock. "No, that can't be right. Perhaps no one has just taken the time to know or understand them." I step forward, I take a big gulp and form my hands into fist refusing to back down.

"Don't bother him, no matter what you think. I do want to help you." He pushes his form forward not seeing me back down like he would like. "He can end your life if he views you as a threat or imprison you if he wishes, or like a billion deadly other things that are not going to be to your liking. Mostly they prefer death that is why they are called death dealers and aptly so. They enjoy and feed off erasing one from the cosmos and not having to deal with that being any longer. Their only downfall is that they like wealth and shiny baubles. It's why they were not eradicated and are held so high; their powers are useful and can be bought for the right price." He seethes in anger.

"That is just sad, and I am almost angry on his behalf, against you all!" I call out. "How can you say you care what happens to me if you don't even care about him or his kind? Do you view half breeds as bad as them?" I watch him fumble under the robes for what he is looking for and he bends down towards Lexi, mumbling and whispering something.

"I am sorry that is the way our world is. They are the monsters of our world. They are assassins for hire. They do not play to sides they only work for the one that has the right price at that given moment. Most are too scared to confront one let alone face one down. You do not want to be on their list, my friend."

I roll my eyes and scoff at him. "You forget... I am not your friend." I step away from the hunched figure back to the door and with all my might and weight I grab the door and pull it shut before Quintan can ghost his way back in here. I wait a moment waiting to see if he will just pass through the wall, I check around to make sure he isn't at the ceiling. I nod and turn back to the death dealer and Lexi. He didn't stop what he was doing even though he had to hear the door shutting. "How was I able to move the door again with Lexi out cold, if this is just a memory?" I ask the door, Quintan not here to answer that.

I turn back to the man in dark clothing. Even with him kneeling in front of my younger form his form still reaches up to my neck. I give an audible gulp and reach out my hand, it shakes but I place it on his shoulder.

A low growl emits from him.

I keep my hand there trying not to put force behind it, leaving it there in kindness. His arm bunches beneath my fingers and under his clothing. His honey eyes flick to me once again and hold my gaze. "I'm not a threat." I whisper my voice gives a croak at the end.

His eyes roam over me, really looking at me. He nods in agreement; he glances at my hand and frowns.

I swallow and lick my lips, my eyes flick to the closed door. "Quintan said you wouldn't like touch but I needed to get your attention, I will remove my hand but I ask that you listen to me and what I have to say." I carefully remove my hand.

He cocks his head to the side and studies me.

I hesitate looking between my past self and him. "Umm... Do you speak?"

He keeps staring at me but does not move or utter a word.

"Okay." I say nervously. "Where is Natasha when I need her, she would be great at this?" I utter. "You see she is my roommate from where..." I stop and think. "When I am... She is amazing and can talk to anyone, she takes no shit and isn't scared of anyone. She knows herself and she has the best ice powers, you should see her ice form." I give a breathless laugh.

"She is dazzling... Come on Alexia just spit it out. He doesn't want to hear about your friend." stomping my foot I berate myself.

He growls and turns toward me lifting one knee up to stand.

"No, no, no. I am sorry." I place my hands up in front of me. "I am just frustrated with myself; I don't know how to ask for help very well."

He is still turned fully towards me but does not bring his other foot up to stand up fully.

"If you don't help me here in this time, I wonder if I will even have a future to go back to." I cry out. "I am not sure how time works or what magic has to play in it but I think if I don't make sure you don't do everything, you're supposed to that I won't be able to break out of whatever spell or curse you land on me."

His eyes light up with laughter as he looks back at my younger sleeping form. His hand reaches up and he caresses my cheek as he had my younger form.

I am caught off guard and not sure how to continue. "Perhaps you will not help me after all." I sigh. He bunches his burly fist in front of me and lays one finger against my lips holding it there shushing me.

He stares at me as if he was trying to convey something with his eyes alone.

My lips tremble. "I do not know what you can do." My gaze snaps back to myself and then back to where Quintan who stayed hidden behind the door. "He said a lot, that you had power." The beast of a man looks over at the door as well, dark bangs fall down over his one eye. The hood of the cloak masking the rest of his hair from sight.

"He stated your kind can see things that not everyone else can. Is there a way that you can, maybe get me out of here? I get it but give me an exit so I can get out of here myself. I obviously get powers or they become unlocked to me at some point. Can you have it where I can wake up once I can tap into them? I am still not clear on the logistics but I want to make my future a reality so I can go back to it." I rush out, confusing myself in the rush of it all. I smile at him. "Time, traveling, and this memory stuff is very confusing. I fear I will have to either get used to it or figure all this out one day." I chuckle. "Wish I had your help to teach me some of this stuff, you don't seem so bad no matter what others say." A tear slips down my cheek.

He nods slightly, barely even uncocking his head.

I smile and then frown as he goes back to what he was doing before I bothered him. I think for a moment and am not sure what he is nodding his head yes to exactly. "Was that a yes you will help me or a yes you are going to go back to your work that you were doing before." I stumble over my words. "Are you going to help me or are you going to let me sleep forever until they find a way to end my life. I need some context." I utter.

A growl emits from him once again he throws his hand at the door and it bursts open. Showing a pacing Quintan on the other side.

I squeak out a small scream, I raise my hands once again in a defensive and apologizing gesture. "Sorry, sorry, Do your thing."

"I did warn you." Quintan quips.

I walk over to him so as not to bother him. "Yeah. Yeah. Shut it you big purple gas ball. I think I got him to help me so you can shove it." I push him away as he floats closer to me.

"Watch it girl!" Quintan bellows out furiously. "We aren't out of the woods yet."

"What are you so worried about; you would be happy to get rid of me." I sneer at him. "Death dealers, are they like reapers?" I say mimicking a scythe slicing someone's head off. "If they, are they will be reveling in their jobs when they come across the night, I take out the people in this place." I laugh out. "Too bad you won't be there."

"They can cause death, they don't collect souls or ferry them to the other side in any way, that would be a reaper that does that. Don't assume you know what someone is and what they can do because of what they are called." Quintan yells out storming away causing a purple cloud to trail him.

"Yeah, I kind of figured out that from Blaise being a snake charmer, have no idea what that means, why not just snake shifter." I call out absently, perhaps I could get some information on what the charmer part does.

"Because he is not just merely a snake shifter." He throws back.

"Hmmm so he explained." I say not really paying attention to him anymore. I see the bulky form lean over Lexi and then stands up and makes his way over to the stairs. He stops near me and stares then looks toward the door and then back at me.

"You want me to follow?" I look back at Lexi and see her hardly breathing as if she was in a deep sleep, her pallor looks better than it had and she seems renewed rather than looking as if she had been kept locked away for a very long time. I nod at him.

He turns away and continues up the stairs knocking on the door. The door opens to Tom and he lets the big figure out of the basement. I squeeze behind and to the side, so I can get through. Quintan floats up above to the ceiling, easily finding his way way out while I slip below.

"Is it done?" Tom frets, glancing back at Jade before he closes the basement door and locks it.

He nods silently, keeping to himself, still not saying anything.

"Your payment bonus then." Jade dangles something from her hand pushing it out in front of her for him to take. He comes forward and snatches it from her hand before I can perceive what it even is. He makes the item disappear into one of the many folds of his cloak. Which means he probably has many weapons hidden on his person as well.

Jade and Tom move to the side out of his way as he steps closer to the door, but stops halfway there looking back at us all there in the living room. Glancing at everyone pointedly. "You are not alone. We will discuss later." He states in a gravelly voice as if it had been damaged by many years of abuse or misuse. His gaze lands on me as he says the message. I knew he was talking to me. He would need to collect payment for my request. I nod but frown, not knowing what I would have to offer for someone that has to have vast amounts of wealth.

"What? What do you mean by that?" Jade asks. She sees him continue to the door and looks questioningly at Tom. They both turn to the room and look around seeing if anyone else is there.

Quintan floats over to me and stands in front of me. "What did you do?" he says haughtily.

"What?" I give a look of innocence. "I don't know what that was all about, he probably was trying to tell them that we are here." I say with a shrug.

"You're a bad liar, you know." He gives a shake of his head.

Tom shrugs at Jade. "You never know what those death dealers mean." He watches him leave out the door, closing it behind him silently. "It will be easier now to make her forget everything at least and it makes that creature on her easier to control without her fighting us all the time."

"Wish we could have afforded them before this, we have had to fight with it for quite a while," Jade states. "Their price was steep enough just to keep her asleep. I didn't want to know what it would have cost for more, when we are so close to the answer I feel."

"True the death dealers were able to tell us that the spell was connected to her and as long as she was under or unconscious that it would be as well. As long as we don't deal too much physical harm nothing will happen no death curse will be activated. She can rot down there basically while we find a cure for you my dear."

Tom walks over to Jade and she laughs as he sits down and she snuggles up to his side. "The spell that we made we can inject her with so she will forget everything and continue to if it has anything to deal with the supernatural, we will make many batches to make sure it takes this time. We will scramble her brain so much, she will only know how to do mundane stuff she learned but people, and places she will have none of it. That way if she does wake up or is ever taken from us then we have a failsafe." She walks her fingers up Tom's chest suggestively winking at him. "Perhaps when I do find the spell or thing to unbind us, we can wake it up and play with it a bit before completely offing it... huh?" She bats her eyelashes as she unbuttons the top of his shirt.

Tom's arms snake around her waist and hugs her to him. "Anything you want darling. But before we start planning things let's make sure you can be unbound first. We will have a doctor come look at her to make sure we can hook her up to something to keep her body sustained while we search for a cure for you and make sure to get with them to see how much of that spell, we can give her to make sure she still stays healthy enough. Plus, the illusions I have put in her mind will guide her toward the normal childhood of a normal kid in case anything ever happened to her or us."

Quintan gives me a raised eye. "Do we want to stay here for this?" He coughs into his hand.

I eye Tom and Jade; they are already kissing and their hands are roaming over each other. I cringe away heading back away from the room. I go into the hallway and sigh leaning against the wall. "I am exhausted." I lower my head and tears drop from my eyes pattering on to the wooden floor.

"I can understand that." Quintan says matching my stance.

"How do we get back home?" I ask in confusion. "We ended up here by accident. Do you even know how we go back?"

"We ended up here because your emotion was high and when that happens it causes chaos. Give me your hands I can get us back with no issues, as long as your emotions are in check now."

I place my hands in his hazy purple ones. "I feel so drained."

"As you should. It was mostly your energy that sent us here, and the emotional turmoil you just witnessed. I would say that you need a lot of rest to recover from all of that." He rubs my cold numb fingers. "I will only borrow a bit of your power, not even that much and we will get back in no time.

I nod as the scene starts to fade away and change.

CHAPTER 10

M Y HAND FLINGS OUT and pain rushes through my mind. "Ugh!" I reach out to stabilize myself. I hold my head in one of my palms, touching it tenderly. My eyes are crusty and bleary. I can barely make out anything. "Are we back?"

"Are you okay where did you guys go?" Blaise asks loudly as his form comes closer.

I open my eyes up as wide as they can go and quickly rub the crust from my eyes, blinking quickly. I notice him back to his normal form and fully dressed. "How long were we gone?"

"Not too long, just a couple of hours." He states, he moves my bangs to the side out of my face.

"Where is Quintan?" I slur my words together.

"Here." Quintan croaks. He groans and just lies there on the mat not moving.

"I thought you said no issues." I whisper not being able to talk very loud, neither my throat or head would allow it.

"Relatively no issues, I can't say what our bodies or minds went through as we traveled." He whispers back vehemently glancing side wise at me.

"Sure, blame me." My voice breaks, I bat at Blaise's hands as he tries to make sure I am well enough. "Stop that."

"I am just making sure you are okay." He states.

"Yeah, well tell Quintan to stop doing weird magic shit that causes all this chaos." I sneer.

"I already explained it was your magic."

"Yeah, and would my magic have activated if you didn't start things or piss me off." I throw back at him, I groan as my voice and head throbs in time with the anger and loudness that echoes around us.

I slowly sit up and groan, Blaise helps to push me up and hold me in a sitting position as I sway a bit. "How long is this going to last?" I belch out not feeling a hundred percent.

"Are you going to get sick?" Blaise asks, looking me over carefully.

I pause and think for a moment, letting my stomach settle. "I don't think so as long as I don't move much."

He nods and just leans against me to keep me in that sitting position. I look out the window and notice the sun has fully fallen and darkness has taken over. "What time is it?"

"Around eight." He whispers.

I feel a flutter on the left side of my ribs.

"What happened?" Blaise asks.

I squeeze my ribs with my arm, closing my eyes as the lights in the room are harsh. "You attacked me." I glare at him. "We got sent somewhere." I glare at Quintan. "Lots happened and we got sent to the past."

"Don't listen to her Blaise. I will explain it to you later." Quintan utters.

"Quintan likes to blame the one that doesn't know how to use magic for it messing up." I interject. "But there were reasons I suppose. Apparently, I get angry and every little thing is my fault."

He hums neither agreeing or disagreeing with what I say. The fluttering on my ribs eases up as I and my surroundings stay calm. I was really worn out after that adventure.

"I just need to rest." I murmur to Blaise.

"Understandably so." He nods. "Quintan, did you want to go over anything before I take her back or am I free to do so?" He utters before looking back at me.

"No, no I don't need any of your help." I spit out but then place a warm hand to my warm forehead as the room decides to spin.

He looks into my eyes; his eyes dilate almost shrinking to a line but they stay in their human shape. "Of course, you need help. I will take you back to your room." He stands over me and picks me up easily.

I wrap my arms around his neck, not sure where to put my hands or arms but didn't want to fall. I give a little yip.

"Will you be fine till I get back Quintan?" He asks, I feel the rumble of his voice in his chest as he holds me close.

"Sure, sure." He waves us on. "Melissa, if you bump into her just send her my way."

Blaise nods and turns to leave the room pushing with his shoulder out of the room.

I snuggle down in his arms quietly enjoying this. "I could have walked myself..." I look around the twisting halls and gulp to myself and close my eyes, not trusting the room to stay put. "But thank you."

His arms bunch beneath me and he pulls me in closer. "Of course."

I open my eyes and peer up at him watching him closely. I hear whispering from others around us. I feel heat travel up my cheeks as I continue to stare.

"Did you do something to me? Charm me?" I ask shyly.

He looks down at me as he continues to walk forward. "No, but I will tell you what it could mean, as long as you promise to go to the library and read up on it more and research then decide for yourself."

I nibble on my lips and then nod.

He continues to look at me than makes up his mind and nods to himself. "When we did what we did... I hope you know I would not entertain doing something like that usually."

I nod not looking directly at him and not trusting my voice to speak.

"I felt a pull to you, something I could not turn away from." He pulls in a big breath of air. "I did not want you to be scared or harmed you're first time." He leans his chin on top of my head, almost hugging me. He takes another steadying breath. "When we were doing what we did." He repeats. "You marked me as yours."

I struggle to sit up. He stops and waits for me to calm down. I place a palm on his chest. "Wait, hold on, what does that mean?"

"I am not going to lie to you usually when there is a pull such as the one, I felt it usually means mates are involved. Both of the participants accept and mark each other for the bond to solidify." He breathes out, He nods. "We are almost to your room." He continues forward.

"Are we mates? And what does that mean?"

He shrugs. "Depends on what philosophy you follow on if it's fate or a sick joke." He chuckles. "That you will have to research for more opinions. In order to solidify it I have to mark you in turn and you have to accept me not just with the mark, so there is more to it." He rumbles. "So, you needn't worry. I did not want to cage you like I have been most of my life."

"Did you want to bite me?' I ask nervously.

He looks down at me as he comes to our door. "I don't know. We don't even know each other. Perhaps in another time such a thing would be possible." He looks back to see if anyone was in the hallway with us, it is empty, most were in the mess room when we had passed there. "A part of me did, I think, but it is not an option I would not take away from you. Especially with what you have gone through." He slowly drops my legs down his body but keeps his arm around my back pressing us close.

I slide down him until I stand on my own feet. I look into his eyes as he stares down into mine. I uncurl my arms around his neck and slide my hand over the bite that I had left him. "What does it do?"

He shivers and closes his eyes. "I will let you find out on your own, minx." He pulls my fingers away from his neck.

"So, what is this?" I give a look of confusion.

"I honestly don't know. There are things going on you don't know; I am not here by choice. You are not here by choice."

"You know nothing of me other than what my file says." I frown.

"And you know nothing of me other than my shape is that of a snake. I think we are on even ground here." He places his knuckles under my chin and brings my face back up to his.

I raise my eyes to his as he brushes my cheek with his knuckles. "You would not like me if you knew what I really was."

"Yet you do not fear or run away from what I am or what you know of me... most would. For I am cold blooded and some would say unable to show warmth of any kind."

I rest a palm against his chest feeling his heartbeat there. "Then they do not truly know you." I giggle.

He laughs low in his throat. "I think not. Perhaps we are more alike than we thought."

"Perhaps, or we see what others do not want to." I shrug.

"If you need me, you know where to find me?"

I give a wicked smile. "Yes."

He winks and turns around and walks down the way we came.

He looks back. "What am I getting myself into?" He mumbles, I shake my head to myself.

The door unlatches quickly and an icy cold hand reaches out and swipes me inside.

"Whoa." I spin and catch myself on the bed frame and breathe in through my nose and out through my mouth in small breaths calming my stomach once again.

"Girl, you have some splanin to do!" Natasha closes the door firmly and stands in front of me with her arms crossed over her chest with her right foot tapping.

"What." I say trying to hold on to my stomach. "I'm queasy and not feeling the best." I call out.

"That is Blaise!" She squeals and throws her arm out behind her causing an icy blast to spray at the door. "Oops." She pulls her arm back down and rubs her hand.

"That's a big oops Natasha." I laugh out.

"And you, you trollop, are the talk of this place! With Blaise! I saw the bite you put on his neck. It was you that bit him was it not?"

I rub the back of my neck. "Yeah, this is all crazy I don't know what any of it means. I didn't mean for any of it to happen."

Her mouth falls open. "Happen... What happened!" She screeches. "Tell me everything." She helps me at my elbow, helping me to the bed.

I flinch at the ice-cold touch but follow to appease her. She doesn't even notice but pulls the blankets down and waits for me to climb in. She grabs her pillows and races back over waiting. "Scootch, you mooch." She fluffs the pillow at my face.

I growl and bat at the pillow and move slowly over for her to climb in. "You just are saying that because you want the deats. The low down."

"Duh." She climbs in and pulls the covers over our legs and leans back comfy and waiting. "Now tell me a story and it better have a spicy ending."

I play with the edge of the blanket needing to know something. "Can you answer me something first?"

"I knew this day would come..."

I sigh in relief.

"No, I am not a lesbian." She pats my leg under the blanket. "I know you're disappointed."

I burst out laughing and she giggles as well. "Why would you even say that?" I lean back in ease. "Take it from you, you know how to put anyone at ease and make an awkward situation even more awkward."

"Was that not your question?" She bats her eyelashes.

"No, not even close. My question was what is your take on half breeds?"

"I mean I know they happen because we are interacting with humans more and more as the years pass, as well as other worlds with other creatures. But..." She shrugs.

"Well good to know but no I mean an actual half breed with like powers and shit." Worrying the blanket before me.

"I guess I never really met one before so I dunno. I guess I would have to find out. But you know I have been judged my whole life. I wouldn't judge another who I would hope not judge me." She nudges my shoulder with hers.

"You're about to learn a lot of things, I don't know how much could be packed into one day?"

"You would be surprised."

"Hey, can you make sure that we head to the library tomorrow? I have to meet a friend there and also check out some more research, unless you know about mates."

She nods once and then freezes. "What the mother fucking hell Alexia!!! Are you holding out on me girl?" She screams. "Is Blaise? Wait, I thought you were a witch?" She looks confused.

"Slow down all in good time. Library?"

"Oh yes, yes. I have to meet the guy you met at lunch there anyways." She states simply she leans far over and opens her drawer that is next to her bed and shuffles things around. "Here." She pulls back slowly trying not to fall and sets some crackers down in front of me. "You said your stomach wasn't feeling well. Did you eat today?"

I nod.

"Other than breakfast?"

I think over the day then shake my head but stop mid motion. "I did have some bread, I think." I open the crackers with shaky hands. "I am a half breed." I say sullenly.

She sees me struggling with the crackers and grabs them from me unwrapping them and then placing them in my lap. "Continue. I mean unless we need to stop to throw a party for being different. If so, that might make this place better if everyone had to throw a party for being different."

I grab a cracker and place the full thing in my mouth giving me a moment to collect my thoughts before I go into things. "Where to start?" I think. "Well for starters I am a half breed."

"Ugh you said that already why not start with the most interesting news first like Blaise?" She spreads her hands out disrupting the crackers.

I grab for them and laugh out. "Calm down, horn dog."

She grumbles but settles back. "You would be too; this place is lacking in the hot male department."

"I can do magic like a witch apparently and am also a badger shifter." I wait to see if Natasha is going to say anything but continue on when she also takes a cracker to nibble on herself. "When going to see Blaise I guess I did something or we were both triggered but things definitely got hot and heavy." I again feel my cheeks getting warm.

"You dog!" She bellows out. "Don't tell me you didn't."

"Umm." I again nibble on a cracker. "Kinda did."

"How was he? I need details girl. How big was he?" She holds up her hands showing length

"Natasha you wretch!" I call out. "Truth, is I don't know how to compare it." I bite at my lip.

She looks at me and then away. "Oh." She looks up to the ceiling. "Well, that's okay. Tell me at least that it felt so good, and he made it good." She melts into her pillow.

"Oh yeah." I melt right beside her. "It was so very, very good," I whisper.

Natasha shudders.

I lick my lips and breathe out slowly. "It was very hot, and intense."

"So, you ended up marking him? Are you into that kink? Marking is supposed to be important between shifters is it not?" She asks.

"I dunno, he said it can be but he wants me to research it more. I think he worries about taking advantage of me, of me making sure I make my own decisions." I pick at my fingers. "Which is kind of nice but I also don't want him to treat me like I am delicate and may break at any moment." I growl out.

"Girl, I say if you are careful and do your homework you can work this for the better." She motions her lower body gyrating. "Though anyone even brings up the idea of mates around me I am running in the other direction."

I chuckle. "I am going to definitely read up on things so I don't inadvertently get a husband or anything but having fun is something I am sorely lacking. It will be nice to have a little fun." I shrug my shoulders.

"What happened after that?"

"Melissa happened!" I give her a deadpan stare.

"No, that bitch!" she yells out.

I pat her leg to calm down. "After we finished everything though."

"Well, at least she didn't come in to break up the good part." She breathes a sigh of relief. "Or you might be sexually frustrated. No one likes a sexually frustrated woman let alone one in heat."

"Heat? Though I feel nice, there is a bit of soreness." I wrap my hands around my stomach, noticing Natasha looking at me. "But I wouldn't say no if it was anything like the previous time." I waggle my eyebrows.

"Yeah, heat is what most of the shifters go through, depending on the animal. So, with Melissa breaking things up when did the magic come into play?" She asks.

"Things happen where a fight starts and Quintan comes in and our magics collide when they were trying to restrain me. Apparently, I picked up an artifact that kind of took over, we then got thrown into the past. Which he blamed on me."

"How did you go to the past?" She exclaims. "Did you at least meet anyone interesting." She waggles her own eyebrows.

"Keep it in your pants. I did meet an interesting tall dark and scary guy; wish you would have been there. You would have been able to intimidate him and make him do what I needed."

"You know I like a challenge." She holds up her fingers and examines her nails. "Tell me about him..." She throws out her hands and leans back.

"He is definitely tall and dark. Kind of had grayish skin. Not sure if he was handsome since he kept to the shadows and had a cloak on."

"Handsome? You think you have me pegged and know my type after only one day? Now you're playing matchmaker?" She pushes me to the side, cramming me against the wall.

"I got a feeling about this one."

"Ooooo." She swishes her fingers in front of my face.

I shrug. "Who knows."

I talk with her over the next couple of hours before she finally lets me pass out. Going into detail about what happened and the past I visited and how I felt about the whole experience. It was an emotional roller coaster going over it in a small amount of time. Hopefully I could be done with it and not really think about it for a while. My eyes drift shut hoping that I made the right decision and with putting my trust in Natasha. I hoped she helped me through things, her breath is already even as she snores softly next to me. Her even breaths pull at me and cause me to get drowsier, my thoughts drifting off.

CHAPTER 11

I GROAN AS I wake up, the light coming fully in. My head and stomach have settled down from last night.

"Well, we don't have to do what I was thinking of, I was going to have you do a spell to see if you were a witch and to see what kind. But we already know you have magic now," she says to me as I start to come around.

I glare out seeing Natasha sitting at her desk already dressed and ready for the day. "Do you ever sleep? Why are you up so early!"

"Depends on what you consider early. I only sleep a few hours and usually am up by four or five. It is almost ten basically you are the one that is sleeping through most of the day! Haven't you ever heard that the early bird gets the worm?" She pops a piece of gum and then goes back to chewing. She looks down at her papers and then throws her pen down on top of them and fully turns to me. "Plus, you were in a small coma a few weeks ago haven't you slept enough." She gets up and places her hands on her hips.

"Yeah, but after the day I had yesterday can you blame me?" I stretch out on the bed snuggling down deep into the covers. "How long have you been here Natasha?" I ask seriously.

"Which time?" She fires back.

"Which time? You have been out of here? I thought this was just a place to send the broken and worthless and for them to stay here till the end of days."

"Nah. They let us out if we do better." She cocks a head and stretches the gum between her forefingers and teeth.

"Everyone other than Jack looks pretty normal for the most part."

Natasha gives a laugh. "We are. Other than the trouble makers and the ones that need to learn more control. Others might be here for a while or ever depending." She frowns.

"What is this place exactly? Is it more like a school, or something else?"

"It changes to what is needed. Most of the time it is a place to send problematic people for them to have a time out or learn control." She puts air quotes around control.

"What about rogues? Why are people considered rogues, and where are they, more importantly what are they?"

Natasha rolls her eyes. "We definitely need to hit that library today. In this world you are either considered light or dark. You are either born to serve the light or born to serve the shadows. We as creatures have come a long way since the old days and old ways of thinking. Some species can intermingle as long as they are on the same side. Rogue's like to have choice and don't want to choose either side. They didn't like either the light or the dark so they decided to choose their own side or create their own. It all started with love." She sighs. "Doesn't everything stop or start because of a romantic gesture, a grand power play!"

"What do you mean?"

She waves a hand up in the air. "It doesn't matter. Apparently, this world was going to bond together the top house from the light side and the top players from the side of shadows. They were going to wed together but it didn't come together as it was supposed to or some shit." She shrugs. "It's all in the past and the story changes depending on who you ask."

"What jurisdiction does this place fall under?" I look around and push myself off into a half sitting position leaning my weight mostly on my hands. "Light or dark?" I clarify.

"There are not enough of us that they need two separate places. With that they combined us all in one and this is the only time where dark and light come together to keep the problem children at bay or the crazies together. This is a bad place to associate, they think this is just one step up from being a rogue and basically being condemned to die!" She chokes out. "Problem is they are creating more rogues that way and they are making sure these people don't have a place they can turn to other than people that are in the same situation."

"What about the teachers and other people that help this place keep going? What are they? It sounds like there is a council or something from what I heard from Quintan."

"They all have their own agenda but most of them are on the light side. Only a few are dark at this point. This place goes back and forth on that though. The first time I was here it was more dark than light teachers. I think they take a vote on who is in charge of the idiots that decade or century." She rolls her eyes.

"Dorothy, we are not in Kansas anymore, are we?"

"I'm hate to break it to you, you're not even in your own world anymore let alone whatever city or state they picked you out of."

I scramble up off my bed and look out the window, though it was dreary and the sky was gray it looked very normal. "It looks the same?" I see the circle of woods and a side of the building I am in. "But I heard the same thing from someone else. How did I get here even?"

"I mean they took you through a portal." She sighs out and places her arm on top of the chair resting there she leans in and puts her chin to rest against her arm. "Duh. Though it looks a lot like your world, it is not. We are in the magic realm that feeds off of the mortal realm and coexists. For the longest time my family moved us over to the human realm to get away from the politics but my mother and I caused too many problems or something." As she sits there with her chin on her arm, she draws with her other hand on her thigh drawing a pattern, ice emerges slowly taking the form of a dagger.

"No, you cause problems I think not! They have got to have the wrong woman." I brush off.

She gives a sad smile.

"You have been helpful to me which is something I needed when I had nothing, literally nothing, no memory... nothing at all." I try to cheer her up.

She nods as if she is listening but not completely.

"What side do you belong to?" I ask.

"Light but my father swears I am the epitome of all chaos." As the full ice dagger forms, she takes aims and throws it at the side of the wall causing it to stick in.

I look over at the wall and notice that there are dents and small thin holes from many sharp edge things being thrown at it. "Do you get bored often?"

"I would say that's a yes." She starts on another ice sculpture this one smaller and more like a small pole

"So, what side does that put me on?" I ask fully sitting up now, sleep not happening again till later tonight.

"They don't put people together, bunking together if they are not of the same class. Meaning that you are part of the light side most likely. They must have had your blood from the previous place you were at so they would put you with the same side. I mean they did think that until you told me that you were of both sides."

"What does that mean though? Does light mean you have light powers versus shadows or what?" I rub my eyes trying to clear the sleep from them and fully comprehend what is happening. "Quintan said I have magic or power but not what kind."

"No and unfortunately you can't just tell either by looking at someone. When they use magic or shift or do what they do that is the moment you can tell someone has power but not what type it is. It is a sense, not really a smell and you definitely have to be paying attention because it is subtle. It takes a lot of years of studying and practicing to find out your specification."

"Why though, why were things separated, why even keep up this archaic tradition when people are starting to come together and blend?"

She throws the pole into the wall and her fingers twitch as she creates another long thin needle looking dagger. The first ice blade is already melting, making a puddle on the floor. She pulls back her hand and lets another one fly as it hits the wall it makes a thump and then breaks off and shatters against the floor. "It would be better to just show you the history from way back when, when the world was just a thought." She stops drawing with her hand and brushes ice dust that is on her jeans.

I nod and motion up out of the bed sliding my feet into my shoes that were placed right next to the bed. "To the library then?" I call out.

She nods once more and stands up looking out the door before opening it up.

"What are you doing?" I look at the door and then out into the hallway.

"Nothing." She calls over her shoulder ignoring me and expecting me to follow.

I give her a peculiar look but shut the door and continue down the hallway following her. As we come across the mess hall I pause. I sniff the air and could smell roasted meat of some kind and my stomach let out a low growl. I moan a bit. "That smells delicious."

Natasha pauses as she sees me not moving. She looks into the mess hall and cringes in pain. "Fine let's get something quick and then we go." She urges me towards the line and lets me go before her.

I eye the plates of food in front of me bypassing the weird looking foods and piling on some bacon, eggs, and hashbrowns. "Breakfast." My mouth drools as I pull on more and more food. I definitely felt like I needed it after using magic and shifting yesterday among other things. My cheeks heat up remembering what I did yesterday. I wonder if I would come across Blaise again, part of me hoped not, but another part of me, one that just ignited yesterday, hoped I did see him once again.

"Hello slut!" A bark calls out after I fill up my plate.

I jump slightly not expecting someone to yell right behind me. I look over my plate noticing nothing was in danger of spilling, so I turn slightly. I see Natasha on the other side of me, she is not turned to me she has already turned to the speaker.

"What do you want Tanya?" Natasha sneers as she looks up and down at her she also flicks her eyes to the side at the girl and guy that stand behind her they are both dark of hair and very similar to one another. She nods to each of them in turn. "Twins."

They nod back, but do not say anything more.

"Who's the whore? Did you not explain the rules? Or does she want to end up dead?" Tanya raises a blonde eyebrow. She wears a blonde ponytail and flips her hair from her shoulder.

"Well, the whore here is Tanya." Natasha stares right back at Tanya motioning to her. "And you know more than anyone rules are meant to be broken."

"She's going to end up just like your mother." Tanya taunts.

"What is she talking about Natasha?" I ask confused about what is happening but I was definitely getting that Natasha did not get along with this person.

"Nothing." She barks out.

"Oh, it's not nothing... Not nothing at all." Tanya gives a tinkling of laughter. "She doesn't even know." She looks to the girl and boy beside her as they continue to stand behind her not even hinting at a smile. Tanya keeps on laughing trying to catch her breath.

I look at Natasha trying to catch her eye to figure this out. I look out to the seats with others sitting. There they look over at us but quickly look back down at their plates, soon whispers start around the room.

I step in trying to distract her from Natasha. "I slept with Blaise so what, is it wrong because he is like a teacher here or whatever you want to call it. We are both adults. What does it matter?"

"I'm sorry sweetie grownups are talking now, though you should know he is part of the dark side, and since you are a light that is never going to work." She eyes me distrusting.

"What?" I gasp out. "What is Quintan then? They were so friendly to one another?"

"They are just coworkers coexisting with what they do but are totally opposite, Quintan is on the light side." Natasha utters before Tanya can.

I nibble on my lip. "Why did Blaise not say something or do something?" I try to whisper to Natasha.

"You should definitely warn her, before what happened to your mother happens to your little friend, their ice bitch. It's one of the reasons you were put here a second time. Did she tell you that, newbie?" She looks expectantly.

I glance at Natasha waiting and looking expectantly. She eyes each twin but does not say more.

"Well, this is boring now, have her tell you all about her mother won't you newbie..." I nod since she didn't want to let that go and wouldn't seem to stop looking at me until I gave her an answer. "Let's go reapers." She tosses her blonde hair over her shoulder and turns to take her leave. The twins stay for a moment.

Natasha whispers out. "Remember who holds your actual leash, Dalia." The girl twin flinches and the guy turns and glares; he grabs his sister's arm before he turns her from us. They walk away with Tanya.

I look shocked and am surprised that I did not just drop my tray through that whole debacle. "They are reapers? They look alive to me."

"Just because you reap the dead does not mean you are also dead." Natasha laughs as she watches the three walk away back the way we had came from. "And before you ask, no Tanya is not a reaper, she is a kind of witch, very strong and her family blood is old, it is why she feels threatened by you and that you are hanging out with me. You being a witch should have drawn you to her regardless if you are from different sides. Or not."

"Because I am a witch, does she not know that I am also a shifter? I have mixed blood and am rabid." I make a little claw with my hand and hiss as I hold the tray close to my body with the other. I edge towards the lady to finish up so we can eat and get to the library quickly. "If the Blaise thing is out how is it that me being of mixed blood is not out?"

Natasha waits a moment, goes back into the line disrupting a few to grab a bowl full of golden jelly squares and then meets me over by the check-out attendant. "Short answer no she doesn't know that part of your story. Just that you are of light and have witch power that she can sense. You have to be actively using it while she is around in order for her to pick up you are not just a witch. Other than me and the teachers no one else is the wiser, for now."

We both take a few minutes to situate and find an empty table. Since witch and reapers had left the people have gone back to just conversing quietly and eyes don't follow us around, it has gone back to normal.

We sit down and I dig in right away. Natasha toys with her golden jelly but does eat some of it. "I wanted to explain things to you since you are new to this world and I wanted to do it in a place where I could make sure no one would judge or hear what was said... Hold on." She runs out of the room and grabs someone that had just walked by, she walks back dragging the boy I had seen yesterday with the dreads.

"Sit." Natasha pushes him down to the side of me and takes a seat back where she was sitting previously.

"Oh, was this now?" He looks around confused.

"Yep, we are doing this now, you know what to do." She nods to him.

"Hi Alexia, how's Blaise doing, I hope well, did Natasha tell you her big plan." He looks at Natasha and sees her shaking her head. "No, she didn't yet no that's not yet." He looks down and thinks for a moment.

"Jack... please." She whispers quietly.

"Right, right not now... right now is this. Focus." He claps his hands and rubs his hands together causing friction. He forces his hands out away from them as if pressing something outward.

I feel something wash over me. It feels like spring rain or a light mist washing over me.

"Set. You are free to discuss now, I stay yes." Jack states.

"Yes, you stay." Natasha nods. "Did he tell you what he does and who he is?"

"Not exactly the lunch lady says he sees possible futures or possible timelines it was really weird and stressful the lunch lady didn't really want me to talk to him. She said he was lost and having a hard time that day."

Jack rubs the back of his neck. "She's harmless she just tries to look out for me and since you are new didn't want you taking advantage of me or being mean to me. She will warm up to you don't worry."

"Yeah, she is harmless," Natasha agrees. "There are good days and there are bad days where he does get lost in the future, but he always makes it back. With that power he also has a minor one in being able to create barriers where he can hide if needed and cast this so we can talk freely but only us three can hear what we have to say. If he learns control, he may even become the next greatest prophet."

"Really? No way!" I say out loud. No others, even those closest to us, make a noise or even a movement towards us. "That is incredible. But they can still see us though right." I wave my fork in the direction of the other people.

Jack shrugs and fiddles with a strand of one of his dreads. "No big. Yeah, they can still see us, I am not really good at visual barriers yet."

"Okay let's get down to business." She leans forward as she finishes the last of the Jell-o. I nibble on my food but still stare at her waiting for her to continue.

"From what you explained to me yesterday and what you witnessed in the past with your mother you can't just be any halfling. I think you are the lost princess from the rogue group. Someone that many have been searching for, for many years. From the stories I have heard the woman or your mother I suppose was from a group of light witches, but a half blood meaning she was not a full witch she had a sister that was full blooded though. Your father was a shifter and very prominent in the night court, their families were to come together and become one and create a union to heal and make us all whole. Unfortunately, things did not go according to plan and your father and mother fell in love, instead of with the full-blooded witch sister. Both parties did not bless that union though could not keep it from happening. Both sides rejected this, a priestess foretold of the union and said it would only bring heartache and chaos and the end of our world here." Natasha spreads her hands out shaping a world and then her hands expand out as if in an explosion.

"More, there has to be more." I urge.

"I don't know much more than that, it didn't work out. They ran away and created a band of rogues to fight against the light and dark side and live in peace. Of course, peace did not come, chaos definitely descended especially when there was word of a child, everyone thought back to the telling and what that could mean. It got many older people scared for what may follow." Natasha breathes on her fingers, chilling them causing them to freeze over and watches them slowly warm up, the ice drips down her fingers, she continues the cycle as she speaks.

"Who else could guess at this? Could there be another family with my story or a couple that wanted to get together to create me that are on the same side."

"That's not how that works, remember. Badger shifters are of the dark side all of them and witches are known to be of the light side the only exceptions are dark witches and necromancers. Shifters that are of the predator families are dark. With what you explained Quintan has probably figured out who you really are. Blaise should have found out what you were when you shifted and then also when you used magic, I am guessing because I have not witnessed it myself yet but there should be a sense you give off depending on where the power originates from you mother's light side or your fathers dark side."

"What would they do with this information? Would they kill me?"

"Melissa, would she know?" She asks quickly.

I think back and shrug. "I am not sure if she could tell from my powers, maybe if not, she might find out from Quintan or Blaise."

"Okay we have to keep that much on lock down as long as possible and keep an eye on you so they don't make you disappear. Either that or find a way out of here for you pronto."

"There's a guy." Jack pitches in.

Natasha looks at him and then back to me. "Apparently there will be a guy, not sure how that happens but okay then. After you are done, let's go to the library and get you some books on lore and shifters so that you can learn more about the past and more about your kind. The part of you that is driving you wild." She wiggles her eyebrows suggestively.

I glare at her. "And what was Tanya talking about, what happened with your mother? Is that why you are being nice to me? Are you a rogue also?" I whisper the last question because I am still afraid for anyone to hear me say it or see me mouth the word.

"My mother joined the rogue forces after she left us, she tried to bring me with her but we were caught and I was made to look like an example of what would happen to those that defect. My father is very powerful and the only reason why I am not dead right now," she pauses here a moment as the ice settles further down her hand. "He is a difficult barrier and if something is happening and he wants to know about it he will find out." Her eyes turn dark blue with a black starburst pattern in the middle as she pushes ice to flow out of her into the room. The temperature drops in the immediate vicinity, and just as easily her eyes turn back to normal and the ice slows down and only covers the center of the table where her hands sit.

"Okay memo to self don't bring up family issues unless I have layers." I shiver to myself pushing away the rest of my plate since it has now chilled. "I am ready I suppose." I frown.

She smiles and claps. "Goody." She jumps up from the table and pats Jack on the shoulder. "You will know when we need you next." He processes that for a moment and then nods.

"There will be a time where I am in the gray but I see it."

"Good." She pats him and turns once again not waiting for me, just expecting me to follow.

"Can you throw this away?" I slip the plate over the ice to Jack.

"Yeah, I can do that... Hey, Alexia?" He waits to make sure I don't move for a moment. "Things will make sense eventually. I know that much is true. Many will help you but four people will be your pillars." He holds up four fingers. "One is made of ice and can be just as fragile."

"Natasha?" I look over my shoulder, seeing her already disappear around the corner.

"Two are made of shadows." He continues.

I wrap my arms around myself and rub my shoulders. Shade, I think to myself can he be considered a person?

"And the fourth is hard to see clearly but is the strongest pillar and most needed. It is one you get to choose freely."

"What does that even mean?" I ask, my voice echoing a bit as sound starts to reverberate around us again. I didn't realize how quiet it was. I look around and then back at Jack.

"Time flies," He smiles. "Oh hi, when will Natasha be here?" He giggles and laughs.

"She was just here; you were talking with her." I look over at the clock making sure time did not pass by again or something.

He gives a look of confusion. "Oh. That's nice." He smiles. "You may know this one. Why did the snake eat his own tail?" He giggles as if he is telling a joke.

"Alexia." Natasha calls for me, I quickly glance over my shoulder and see her waiving me over she was already around the corner.

"I am not sure Jack but I gotta go, I will see you soon." I wave back and head over to where I had seen Natasha. She was already gone.

"Of course, very busy, war and all. The death dealer will see you soon." He cackles.

I run to catch up to Natasha's quickening pace. "Hey, some of us don't have long legs here, let alone wings."

"Then you will be left behind I guess," she says easily enough.

I huff not letting her comment affect me too much since she was still hurting from thinking of her family. "Did you tell Jack about what I explained last night? My dealings with the death dealer specifically."

"No." She thinks a moment as she keeps walking. I struggle to keep up with her. "Though it doesn't mean I don't eventually."

"How do you keep up with what he is saying or what he even means?"

"I don't try to; I just listen and try to remember and keep a careful eye or ear for when it happens hopefully I remember or am ready for what was needed and then realize he was talking about this time. Sometimes I can guess by the clues he gives or leaves but he barely understands what he sees and again it is just one possibility. Let alone if he says the wrong thing it can change things drastically, and being in his gray area nothing comes through very clear so that helps him, but not others, it's a very delicate balance." She shrugs. "All you need to know is he is a major help and cares what happens to the lost ones. The ones that no one wants." She comes to a stop in front of two large wooden doors.

I crane my neck up at how gigantic the doors are. "This is the library?" I squeak out.

"Not just the library." She smiles as she struggles to open one of the doors. "A portal to The Library, we only have access to certain areas being where we are from but this place is amazing if you ever get the full access." She opens the door a smidge enough for her and I to slide through. There is white light that emits beyond the door. She slips in and her body disappears. I worry at where I am being led.

I see many people passing by they stop and give weird looks but none seem upset about where I am heading with Natasha. I slide through and the light passes over me, squeezing my eyes shut I expect the light to sear my eyes and brain. I blink the dots that dance in my vision away as I land in a small room.

"That didn't feel weird or magical?" I look back in confusion and just notice a blank room and wall, another dragon like form is behind a desk this one pink instead of purple as well as skinny and long, the room is bare and sparse the only thing taking up room is the creature along with the desk.

"I thought you said this would be amazing." I look around in confusion huddling up to Natasha and keeping close to her.

"I said if we had access to the full potential then yes it would be glorious. But no, we get dumped into this section and then the Teager here gets us a room and allows us to research or do what is needed. All we have to do is send a request to her." Natasha waves. "Did you meet her sister in Melissa's office?"

"Oh. Yea I did." I look at the Teager who is pink in color with purple hues. Her form is slim and agile. Instead of claws there are suction cups at the end of her fingers and she has wings tucked into her back. "You look a lot different compared to your sister," I call out.

She looks up at me from what she is doing, like her sister she stands behind a big desk but these desks are made of glass. Surface light flickers and she dashes to the side and taps on the glass a few times, swipes this way and that and then taps a few more times and swishes it away before walking back over to peer down her nose at us.

"Why look at you, cute little things, oh I could just eat you up. Yes, sister did say you would be stopping in now didn't she. My name is Scarlet. Nice to meet you." She puts out a hand, there are only four digits on her hand. Her voice echoes in the small room and is very loud.

After I flinch and cover my ears with my hands, I shake her hand. "Right, Tallia gave up her voice," I blurt out. "I almost expected you to speak through my mind like she did and it would be soft and gentle."

"Oh, my other half she always was the quiet one. Was surprised that she didn't want this job instead of where she went, though she wasn't too good with technology, which is my area of expertise." She notices another box appear, her fingers dash over the screens skillfully and soon that box is no more. "Tallia said that you would be stopping by." She flutters her wings a bit and taps at something on the wall which causes a door to pop open. "She said that I was to give you this when you stopped by." She slithers back to us holding up a pendant on a chain.

I look at the pendant. It is in the shape of a flower that is metal. "What is it?"

"It's a flower and has power inside it." She smiles. "It will allow you to speak mind to mind with your creature, as long as you are touching in some way. As long as you wear the necklace and you are touching the shadow you will be able to talk to one another."

"That's amazing!" I say in awe.

She waits for me to take the chain from her scaled hands. Another screen pops open and she races back to her table.

I place the chain around my neck. I would need to test this out soon. "What are you doing with the screens? Are they all over?" I lean over the glass to see if I could see through it to see if the whole glass table was a monitor.

"Oh, these things are all connected to the rooms that people are in. They send requests over to me and I send them what they need. Unless of course it is restricted from them then they get denied or if they actually do need it then it goes through a request from others higher up for special handling and supervision." Her voice has a deep twang and almost drawl to the tone.

"Oh so no searching through the stacks for books? No rows and rows of knowledge to peruse through?"

"As the human age progresses forward so do we, mostly anything can be found through the request to me if you were in the actual library and had full access to it yes you would be able to peruse stacks and rows of books even get lost if you aren't carefully." She whispers. "Spooky stuff can happen there." She twitches her fingers.

"Well good news." Natasha says just as loudly and boisterously as Scarlet. "We need research, so I came to the best place I knew where to get that. We will need a room and a couple of things to start. The history of the start of this world and how it was divided between light and dark, some stuff on." She looks at me and mouths the word, Badger. I nod. "Badger shifters, and another on mates."

Scarlet eyes Natasha and her right eye begins to twitch. "You know darlin you are supposed to use the request channel because it will help you get exactly what you are looking for since there are so many books on all three of those subjects you just named."

Natasha twitches her fingers right back. "Just the beginner friendly ones we need to start her off easy. She is brand new." She pats my head and then claps her hands. "Okay, bring the room up, we will be waiting." She pulls my hand into the crook of her arm and we walk away from the desk.

"What are you doing?" I whisper, eyeing the wall that we are walking up to. "What room?"

"Natasha Marie Bragin, you know there are rules in place for a reason and you are the reason for those rules in the first place." The Teager grumbles, hard taps sound from the glass as her hands fly across the keyboard.

Sliding doors appear in front of us and the doors slide open showing a room that is big enough for the two of us with chairs and a desk.

"Yeah, but you like our banter and wouldn't change it for the world," she yells over her shoulder as she pulls me into the room.

The doors slide shut but before they do I notice Scarlet's wings unhinge, she opens them up flapping them in frustration. The door shuts with a snick and we are closed in the room it is quiet and silent.

"Aren't you afraid she will take away your access or not send you what you need?" I ask.

Natasha lets go of my hand and takes a seat. I sit down in the other chair and look down at a desk similar to Scarlets where a display lightens in front of each of our work stations. "Everything is digital?" I say in wonder—and a little sad.

"Scarlet is sweet. No I am not worried about her, because she knows I know my way around these things. Since my father is the one who invented them, so I know all their secrets." She smiles. "Scarlet also is not a fighter at heart and she knows I mean well and am just having some fun. It keeps both of us out of trouble." She huffs tapping on the glass waiting for the information to pull up.

"Does it take a few moments? It looked almost instantaneous out there?" I shuffle my feet.

"This is part of our game. She makes me wait a little while, thinking about what I have done or what not. She doesn't wait too long because electronics don't work well around cold things." She snickers.

"I wonder what she traded for her claws." I say.

"What do you mean?" Natasha asks, taken aback. "You mean like her sister? How do you know about that?"

"Her sister gave up her voice for more knowledge or something like that. At least that is what she said. I wondered if she gave up her claws for something like Tallia did. She said that they could give up treasured things to them to get something in return."

Natasha's face falls and she frowns in sadness. "No, she didn't willingly give up her claws. And no matter what Tallia said about giving up her voice for knowledge there is more to that story than you know." She shakes her head. "Nothing like what happened to the sisters should ever happen to anyone, but they couldn't touch them so this is the way things must be for the time being." She taps on the glass again with a bit more pressure.

"I didn't mean... I am sor...you know. I am glad I didn't say anything to her about it then." My face falls. "I could have been so mean and insensitive at that time if I would have said something."

"Don't worry about the maybes and possibilities, you're not a prophet, leave that to someone else; you didn't know all is good and even if you did it was a long time ago and she gets it, they both do." She shrugs.

At that moment multiple windows start to pop up and light up the large screen in front of us. Natasha widens some of the screens and throws others over to my side. I have a few windows open on my side and she has a main page on hers. She scrolls through pages and lands on a picture, a very old looking picture. She widens it with both of her hands and makes it cover the whole desk and both of our working spots. The map fills the area on one side it is marked Shadows and the other is marked as Light.

"The pages I sent over to you are about badger shifters. I opened it up to badger habits or times where you will be extremely sexually charged. The other is on mates, I would probably focus on the mate one since you had more questions on that one and it seemed more pertinent. It will tell you what to do and what not to do, depending on what way you want to go." She nods to the screen. "But before we start with that, I wanted to give you a quick history lesson. When magic and more human looking creatures stumbled upon this world it was divided between light and dark. Yes, the creatures here were split but so was the land, it was eternal darkness on the shadows side and eternal light on the light side." She scrolls through pictures of the world before it was what it is like today. Showing total darkness or bright sunny weather.

"That sounds amazing!" I pour over the pictures and keep listening to the story.

"It was split evenly, though there were skirmishes, the sides were balanced and even. Some of the creatures were accepting of the people who visited this land and welcomed them on either side. Through the ages the lands grew and were prosperous with all the magic and soon the lands started to blend. There were still parts that were dark and others that were light but it started to take on more of a human element like worlds do where there is a night and a day. Change is hard for anyone and especially at that time people and creatures were scared of what that meant or what this would bring. Sides began to form alliances and were drawn. Still through it all it happened where we mixed fully or tried to. The first defect was born from a light and a dark coming together, unfortunately the magic washed over them and did not stay with them. The defect, the first void creature was born. They are almost human right so why not just scoot them out and throw them in the human world and make them live their lives in that realm. Simply put they knew too much by the time they figured out that it would never get powers or be a part of either side that thing grew up dangerous and knowledgeable in magics. Being a void means magic does not touch you meaning we could not fight or use anything containing magic or holding magic of any kind to fight. In a land where everything is embedded with magic it makes it hard to fight something that can't be touched by it." She smiles.

"How did they rid it from the world? It was just one person?"

"Actually, there were seven I believe created by that time. They ended up binding together and pairing off, three couples if you will except one. The elders ended up trapping them all in a cave system way down south, it is a labyrinth of twists and turns and never meant to let anyone free of its clutches if the person is not prepared when they enter. It was blocked off for a time. Others got worried throughout the centuries and decided to open it up thinking there would be skeletons near the opening. Many prepared over the years to wander the cave system to find what they were looking for and never came across what they were searching for. There were no clues or tracks or anything to do with the seven people that had been trapped. Those mountains have minds of themselves, some say they asked the mountain to help and the land provided when their own people would not."

"But I am not a void creature. So, mixing the two sides doesn't only create voids." I say in confusion.

"No, you are right, it has changed. The magic back then was more fertile and wilder, it has changed as the world here has changed. A prophet, one of the strongest who has ever lived, foretold of another time when the mixing of the species would happen. It was foretold that if the strongest of the two sides could come together and unite, a savior would be born. The people have been needing this to help our world and to continue to survive and thrive. If it was anything else he only saw dark paths that would lead to this world's destruction and not only this world but others as well, since ours is off of a focal point."

I look over the map and notice cities and towns but to the south there are just mountains that are at the edge. They carry around the border encircling this whole place. "What is past the mountains?"

"Nothing, it is all the mountains, they move how they want and allow or do not allow certain things to happen as they want." She slides to a new more modern map.

"There is nothing but this land and nothing else? Other than the mountains? What about oceans?"

"Correct, some places are like that though. Unlike yours where you have a whole planet and universe to explore, others have just a slice of living space. Outside the mountains it has not been figured out or discovered. There is water but again only what the Mountains let through. Perhaps one day the mountains will converse with us or help us know the true potential of this world." She sighs. "This is a more modern looking map. To the north there used to be a rogue headquarters somewhere." She motions at the top but no markers are there to show it. "Here is where we are." She points to the center of the map in between both sides.

"This looks smaller than the previous map."

She nods and frowns. "That's because it is. Ever since those seven were born the mountains have started to encroach on us and push into ourselves. If we do not keep ahead of it, whole towns disappear overnight. Ones that are on the edge. The mountains swallow up anyone or anything that is in its path. We do not know where they go. We assume into the cave system to be lost forever."

My voice croaks and is parched. "What happens when the mountains take back the land and covers all of it?"

Natasha shrugs. "Not sure we can only theorize; many have tried to figure out the shift of the tunnels and mountains but they are confusing and there are too many possibilities to help with planning anything substantial. It is partly why I am here. My father is focused on stopping the destruction of our world and protecting the people. He is in talks with the dark side to try again but they fear that it is too late to create a savior. Especially if they find out about you and think you are the destroyer of this world instead of the savior who knows what they will do to you."

"I am not a savior or a destroyer." I pull on the collar of my shirt, finding it hard to breathe at the moment. "How can there be a prophecy about a savior and a destroyer born of mixing the sides?"

"That is not what others are going to think when or if they find out you are mixed with both shadow and light. The light side or part of the light side had a hold of you and you saw what they did." Natasha reiterates. "They probably are hoping that they can create the savior that the prophecy foretold so they can control it. That or destroy you in some spell they make to help keep everything light and good."

I eye her carefully. "And what are your thoughts on everything, where do you land?" I eye her, seeing her scrunch her face in anger as she talks.

She looks right back at me and swipes the maps away so it is just a blank screen. "My mother wanted her and I to be a part of the rogues, so that should tell all that is needed."

"But you weren't successful so you never became a part of them."

She smiles. "Why do you think I'm here? Just because my father caught me does not mean my heart is not there with my mother. Believe me there are other reasons why I am locked up here right now rather than out there with my father or out on my own. I think prophets barely know what we do. Usually, it is in the moment right before whatever happens, happens. Where you can see all the ties that come together to create that one moment and if one thing changes or is not done correctly it all falls apart. How can they believe a telling from way back then to be actually correct? Who knows why they fear everything, it's like they are almost as bad as humans?" She scoffs, but continues, "Remember I have seen a couple of worlds in my time and mostly this one and the human one. They are all making some of the same mistakes. Time and time it happens again, they tried a form of segregation in each world and it didn't work for them it's not going to work for us, yes ours involves magic and can make or destroy worlds but you would think we would learn, be better than our ape cousins," she says.

"Until recently I thought I was human so I take offense that you compare us to animals and we are viewed lower than you."

She rolls her eyes. "But you are not human, though you grew up as one, you are not one. You would understand if you only knew."

"Because I just have the capability to understand as my human equivalent and apes," My hands clench. "No..." I stop her. "I'm sorry that's not right. Separating magic users and non-magic users is the same kind of segregation that you were just talking about."

"No ugh. Saying sorry is going to make you go into debt!" She grows frustrated and stands up. "You don't realize humans come to destroy and judge; they are good for fun but that is about all. Our magic is powerful and it is easy to make the weaker whatever we wish. The ones that want the power for themselves cause more trouble and bring about horrible things in the process."

I stand up as well. "Perhaps you are more like your father than you care to admit! It is the responsibility of the strongest to look out for the weak not to punish them for what they were dealt. I am not saying rush into anything quickly and let go of all the precautions but don't let that fear keep the world from being great." I stare at her.

Her eyes open up wide and she stands there frozen and shocked.

"And if you really thought any of what you just said, then why get to know me in the first place? Why be friendly with me? No matter the life form we all have the capabilities of doing great and horrible things, no one is immune to that and I mean no one." I point a finger at her.

She crosses her arms in front of her. "Good." She looks me up and down. "Keep that up and you might do some good here yet." She turns and pushes a button on the wall, the doors slide open.

"Where are you going? What do you mean good?" A flutter and tingle zings through me as I see a shadow float under Natasha. My eyes dart to him as he hovers under her keeping to her shadow.

"Out I will be back, go ahead and read and do some research I will come back for you when I am done, if you need anything else on the top left corner you will see a box you can click in there and type whatever you need to ask for. This world is in a war whether they would like to admit it or not. They don't need someone that will just be meek and afraid. And they don't need someone that will run away either." She chews on her bottom lip.

She walks away without further instructions and the door slides back into place leaving me alone with my reading material. "Weird he must need to go check something out while I am safe here." I touch the screen and one of the boxes follows my fingers around the screen, I remember Natasha spreading her fingers away from each other to make the page bigger.

It enlarges and fills the screen and the text becomes larger. I play around for a moment trying to learn the lay of the system and how to work it and try not to break anything. I pull up the other article, since this one went straight into badger shifters. I read at the top of the article, Mates and what that entails!

After scanning a few of the stories, it was very confusing and sometimes unfair. Not all mates get along just because you were destined to be together. It did not always work out. It warns people before continuing forward that both parties need to make sure this is actually what they want.

There were some stories of where that did not happen, where it was forced. The magic makes it where it can't be forced easily but like with anything it can be possible. You have to fully mark one another. The female has to take the male into her without his help and join fully holding one another and repeating some words before drinking from each other. It solidifies the bond and makes it almost impossible to break.

"What if I don't want to be a mate?" I grind out.

My gaze wanders to the left-hand corner and flicks to the box. It enlarges and a textbox and a cursor pulls up along with a keyboard. My hands fly across the keyboard not really knowing what to do. I notice the letters and touch each one of them to start spelling out the words.

"Does not want a mate," I typed.

It stayed there and nothing else pulled up on the screen. I stare in confusion. And see another button that says find. I press that one and another box pulls up to write in. I shake my head and exit out of that box. It goes back to my normal one that still has the question in it. I notice another one that says enter. I press it hard hoping that it does what I need it to. The box goes away and another small article pops open.

Mates should think before they reject the other one, because until one perishes another is not marked as a mate if ever. Most do not recover and both may end up only living half-lives or incomplete lives, there is not a lot of data on this as of yet due to them being traumatic or harsh experiences. The good news is that mates can wait before deciding either way and take it slow so neither is harmed throughout. "Well, this is just some bullshit. What loser set mates in motion; I would like to meet with them and have a discussion. So not really a decision to make here." My face scrunches in anger.

"Hello, Alexia," a low gravelly sound emits behind me.

I squeak in surprise and turn around rapidly climbing up on the table and screen to get away from who was standing behind me.

"Death dealer!" I look around and the door remains closed. "How did you get in here?"

"I did warn you I would find you and come for you did I not?"

"I suppose you did." I remain posed up on top of the desk furthest away from him. "What do you want?"

His eyes flick down to my work space. "I have come to collect."

"Collect what. I don't have anything," I say.

"But you do." He inclines his head. "Did you know mates can happen to anyone, not just shifters?"

I look down at what was still pulled up on the screen. I see the title in big bold letters at the top and glances back to the death dealer and shake my head.

"You just need to know how to listen. Some worlds have marks that appear, others there is just a knowing." He cocks his head to the side; he slides down his hood to show his face and hair.

The harsh light makes his skin seem extra gray but his dark hair is cut to about his shoulders. Part of his hair falls over his eyes covering one of the copper irises. His jaw is square and there is a rough day's growth coming in on his jaw, he is still dressed in a dark cloak that flows down to his dark boots. His hands are covered in black leather gloves.

"Don't you get hot in all of that?"

"Not how and where I travel, no."

I nod, not sure what else to say. "You said you have come to collect? What would that be? What do I have that you are trying to collect?" I ask hoping he would give me a hint.

"Being a death dealer can be challenging," he growls.

I stare at him acting as if I understood what he is dealing with even though I had no clue other than what Quintan had told me before.

He ignores me and flips through the screens that I was reading through and even the one I had not gotten to yet on badger shifters. "Don't read that one." He flicks it away. "Shifters learn control as long as they learn to embrace their animal, or at least not fight it at every chance they get." He eyes me and then eyes another article the question Mates or Frenzy what's the difference?

"Okay, I figured I couldn't learn everything from a book, good to know. What's this about?".

"When you are around this other person, is there a pull, a yearn for them regardless of what you are doing? No thought, nothing logical can stop things."

"That could be because he is a snake charmer, I mean it's in the name he is supposed to charm people. I don't really know my own emotions let alone what he is feeling."

"In a manner of speaking, but snake charmers are known for what they do and do not lose control. Did he?"

"I think so, I don't know… I feel like I lost more control, I ended up marking him. He seemed pretty in control when he asked me to make the decisions." I bring my feet up on the chair and just sit on the table with my arms resting on my upper thighs.

"If a snake lets you mark him willingly then these are definitely what you should be reading." He pulls the mate articles back up.

I push myself to the edge scoot away from him as far as possible in this small room, to see what new ones he brought up. "I did see scales flow over him after I marked him. I thought that was for protection, that he wasn't expecting it and didn't want me to cause any more damage. What can I offer him, let alone you?"

"Then he lost control." He smiles. "They rarely do that, even in death." He taps on the glass and leans against the table, not looking at the screens anymore. "You mentioned a woman, previously in the past."

I move my knees away from him and try not to make myself a large target especially when he mentioned death. "Natasha?" I ask.

His eyes turn blood red. "Yes, her... Natasha." He tries her name out. "I need you to introduce me to her."

"Why?" I ask full of suspicion.

His eyes bore into mine. "Because it's either that or our deal will have to be paid in another way."

"That was a deal? I didn't put up anything for us to make a deal?" I complain.

"Careful what you say to one of our kind especially when pleading for help, we can require any form of payment if one is not put forth. Mine is a meeting with Natasha." He taps his boots against one another, dust breaks loose from them.

"But just like an impromptu meeting, not like you will take her away or anything? Why do you want or need a meeting with her?"

"She is free. I will not take her away, but I do require you to introduce us."

"Why? Why couldn't you just bump into her anywhere."

"The outcome I am needing requires this."

"That you will not tell me about?" I ask.

"Correct," he growls.

"This seems very important to you that I do this, am I correct?" I say a little more straight forward.

"Perhaps." His lips form a grim line.

"How long have you been... alive?" I want to say *alone* instead of alive, but don't think that would be received well.

"Since the beginning," he utters.

"Beginning of what?" He looks at the map, the one that is cut in half of dark and light. "That's a long time." I stand up and lean against the wall letting my head fall back against it as I look up at the ceiling.

"I am going to require an answer soon," he states, he opens something in his hand and then closes it and puts it in his pocket.

"Can I know your name?"

"No," He grinds out taking a step forward with his fists clenched at his side.

I cross my arms in front of my chest. "Well, then how am I supposed to introduce you if I don't even know your name?" I give him a pointed look.

His eyes turn a muddy red color and takes a step back shrugging his shoulders releasing the tension built there. "It's Zeek."

"Zeek," I say. "What would another favor from you cost me?"

"What sort of favor?" He leans against the desk and parts the cloak showing off a slim figure with dark clothing on, there are daggers and pouches slung around his hips and a belt crossing over his chest that disappears up near his arm into the cloak.

"Could you get us and some select few others out if needed? No killing or harming, just an exit out of this place."

He rests a hand on his hips and thinks about it a moment before speaking. "Yes, that could be done, for the right price. Nothing too much would be needed, just a token of protection."

"What does that mean?"

"It means all death dealers are considered dark creatures, creatures of shadow. Though we are used and employed by all, we are born from the darkness itself since the beginning."

"And Natasha is part of the light."

He nods. "If I help you with this and go down this road, I need a token of protection to secure me and mine." His eyes burn bright red once more.

"A token? Like a trinket?" I ask.

"Something more substantial than that we can make a blood pact or we can infuse something with magic from both of us to create the pact."

I take a gulp. "Blood?" I flash back to the bodies that littered the room and blood was soaked and puddled everywhere.

He steps forward before I fully snap out of things and plucks a piece of my hair from my head. He does the same from his own. He keeps them separated and holds mine in his right hand and his in his left hand. "A spell it is then."

I breathe out a harsh breath that I had held.

"Give me your hand." I raise my hand and place it next to his palm face up. He empties my hair into my palm. It curls in on itself and lays there barely moving in the air-conditioned air. He mumbles under his breath as he starts to chant. "Do you promise to protect me and mine within your powers and abilities?" He looks to me waiting, the hairs have started to float and are held there next to each other mine longer than his.

I concentrate between the two hairs and then back at Zeek. "Oh. Yes. I promise." I give a questioning look; my palm falls down to my side since it no longer holds the hair.

"Accepted, For the price of getting you and others out of here we bind it from henceforth." The hairs twirl around each other and become locked together, once completed it falls limply into his open hand.

"Sealed," he says finally. He goes ahead and pockets the hairs and nods. "When?"

"A few days I think I will work with Natasha to get this set up and we will need to plan some things out. If it is sooner, is there a way I can call upon you?"

"I will be listening, you can call out my name and I will come, though I warn you to be in a place that is secure and hidden from sight. I may not answer right away, depending."

I nod, as he sighs. I blurt out a question wanting to ask before he leaves. "Zeek?"

He waits.

"Do you think Natasha is your mate, you said before people other than shifters can get them?"

"No." He shakes his head. "My kind have given up on mates long ago, when we were cursed. There is nothing but this for a death dealer."

"Then why do I have to introduce you two?"

"It is confusing and I will explain it in the future. First, I was told through a deal that was made, so it is a requirement. With all curses there is always a way to break them, perhaps you are the way to break that one."

"Me?" He nods. "So, you're saying there's a chance."

He shrugs. "I only try to think of the present, but I do have a weakness for hoping I have been told." He gives sad eyes.

"That is hard to believe, you having a weakness."

"We all do."

I walk over to him slowly and place my hand on his shoulder. "Zeek as long as you are on our side, I will try my hardest to make it a better life for you and your own."

He brushes a thumb across my cheek, a tear breaks free. "Be careful what you say to barter with my kind." He licks the tear from his thumb and closes his eyes for a moment. "But thank you little one." He raises an arm in his cloak and disappears in a blink of an eye.

"Well, okay then," I huff out and lean back against the wall, just closing my eyes.

I have no clue what this all means, but I stand there for a good amount of time. I sit back down and research through things and try to learn more about myself and this world, and a little bit on death dealers. Everything I read though is warning not to work with them. They brought reapers wherever they dealt. Which brought death.

For a world that had been around for as long as it has, there is little known about it. Some of knowledge came from the inhabitants that came with the land most had come from other worlds.

Many hours go by. I read up on witches and shifters alike, not just badgers. I tried looking up the prophecy on me or prophesies in general but got an error saying that I could not look into that without further clearance. Same thing happened when I tried searching spells, even basic ones. I lay my head against the desk and just rest my eyes, lying there breathing in the recycled air.

Warmth brushes against my back as I hear the door behind me snick open. "Have I killed you yet?" Natasha asks.

I give a chuckle. "No, but I think I have a way out for us."

"I leave you alone for hours and you come up with a way out?" she whispers as she fully comes into the room and the doors slide shut behind her. "This I gotta hear."

"Remember that death dealer I told you a little about."

"Did he bother you? Do you want me to beat him up for you?" Natasha asks.

"I don't think you are supposed to be the one threatening the death dealers," I say. I lift my face up from the desk. "He said he would get us out."

"What did you have to give him to get us out, and what did he come to collect?" she asks as she goes through the history of what pages or things I looked at.

I chuckle deciding on whether to tell her the full story or not. "Wait till you hear this." Natasha looks back at me and raises an eyebrow.

"I have a feeling that I am going to be pissed soon, am I right?"

"Let's find out. All he wanted was me to introduce you two."

She stands up from leaning over the desk and then partially sits on the desk and glares and giving suspicious look. "Why?"

"Wouldn't say much other than I had to introduce you two."

"What did he want for getting you out of here?"

"It's me and anyone I want to come with. He wanted a token of protection for him and any he calls his, as long as it is within my power."

Natasha stands abruptly and squeezes my upper arms with her hands, the temperature plummets. "Alexia, tell me you didn't!"

"What!?" I ask in a high-pitched voice.

"He could literally consider anyone his and you would have to help. He basically made it where you have to play whatever plan or hand, he deals you. And if you have the power or the capabilities to save him or his then you have to do so even if it means dying yourself!"

"But he seemed so... nice... and alone he couldn't have meant it that way."

"Girl he is and has been a death dealer since he was made don't think he doesn't have an agenda, and believe me he is not going to be happy when we meet." She places a hand down on the console and it promptly freezes over and short circuits the desk in very quick succession.

"Natasha!" a voice bellows.

She rolls her eyes and hops off of the now frozen table top. "Calm down, just get another one brought up from storage," she calls as she punches the button and the doors swooshes open.

"You are the reason why we have the extra supply." Scarlet flies over; she tucks her wings in before she bends to enter into the room.

I move around and out the door to give her more space. Her tail whips back and forth banging against the doorway.

Natasha grabs my hand as I back out. "Let's go before she gets started and gets really angry. It's getting late anyway," she says over her shoulder as she runs with me back the way we came. "Bye Scarlet."

"Yeah, you two better leave before I get this fixed," she huffs. Natasha breathes into her palm and throws something at us.

I look back seeing a blue glowing orb and duck down, pulling Natasha down with me. She looks up and laughs as the ball hits the wall we were running towards. Once it hits the wall it blasts out and creates a portal to head back to the Morning Star.

We scramble up from our crouch and run through the light, we come out the other end back into the place where we left and the door is still partially open as we turn back. The door then slams shut as if it would not allow us to come back even if we wanted to.

"I won't be able to go back there for a little while, hope we didn't need any more research for the moment," she states. Her voice echoes in the empty corridor.

"Where is everyone?"

"It's pretty late, everyone is either getting dinner or hanging out with friends."

"Wow really? I didn't think we spent that much time there." I check the clock in the hallway to see what time it is.

"Time works a bit differently there and also like I said you were smooth out when I came into the room to get you."

"Was I? I could have sworn I just closed my eyes to rest." I yawn. "And I am still tired. How can that be?"

"You forget you did a lot yesterday so that probably has a lot to do with it. You used a lot of magic and shifting along with bow chicka wow wow." She nudges me with her elbow.

"Shut up," I call and head back to our room.

"I get it you're not used to all this excitement you need your beauty rest," she digs. "I am going to find Jack then I will be in later but you go ahead and head back if you need.

"Thanks, we will start planning an exit strategy tomorrow. You let Jack know what's happening, we can bring him with. I am going to head to bed early."

She nods and waves as I walk away from her. I head back to the room and don't take much time to get ready for bed and pass back out.

CHAPTER 12

"**M**INX," A LOW RUMBLE calls.

"Blaise?" I call. "Blaise where are you?" I am in a hallway that is deep red. I race around the corner thinking he was right there. "Where did you go?"

"Where did who go?" a low voice calls behind me.

I give a shriek and jump as I spin around. "Blaise. There you are."

"You called for me, of course I am here." He brushes my hair away from my face.

"Right, where is here?" I look around.

"What do you make of it? This is your dream." He caresses my cheek with his hand. "Are you okay?" He stares at me and my lips.

I lick my lips not knowing what to do or say, my voice leaves me. "A dream? I just went to sleep or I think I did." The scene changes to a bedroom set in deep red and black tones.

"Did you need something little minx?" His thumb trails down to the corner of my mouth as he steps closer.

"Did I?" I echo.

"Why did you call for me?" He licks his lips, which causes my eyes to zero in on him.

"You said minx. You called to me, didn't you?" I take a step forward and my hand rests on his chest.

"Did I?" He looks down at my hand resting on him.

"I researched and read some things," I say almost hesitantly.

"Hmm," He hums, but says nothing else.

I reach up and turn his cheek gently so he is seeing me fully. "Are you okay?"

His arm comes up and cups my hand to his cheek. I see a flash of metal on his wrists but it doesn't stick and the next moment his wrists are just plain.

"Yes, though I fear I need you more than you need me," he rasps out.

"Let's put that to the test." I give a wicked look as our clothes melt from our bodies. "Let's play." I push him onto the bed behind him and watch him flop down.

He laughs out. "What are you going to do, wild one?"

"Last time I didn't get to explore much so this time you're going to let me do what I want and figure things out." I run my nails up his inner thighs gently as I take hold of his hardening shaft. I lean down, flicking my tongue over his head.

He hisses and his head falls back and his hands bunch in the comforter. "Why did you bring me here?"

I take this as a good thing and continue. Kneeling on the bed as I lick and suck my way down his hard length. I scrape my teeth gently; and cup his balls stroking them in time with my mouth.

"Woman," he utters.

I grow eager and happy with how I can control him with just my mouth. I lean over him to get a better angle and as I push all the way down as far as I can. I rumble my throat.

He dislodges me as he yanks my lower half over to him, forcing me to kneel over his head and chest. I lick the tip of him and taste him there. He follows suit and licks me clear from front to back, not stopping. His hand massages my back, pushing me back down as I stop, not knowing what to do with all the sensation.

I wrap my tongue around him and then take him into my mouth once again, moaning as he licks and presses a finger into me.

I suck hard as I pop him out of my mouth. "I need you."

"Yes," is all he utters as he continues to lick.

I move up off of him taking myself away from him, he growls and rolls to the side. "Come here."

I crawl up to him, but he moves me to face away from him, and am pulled tight to his front. I feel him hard against my backside. I brush against him. The silken blanket rubs against me heightening my senses.

He pulls my leg up and holds it so I am open and ready. His other hand holds me close and caresses the underside of my breast. He nibbles on the bottom of my earlobe. "Create a mirror."

"But," I whine, rubbing myself against him, making sweet friction.

He presses the head of his penis to rest against my lips and rubs them there a bit. "Mirror."

I lose all thought as I squirm to keep him there. What did he ask for again? Mirror why? A wall of mirrors appear next to the bed reflecting us back. I see him looking at me, looking as if he wants to devour me.

"Feel us," he breathes into my ear and nibbles down to my neck as he pinches my nipple very lightly.

I brush my hand over the curve of my hip and through my curls sliding down over my lips where his length rests. I rub the tip of him and down the underside of him pushing him into me. He twitches against my lips, happy that I am touching him. He continues to rub back and forth moving slowly.

"Guide me, and watch."

I look at the mirror, watching him caress my lips, only parting them partially. I guide the tip of him to enter me, and he pushes fully in. I leave my hand there, my fingers spreading my lips for him. He pushes deeper inside me, filling me fully. He angles my leg up, giving him more room. He slides in and out in a steady rhythm. I continue to watch and feel him move inside me. I moan and grind against him, wanting more friction. He scrapes his teeth against my neck.

"Is this how this will always be?" I ask breathlessly, not sure what I am exactly asking and also afraid of what I am asking.

"Do you want more? Do you want it too always be like this?" He teases at my neck. He speeds up and hits harder, hitting the spot over and over again.

I feel the heat rising as he continues to move. "If you bite me in a dream, does it transfer over to the real world?" I was having a hard time sticking to the conversation. I just need more.

He looks down at me and pauses his movement. "No, it is just a dream, minx."

I squirm and move against him, groaning. He continues his strokes, his breath coming in as choppy as mine. "Bite me." I grab his hand that is caressing my breast and hold it there. I caress myself and him with my other hand. The precipice right there, I can feel it. He must as well because he lowers his head over me and kisses my neck before gently sinking fangs into my neck. As his teeth sink in a moan shoots out in pleasure causing me to go over the edge.

He continues to pump into me faster and harder, the rhythm not there anymore, as he nibbles and sucks on my neck. He comes as well as he grinds against me pulling me on to him, he lets my leg go. I leave it draped over his legs. He wraps me up in his arms fully against him. My eyes fall close and I relax against him.

He removes his fangs from my neck and licks the wound. "Alexia, promise me something." He tips my head to the side to look at me.

I open my eyes slowly, sleep real sleep calling to me. "I don't think you have ever called me Alexia before. Other than when we first met," I comment as I move my leg up.

"You can't return home, do you understand?" He looks worried; his eyes dart over his shoulder.

Metal bands show once again at his wrists and at his neck. I sit up and start to get confused and angry. He slips out as I move around to face him "No, I do not understand," I yell back at him. Chains link to manacles that are at his throat and wrists. They pull tighter and tighter against him. "What is going on?" I shriek.

"Do not go home, Alexia," he calls before he disappears all together.

"Blaise where are you? Where did you go?" I call. I raise to a kneel on the bed, looking this way and that. I cover myself in a black simple dress, wanting to be dressed before continuing looking for him. The room turns cold without him there to warm me.

I wrap my arms around myself. Cold metal links shoot out from one of the dark corners of the room, wrapping around my whole form starting at my neck and curling around me to my waist. I try at first to scratch and call my claws but they elude me. The chains pull me curling around my neck and chest, reeling me into the corner holding me there tight. Not letting me go. "How do I get out of this dream?" I yell. "Wake up!"

"Little lost soul can't find her way out." A voice that is disgustingly familiar calls out. Shoes clap on the hardwood floors as they come forward. "He thought he could hide the little lost lamb." The chains tighten.

"You're supposed to be dead," I call as I realize where I had heard his voice from.

The shadow's part and he moves closer. "And you were supposed to stay locked up in our basement until we found a cure for my wife!" he calls back.

"Tom? How did you make it out alive?" I ask, fear coating the back of my tongue.

"You honestly think we are that easy to kill." He laughs. Closing his fist, the chains tighten around my chest, making it harder and harder to breathe. "I escaped but the others that were there for the ceremony did not escape you were too busy destroying their lives. You are truly a monster, but we have a solution for that." He chuckles. "Fortunately for us only a couple knew of your true nature and will be easy to dispose of. Or can be confined to places until they happen to forget. But those are details you do not need."

"Where is Blaise?" I squeak out.

"He is here with us." Other chains rattle, but I can't see through the dark shadows. "It was such luck we came across him, Melissa had told us where to find him to use as leverage. Word does travel quickly, especially when there is a possible mate involved."

"What do you want?" I growl out low barely able to get enough breath. I had no one in this world and as soon as I had a tiny bond the world takes it from me.

"Well, you of course my dear, we have big plans for you." He claps happily.

"Come get me," I call, pushing him.

"Sadly, that place is under another's, one that does not feel the same as we do. So, you must come to us." He crooks his finger forward and loosens the metal links pulling me closer to him. They unravel but there is still a chain holding my neck so I can't move other than stand in front of him, but it did make it easier to breathe. "We have made it worth your while."

"Blaise? He is not a part of this, leave him alone."

"Find an exit and follow this trail northward to your home where it all began." He makes a map appear and a red line marks the way I am meant to follow. "There are many exits in this place you just have to find the right rock to look under, but hurry time is of the essence." He tsks as I am pulled by my neck backwards. I grip the chain holding it a little bit away from my neck which lets me breathe easier. I am thrown backwards and fall into a soft plush mattress. I try to break free but cloth holds my arms down. "Let go," I growl out.

"Alexia," a light voice tinkles.

I growl as the anger rages through me, claws pierce out of my fingers and I slice my arms around me cutting through the fabric that was holding me in place. I hiss in pain as one of my claws catches me.

A powerful cold blast climbs up and holds my arms in place, ice encases my hands. My eyes focus as I look around me, I am back in my room and Natasha is fluttering up against the ceiling in her blue

Fae form. Her cool dust falls to the floor creating snow as ice still shoots out of her hands.

"Natasha what are you doing?" I look around the room. "Where is Blaise?" I think back over just what happened and my face falls and darkens. "Where is Tom?"

"Me? You're the one that came out of dead sleep swinging," she yells back, the ice slowing down and stopping.

I hiss as the ice is touching my skin and starting to burn where it touches. My hands melt back to normal but the ice still hangs around my wrists.

The tattoo flutters and slips from me crawling to the front of my shoulder. It slips between the ice and my skin, he slides down and expands around my wrists and causes the ice to break. Shade falls to the ground and races over the shards of ice collecting them and then stands like a wall between Natasha and I holding the shards up on one arm.

"Shade, no, stop." I try to pull at the back of the inky darkness, but he is not substantial. My hands pass through him.

"What is he doing?" Natasha asks concerned.

I push all the way through him so I am in front of him forcing him to see me. "Shade." I put my hands up in front of him.

"Call off your spell," Natasha bellows. I feel coldness creep down from her. I turn to see her creating a long sword almost like a rapier.

"Look, I am fine. Yes, a little scared and banged up but that's it. Natasha is a friend and was only helping. I got scared when coming out of a dream and lost control."

Natasha's wings flutter slower as she lowers to the ground but she still has her sword pulled up in front of her.

"That's right, shadow creature. Alexia was screaming, and I was trying to wake her. She then promptly started slashing with claws. I knew the fastest way to both save myself and wake her up was doing what I did." Natasha shoves the point into the floor and it causes ice to spread out from where it hit.

Shade cocks his head to the side and grows taller. Maybe I could try talking to him mind to mind. I grab the necklace that was still around my neck and reach out my fingers to brush against the shadows. The shadows are still not tangible but maybe that is all I need to do is touch the shadow part.

"I am stressed and still scared; I know but that is something different from this." He bows down and looks at me inches away from my face. "I swear it." Since he seemed to need a bit more. I talk out loud so Natasha will know what I am saying.

No words enter my head or are spoken to me. He shrinks and flows over my body covering my arms and legs, covering all but my hands, feet, and head. I look under the shirt I am wearing and see the dark shadow flowing over all of me. I poke at the darkness on my arm and on my stomach seeing how much I can feel. The first poke I touch him and don't feel the poke myself, he settles down more and the second poke is more like a tattoo and I can feel it now. "You can do a full body armor!?" I say, surprised.

Natasha pours ice into her hand like little needles. "Wanna test it?" She grins.

"No, we have to get moving!"

"What are you talking about?" Natasha mutters. "It is barely past four in the morning." She looks lovingly over at her bed. "You woke me up with all your moaning and screaming."

"Did you see Blaise yesterday?"

Natasha thinks for a moment then shakes her head no.

"I think someone may have taken him, we have to get out of this place and now."

"First, we don't know that. Second, I thought we were supposed to plan something, where would we go or head?

"They used Blaise to get me to come. To where it all started where I was taken, the old Rogue encampment. Tom, who I had thought I killed, said to meet him there," I say.

"When did this become a story where the girl saves the guy?" she sneers. "He can get himself out of the trouble he got himself into. Tom isn't that Jade's husband? I thought they were both dead."

I pause and sit for a moment back on my bed. "I don't know, something is pushing me to act." I twist my fingers in worry. "Apparently in my rage I missed Tom and he was able to get away, and now has it out for me since I killed his wife."

"Did you see Blaise in your dream or wherever you were?" she asks questions, keeping me talking and thinking things through.

"He specifically told me not to come."

"There you have it, smart man, it makes me like him a little bit more. He is logical."

I give her a look.

"Don't look at me like I'm crazy." She stomps her foot. "You want us to go up against who knows what with no weapons or defense to get a guy you slept with once... With no plan in place on how to even get there?" She gives me a pointed glare. "Is that about, right?"

"Well, when you put it like that it sounds like I am doing something dumb but what would you have me do instead." I run my hand through my hair. It had come loose from the ponytail as I had slept.

"Let's at least think this through. Get a plan in place like we were going to do."

"I need to make them pay my aunt and her husband; they started all this. Something is urging me to save Blaise, I know it in the pit of my stomach that I must. Tom also showed me where the location is to my family home."

"All good points. Don't you think that you should slow down and think it through. Why would we trust his information when he did all this horrible stuff to you to begin with?" She walks back and forth from the door to our bedside tables. "First step if we do go, how are we getting out of here and who are we bringing?" She holds up one finger.

"Zeek he will get us out of here," I start.

"You're ready then." Zeek appears next to the door and leans against it. He looks between Natasha and I as if he was waiting there the whole time waiting for his name to be said.

My mouth hangs open. "Shit, I said your name I wasn't supposed to until I was ready." I hit my palm against my head. What more could go wrong.

"Zeek?" Natasha's wings flutter again, stirring up the air.

I look up in time to see Natasha's feet come off the floor.

"Natasha, Zeek. Zeek, Natasha," I introduce. I bet he wasn't thinking this would be the introduction he was looking for.

"Death dealer I presume." She glares and purses her lips. She throws an ice dagger near his neck and flies across the room bringing the rapier up and points it at his throat, her wings keep her level with him so they were the same height.

"Kill me if you think you can." He pushes against her sword, causing a bead of blood to slide down his throat.

"Don't threaten me with a good time," she growls back. "But before we get to the fun part, you need to release her from your bond."

He eyes her carefully. "Why? Would you like to take on the debt instead?"

"You know why and of course not!"

He whips his arm through the rapier breaking it into pieces causing Natasha to come closer. He wraps his arms around her waist holding her to him a dagger in his hand caressing Natasha's cheek. She glares at him and sends one of her wings into his shoulder and the spikes on the edge of them spears into his shoulder.

"I am fine with it Natasha. Just stop." This just got a lot bloodier than I was anticipating.

"No, he is going to release you," she says through gritted teeth as she pushes in harder and sends ice cold temperature throughout the whole room.

Zeek's hand never wavers and only stays light against Natasha's skin. "Explain to me why you think I, who is a death dealer, would ever do something without a debt to be paid." He states as if he was not feeling any pain from Natasha's wing.

She bites at him with her black teeth. "Because if you don't, you won't see me or her ever again. It is not fair for her to have to keep you and who you call yours safe. That is a fool's bargain." She smirks.

"Hey!" I remark.

"I'm not worried," he bites back at her. "She's young she will ask for another debt at some time, I will find her and you then."

"All right then." She nods her head as if she has made a decision. She moves her hand to turn towards her face and creates a long icicle. That is crawling closer to her own throat inch by inch.

Zeek eyes the ice watching it push towards her own throat. "What are you doing?"

"You said you weren't worried; I am making sure you do not see me in the future. It's a win, win for me I don't have to watch her make stupid mistakes with creatures such as yourself and I won't have to see your face again."

"Hello, I'm right here!" I yell out, but neither pay me any attention. I huff in annoyance.

The ice pricks her throat but continues to move forward. "That is not what I meant." He pulls her hand away so the ice moves away from her throat, blood falls down her neck but she freezes it in place shortly after it drips. The dagger-like thing begins to grow back towards herself. The ice also encompasses his hand making it harder for him to have control of her.

"Stop," Zeek growls. "You're starting to piss me off."

"It is why I am here to continue to piss people off. You know how to stop this," she says sweetly as the ice is inches away from her neck once more.

He pauses, looks over at me, I shake my head. "Oh, now you want my help. Nope you're on your own now." I grumble and wait close by, unsure how far this is going to go. "When Natasha puts her mind to something it usually happens, I just met her and can tell that much about her."

"Fine." He doesn't see the ice stopping and it begins to prick another spot on her neck. "Release me, I will break the debt bond."

He continues to hold her close with the one hand but the other one that has ice down it and grips hers, the ice begins to melt off of his hand and free them both. He looks at her as she is still eye level with him and holds there for a moment. "You knew."

She arches a brow at him.

"You know what my kind can do. We are not easily swayed."

"Yes, and you could have easily disarmed me, it would have hurt mostly me." She flinches. "But it was doable whatever you came here for I needed to be a part of the picture." The temperature starts to warm back up and their breaths no longer coming out in puffs. "It was a gamble, but I liked my odds."

He steps back and shuffles his cloak digging into one of the many pouches that are equipped to his belts. He pulls out two strands of hairs that are still curled around one another. "I unbind this spell," he says and then blows on the strands. A puff of smoke from a tiny ember puffs up as the hairs are burned away.

"Count yourself lucky. I don't unbind my contracts usually," he says gruffly towards me.

"Be glad that is all I made you do." Natasha barks back eying him as she removes her spike from his shoulder ever so slowly. "That never even slowed you down, so don't act like it did."

"Okay, can we move on now before you guys make me sick?" I call out trying not to look at their 'friendly' banter. "I can't tell if you guys will kill each other or what..."

Blood drips down the spike and she flutters her wings causing the blood to whip onto his face. She laughs as she flutters back over and comes to land on the bed behind me. Her icicle hair clinks together, she snaps her fingers and she is back in her more humane shape. The creek of the bed complains as she comes to sit there.

"Of course, but on a more serious matter don't deal with death dealers unless I am around." She smiles over at Zeek.

I look over at him as well, and he stares back at me. "As entertaining as this was, I will refrain from making deals." I rub my stomach feeling a bit queasy.

"Are we ready to leave?" He slumps against the door.

"What about Blaise?" I ask Natasha.

She rolls her eyes. "Can you tell if someone is still here or not, I mean in this building or in the vicinity?"

He thinks for a moment then nods.

"Can you tell if there is a snake charmer here in the area?" she asks since he did not continue on.

He closes his eyes and hums to himself. "No, no snake charmer."

"They have him then, Natasha." I turn to her, taking her hand in mine.

"Are you sure this is what you want to do? We can forget them and continue on with our journey without them. Trust me men suck most of the time anyway." She glares at Zeek once more.

"You wouldn't understand." I squeeze her hand. "I have to." My eyes bore into hers urging her to understand, to see what is riding me underneath that urges me forward. "I have never had anything to call my own and the first little flicker of light was taken from me. I was never given the chance to mess it up myself or see if it was something I wanted or not."

"I understand all too clearly." Natasha frowns. "I have seen what love can do and I know how it can tear people apart, it is why most of the time I run the other way." Natasha pats my hand and sets it beside her, she looks out at the still dark window. Looking out as if she could see something out there.

"The deal was to get you out, not take you somewhere as well," Zeek points out.

"Fine, what would you want for getting us to her parents' old place?"

"Just a small token." He chuckles.

"Not that again." I fall back against the covers with my arms spread out to the side. "We will just take the long way even though he said time is of the essence. We are not doing another debt bond thingy."

"I won't be able to drop you off at that place since I have not been there and am not sure of the surroundings, but I can get you about a day's walk from there in a neighboring village," Zeek states. "And that will even require a smaller token, hardly even an ask really."

"What is it?" Natasha edges to the side of the bed, she gets up and goes back over to his side of the room. "I have many trinkets that could be of use to you." She reaches a hand for one of the drawers in the dresser next to her desk.

"Nothing like that." He moves in behind her, placing a hand next to her, keeping the drawer shut and in place.

She turns around and eyes him warily.

"It's rather simple really." He crowds closer to her just a breath away. "It's not a high price at all," he whispers.

"You don't have the right equipment." Her eyes squint at him, zeroing in. "I like girls."

His eyes stay trained on her, he reaches up his hand cups the back of her neck and pulls her in quickly, their lips touch.

I quickly avert my eyes but find my eyes sliding back over to them, not being able to look away. "That is not what she told me," I whisper to myself amazed she wasn't fighting him.

She leans into him for all of thirty seconds, enough for him to deepen the kiss but then begins to struggle and fights to get away from him. He holds it a second more than lets her get away from him.

Natasha doubles over coughing, she hacks and wheezes, trying to cough up something.

"What did you do to her?" I get to my feet and race over to her pushing him out of the way.

"The deal is paid for and another is completed," he says.

Natasha continues to cough; I pound on her back. A black inky blob falls onto the floor melting into a puddle. "What is that?" I screech.

"A spell her father fed her," Zeek answers in kind.

Natasha continues to cough, she slowly eases to the floor and tries to catch her breath, the coughing subsides. She peers through teary eyes at the inky substance. She scoots away, not wanting to look at it. A numb voice echoes out of Natasha's mouth. "We will need to bring Quintan with us, as well as Jack."

I nod along with her to Zeek. His head turns down at both of us as he clutches something at his belt. "Will that be all, just you four?"

"Yes," she says in a sad voice. "You have dealt with Patricia I am guessing then?" she asks in afterthought.

"I have."

"Then stay away from me." She pulls her legs up to her, her arms wrap around her legs and holds them close to her. "Go get Quintan and Jack first. We should be ready once you get back."

He nods and takes his leave of the room, backing out watching Natasha the whole time as he leaves. She did not look up or at him once.

"Natasha, are you going to be, okay?" I ask hesitantly, not knowing exactly what to say. I wanted to ask so many questions. "We can talk while I pack." I go into packing mode; I keep an eye on Natasha's silent form.

I go around and bag up what I need, which wasn't much due to me not having much to begin with. Natasha, on the other hand, has way more stuff. I grab a bag and open it up not knowing where to start.

"What do you want me to pack for you? Or do you need to talk first?" I ask.

"I can't be like them," she states.

"Like who?"

"Them, my parents." She motions to the inky residue still on the floor. "I am their battlefield; I am their war ground. I can't trust anyone that has had dealings with either one of them."

"I know how that is." I sit down on the floor with her. "I don't think there is a creature alive that hasn't dealt with Zeek it seems." I try to atone for him. "I didn't know he was going to do any of that," I say, guilt ways down deep in the pit of my stomach. "Is that who Patricia is? Your mother?"

Natasha touches her lips. "They were like that fire when they came together but, fire burns even the best of people." She lets her hand fall away from her mouth.

"Not all are like that. What was that spell?"

"Only because you don't know enough of your snake to know better. Regardless of the creature they are all the same. That is why I refuse to go through that. Better alone than hurt, or worse. Something that probably would have activated when I cam close to my mother to capture us both."

"I get that you are hurting and that I may not know a lot of what is going on or if something is wrong or not, but snap out of it. Just because it is like that for many out there does not mean that is how it is for everyone." I get up off the floor, not wanting to let her continue to wallow. I grab the bag and go through the drawers and start picking things out that seem like something she would wear. I hesitate at the desk.

"Top right drawer. The book there," she mumbles. "It is hard for you to see the other side of the coin when you have not been burned by the terribleness of love."

I pull it open and see a plain book sitting there. I grab it; the black leather is soft to the touch. A picture slides out from the back and I see her between a woman and a man. "Is this you? Is this your parents?" I look over at Natasha, and she hasn't moved yet.

"Yeah, before when they liked each other, and I wasn't some trophy to win."

I slide the picture back in the book and throw it in the bag. I go back to her bedside table and place her toiletry bag and some sweets that she liked to snack on in there as well. I place both bags on the bed next to one another.

"Natasha looks at me."

Her head pulls up gradually weighing down as if the weight of the world was on her shoulders. "Even if they did not deserve what they had and squandered everything, please do not squander it if you ever do find it. For like my parents you never know how long one has," I say.

"I definitely can't promise that." She shakes her head.

I reach down to help Natasha up.

She looks up at my face and accepts the help. As she gets up, she holds on to my hands, keeping them there. "But I will think on it." She gives a sly smile. "And maybe have some fun along the way."

"I thought you weren't into girls?" I ask, not being able to keep that question in any longer.

She bursts out laughing. "I'm not," she says. "But he doesn't know that. Have to keep them always guessing."

I roll my eyes at her and shake my head.

A knock sounds on the door, whoever is on the other side waits a moment and then opens it up. Zeek pokes his head in. "Are we ready, I've got Quintan here?" He fully opens the door and it is only him there without Quintan.

"Where is Quintan and Jack?" I point behind him.

Zeek looks around the door behind him. He growls and walks back down the hallway. "Don't make me chase after you."

I hear Quintan whining down the hall. "Listen, there has to be some misunderstanding. I don't want to be a part of this." His voice quivers.

"Natasha said you were needed so you will be a part of this regardless if you want to or not." He calls out as quietly as he can.

I peek around the door and see Zeek grab onto Quintan's shoulder and drag him back to the doorway. I grab my case and Natasha already has hers. "We are ready. Where is Jack?"

"He stated that it was not time for him yet he will come later. I will land us in a town with a friend near where you need to be," Zeek reiterates.

"Hold on one second!" I hold up a finger and go to the dresser and slip something out of the drawer and slip it into my pocket.

"Are we ready now?" He looks to all of us for confirmation.

We all nod to this. Natasha and Quintan step behind Zeek and rest a hand on his shoulders. I step up to his side and hold on to his cloak at his elbow.

Shadows crawl up our legs and squeeze us. They feel very cold and hard. My teeth begin to chatter as it begins to climb up my stomach and higher. I look around to see the others but they just stare forward as if expecting this.

As the darkness encompasses my whole body, I start to panic as it keeps squeezing on my whole body. I breathe in and out in quick succession. The ground starts to move and I do not know which way is up or down. I am spinning further and further out of control. My mouth begins to water profusely, though I keep gulping it down, hoping to hold it all in. The only saving grace is I couldn't get enough air to get a full breath let alone my stomach having enough space to up chuck.

My fingers were losing sensation along with my toes. They felt as if there were thousands of needles pricking my skin. The darkness is all encompassing, I try to scream out and could not utter a sound. It was all too much. I couldn't keep a handle on things, my grip slips from this world and lack of oxygen makes me pass out.

CHAPTER 13

As I come to, the room continues to spin, I scramble up and look for the nearest trash bin. The lavish bed I am in has a small plastic trash can that sits next to it and under a small table, leaning down I grab at it to retch into the bin, my hands start to shake as I curl around the bin. I try to peer around the room but can only make out that I am in a very extravagant room before it starts to spin once again. I shut my eyes not being able to stand it.

After my stomach rolls once again, and wiping my mouth on my sleeve, I rest my head against the bed. It was very plush and warm against my face. My skin feels clammy to the touch both warm and cold. I slip down to the cold floor of the wood needing it against my legs. Requiring warmth still I yank the cover down on top of me and sit there for a moment, trying to get my bearings.

"Where are we? Did we make it?" I uncurl my legs from underneath me as the shooting feeling of pins and needles race up and down my legs.

Shade flutters against me; he is still covering me mostly from head to toe. He pools down to my hand sluggishly as he mumbles to me, as if he was feeling the same effects as I am.

"Where are we? Why did we pass out?" Shades voice grumbles softly. "You were fine and then the next second it didn't feel like you were being attacked but there was something wrong."

"What affects me seems to affect you as well has that happened before? Maybe you don't feel things as intense as I do but you still do feel them. I think I passed out when Zeek tried moving us or traveling us. I am not sure though." I place my other cool hand against my warm forehead. "When Quintan and I traveled together it never felt like this, was the magic different or something else?" I ask confused and not sure.

"You understood me?" Shade asks.

"Wait, I can hear you!" I say at the same time. "Wait, what?" I didn't hear him over my own freak out.

"Why can we communicate all of a sudden?" A small head pokes up from the puddle of shadows that poured into my hands.

I play with the necklace the metal in the shape of a flower still sits around my neck no one had removed it. "This, the Teager's gave it to me to help me communicate with you but we can only do that if we are touching. If we are apart, we won't be able to hear one another." I rub my fingers over the metal, soothing myself by smoothing it with my thumb. My hand falls from the chain to my pocket I pull out what I had taken last from the room. I pull out the black stone and rub my fingers over it. I glance at the side table and see a drawer there. "I will have to search for something to maybe attach it to the necklace so I can have both of them on one chain. But for now it will be safer hidden."

"Back to what you said before, that is not right when they knocked you out with that medicine, I was still able to move around freely and not feel any effects from that." Shade recalls. "The only time that it did affect me was when that larger man did something when I was attacking the wolf."

"Oh, yeah, that is right. Perhaps it is only when magic is involved that it twists things. Perhaps whatever he did affected you the same, did it do that to Quintan and Natasha as well? Where are they?" I look around and the walls and floor are not moving this time, though I do still feel like crap. I test myself as I rise up on shaky legs leaning heavily against the bed.

"Shade, can you go look around a little and tell me where everyone is? We can talk a bit later and get to know one another now that we know we can talk together." Shade flutters into the shape of a butterfly and flies off of me over to the door, he slips under it sitting there a moment, then flies right back to me. He lands on my hand before words pour into my mind. "The large mage is coming, Quintan, I think you called him. I don't want to be away from you in this strange place, I will wait."

I nod as he slides down to my ankle. I maneuver my hands over the bed walking to the edge where there are tall columns at the corners. I lean against one letting it take most of my weight. I brush my hair back out of my face trying to appear with some semblance of normal before he enters. A small knock echoes from the door.

I glance up and wonder why he doesn't just barge in. "Yes?" I hiss as my stomach twinges but holds it together.

The door opens slowly showing Quintan standing there. "I was coming to check on you," he says simply before he sees me standing. "What are you doing?"

"About to come find you guys. Did that mess you guys up as much as it did me?" I ask while looking Quintan over. He looked all right but perhaps since he was a mage and used magic on the regular maybe he didn't feel it much or was immune.

"That did a number on you didn't it?" he throws back at me, coming into the room and opening up the curtains to let more light in. The sun glints in, almost blinding me where I was standing.

I raise a hand in front of my eyes before he does any more damage. I move back towards the bed, slipping on the covers that are still on the ground, my butt hits the floor hard since I did not have a good grip on the bed.

"Looks like you are still feeling it. The way death dealers travel can be a bit tricky for new magical users. They travel through the coldest darkest channels because to them they are easier than some of the others if you are not used to it, it can play havoc on your system." He walks over to help me back up.

I edge away from him grabbing onto the bedding to hide behind or use as a barrier.

Quintan's rotund form blocks some of the sun making it easier to see. "Do you want to spend all day on the floor?"

"No." I grudgingly admit, smelling the contents of the bucket next to me I wrinkle my nose.

"Okay then." He moves over me and waits for me to stretch out my hand and arm. He helps pull me to my feet and sets me on the bed as well as the covers wrapping them around my shoulders.

He peers down and sees the contents of my stomach in the bin and grimaces. "We will get someone to get that cleaned up for you."

"Why are you being so nice?" I ask Quintan.

"Well, if you haven't guessed yet we are out of Morning Star, and we made it to the town Zeek said he had friends at."

"I figured that much." I look around and down at the bed. "Sorry to say, but Morning Star is not really a place for comfort." I press on the bed for emphasis. "See no squeak."

"After I found out what you are or guessed at what you are, I went to Natasha to double check and keep an eye on you and anyone else around you."

"Natasha is in on this, you two are working together but she said she understood."

"She does, we do." He puts stress on the end of his sentence.

Natasha knocks at the doorway, holding a tray of food and liquids. "My father knows a lot but he doesn't see all. Though knowing him, he will soon be aware that I am no longer at Morning Star." She comes through the door fully as my eyes train on her. "Quintan is a part of the rogue's but keeps up appearances on the light side." She walks in and places the tray on the bed. She scoots it closer so I can reach it.

"I thought you said you weren't able to make it with your mother." I pull the tray closer and look at the soup and water. I take the bottle of water and sip on it, but push away the food for now. My stomach is not up to it at the moment.

"I wasn't able to get there with her, no that is true, but she, like you saw last night still has other ways to make things happen apparently. Quintan though has been a shining light in all of this and has helped me move past some of the things that my parents have put me through, and why I also just don't hate everyone." She gives a sheepish smile.

"This neighboring town is a rogue community." Quintan picks up. "Many of the neighboring towns are rogue villages. Your parents' house was at the center of all this. It was meant to be your kingdom. This village as well as many others stay hidden due to your mother's spell. We are hard to find."

"My kingdom?" I spit out a little bit of water that I was finishing.

"Yes, the group of in-betweens, the rogue community, it was all supposed to be yours. Didn't you explain that to her Natasha?"

"I thought the rogues were all disbanded. Both sides broke them up other than a few here and there."

"It is true most are in hiding or under disguises of sorts. This town is surrounded by a barrier to keep hidden, others are underground or hidden in plain sight. Your mother helped with the spells around these hidden rogue camps, she is still helping out even now."

"Wait then how are Tom and them at my parents place? Why can't Miss Ice Queen be in charge instead? She would be better at ruling people and keeping them in line. She would be better at telling people what to do." I motion to Natasha.

"First off, I am not of both sides like you, so if I tried to take over the other side would not trust me as my side would. Since, you are born of both they can't hold that against you and you were out of both courts so they won't claim that either side has your ear like they would with me. Though they might hold your time in captivity against the side of the light, I will be a major pain in your butt, don't you think I won't." Natasha gives me an evil eye. "Rogues don't last long these past twenty some odd years. The ones who have remained are lucky or that good," Natasha says.

"Natasha!" Quintan exclaims. "Slow down."

"What?" She looks coolly over at him dropping the temperature a few degrees.

"Do not worry her with stuff like that. We need her to be the hope that the Rogue's need. You Natasha don't need to do this. Calm yourself before you go running from your problems again."

"How can she be the hope that helps us if she doesn't know what she is up against. How do you expect people to follow her if she is not in the know of what is actually happening? People will think she is the destroyer not the savior."

"Princess, I am sorry for her outburst." Quintan turns back to me. "To answer your previous question about your parents place is that there are no people left to protect there. They dispersed or perished that night and the magic she created went to help the other places that were built and hidden."

I hold up a hand. "Stop." My head swivels between Natasha and Quintan. "What did you just call me?" I ask.

"Princess." Quintan gives a smug look.

"Quintan and some others want to call you that or give you a title so others will be drawn to you for leadership and guidance, they are hoping that others will follow and it will help accentuate your birthright." Natasha continues as she sees my frown, she walks forward her hand mimicking a talking puppet.

I hold my head in my hands thinking what would calm the severe pounding that is going on somewhere in my skull. "Well, Quintan is wrong."

"I told you, she would not like that," Natasha crows in amusement and puffs out her chest.

I look over at Quintan's red face, seeing him about to argue.

"Is Zeek still around?" I ask, interrupting his tirade.

"No, he had something else to do." Natasha flits her hand in the air, looking highly annoyed.

"Where are we or who are we staying with?"

"This is an inn sort of and a library, we are with the friends Zeek had mentioned, we are on the dark side's border so we should not use magic if we can help it and stick to only people that are his friends just in case. Not everyone here is friendly, for that matter," Quintan explains before Natasha can, wanting to speak freely.

"Okay, that being said, since you know more about all of this stuff and what is happening in this land, I need to lay some ground rules. I need to know the truth of what is happening even if it is hard to hear. Natasha you will be my trusted advisor or person that is of high rank and knows stuff." I look at Quintan. "You can be there too but I don't trust you," I say honestly.

"But but, but..." he blubbers out.

"No!" I raise my voice. "First of all, you didn't ask me if I wanted any of this so you don't get to tell me how to do things. Second, I tried to tell you to choose another you did not want to." I argue.

"Greatness is never chosen; it is thrust upon someone," Quintan states.

"That may be but you have not proven to me that you are some-one I can trust either." I eye him.

Natasha lays a hand on my arm. "We will need his help, Alexia."

"I figured that is why he will still be here but—" I look over to Quintan. "—know I will keep an eye on you."

"Many will be keeping their eyes on you as well, Princess. If weak-ness is seen you will not last long."

"Yes, you can work with Miss Frosty on figuring that part out and then coming to me if you guys agree upon something." I point to each of them in turn, emphasizing my point.

Natasha and Quintan smile together. "Your parents would be proud of you," Quintan says.

"Did you know them?" I ask curiously.

"No, not personally but we knew of them both of us did." Quin-tan motions to Natasha as well.

"No one over here has normal ages, do they?"

"Not human standard of ones," Quintan reassures.

"Are we ready to go to my parents' house to get Blaise and take back what is rightfully mine then? I may be able to learn about them while we are there," I reiterate, trying to get us back on track of why we came here in the first place.

Natasha fidgets nervously. "Yes, we are still planning that attack but we need you to go through some training first," she reminds me sadly. "What do you plan to do? Just give yourself up and hope everything works out your way?"

"Blaise is a big boy, he can handle what they are doing to him," Quintan says.

"He didn't sign up for this," I yell back.

"No, he knew what he was signing up for. Natasha said that he told you not to come. I don't think he minds; he knows what he is doing," Quintan says.

"He might not mind but I do," I growl out.

"We will have time to go over all that later. First, we have to see what kind of skills you have, or don't have." Natasha smirks guiding the conversation where it is needed.

Shade whispers into my mind at that point. "What about me? I can be of use."

"What about you?" I whisper back wordlessly, massaging my temples to cover up why I was not saying anything for a moment.

"Explain to them what I am and how I can be of help." He nudges against my foot.

I look down and stomp my foot. "Why?"

Natasha and Quintan look down as well once I stomp and give me curious looks.

"We can both become stronger and don't act like you won't need my help in the coming days, I also need to learn how to protect you better," he flutters.

"Fine, pull off and be visible for them to see you, but this is all your idea," I say.

Shade slides off of my foot gliding on the air currents becoming a bigger and bigger butterfly of his original shape, he pulls out of it and shapes more like a man or a figure of some sort. Natasha plops down on the bed as her mouth opens wide hanging open.

"Is that your spell? The creature?" Quintan exclaims.

I wave my hands. "This is Shade, he is my protector."

Natasha turns to me, her mouth still hanging open but closes it and looks back at him. "I don't think that. That will ever stop amazing me."

"What's a shade?" Quintan breathes. Natasha breathes into her hand and creates ice stars and sits them there waiting to be thrown. "Wait, is that the same thing that was summoned when I had to come in and help with Melissa. I thought that was a spell you created." Quintan looks back and forth between Shade and my foot. "Is it not a spell? You didn't have a tattoo on your foot earlier... Did you?" He pinches the top of his nose, rubbing his eyes.

"Shade isn't a what, he is a who I think," I say as Shade waves a shadow hand. I place a hand on Natasha's arm stopping her from launching the throwing snowflakes at him and starting a fight of some sort.

"My mother ignited a death spell, one that protects me," I say hoping that explains it. "Natasha, why do you like to antagonize him?"

Shade fades out as he walks back into the shadowed areas of the room.

"He started it." She throws one of the snowflakes up before catching it between her fingers.

Quintan turns around looking through the entire room. "Wait, now the tattoo disappeared, where did he go? Was that the death curse that you were talking about from the past memory? Did she use a hollow spirit?" he says in quick succession.

"He just moved into the shadows so you wouldn't attack him. Yes, Jade is the reason why the death curse is in place from that past memory. Hollow spirit? I am not sure what that is." I look to Natasha, hoping she would explain since Quintan didn't seem capable at the moment.

Natasha fiddles with the ice star snowflakes, breaking them as she turns them. "A hollow spirit is something without a soul when it is created, it definitely takes strong magics to create said thing and not indefinitely. It has to be tied to something or someone in order for it to survive. Can you still see it even in the shadows?" She switches to asking me a question.

"I can tell where he is at, yes." I look at her in wonder. "Can you not?"

"No, it seems like only you can perceive him or others most likely could if they were searching hard enough or with a spell. But the tattoo can be seen when it is on your skin, just not perceive its true nature. Interesting," she says in thought.

Quintan stops and stands still sensing beside him with his hand pointed to the shadows where Shade disappeared. "Is this the creature I felt snooping around me the other day?" He gives it the evil eye, and then glares at me since he could not see where Shade went exactly.

I chew on my bottom lip. "About that." I grab one of Natasha's snowflakes to fidget with. "When I am threatened or hurt, he protects me. When we went back into the past he was worried after that event and most likely kept an eye on you. Though he does protect me I don't tell him what to do and how to do things. If he was snooping on you, it was without my knowledge of it but can you blame him."

"And if I was doing something more sinister or would bring harm against you, he would have finished me off?" Quintan explodes.

I hesitate, not sure what would have happened. "Nothing that severe probably, I am guessing he would pay you back the same amount of pain you put me through. Or would have just gotten information and come back to me with it." I shrug. "We are still figuring out our balance."

Quintan still is angry but contemplates as he nods his head. "I can understand that but am still perturbed."

"You must have some magic; I mean what you told me of it mixing with Quintan's to send you back in the past. That means we are halfway there we just need to get you trained up on fighting with it." Natasha hops up and down before she pushes the crumbs of ice to the floor and fully stands up.

"Shade is not my magic though he is a byproduct of my mother's spell but she did tie him to me to keep me safe. Other than that, I have not seen any physical magic come from me. Yes, Quintan said my magic had to mix with his to send us to the past, but do we really know that?" I ask, narrowing my eyes at him in question.

Natasha slouches against the bed. "Okay, strike what I just said from the record then. All we have to go on for sure is that when you're angry you can shift your hands into claws and this shadow dude can come out and protect you if you are hurt." She motions to the shadows. "Is that the gist of things so far?"

Shade comes back out seeing as there isn't a threat at the moment and everyone seems to remain calm.

"Is there a test that I can try or something a beginner can learn to get the hang of magic or see if I can even do it," I ask, unsure of where to go from here. I see both Quintan and Natasha's faces fall. "I can study if that is what it requires."

"That's not really how that works. I mean to know the spells you have to study and know the right ingredients and words, yes, but to actually perform the magic that more has to come from within and your heart and power that you have and being one with yourself as well as understanding your wants and dreams," Quintan corrects.

Natasha quickly adds in, "Perhaps that is why your magic has not fully manifested yet because you don't yet know who or what your true self is, let alone your wants and dreams. How can you be expected to know that without understanding your past and where you came from?"

"Or she could be a defect," Quintan continues. "A void."

Natasha glares in Quintan's direction. "And what she is going to bring about the end of the world as we know it. She is not a void; magic has affected her. Come on you know that much."

Quintan eases my way and just stares; I stare back daring him to say something. He shakes his head and looks away. He coughs and moves away from the conversation. "Maybe she is a defect in another way. We have not seen a void since the beginning of time.

We don't even know what they really were other than the stories we have. Maybe a void has evolved over time, like we all have."

Natasha studies both Quintan and me. "Let's not think of that right now and just focus on what we can do and what we know as of right now." She bustles forward.

"That's your answer to everything isn't it," Quintan bellows. "Just run away from everything and hope it will go away at some point or gives up."

"It's worked so far hasn't it," Natasha yells right back at him.

"This is not about you and your shortcomings; this is about Alexia." He motions toward me.

"Are you going to be teaching me magic, Natasha?" I interrupt before they can get to into their bickering.

Natasha glares at Quintan before turning back to me. "Yeah, I can do that, now that we are out of that horrendous place that Quintan likes to run. We have access to lots of things as well as people."

I rub at the side of my right temple. "Okay, sounds like a game plan. But first, can we please get something so I am not dying over here?"

"Yeah, I thought you might not take that kind of traveling well so I brought this with me." She pulls out a small bottle and shakes out a tiny round disc. "Take one of these, they are powerful so no more than one in a day but they heal aches, pains, and fights anything that ills a person. More powerful than a normal aspirin."

I take the small pill and toss it in and gulp down many mouthfuls from the water.

"We can also work on Shade and his training. Him? It? Her? What did you say it was again?" she mutters to herself confused on how to talk about him.

"He," I say once I have finished the glass of water. "I had the same questions at first." I put her at ease.

Shade moves closer to me to touch me so that I can hear him. "Yes, I want to help," his voice rumbles through my mind.

"What is he doing?" Natasha looks at where his shadow form hovers over my arm.

"He is communicating with me through my mind, but we have to touch in order for me to hear him. The Teager helped us with this ability, remember when she gave me the necklace in the library," I finish before more questions are thrown out. "He wants to help out, which is great because with all the supernatural's that are around here and with what I don't know I am going to need the help." I shoot that part more towards Shade.

"Oh yea! I forgot about that part, I thought it was just a nice bauble and that they liked you."

Quintan walks up and brushes against the shadows. "As long as he sticks to the dark or shadows, then he should not be sensed by others at all. Though he will have to learn to fight from the shadows instead of coming at people forthright," Quintan states.

"Also, creatures like I, who can see other dimensions or planes will be able to see him so he will have to learn stealth," a gruff voice quips at the door.

Looking over we see Zeek standing in the doorway leaning against the frame.

Natasha moves closer to Shade and me. "Are you going to train him? Neither I nor Quintan have any practice in stealth."

"I will not, no."

Natasha's face falls a bit as she bites her lip.

"My brother can, though he is the one that owns this house with his wife."

"You have a brother?" both Natasha and I ask at the same time.

A low rumbling laugh emits past Zeek. "He has many brothers." A guy that is tall, bronzed and has nice short brown hair claps his hand on Zeek's shoulder. "Brothers from many mothers that is. Though we are a brotherhood of sorts." He looks at our group in the room and nods, moving forward past Zeek. "I'm Robert."

"This brotherhood is it like a group of assassins or something? Or are you all death dealers?" I ask.

"Or something," Robert hedges.

"As I stated before I have things to do, I just wanted to make sure to introduce you guys and make sure all came out of the trip all right." His eyes stick on Natasha's for a little longer than the rest of us.

"Thank you Zeek." I look at Natasha. "I can say that right because he isn't Fae?"

She purses her lips but nods that is correct.

He shuffles his shoulders a bit. "No thanks needed; it was a contract is all."

"You guys aren't annoying our guests, are you?" a woman bellows from below.

Zeek nods and turns around leaving the room and walking away.

"No Margret darling, we wouldn't dream of it," Robert calls, smiling. He turns back to our group. "I can start training with Shade and seeing what we can do tonight."

I nod my head and so does Shade. Robert walks out following Zeek. I let my head fall back. "Is it always going to feel like this?"

"Like what?" Natasha asks.

"Like the information is never going to stop gushing at me making me feel like I am drowning." The medicine has already started to work so the ache was fading away quickly. "Speaking of things that are tiring, isn't holding your glamor up exhausting work?"

"Eventually the information will slow to a trickle unless you plan to go outside of our world then most likely not." Natasha answers the first question, her eyes not quite meeting mine. "The other answer you are wanting is complicated, I barely feel the magic I am always using for the glamor any more but it would be nice letting it fade of course but there are many reasons I hold a more human form than just to hide what I truly am."

"It couldn't be you know because your father is who he is and you would be known on sight in your other form or that others may attack you on sight for who your mother is, nope that isn't something that it could be," Quintan adds in.

"We are not in a session and you are not helping me through issues you think I have," Natasha growls.

I walk over to the window as they squabble and notice a little balcony that the window doors open up to. I open it and look outside at what there is to be seen. We are on the second floor and the village is relatively small. I don't see many houses not like a city would have, maybe twenty at most. There are people and animals walking around but none look up. I stay back not wanting to be seen. Trees surround us and are very heavy. I can't see past them.

"Where is my house, or my parents' house?" I take an audible gulp. "My kingdom? Did they have a whole village like this or was it larger?" I whisper.

Quintan hears my questions and comes forward seeing what is out the window with me. "Your parent's kingdom was small, much like this village but it was called a kingdom for they wanted to grow it bigger and make it something to contend with like the light and dark sides. The estate may not look the same as it did in your previous memory of it. Some things have changed while you were away."

"Don't sugar coat shit," Natasha growls. "It has gone to rubble after that night they knew where the main headquarters was located. They burned it to the ground and made sure your family along with anyone else thinking of doing the same was shown what would happen if they even thought of it."

"We have worked on keeping the people together and the movement strong, the place does not matter as long as the thought and fight is there," Quintan states.

"Why are we wasting time here when we should be going to find Blaise?" I urge, searching the top of the tree tops.

"Is that why you are wanting to know where your parent's place is at?" Quintan asks. He looks at me, but I keep my eyes focused on the horizon, searching.

"We have to regroup, we have to get things ready and then we will go in with a plan, if we don't have a plan then he will be dead before we get there," Quintan tries to reason. "Or we will."

"Let's let her get some more rest before we start training, we will start later today." Natasha slinks toward the door.

Quintan hesitates a moment before walking heavily towards the door he waits at the door. "Though he was newer there he was a friend of mine as well."

Though my head does not move I look back out of the corner of my eye. "Do not pretend to feel what I am."

He nods and closes the door both him and Natasha out of the room.

Shade slides over the floor and touches my arm climbing back up on it to settle as a full sleeve down my left arm. "I feel your pain when we are connected," Shade whispers through my mind.

I ignore what he says and ask my own questions. "Will you find the house? Will you find Blaise?"

Shade lifts off my arm creating a small snake like shape pointing at me but still latches around my wrist. "I can try to find him and the house, are you sure you don't want to wait for your team?"

"I am tired of waiting for things to happen to me, it's time for me to do something and attack instead of being attacked."

He nods and slides down my arm. "Consider it done."

Before he fully falls off my arm I call out. "Tell me as soon as you know, then we will start making our own plan."

He slips fully off and slides over the floors and out the window sticking to the shadows, I continue to watch his progress till he gets to the woods the shadows and leaves cover him fully making it so I can no longer see him.

CHAPTER 14

"**I** DIDN'T THINK YOU meant this when you talked about spell training." I huff out a tired breath as I dodge to the left and fall into a roll. Once I fully roll, I land in a crouch on my knees.

Natasha throws another ice bomb at my head. I scramble to the side barely getting out of the way. "What are you going to do if you can't rely on your magic or shifting form for defense?" she asks, powering up an ice dagger this time.

"Well, aren't you and the people you say I have in my corner supposed to help?" I ask, grunting as the knife grazes me, not dodging fully out of the way.

She raises an eyebrow at me; my chest is heaving from exhaustion. She angles her hands down towards the ground, and ice pours out of her finger tips covering the floor. It flows up over my shoes and covers them. I backpedal, trying to get out before it solidifies. Luckily, it breaks and doesn't hold me in place. The ice keeps coming and continues to cover the two holes my feet leave. The ice slides over as my feet continue to leave holes, filling in any gaps.

"Think you're queen? That you have what it takes to lead now? Let's see you lead and how that will work against your enemies."

Natasha waves her arm away from her causing cold bitter ice and wind to hit me in the face.

I cover my head and it throws me off my balance. My legs slide out from underneath me and I tip over slamming down on my side.

Natasha's eyes bleed back to the blue and black starburst eyes that are of her true form. "Pathetic." She quips.

I hiss in a breath and sit up holding my arm, I take my time before getting up once again. "Easy for you to say you have lived in this world your whole life, you were born for this."

She squints her eyes a bit. "You have to take this seriously, and it's not like I asked for this. Trust me my life isn't any better." She puckers her lips in anger.

I wipe the hair that sticks to my neck away even though the temperature dropped, sweat keeps running down my neck and forehead. "I am serious, I just thought I am supposed to be learning, you know, some spells. Try to train, not just dodge any and everything you throw at me."

Natasha throws her hands up in the air causing another swirling cold wind to take place up above us in the small enclosed space we are using. Large pointy icicles dangle up above us. "Trust me I know from experience people don't just take it easy on you because of who birthed or raised you. You said anger or sexual attraction is what pulls out the shifting. I am trying to pull out more." She waves her hand in the air and yanks it to her body.

My head comes up just in time to be hit in the face by a small icicle. I look back at Natasha, shock written across my face.

"That was a warning shot, next one you will either bleed or you won't." She shrugs as she waves her hand upward again. I notice another larger pointier icicle right above me starting to wobble.

The ice is still very slippery, and I struggle getting to my knees. I look up and see she has yanked her hand back to her. I roll away as I feel the cold air move behind me. I stay low to the ground crawling and dashing around the icicles that fall. Natasha's focus is on the ceiling, as she continues to yank the ice to the ground as well as creating new ones in case I move backwards. I circle her trying to calculate, my anger is rising as I am growing weary and tired. She notices me getting closer and closer to her so she drops them in faster succession keeping up with me easily.

"I can't," I utter as one tags my shoulder and brings me fully down spinning closer to her. I lie there breathing heavily on my stomach. I feel ice fall down around me but it doesn't connect though it does come close.

"Get up," she yells.

I shake my head.

She lowers her voice. "Get up."

"Do what you want, but I am not going to be a part of it. This is not the way to get me to learn." I raise my head and look her dead in the eyes. "If the people that could get me to trigger these things couldn't get me to keep doing it, how do you think you will?" I ask in a serious tone daring her to continue.

She stares right back at me for a moment then nods. "You will be good for us if you can survive this." She wipes the snowflakes away from her cheeks that flow like beautiful tears down her face.

I nod back and lay my head back down on my arms. "Do you have something else that I can try now to learn a spell?" I glance up. "Can't say I won't miss your snowball throwing."

Natasha eyes me and gives me a once over. "Fine, it won't hurt to try it your way. I mean, whatever gets it working right." She nudges my arm with her shoe. Come on." She skates and slides over to the door. She has to lean into the door to push it open so the ice can break away.

I roll my head against my arms and contemplate just lying here but the cold is starting to seep into my bones and the heat is escaping and cooling down quickly. I get my feet under me and slowly make my way toward the door that is left open. Natasha has turned left and down the hallway not waiting for me.

"I brought these down," she calls loudly behind her knowing I was still making my way to her. "I knew we would eventually get to these or worse thing I could do is throw them at you." I peek around the door and see large books stacked on a small table, three of them.

I grip the side of the door. "Would you even be able to throw it very far?"

"Curiosity killed the cat," she answers.

"Good thing I'm a badger."

"Now before you get your mind reeling these are only the beginning tomes most witches learn these before they hit puberty." She thumps one of the hard covers

"All of this?" I motion with my arm; it shakes as I drop it back down quickly. I open one of the large books that if compared to my torso would be as long. I thumb through the pages noticing the pages are thin. "Do they just have to know everything in these, master it all?" They couldn't not when so young that takes longer, had to.

"Master it," she answers. "Most are raised knowing the basics, the rest comes naturally to most." She shrugs as she looks down at the stack again. "Also, in this world we age a bit slower than in the human realm so there is plenty of time."

I move around the large books haphazardly. "But I have only been in this world for a couple of days." I say in defense.

"You said you were a quick study though," she throws back at me. Her fingers caress the tomes lovingly as she plucks one from the many stacks. "We will start with a defensive spell which is located in this book." She plops the book down into my arms and slides back the other stacks of books. "And... this one." She stacks another book on the previous one. Both of them are very different from one another. One is tiny and dainty compared to the ginormous monster of a book underneath it.

I pick up the small dainty one first.

"Of course, you would go for the smaller one first. That one is to learn about the essence of where your magic is derived from and how you are supposed to use it. Blah, blah, blah. Total snooze fest if you ask me. But everyone needs to know the basics so that when they get into the more difficult spells you know the why's and what's of the spell. So, you don't inadvertently blow yourself up or something to that effect."

I leave the giant book behind and walk down the hallway to the kitchen. I see another table there and pull out the chair to sit down. There are knives and other smaller weapons covering half of the table. I sit down on the other half, not wanting to mess with anything they were in the middle of doing. My fingers itch to pick up one of the throwing daggers. "When do we get to play with these?" I ask pointing to the weapons.

She looks at the book in my hands and then back at me.

I sigh and flip through the beginner's book, seeing how tiny the writing is for such a small book. I groan as I become discouraged, I flip through the thin pages trying to find hope written there within. "No pictures, no diagrams. Nothing but small tinkerbell writing."

Natasha shakes her head at me. "'Fraid not. Most spells you have to create and have a strict dedication and have your soul focus on that alone. Which usually requires preparation and has many variables that you need to take into account. The one I want you to learn is in there and it takes little to no preparation or work so you won't mess it up but it will be harder since you haven't really shown us that your powers have awakened yet." She comes around behind me and helps me flip to the page she is wanting me to see in the book. "Here it is." She points to the page in question. "It is a barrier that I want you to learn how to use so that it can protect you and others who need it. If you become strong enough, we can move on from there and you will be able to protect not only yourself."

"Come on," I call. "I can do more than a barrier," I urge.

"Without Shade's help?" She gives me a pointed look as she moves back around the table towards the weapons. "It didn't seem like you could when you were dodging snowballs and ice?" She picks up one of the daggers and caresses it against her skin.

I grumble to myself and flip a couple of pages to the beginning to settle in to see what it is I have to learn.

"I know it is grueling to wait and be patient for you to learn but for now I just want you to learn how to place the barrier around yourself. If you can do that at least it means that you have magic that you can tap into. The larger tome gets more into defensive and offensive magics. This beginner book will help see if you're an elemental or have better luck with a certain element." She pauses and then puts down the dagger before turning to leave. "Happy reading."

I nod and set into reading through this tiny book.

"Where did Shade go? Is he around?" Natasha stops down the hallway near the books.

I shrug, but as I look up, I see she is facing away from me. "He's around here somewhere, probably scoping out the place. He will be back later to fight with what's his name." I flit my hand in the air.

"Robert, right." Natasha fiddles with the books stacking them in an order that she thought they needed to be read in. "I was hoping he was around to see what kind of power he has."

I bite my lip not wanting to give away where he actually was. "He will be back soon hopefully; I will send him to come find you once I see him."

She nods and walks around the corner back to where we came from, out of sight. I sigh to myself and try to concentrate on the words in front of me. Trying not to feel too bad about keeping things from Natasha. She was the most honest person with me but I have learned especially over the last couple of days that a person needs to keep something to themselves otherwise, others like to take advantage of the situation. They wouldn't let me go find Blaise, they didn't understand, it's not like they have a possible mate on the line. I scratch at the back of my hand in nervousness, a red mark appearing.

I read the first page aloud. "First things first there are four main elements. It is best to know what elements will help you and which ones are the best to call on for your person. The best way to do this is to get items from each element and concentrate on them to see which one calls to your soul, your magic." I search the kitchen and find a plant. I take a small leaf off the plant and set it on the table. I grab a glass of water and set it next to the leaf, taking a small drink before grabbing an already lit candle that was sitting on the counter. I look around for something that could represent air.

"Air is all around us. I think that will be good enough." I shrug and just stick with the three I have on the table already.

I puff out a tired breath and stare longingly at the three elements in front of me. The fire catches my eyes as I gaze into the fiery depths of the candle. I watch the little flame dance back and forth as I puff out air in front of it. I stare at the center of the fire where it burns the hottest and where it is most solid. I lay my head on my arms that rests in front of the old tiny book and just stare at the dancing light.

My eyes continue to gaze determinedly at the candle, as everything else seems to vanish from view, white noise replaces the rumble of conversation elsewhere in the house. The heat from the fire embraces me, warming my cold center. It flicks back and forth at me as if it calls me forward, wanting me to come closer as if to tell me a secret.

"We want to play." Tiny high-pitched voices call out from the flame. My vision begins to blur and multiple flames kick off from the main one.

"What?" I ask groggily and rub my eyes, trying to clear them. The multiple flames do not dissipate as I try to clear my vision. "How does fire play?"

One flame jumps excitedly around, I keep my eye on it and it begins to move around more as I continue to pay attention to it. "We like to play! Very much!" It screeches and swirls around the wick wanting to find something else to find purchase on, it jumps over the water glass and lands on the leaf the fire making it light for a moment before it crumbles to ash.

Little burn dots dance around on the table cloth as the flame makes its way back to the candle. I smudge out the burn spots on the cloth not wanting it to catch on fire. "How would you play without burning everything down?" I ask roughly, not wanting to be the cause of burning down Robert's house after they have helped us.

Another flame breaks off from the main light and splashes in the wet candle wax kicking it this way and that. "We good... Unless we bad." She sing songs with the same high-pitched voice as the other one.

I scrunch my face up. "Well, I can only play if we don't burn down this house because it's kind of not mine you know?"

A last taller light breaks off from the main candle making it very small. "We will be good. You will see."

"Are there only the three of you?" I ask, seeing the one still playing in the wax making it dry in different shapes and then melting it once again. The smallest flame skates around the edge of the candle glass and the third one the tallest comes closer to me peering at me.

"Yes, we are three sisters. Made of pure fire." She rubs her flaming hands together. Their forms begin to take a more solid shape as they step away from the flame itself though they still keep the fire surrounding them.

"Can you take on a more human form? Not on fire I mean."

The tallest looks up at me. "When we get older mama said we could."

I smile down at the three as they all look up when the tallest one says "mama"

"Oh, that is nice. Where is your mother, is she here somewhere?"

The little one's light snuffs out all of a sudden and each are black and dark, a high-pitched screaming begins and then sobbing and crying. I look at the three little ones and they are all in a state of duress. The candle itself also burns out and a line of smoke sways away.

"Oh no. What is going on here?" I look up to see a woman bustling in

Her voice is similiar to earlier. "Margaret?"

"Yes that's me."

I give a sheepish look as girls continue to cry. "Do you see three little flame girls?" I catch myself asking just in case.

Margaret shakes her head. "Well not anymore." She walks over to the counter and grabs a match and strikes it against the side of the box. She lights the candle once again and touches the fire to each girl's head. "It will be all right. What happened?" Margaret frowns at me and gives a fierce look.

The smallest light was sitting on the edge of the glass kicking her feet. "Trill brought up mama." She sniffles her light flickering as she wipes at her face.

Trill jumps down onto my hand. Her heat warms me but does not burn as she hops down hiding behind my arms that are piled in front of me.

"Oh, that's okay," Margaret soothes. "The best way to remember someone who is no longer with us is to talk about them."

"But it makes me sad." The littlest squeak comes out, and her light smothers out.

"You will be sad for a time but eventually it won't hurt so much and as you grow you will want to remember more since it happened when you were so young."

Trill nudges my hand and sinks in there seeming to disappear. "Whoa, what happened?" I scoot myself back. I push my chair away and look around, searching for the tallest light. "Where did she go?"

The middle one that was playing in candle wax jumps over the edge of the glass and plops down sending wet wax all around her. "Are you sure Trill? Mama said to trust Margaret?" She looks back at Margaret, still consoling the smallest flame who is having a hard time staying lit.

Unlike her sister she had no such issue, her fire was hot and bright. She stomps her small foot on the table and the cloth starts to burn below her. "Place your hand face up here," she demands.

I place my hand down slowly, unsure of what to expect. I brace myself, expecting to feel white hot pain as she steps on my hand. Though she is hotter than her sister, her heat does not sear me as I expect, she melts into my palm and the liquid wax puddles in the middle of my hand as she disappears.

I stare at my palm and ask. "Where are you guys going?"

"They have chosen you." She looks down at the smallest one. "Your sisters have decided where they are wanting to stay, are you going to go with them?"

"No, I don't wanna," she huffs out.

"But wouldn't it be more fun with Alexia and your sisters?" Margaret smiles at me.

"Who wait, what does that mean for me? Don't I get a say in this?"

Margaret laughs out loud. "Nope... True elementals choose their owners much like a cat does. You are bestowed with their gift regardless if you wanted or asked for them."

"Sisters are mean, I don't like them anymore." She pouts and runs back to the flame of the candle dancing in the middle.

"Okay well you know you can stay with me but you will be all alone, and they will go on many adventures without you."

"They do that already," she puffs her chest out.

Both of my arms are warmed by where they touched but both stay where they are not wanting to come out. I felt their heat travel around as they grow used to their new place.

I catch a shadow to the right and notice Shade has squirmed his way under the door. He sits there behind Margaret, waiting for her to move and leave. Like me he was wary of who to trust in this world.

"Oh, I don't know about that, but you know you are welcome here for as long as you want." She nods but busies herself. "And if you do choose to go elsewhere, always know you can come and visit if needed." She walks over to me and looks down one last time. "Please take care of them. Zeek said you were good but I don't know you like that." She stares for a moment more.

I am unsure what I can offer her. I don't know her either. "I will do my best," I say hugging my hands around my middle.

She stares into my eyes and finally nods as if she reads something there. She continues on down the hallway towards where Natasha went.

I wait till she has turned the corner and wait a little longer before I know she is out of hearing distance. I look down under the chair into the deepest shadows. "What did you find?"

Shade morphs into a shadow butterfly, his favorite form as of lately and flutters over the table. He flies near the candle which causes the tiniest flame to come out of the fire once more.

"Pweety." She dances to the side of the glass once again.

Shade flutters just out of reach but goes in a circle for her to chase.

"Fun, fun." The flame chants and dances.

Shade flies up and dives down fluttering against my cheek. As he touches his mind melds with mind and once again, I can hear him. "This world has some interesting creatures." He laughs.

"He belongs to you?" She cocks her head as she stares at the butterfly shadow on my cheek.

"I wouldn't say belong, but he was gifted to me and helps me," I say honestly.

"Do you have fun?" Her voice wavers.

I caress Shade on my cheek. "To be honest no we don't have much fun."

"Oh." She wilts, sad about that answer.

"Perhaps, we need someone to show us how to have more fun." I say encouragingly.

She slides down the side of the glass and takes a hesitant step forward. "I'm fun."

"I've seen." I nod.

"I wanna travel with the shadow." She points to my cheek where he is resting.

"Shade is that okay."

He flutters down my neck and rests over my heart on my upper chest. The tips of his wings can be seen peeking out of the top of my shirt. "It won't hurt you?" Shade asks.

"No, her two sisters are already here with us. Do you not feel them?"

"Not yet, but I have not been here long yet," Shade comments. "Yes, she can hitch a ride with me as long as she doesn't cause you pain."

I nod. "Shade states that he is okay with it and just asks that you not cause me pain." I reiterate his wishes.

"Fun." She squeals as she jumps up and down, I lower my chest so she can reach and touch Shades wing she dissolves into my skin much like her sisters did.

Shade hums in pleasure. "That feels nice."

"Kind of toasty right?" I agree with him. "So did you find anything?" I hurry forward wanting to know what he found out.

"I think I found the place up north that was your parents' home. If you stay straight from here headed north you almost run right into it. Of course, there are guards and traps here and there but other than that it seems very dead the place is in ruins."

"So, you didn't see Blaise? But you said there were guards."

"It must be spelled to where I can't even get into where he was being held, I did hear talk about Tom though."

"I still can't believe he is actually alive. That he made it out."

"That time is hazy for me as well."

"So, no talks of Blaise or sightings?"

"Again, I did search but there were spelled areas I couldn't get into and I didn't want to take too long or get caught."

"I will go tonight then and see what I can find out."

His thoughts turn quiet. "Are you going to ask Natasha and Quintan for help?"

I shake my head. "Quintan wouldn't want me to go and Natasha, though she seems down for a good fight, is better at running away. They have both blocked me when I brought it up before."

"She may surprise you and she has helped us so far."

I bite my lip but shake my head solidifying my answer. "Natasha was looking for you earlier, by the way."

"Why?" His voice wavers.

"I think she wanted to see what kind of fight you have since apparently I am just a moving target." I roll my eyes as I scan the pages of the book.

"I can go by myself if you want to continue reading." He moves over to my arm taking the warmth with him. "You do need to trust some of these people though, not all are out to get you."

I thump my fingers against the side of my arm, bumping up against him. "I know, I know. They need to stop hiding things from me and get on board regardless if I have powers or not. I have survived this long haven't I."

"Have you?" Shade comments softly.

"Whose side are you on?" I stand up and grab the tiny book from the table. "Let's go find Natasha and have her knock some sense into you."

"She can try." Shade chuckles.

"Natasha?" I round the hallway and go down to the room that we were practicing in. I find Natasha there among the Icelandic wonderland she had created. "I found Shade," I call.

Natasha turns around and notices us coming into her wintery mixture. "You did?"

Shade pulls off of me and elongates into a shadow humanoid form. The warmth from where he had touched my skin disappears and I know the little flame has gone with him.

Natasha's eyes light up with mischief as she lets ice fall from her fingertips. She throws a blast at his legs and catches him there off guard, freezing him in place.

"Wait, aren't you supposed to train him, not turn him into an ice sculpture?" I cringe as Shade elongates his form further making his darkness stretch and thin out.

"The whole point is to put Shade into situations that he has never dealt with before; he is as much of a newborn to this world as you are."

"Yes, but where I have been made to forget who and what I was throughout my life he has not, I think you will find him more of a challenge," I say coolly, not liking that they think we are weak.

"He is used to humans not magic and not having to deal with the creatures that have been honing their skills since they were young." She closes her fist the ice encompassing more of his form and gripping on to him so he can't escape. "Has he ever had to defend against magic or fight against it before, that you can recall?" Her voice turns soft, keeping it more of a light question.

On Shades back a small red flame flows down into his leg that is stuck and holds there glowing in light. The flame keeps to the back hidden from Natasha, but the ice starts to melt and Shade wiggles out of the ice that continues to climb. Shade moves down into the ground hiding amongst the shadows.

Natasha turns around and smiles to herself. "Well done," she calls.

I back up and lean against the wall watching how this will play out. I notice Shade move into Natasha's shadow that casts behind her. He pulls off of the ground, catching her ankles and making her trip backwards. He pulls up his form, taking on hers.

There is now a Natasha and a shadow Natasha.

"You two have fun!" I call as I pull open the book that I did not forget in the kitchen. I keep an eye on them as they continue to fight.

After several pages I yawn and look up from the midpoint of the book. "I will say this is no thriller," I mention. I notice Shade is almost in a puddle like substance. "What did you do to him?" I throw the book down and walk over to Shade. Natasha is down in the snow as well puffing out hard breaths of air into the cold room. Her human features are gone and her Fae features have taken over.

I kneel down beside the black puddle and run my hands through the black water. Though it is warm to the touch, I know the fire burns there somewhere. A silent rough voice enters my mind as my fingers run through the black liquid. "If I were actually alive, she might have killed me twice by now. Were you not watching?" At the end, his voice tapers off and is more of a whisper.

"Don't be hurt, I was trying to focus on learning something from that book." I motion to where I dropped the book into the ice and snow. "You know if you were actually in pain or fighting, I would be there for you just like you are for me." I look over at Natasha who hasn't moved or stopped breathing heavily. "Maybe you guys need to chill out and take a break."

Natasha laughs out and grabs her sides. "Chill out, nice one."

I shake my head and chuckle with her.

"Sure, just leave me here to die!" Shade whispers through our mind link dramatically.

Natasha gathers snow into her hand and throws it on top of Shade. "He's complaining, isn't he? Blubbering like a little baby." She rolls over on her stomach and her ice-like wings start to flutter to pull her up into the air. "Typical, I meet a decent fighter and they are a pansy."

I give him a look as I quirk up my eyebrow. "You going to prove her right by just sitting there or are you going to do something about it."

"That's not what you said to Zeek when he tried to fight you. Better yet I think you ran away when he asked if you wanted to spar," Robert says from the doorway. "Also how dare you tire out the person I was going to train with tonight."

Natasha sputters, her wings slow down as she is lowered back onto her feet touching the cool ground. "I didn't want to fight Zeek. I don't even know him really. Plus, it's good to know where we are with both of these as a baseline before we start training too heavily." She covers.

As Robert gives Natasha a look, Shade taps my foot as he pulls himself together and slides up on my shoe. He pulls himself up but just barely and motions me to bend down. I extend my arm down to him, allowing him to crawl up my arm and swirl around it finally coming to rest on my bicep in a tribal pattern that just looks like a bunch of swirls. "Too tired to even form your normal intricate tattoos." I say out loud and right after a yawn catches me unaware.

Robert knocks on the side of the doorway. "Perhaps we should pick this up again tomorrow instead. It was a pretty rough day with all sorts of new experiences."

I rub sleepily at my eyes and nod along with what he was saying.

Robert looks over to Natasha. "Zeek will be back later tonight if you still want to school someone on fighting."

She stomps her foot and growls. "As if, I will most likely be busy with Quintan. He wants to run some things by me." She pulls her human covering back to her so her wings and other things are hidden. "It will be a late night for us, if we are to help Alexia with getting Blaise free." She rushes past calling out behind her. "He should be in the study next to his room, correct?"

"Yes," he grumbles. "I will send Zeek up to see if you need any help when he gets here." Natasha doesn't say anything else.

"You can't push her towards her destiny any faster than what she is going to do." I eye him.

"She does have a way of running away from things." Robert states.

"I haven't known her for long, and yeah, there probably are some things that she can work on, shit who doesn't? But I don't blame her for not wanting to deal with certain things yet."

"She has been in this war a lot longer than you have, along with all of us and she needs to start facing the music. I can easily understand, with everything you and she have going on, but life even for long lived beings can be short when you are unhappy." He looks down the hallway to the kitchen. "Trust me I know."

"Are you and Margaret soul mates?" I ask.

"What do you know of soul mates?" Robert looks down his nose at me.

"Just what I have read, and Blaise, who I want to go rescue, said we might be soul mates."

"Soul mates is not everything it is cracked up to be, at least not for everyone. No Margaret and I are not soul mates, we work hard to keep our relationship in working order," Robert bites out.

I take a step back and rub at my arm where Shade lies. "Oh, it sounded romantic, and—"

"Of course, the book will make it sound romantic, and they want everyone to find their perfect match. Problem is that the book doesn't take into account how we as people work. It doesn't take into account who or what you are born into. Don't be so naïve, read more than one book someone gives you, find out for yourself." He takes a step forward. "Tell me about this soul mate."

"Blaise?"

"Yeah, they said he was a snake charmer, correct."

I hedge back once again as he advances. "Yes."

"Do you know what a snake charmer is? What they do?"

"He transforms into a snake." I whisper out unsure of my answer. "And can charm..."

He lets his head fall forward and chuckles. "Why do you think Blaise is telling you the truth about you being soul mates?"

I lick my lips and eye the door, not wanting to be here anymore. "I—he—we," I stutter out.

"Tell me what happened, what you went through." He walks back giving me some room but shuts the door keeping us both in the ice fortress.

I feel a drip on my arm and look up seeing the ice starting to melt with Natasha no longer able to keep up the coldness in the room. "Well, I was going to go to bed and rest but I guess we can do this instead. Why do you care?"

"Margaret told me who you now carry with you, I want to make sure they are going to be well taken care of wherever they go. Zeek and Natasha have their own thing that they will work out or they won't." He shrugs. "But I usually do not look kindly toward soul mates, I have heard too many and been a part of too many bad ones to know better. Just color me intrigued to say the least. Or think of me as a concerned father, with the children you will be taking care of."

I cross my arms in front of my chest not wanting to talk on this subject with someone I don't know very well.

"The sooner we go over this the sooner you can get away from me." He smirks, crossing his arms in front of his chest as well.

I turn away not wanting to look at him while I go over this. "My anger got out of hand those first few days. It didn't seem like there was anyone that was in charge that I could trust and then Blaise came in and tried to calm me down, everything seemed to piss me off that he did."

He chuckles. "I'm not surprised. Badgers and snakes usually don't get along."

"But we are people, not just animals."

"Tell that to some that don't even have animals locked up inside them," he booms.

I look over my shoulder and stare at him. "This is not funny."

He coughs into his hand and motions with his hand to continue.

I let out a loud exhale. "I don't know just something happened after he pinned me something changed where either I was going to kill him or fuck him," I throw out harshly.

He nods and slides away from the door kicking one of the melting ice piles. I turn to watch him as he moves keeping him in my sights, I give a look of longing at the door but move away from it as we delve deeper into the room.

"I didn't want to kill or harm anybody so I chose the option I was left with. He didn't push me towards that or anything, it didn't seem like it. It all happened really fast."

"Did you ever think that he was there to seduce you?"

I growl out.

He holds his hands up and backs away from the fallen ice sculpture he just kicked down. "I just want to make sure you see a full picture and have thought of all the possibilities, because the truth of the matter no one knows really who Blaise is or who he may work for. He was there for a reason, put there by the dark side, him and Melissa."

"But then why the sudden pull, there isn't anything that appears like a mark until both of us accept one another whatever that means." I kick snow, covering the ice sculpture he knocked down.

"Yeah, that is the bad thing about this soulmate business you don't know for sure you just hope kind of like with real love. They say there is a pull you can't escape and a tie that binds you metaphysically as well as with animals a pull to claim the other."

"Yeah, I had all that I bit him while we were." My cheeks heat up and I turn from him once again. "Yeah, and I had a dream that felt so real and that is how I found out they have him captured."

"Wait." He stops and stomps toward me.

"You are following a dream that you had with Blaise?" He stops in front of me staring down at me.

I look up and search his gaze. "Yes, another interrupted the dream, Tom is who took him."

"He is known to be a powerful mage and can bend realities." He searches around us and massages his temples with his fingers. "Blaise might not even be there; he could have made up that whole dream sequence."

"I know he is there," I whisper out between clenched teeth. "It was Blaise, no one else."

"Oh, is that so?" he asks.

I back pedal and move away from Robert closer to the door making my way out of the room. "I just feel it. The book I read today said to trust in that intuition when you are a witch it may lead to some valuable insights."

"Yes, but it also takes years of honing that kind of power to actually be right and something come from it." I hear his boots follow mine as he moves after me.

I don't turn back as I reach for the door knob wanting this over, he was trying to talk me out of saving him trying to talk me out of I don't know what. "You already said you don't like soul mates so I can't talk you into understanding it."

His hand comes down on my shoulder stopping me in my tracks before I can open the door. "Alexia," he says calmly.

I stop and wait for him to say more.

"I just want you to know what you are going up against and be prepared for the worst if needed."

I inhale a breath about to yell at him.

"I won't stop you," he says quietly.

The air comes out of me in a rush and I look back over my left shoulder where his hand is still resting.

"I won't stop you, but I want to prepare you for the possibilities and give you every fighting chance. I can follow behind and make sure you don't get into trouble."

"Natasha and Quintan?" I ask.

"We can go just us two and at least see what we can find out?"

I nod slightly. "Deal."

He nods and we continue out of the room to go change. "Meet me at the back of the house outside in about an hour." Robert whispers to me before I round the corner going up to my room.

CHAPTER 15

A S BOTH ROBERT AND I exit through the back of the house we find a path to the right that leads to a stable. I stop next to Robert. "Where we headed to?"

"First we head there." He points to the stable in front of us.

"Do we need horses? I didn't know it was that far away." I look into the woods that are nearby.

"Why did you think it was not? If you walk it would be a full day going there and back, but if we go by horse, it should only take a couple of hours max." He gives a solemn look at me.

I rub the back of my neck. "I had Shade check it out and he wasn't gone long or what seemed very long." I think about what I was doing while he was gone and it could have been longer than I initially thought.

"He wouldn't have to be very careful making his way there; only when he got there would he have to make sure he was not spotted. We will have to be and take care not to attract attention. Plus, I think your little guy travels faster than horses somehow," Robert says.

We make our way to the stable, I hear neighing inside. "What gave me away?" He stops and eyes me carefully. "How did you know I wasn't going to stay put."

"You mentioned it once or twice and your face did not like that no one was listening to your wants or needs." His long legs cover more ground faster than my shorter ones.

I try to walk faster to keep up with him and not be left behind. "My face gave me away?" I touch my hand to my cheek and wonder what else I inadvertently gave away.

Robert smiles as he opens the large door to the stables. "That and Zeek warned me to keep an eye on you."

I roll my eyes and duck inside before he closes it on me and leaves me behind. I grin as I see and hear many horses down a long row, some have their heads peeking out others are deep in their stalls. "Are all of these yours?" I quickly walk up to one and see a horse munching on hay in the back. I walk to the next one where a head is poking out.

"Easy, easy." Robert follows me and backs me away from a midnight black horse that I was about to go up to and pet. "No these are not all mine; they belong collectively to the town. That one there is a biter." He nods, patting my fingers and making sure I keep them to myself.

I glance back at the black stallion; he gives me a snort and eyes Robert giving him the evil eye.

"I bet he is cursing you up a storm that you didn't let him have his fun."

Robert laughs. "He for sure is." He pats the midnight coat. "I'll come back for you in a moment, boy."

I give a surprised look. "He's yours."

"About the only one that can handle him nowadays, he doesn't get along with many in his older age." The horse in question neighs loudly and knocks against his door with his hooves.

I back away further from the horse and another's muzzle comes down over my shoulder. I shriek and dodge away, not expecting another horse to be right behind me. "She, on the other hand, is very gentle." Robert comes up and pats the brown head that had come over my shoulder. "This one is my wife's and is good for anyone that has never ridden or doesn't have much experience."

"That is the speed I am looking for." I spin around to the brown horse and reach my fingers out slowly.

"There you go." He guides my hand on top of her nose and lets me pet her there. He pats the side of her neck so I move my hand up and my other hand to the side of her neck like he did.

"She is completely opposite of the other one." My fingers touch the top of her main which is black. "What's her name?" I ask.

Her name is Gem. She is a Morgan. My wife has had her since she was a little pony. Has also had to deal with that brute over there." He points back at the black horse.

"Do they get along, also what is his name?" I look back but end up moving closer to Gem as the other one knocks into his stall some more upset that we are not paying attention to him.

"That one we got him wild and so he has only allowed very few to ride him, I being one of them. They almost put him down because of it, so for that we call him Lucky."

I hide behind Gem and let out a small giggle. "How original."

"Yeah, that is what my wife said also but what else could I have named him. He better be glad I didn't just name him stubborn." He opens Gem's gate and walks her out getting her ready to be rode.

"You will go easy on me, won't you?" I whisper to the horse. It neighs and rests her head on my shoulder as if answering my question.

Robert finishes up getting her ready, he then moves over to Lucky's stall and hollers out. "All right, all right. We are not leaving you out of any adventuring." He slides open the door, and before it is even fully open, Lucky is banging forward. "Hey, stop that," Robert calls, trying to grab for the reins.

I ease behind Gem as Lucky comes forward. Gem doesn't move but swishes her tail in answer. Lucky tries to bite at my fingers that are still petting Gem. Robert grabs the reins and pulls on them hard, moving Lucky back away from Gem. "You stop that right now." Robert shakes a finger at him. Lucky tries to bite that finger. "Don't be jealous she tried to give you pets but you know you wouldn't let her get to you before biting them off." The horse neighs and turns his head away from Robert not wanting to hear it.

I watch as Robert readies Lucky and he starts to calm down and not dash for Gem and I any more. Once Lucky is ready Robert kicks his leg up into the stirrup and grabs the front and back of the saddle pulling himself up into the saddle.

I look at Gem and then back at Robert trying to figure out the logistics. "You sure made that look easy, long legs would be helpful right about now." I grumble to myself.

"Okay if you are getting up on that side you want to kick your left foot into the stirrup," he calls, waiting with Lucky a little in front of us.

I kick up my foot and get it into the stirrup, but I lean too far back and am holding onto the edge of the back part of the saddle. "This does not feel right." I laugh. I try to bend my knee closer to myself, I hop closer to the middle and can just reach the front I grab it.

"Great," Robert calls. "Now kick off with the other foot and lift yourself up and into the saddle."

I kick off the ground and pull myself up. I lean my stomach on the middle part of the saddle resting there. Gem moves a bit trying to get used to me. I hold on for dear life. "Okay, now what?"

Robert backs Lucky up a bit so he is closer to me and steadies Gem. "Okay, swing that leg over here, and sit in the saddle."

I kick it over and barely clear the back of the saddle, I sit down fully in the saddle. One foot not getting in the stirrup, but I sit there. My arms are shaking. I let out a breath I was holding onto. "Man, that is a lot tougher than it looked."

"It is not easy, especially if you have never done it before. Go ahead and put that in here." He bends down and helps me get my foot into the stirrup fully.

I sway my foot in the stirrup and wiggle in place to get better seated.

"Okay and to move forward you just nudge with your foot lightly to press them forward."

I tap very lightly and she starts to move forward. I hold on to the front of the saddle with the reins and grip them for dear life. I make sure to keep her going forward and not run into anything on the sides. "Come on, I don't know where I'm going."

"You're fine. Keep going, we need to get going anyway, before they get suspicious and try to come out here and stop us." He trots up beside me once we get out of the building. He pulls his stallion to the left, heading into the woods.

I ease up and do the same. He trots ahead easily so I can watch what he does. I notice him set the reins to the side and just keep a loose hold on them as the horse moves forward.

My body settles after a minute into the rhythm, eventually moving back and forward as Gem takes steps. The unevenness of the ground makes me go further to either side.

"Let me know if it becomes too much for you like I said it should only take a couple of hours or so and you shouldn't feel the soreness right away but you may find some tightness over the next few days." It is full night now, the pale moon illuminating our way forward.

At first there was a path that we followed that was well traveled, but as we continue, we diverge from the path and this terrain is a bit more rugged, and the canopy of the trees hides the bright moon from sight.

I growl in frustration once more as leaves hit me in the face. I wave my hands around my face feeling a sticky web cling to me as we duck under low hanging branches.

"You did that on purpose!" I throw back at him.

He chuckles and moves through the underbrush and gently lowers the prickly thorns back, covering the trail. "I didn't see the web, grab something to knock around before you go through or hunch low on the horse's back," he says in answer.

"Or you could, you know, warn a person." I wipe at my arms once more feeling as there is still something on me.

"I thought it was warning enough that you were in the woods." He purses his lips trotting ahead.

I bite the inside of my cheek, biting back an answer, knowing he didn't have to be out here with me but appreciated it nonetheless.

I urge Gem to keep up, but not to close. "Thank you." I hesitate before continuing. "For opening up your home and doing this." I keep quiet, leaving it at that if he didn't want to talk.

A loud hoot echoes in the trees up above us, the crunching noises the horses make as we step and disturb the silent night. I hear a trickle of water up ahead. I sit up in my seat and push up on the stirrups seeing a little stream come up in front of us. It isn't deep, not even enough water to cover the bottom of the rock bed properly. Robert urges his horse to the right and just walks along the side. I stop to look over the side and see how much of a steep descent it is down to the water.

"It's too steep and the rocks might throw the horses off balance. We will follow up this way. It gets shallower and the rocks are not as jagged and the water covers more fully," he says in answer as he notices me still staying behind checking out the ravine.

I push in with my feet to get Gem moving again. The greenery around us was such a deep dark green. Everything felt so light and full of life. "It's hard to believe that there is something evil lurking in these woods," I say.

The heat from the day starts to cool off as the night grows deeper and darker. The moon is further overhead than when we first started. I could see pokes of light still streaming through even though the woods were very deep and fully covered here.

"Careful!" Robert hisses, jumping down from his stallion strolling over to me quickly.

Gem shutters away from some bushes while I was not paying attention. Robert grabs onto the reins and leads her over to where Lucky stands. "What, she basically steers herself."

My head swishes around searching to see what has got him so worried.

He waves his hand as if saying to lower my voice. "Quiet we are close to your lost kingdom." He nods towards a steep hill. "Just over that and then back down the other side is your parents' place. On the other side is a deep riverside, but I didn't think after horseback riding your first time, that you would also want to try rock climbing."

"Yeah, no thank you." I shake my head, looking up the hill seeing as it wasn't that bad, not like a mountain or anything like that.

"As we move forward you are going to have to be more careful and pay attention to where you step and what is in front of you. The dark canopy keeps out a lot of the light, but as long as you step and move where I do, we shouldn't run into any traps."

"Traps!" I exclaim.

"Of course, there will be traps along with people who patrol the woods, but I hope to stay out of their sight and range. If they are keeping anyone out here then of course there are people making sure that they are left alone."

Robert ties the reins up on the saddles so they don't droop down and aren't able to catch on anything.

"Aren't you going to tie them to anything so they don't run off." I lower my voice so we are harder to hear for anyone that may be trying to listen.

"If they need to run, then I need to give them the option to get away safely. Because anything they are running away from, we should be running as well. They will stay if they can but they know the way back home if needed."

I whisper under my breath harshly. "But we will be stranded."

Robert turns around his back ramrod straight. "Listen princess, most things in life are hard, the faster you realize it the better off you will be. Would you rather the horses stay here and die if something was wanting to cause them harm?"

"Well, no, but what if we are hurt or need a quick getaway," I whisper just as lowly as he does.

"Then we will have to just figure something else out at that time, though I am going to try to avoid having a run in with anyone we come across."

"Fine, let's go."

"Here I will lead, I have animal eyes that can easily see traps that are laid out. Zeek said you had an animal to call. Can you call up just your eyes without fully turning?"

I shake my head in answer but don't provide any more than that.

"Remember to follow my footing and the way I move exactly," he reiterates, not continuing on with the line of questioning.

"Yes, I will remember." I bite my tongue, wanting to say more but not wanting to get in it enough to start something while in enemy territory.

We move away from the horses and through the trees crouching as low as possible. I step as he steps and try to move as he does. I hop to the next step that he wants me to take and rocks scatter below my feet causing a noise to echo around us and birds' rustle in the trees.

"What did I say?" He looks around, staying hidden behind a tree and low, almost hugging the ground.

I kneel down low, but have nothing I can move to hide behind since he is behind the tree. I look around to make sure I am not being seen by anything. Then hiss out. "Your steps are too long! I can't move how you move if you don't think of who is trying to follow you." I argue.

I take smaller steps to also hide behind the tree. Almost tip toeing through the undergrowth hoping there were no traps set up between us where I step.

I yawn and rub my eyes, a lot more tired than I was just a moment ago. My temper is getting the best of me.

Robert rolls his eyes and looks once more starting forward through the wooded hill keeping his steps shorter and easier to keep up with.

I lean against the tree and my eyelids grow heavy.

An owl hoots far off in the distance.

I shake my head and take a moment to rest my eyes. I take a deep breath in, and as I release, slowly, I open up my eyes and stare at the forest around me. Robert has continued on without me. I look around trying to guess where he had stepped next or guess at where to go after the first move, he took.

Another hoot echoes around me along with something slithering off to the left.

I look up to see if anything is in the trees around me, I continue to crouch down low behind the tree not sure where to go next. I look around the tree expecting to see Robert somewhere up ahead but I just see darkness and dark green shadows all around.

"Robert?" I whisper trying to be as quiet as possible.

I hear a stick break close by, I put my back firmly against the tree I am hiding behind and make sure I am tucked behind it. I search the woods that were behind me making sure no one had snuck up that way. I don't see anything in the dull light. My heart begins to beat faster and my palms start to sweat. I place my hand over my mouth fighting to not make a sound. I try to calm my heart beat but my breath is so loud in my ears.

They were going to find me; Robert must have sensed trouble and that is why I could no longer see him since he went into hiding and that is why he did not answer me.

A rattle sounds to my right, my eyes dart to that side as I slink down lower trying not to make too much sound. The tree bark scratches at my back as my shirt rides up. I hardly feel the bite of pain as it scrapes. The area and ground grow deeper as the light dims from above the trees.

I could not see the horses below the foliage too thick and the darkness too great. I breathe in and out heavily, my ears ringing with the sound I am making. I try to hold my breath steadying it but it comes out choppy as I exhale as slowly as possible.

Something scratches on the tree up above my head. I look up but the shadows keep me from seeing too far up. "Alexia?" a voice hisses in a whisper.

I stop breathing all together trying to see and hear more. Who was that, was that Robert?

Another shake of a rattle happens from my right and in front of the tree I am hiding behind.

"Alexia, where are you?" another quiet whisper.

"Blaise?" I almost say silently. I peer around the edge of the tree. "Is that you?" I ask a bit louder.

I notice Blaise in his half animal form, his lower half is covered in scales and in the shape of a snake and his torso, arms and above are all that of a human still.

"Alexia there you are." He slithers forward, his tail making another rattling noise as he moves to me. "Are you okay? You're not hurt, are you?"

"What is this?" I ask, not believing my eyes. "How did you escape?" I accept Blaise's hug as he holds me close and checks over me making sure I am not hurt.

"Never mind that now? We can talk about that later. We have to get going. Did you have horses or did you have somewhere we could go and be safe?" Blaise tugs on my hand trying to urge me away.

His tug on my hand is light and my head starts to spin. "What do you mean?" I question. I drop his hand and move away from him towards the tree once more. Only it is no longer there. I turn around searching for the tree that was just behind me and then back to Blaise who is right there when I turn back around. "What game is this?" I put my hand on his chest to keep him at bay.

He smiles and wraps his hands around me, trapping my arms between us. "I thought you liked games?" he hisses, his tongue flicks out and touches my nose, which I barely feel.

"This isn't you?" I say in horror, I duck under his arms but his tail has moved behind me and I trip backwards going down hard. My butt and hands take the brunt of my fall. I look up, and he has crouched above me, his snake-like tail coming up in between my legs. He pins me there to the ground.

"Isn't it? How do you know?" he asks.

My hands scrape against the ground, but the sting of the rocks doesn't come. My eyes dance around Blaise, but they don't catch on anything of substance. Everything has grown dark, and it is just him and me. "Tell me how you escaped," I say as I try to scrabble backwards.

He keeps me pinned where I am, not easing up, his tail rattles once more. "You tell me?" he throws back at me the weight of him crushing over the lower half of my body.

"How did you know I was out here?" I ask, trying to get some answers. Trying to make sense of all that was happening.

"You're not that dumb, are you?" He rolls his hips over mine.

Tears prick my eyes.

"Alexia!" a kinder, gentler voice echoes around me yelling as if from a very far place.

I shake my head and try to push against Blaise and move him but his weight sinks further onto me and his bare chest comes down, his face right in mine. My fingers pat the ground next to me, searching for something to grab onto. Nothing feels substantial, just the ground beneath me. I go to dig my hands into the dirt there for something to throw at his face, but nothing comes up from the ground.

"What is going on?" I fight back, throwing out punches and moving my legs trying to throw him off.

As I fight, the voice calls out, closer this time. "Alexia, get up!"

"I'm trying to," I yell.

"Trying to what, my sweet?" Blaise pins my hands to the side, caging my body more.

"You're not real. This can't be real!" I growl out getting angry now. "Are you even Blaise?" I ask, still uncertain. I hoped the voice earlier was the real Blaise. It sure sounded like him, but I couldn't tell by voice alone this one looked so real.

"Yessss," he hisses out. "Of course, I am real." He licks my lips and presses down on me, the pain increasing as he does. "You are so easy to play with." His fangs elongate and glisten as he lowers his head slowly.

"Who are you?" I glare at him, still trying to kick my legs and move my arms.

"I am the one that tricked you here," he urges. "I am the one that made you fall for my devilish good charms." He rolls his hips for emphasis. "I am the one that has brought you here soul mate." He lowers his head beside mine, and his fangs scrape against the side of my mouth close to my cheek. "The dark side will be very pleased to have you brought to them finally," he whispers. His tail coils around my leg, tightening his hold on me and making me stiller.

I struggle to move, let alone breathe. "I don't believe you," my thoughts yell at Shade, but nothing answers, no words whisper through my mind.

"You better start believing, I will be your only saving grace, if I want it to be." He smiles.

Fire sisters. I think to myself not sure how to call them out to help. All my previous training flitted out of my mind as I tried to scramble for something, anything to break free of this. Whatever this was. This couldn't be real; it didn't feel right and I couldn't grab onto anything other than him and there were no clear surroundings anymore, just darkness and a little light to see by.

"I don't know how to do anything without others' help," I mumble under my breath.

"What are you mumbling about?" Blaise moves up and above me easing some of the weight off of me.

I stare back at this fake in front of me, my anger rising. "You are not him, drop the act!" I throw back at him. My fear is still there under the surface, but I let the anger over power it and let the sea rage on. I growl working myself up, powering myself tapping into that dark part of myself.

The scene skips a beat and shifts, a loud crack booms up above and the ground rumbles beneath us. Blaise looks up to the sky and then back down at me.

My eyes scramble for purchase on the moving ground. "What are you doing?" I try to roll out from under him.

I am able to twist my upper half away from him before he grabs my arm and twists me back towards him with a cold pinch, bites into my neck a burning sensation. My fingers flex into a fist and I pull my arm up but his grip keeps it pinned down. I look back at him and notice a needle being pulled away—no, his teeth. Blaise's form flickers in and out.

"Sleep now. I will talk to you later my dear." He laughs as my eyes flutter close; I fight to pry them back open. They are so heavy I can't keep them open much longer but before they close for the final time, I see Tom standing up above me.

"Wha—" I whisper out before surrendering to the darkness once more.

ID="CHAPTER 16"

CHAPTER 16

MY EYES SPRING OPEN, there are no bright lights but it is not fully dark either. The cold bites into me, I move my fingers and feel cold cobblestone below me. I scrape at the rock with my fingers, the dirt easily coming up. "Real," I whisper and shudder with the cold. I move my head to look around and my stomach rolls as I do.

I don't see anyone around or hear anything. I try to move slowly but my stomach rebels in answer. "Shade?" I whisper out in a croak, my throat sore as if someone had squeezed my throat as I lie helpless.

"Yea?" His voice echoes back at me in my mind. He flutters near my neck.

"Have you been awake this whole time?" I ask hoping he was so I could get some good intel.

"No, whatever got you, got me, too. I felt the tug in the woods but then I was cast into some weird place and could not connect with you," he says, just as confused. "Does it hurt much?"

My fingers shake as they slowly rise to my throat brushing against my neck and him. "It does but I think we have other things to worry about. Do you sense anything or anyone down here with us?" I try to move as little as possible to not draw anyone's attention to bring them here faster.

"I don't sense anything now. But I can see if I can take a look around. What happened to you?" he asks, waiting to peel off of me since we needed the contact to speak to one another.

My head aches, but I think back trying to remember what exactly happened. "Blaise…"

"Blaise was there? What was he doing and he's not here now?" He goes deathly still.

I close my eyes and take in a shaky breath trying to not let the pounding of my head get to me. "It wasn't Blaise though. It was and it wasn't. It looked and felt real… but it didn't feel real at the same time. I couldn't throw dirt, and trees moved. It was weird, almost like a dream." I say my confusion, making me go in circles.

"So not Blaise?"

I sit up in surprise. "No, it was Tom!" I yell loud instead of in my head. My head and stomach roll in unison as they both try to catch up to me. I groan in pain and slowly lower myself back to the floor needing a moment for things to not spin.

"Tom? How could he be Blaise?"

I groan out once more but still answer him in my head. "It's like he was disguised as Blaise. But he didn't act like him or not much, just moved and copied the way he talks but did not say words like he does or know him really."

"Like you do?"

"Hey!" I yelp. I let out a burp as my stomach also fights to answer.

Shade pulls up off of me fluttering away before he or I could say more. Not wanting to fight at a time like this. I wait, knowing it could be a few minutes before he is able to look around and come back to me. I dig my fingers yet again into the mud between the cobble stones and feel the cool earth there. The cold bricks feel good against the heat in my face. My forehead throbs in tune with my heart and the heat is cooled by the ground and bricks. I lie there with my forehead against the stones and my body twisted up almost in a ball conserving heat. I was both cold and hot at the same time.

The room is very cool and dry. My mouth is parched. "How long have I been out?" I ask out loud but in an almost whisper to myself again not wanting to call attention to myself. My arms are covered in goose flesh. I slowly sit up trying not to move too quickly and hug my arms around myself to try to keep warm. My breath puffs out and I can see it in the cold air.

Soon Shade is back, his dark shadow makes his way over to me staying low to the ground out of sight. He pulls up on to my arm and whispers against my mind. "We are at your parents' house where I checked out yesterday." He utters in a low growl.

My eyes fall close, they struggle to open once again. "What did they give me?"

"What did they do to you?" Shade asks at the same time.

"They gave me something though it looked like Blaise bit me and poisoned me." I put my hands to my head trying to think over my last memory. "But at the end before I blacked out, I saw Tom over me with a needle." I rub at my forehead trying to let the information sink in.

Shade elongates his form covering my arms fully and the little heater that is with him starts to warm up my numb fingers. "We are in a cage made of some kind of metal; metal bars surround us," Shade whispers to me.

I look around the room and notice the bars around us. I reach out my foot slowly since I did not want to try getting fully up. A few tingles run up my leg in warning before I nudge the bar. An arch of pain radiates through scrambling my thoughts. I scream out in pain and shock.

Shade quickly slides down and pulls my leg back from the bars that were still sending quick shocks through my body. "I should have warned you, that I felt the vibrations from them to begin with." He squeezes out in a wheeze.

My body shakes with the aftershocks of it, but I am more alert and awake then I was before. "Don't be, I think it helped wake me up at least and not feel as groggy."

Shade stretches out his form to cover my upper and lower half to radiate heat through my body and help protect me from anything else that might happen. Once my body stays still long enough, I try to sit up once again and scoot just a little closer to the bars to see if there was anything on them. "There is scroll work on these bars like the school had on those gloves," I mention.

There is an altar on the other side of the cage along with a bunch of candles that are already lit, and from the candle wax dripping down the side, it looks like it has been that way for a while.

"There are guards everywhere around this place but I did not see Tom when I was out. You are heavily guarded, they most likely heard you and know you're up now," Shade says.

"Are you able to get out of here and go get help?" I ask, thinking through our options here.

"I am not leaving you behind!" he says sharply.

"But we might need help. If you do not want to do that then see what we can use around here to help get me out." I throw my hands out around us taking care not to touch the bars.

He nods and quickly flows into a small slender being lifting off of me to go back through the bars, slipping through the bars easily as a serpent slithering over the stone. I hold my breath watching him move around not wanting anyone to come in and see him.

My body starts to come awake more due to the shock, the drug finally letting go of my mind. I look down at my bare feet, scratches and dirt cover them. I rub at them trying to bring warmth and feeling back into them.

I watch Shade slither over the bumpy floor, making his way to the door. "What are you doing?" I ask in a harsh whisper. I watch him not go under the door as he did last time to find out where we are.

He gets almost to the wall and then slithers away, backing up and moving around as if searching. He backs up a bit then elongates into something larger, a bigger blob and charges at the door.

I hiss, "Stop, you're going to cause a scene." But before he hits the door, he hits something else that is blocking him.

"What was that?" I call out a bit louder, catching myself midway and whispering the last of it. Shade falls down in a puddle as if stunned like I was when I hit the side of my cage. I take care but move closer to the front of the cage to be able to see better. My fingers itch to reach through the bars to touch Shade and hear what he is saying or feeling. "I can't hear if you are saying anything. Are you okay? Move around or something," I ask, worrying.

I bite at the tip of my thumb not sure what to do. I pace back and forth growing closer to the bars but still not touching them. He Mostly stays there in a puddle of himself but a part of him trickles to the side causing a stream of inky darkness that drips in between the bars and pools there.

I dip my fingers into the darkness and feel Shades' mind latch on to mine. "Something is weird." His voice strains as if he were fighting for breath like a normal person.

"Weird how?" I fight my instincts to pull him over to me and keep him close. I didn't want to move him too much to hit the electrified bars and he would be hurt once again.

"Something is blocking my way through, unlike before." His voice wheezes away as if he is trying to find enough breath to talk. "When I came up against it, it would just block me and allow me no further. But when I charged it, it hit back tenfold."

"Was it electric? Like the bars?" I ask.

"No, more like a huge truck running into me it took what I literally did and magnified it somehow," his voice whispers through mine.

I kneel down and try to get my face as close to the bars as I can. "I don't see anything," I say in confusion.

"Doesn't matter, something is still there."

"Shouldn't we have been able to tell when the spell went up or at least you should have, right?" I sit back on my heels and just keep my one hand against Shade holding on to him.

"I should have, yes," he says with sorrow in his voice.

I pat the little puddle of him I could reach with both my hands. "Shade, don't go anywhere. You are my life line." My voice dies out part of the way through, the emotion not able to be stopped.

"I will always protect you." He sends back. "I am not going anywhere, just took a big hit, it's going to take me a moment to bounce back." He chuckles.

"Rise and shine!" A voice booms out as people come through the door. A red beam shoots out at me through the bars shoving me in the chest and causing me to fall back away from Shade and the front of the cage.

The beam dissipates quickly before I can even realize what is going on. I touch my hand to my chest expecting to see blood or see a burn there but there is no mark, just a sore spot where a bruise might show up later.

"What is happening?" I growl out, wiping the tears from my eyes. I sit up and look at Shade who has retracted back into himself and is squirming and writhing in pain. There are people who are surrounding him and they have the red beams turned on him. They are thick and cover his whole body from my sight. They are chanting and focusing on him alone.

"Shade!" I scream out, I run forward accidentally brushing against the bars.

I bite back a curse and step back. I ball my fingers into fists and shake them, holding them close to my body, trying to curl myself around the pain.

"You're not going to get through that way." Tom calls out.

I lift my head up from my fingers and scan the room. Tom is a few steps away from the people that are surrounding Shade.

"You!" I growl out feeling my anger rise. "What are they doing to him?" I yell at him, keeping well behind the bars. The people surrounding Shade pay me no attention, their sole focus is on Shade. "Leave him alone!"

"Don't you feel useless. I have been watching you, you know?" he says casually as if we had all the time in the world and nothing serious was happening.

"Is that what you need to hear to stop what you are doing to him?" I say.

"Him, you realize he is genderless he is nothing but a spell a byproduct, he doesn't have a soul, he isn't anything but instructions made from a spell." Tom laughs.

"He is more than you ever could be, all you know how to do is stalk people and make them feel as if they are weak and useless," I throw back at him.

"It's easy when you have the right participant," he spits at me through bars.

I glare back at him and wipe at the side of my face and arm where his spit had landed. "What did I do to you? For you to do all this? Why go through all this trouble? You said he isn't even real so why are you killing him?" I say in frustration not knowing how to stop the questions coming out of my mouth.

Tom interrupts, "First, we are not killing it. We are turning it human, so you have nothing to use against us. He may die if we can't use him for anything else, but you will die first, I promise you that." He smiles. "You are a rat, a lowly disgusting rat and must be eradicated. You took something from me and I am taking something from you."

"What do you mean?" I ask in confusion and anger.

"You still don't remember?" He laughs very loudly as it echoes around the walls. "Good that means what we did to you really kept you dumb and naive. You killed my wife and a bunch of other people at the house in your rage!" he yells. "You are unfit to be alive, you couldn't control your power when it unlocked and she along with her group was the closest to you, they could not escape like the others. After all we did to care for you, this is how you pay us back." He acts as if he is throwing something at me.

I am hit with a memory. One showing Tom, Jade, and I all happy and having fun at dinner like a normal family. I huddle over and grab my head fighting what I am being shown. "These are lies. This is not the truth!" I scream out. "I remember them going down. I meant why did you do this to me from the start. Why was I captured and kept as a prisoner that whole time I never did anything to you or Jade?"

"Oh, but it is the truth," he presses. "You just don't want to believe you did a horrible thing to a loving family that took you in and just tried to give you a place to live and a home. Especially after your own parents tried to kill you!"

I shake my head. Visions keep coming at me showing me a life that I had, my head started to throb as I kept rejecting them. I laugh at him, I laugh at myself, I laugh at everything that has happened. I let the pain and anger seep into me. I cover my face as I continue to laugh and peak behind my fingers at him, hunched over. "Want to know why I know these are all lies!" I continue to cackle.

He backs up from the bars away from me, looking over at the people that are surrounding Shade making sure that they have not been interrupted. "They are no lies." He grounds out.

"Uh uh uh!" I call out in a sing-song voice. "The illusionist is not a writer of stories; they are filled with plot holes and not realistic. I can't feel the depths of your story. It is a base coat at best." I grin back. "I was told of your tricks. Silly rabbit."

"You believed them when you were younger." He laughs right back at me.

"Then why did you stop with just the illusions?" I bite out.

"Because you were getting too strong and fighting them." He steps back closer to the circle of people. "Jade's coven helped us through all the struggles you gave us. These witches will help clean up this world and let us all get back to the way life is supposed to be."

"What do you mean? What are you talking about?" I rise up on my shaky legs wanting to be on equal ground.

"Your little shadow puppet is your tie to this world, your only tie. If we sever the tie and turn him human so we can easily dispose of him, the one who protects you. Or we could keep him locked up to then get at you before you can turn into the thing that ends this world." He smiles smugly.

"Tell those witches to leave him alone, or else..." I threaten, reaching for the anger that is always there ready and waiting.

"Those are sorcerers, not witches; they are very different from a witch's magic like Jade and your mother," he explains clearly, perturbed by my knowledge. "They deal with life and death magic specifically like the death spell your mother enacted to create that." He points to Shade. "Which is exactly what this kind of thing calls for doesn't it?"

A loud scream and grunt of pain echoes back off the walls to me coming from the circle of people. They have crowded closer, blocking my sight from Shade. I can't see him at all. "Shade! Shade!" I scream not caring what Tom or anyone else thought anymore. "Stop." I cry out.

Tom shakes his head. "The only person you should blame for this is yourself. You started this."

"I didn't ask to be born," I cry and yell.

"And I didn't ask to be a widower."

I feel something brush against my mind. I feel claws dig in at my insides as my anger continues to rise. But this is not a situation that I would need teeth and claws to fix, I need magic. I need raw power. I feel the fur slide down my back and arms, trying to calm me. I feel my claws grow out and my teeth elongate the anger not being able to be held back.

"There she is, the animal I know you are. Temper. Temper." He sings to my face. He grips one of the shoulders of the people in the circle and squeezes lightly and heads towards the doorway. "Finish it; I will be back when it is done to end their pathetic lives!" He shuts the door with force as he leaves, I catch two people on the outside as he begins to talk with them.

The voices begin to chant louder, and my growls pour out. My soul focuses on the group.

A silver fox glides through the wall and dances outside my cage, it glows with a ghostly aura, his form almost liquid like as it moves. It bounds through the bars to get closer to me. I growl out and bite my teeth at it wanting it to stay away. As it moves closer, I move forward. I reach out my claws to swipe at it.

It skips out of range being very tricky. "Lexi, calm down please. It's Robert, we are coming for you. We are almost there. You just have to wait a little longer." Robert's voice comes out of the little fox. His tails swish back and forth.

I take a step back and cock my head to the side in confusion, another rough howl of pain comes from the circle that catches my attention. "Do you think he has that kind of time?" I growl, my voice rough.

"Who is that?" Robert calls out. His fox form skips back out the bars, his form not activating the bars at all.

"Shade! Didn't Zeek tell you about him, he seems to know everything there is about me?" I say, quickly walking back and forth quickly.

"My brother in arms, though he himself knows a lot, gives very little details about situations when they happen." He shrugs accepting this of his friend and brother.

"Shade is my protector, a spell that my mother created to aid me and helps keep me alive," I say simply. "Though he is much more than just a spell." I cringe as I hear whimpering. "Can you not help him?"

"No, I am astral projecting my animal."

"A fox?" I ask.

"Kind of, it's a Kitsune, but not important right now. I can't really affect the physical world in my form right now but wanted to let you know we are coming." He looks back at something only he can see. "I had to go back for help after I saw where Tom took you. There were too many goons around to help you and he had caught you in his mind to bring you along willingly for the most part."

I glare at him, highly irritated. "Why didn't you do anything to help?"

"You were adamant about helping Blaise, if he could take you to Blaise or if Blaise was a part of this setup, then we could go from there. After you and him talked in his made-up reality of a dream world. I figured he imitated Blaise to lure you in. I overheard his people say they did have Blaise at one time but ended up giving him back to his owner."

"You still could have done something to avoid this, I obviously now know I can't do this by myself! I am useless! But Shade doesn't have that kind of time." My eyes glue to where they cover Shade's form. A brush of wind knocks back a bit of one's cloak and I can see shadow turning to human skin.

"I thought I felt someone slip through our defenses. Can't do anything though can you?" Tom walks back in casually checking things out. He holds a very large blade in his right hand. "Good you can watch the show that is about to happen. They tell me you are still too far out to be of any nuisance." He walks close to the cage; his eyes hold excitement for what he is about to do.

"You make me sick," I growl. I stand a hair's breadth away from the bars, itching to pull him into the bars. I stick to that idea and try to think through how to go about it. "My sisters shall come for me. They are fire where I am cool," I try saying cryptically and calling to the two sisters I hold inside me. They didn't tell me how to call them forward.

"Sisters? You have no siblings, or did you forget that also." He taps his own temple and gives me a weird look.

"Play!" they speak in unison in my mind. "We can bring the scary fire!" They sing in my head. Their voices warble in and out.

I wondered if it was because they were so young but I hoped they had enough juice and power to at least help me through this. I didn't know if they could be hurt but they seemed to be fine and not hurt from the shocks I took earlier. I smile back at Tom. "Exactly what I was thinking, we should play with him." I press my hands to the bars, ignoring the shocks it sends through my body, only concentrating on my anger and the pain I want him to feel.

Tom backs up a bit at my words and looks at the Kitsune still next to me in confusion.

"What are you doing?" Robert comes closer, trying to find a way to make me let go of the bars.

"You can't die until the spell is finished!" Tom yells as he looks back and forth between the circle and me.

As he looks away, I feel the change happen more my eyes change and fur erupts over my body. I scream out. "Go!" The bars heat up from the two fire sisters and they bend easily in my hands, the heat has short circuited with the power fluctuation. I bend the metal enough for me to slide through. "Attack!" I holler and cast my hands at Tom.

My hands blaze up in flames, they jump from my flesh to his. I smell his skin begin to stink as the flames sear him to the bone. He dances around and slaps at his clothes and skin to get them off. The girls scream in joy as they hop and skip around his body as if it were a game. They continue to dodge his attempts until his limbs begin to slow.

I laugh at him and walk through the bars to lay my hands on his chest, the flames still eating at him. "I am your judgment!" I seethe at him. "Sisters he is mine." They go from jumping around to hanging their heads but they walk back to me and melt into my skin once more.

"No fun," the younger one whispers to me through my mind.

I would have to remember to play with them later on.

The flames continue to lick their way over Tom's skin and clothes, their threads tearing apart and showing pink and bubbling skin beneath. With the girls back to me, their flames they create do not touch my skin. I crouch down over Tom and grab his neck with my clawed hands raising his head up. I smother some of the flames out as I make sure he does not pass out. He croaks out a wheeze of pain. His fingers clutch around my misshapen hands. The flames die down as nothing is keeping them going.

"Call off your sorcerers." I growl at him, my face close to his so he would not mistake what my words meant.

Shade screams a long and low note of pain.

"It is done." He laughs weakly.

I let Tom fall to a slump on the floor and move over to the sorcerers still huddled around Shade. I call on my anger and strength from my badger side. My hair pools around my face as it comes undone from the pony tail it was in before. As I call more on my badger power, my fur and hair changes color of what it would be as a full animal shift. My brown changes to black, gray, and white. I can see the color twirl its way down my hair as it moves in front of my face.

I move closer to the people surrounding Shade, they pay no attention to me. I circle around, most of them look tired as they catch their breath after casting so much power in such a short amount of time. I launch at one doubled over resting his hands on his knees. I hug my hands around his neck and wrap my legs around his waist. I squeeze and pull back against him, tearing my long claws into his throat and skin. The sharp points easily cut through his pliable skin. The unsuspecting prey falls back in surprise as my hands rip through his throat. I fall into a crouch, my eyes moving on to my next victim.

The four others realize they have something more sinister to deal with other than the man lying naked on the floor. My eyes scan Shade, though I don't see any marks on where they had hurt him, I don't see him moving or breathing either.

They all back up as they see my eyes scanning them. "What did you do to him?" I growl out still in a crouch, the body behind me now silent and lifeless as blood slows to a trickle from his throat.

One takes out a butterfly knife hidden in his robes. "You are a mut, something that needs to be destroyed. That spell—" He points with the dagger as he flips it open. "He's been remade into something useless to you so you have no other power to rely on." He chuckles. The others follow him and snicker, all moving forward as one towards me surrounding me.

I squeeze my hands and realize that there are guts and parts of the dead man's throat still hanging from my claws. I heave the blood and guts at the people in front of me. Smacking them in the face with it to distract them. His words sear into my brain. I scream out as if his words have done physical damage to me.

I dive over to the one who threw such cruel words and grab at him, flinging my whole-body weight at him. He catches me easily and flips me over his side. He tries to restrain my hands. I wiggle and break out of the hold. His arms come across my face as he tries to keep my hands from his own throat.

I bury my teeth and fangs into his arm as it moves closer. I bite into him. I feel the heat of his blood splash onto my tongue. I latch on with force and crunch down as tightly as I can. The man rears back trying to dislodge me from him.

He punches at my face but I bring my arms up to block the brunt of the force. Our bodies twist and now I am falling on to him, switching our positions. He kicks a leg between us and works his leg to push at me as he pulls back.

He screams out in pain. "Get this bitch off of me!" he calls to his buddies. They had stood around in shock at how the tables had changed so quickly. They quickly spring into action and try to grab at my arms and legs holding me away from him, he throws another punch with his good arm into my side. My arms are no longer able to catch some of the force, his punch catches me and throws me off balance. I unlatch and the breath is knocked out of me.

I cough and spit out his blood and skin. I slice my claws out making the other three members drop my hands and legs. I roll backwards into a crouch and huddle into myself as I try to figure out how to breathe once more. "Only I decide my potential... not others," I wheeze out in a low soft voice.

Darkness inches around my eye sight. I try to shake my head clear along with my vision. I hold a clawed hand to my side where I am hit. The three others check on their friend with the arm and hover around him. One does notice Tom and runs over to him checking his vitals. He glances once more my way and makes a decision to lift him up under his armpits and slowly makes his way back to where the others are standing. One is standing in front of the others knowing he will have to go toe to toe with me if I continue while the other two get the injured out. They are closer to the door than I am and can easily trap me here.

I lunge forward growling out making my way closer to the door as well. "You are not leaving me locked in here for your own torture!"

I garble out, I look back at the cage seeing if there was anything I could use as a weapon.

I noticed the fox had disappeared at some point. Fine he was useless anyway

The darkness closes in more quickly and my side shoots pain up and down my side. I inch up my shirt and see red blooming there on my side. I slowly lower the shirt back down cocked to the side so the one that is watching me carefully does not notice.

"We all can leave and go our separate ways. Think about this, we are all members of a world that would miss us and retaliate against you and anyone you are working with to get us back or avenge our deaths. You don't look so well there." He notices me stumble as I continue moving towards the door. "What makes you think you can continue?" he asks.

I glare at him, taking my hand away from my side and straightening up. "Oh, I can continue if you would like." I lick my lips; a bit of blood has sprayed on my face and I taste the copper wetness of my enemies. I laugh.

He smirks back. "You can barely stand, let alone fight. Stand aside little girl and let us by or I will have to force you, and knowing my boys here—" He nods his head back toward them. "They wouldn't mind taking their pound of flesh from you, which may kill you at this very moment." He bends his knees and readies himself either way.

My heart starts to beat fast once again and my vision goes in and out and I start to grow lethargic once again. I growl out and flex my claws and focus on him.

He cracks his knuckles and pops his neck as he twists it to the side. He glares at me urging me to fight him. "Don't forget we also have your friend who we can kill." He looks back behind his group at the man still lying there not moving other than breath that causes his chest to rise and fall.

I notice him breathing and take a step back. "He's alive?" I whisper.

"Of course, he is. We made him human." The man who was ready to brawl stands down.

I snort at him and nod towards the door. "Fine go." My eyes don't stray from Shade.

I stand back ready to fight if needed but I just watch from my peripheral as the group gathers their hurt and ushers them through the door. The door closes and I hear a lock turn in the door, locking us in here once again.

"I knew they would do that," I utter.

I pick my way over carefully to Shade who is sprawled out on his back on the cold hard ground. His hair is dark much like his shadow body used to be. He is very tall and skinny in length. "Shade?" I say my body and voice start to shake. Whether from the cold, pain, or fear I couldn't discern.

I gather him close to me, wrapping my arms around him, wanting to give him what little heat I could. I didn't know what would have happened to his little flame he had with him. "Please say something to me, Shade."

With the sharp movements I make I take on some of his weight. my side and head scream at me.

I maneuver his head so I can look at his face, but his body is still against me. His eyes flutter open and they are piercing green. He scans his surroundings and me, looking at me with curious eyes.

I raise up, a little bit shocked that his eyes are open. "Shade? Are you okay? Say something?" I repeat as he continues to stare at me.

His hand reaches out and grips my hurt side. I hiss in pain and cringe, closing my eyes. His touch is not gentle, but continues to squeeze and pull me towards him. "Death," he rasps out. "For all." His other hand reaches out and grabs my throat, pulling me closer.

My eyes struggle to open and his face is right there next to mine. His face comes closer, his hand tightening on my throat forcing me to stay. His lips slam into mine with bruising force and a thick curtain of darkness erupts from me spilling into him.

Once the ooze slows down, he smiles against my lips as the darkness continues to pour out of me. I feel weak and lethargic as more and more pours out of me. He reaches for some of the dark liquid that splashes beside him, he caresses it, my eyes follow his movements. My eyes fall shut as air and pain is starting to set in. He relaxes his hold around my neck and throws me to the side. I wince as I land and breathe in the ice-cold air. My eyes inch open enough to see Shade follow the shadow and power and use it to help him rise up and stand.

"What did you do?" I whisper my teeth chattering.

"I took what you did not wish to use. I will make them pay with the power that they wish to crush. Unlike you I will not hold back until they are all finished, this world will pay!"

He crosses across the room and rips the door from the hinges, shattering it to pieces as he sends the darkness out with the shards of wood from the door impaling the guards that were set to guard the door. "Shade," I say weakly. Trying to call him back to me.

He looks back before turning out the door. "I will finish this," he growls, his eyes flashing with finality.

I lie on my side, no strength left in me to follow him out or fight let alone stand. A loud rumble shakes the room and causes dust to fall from the ceiling covering me with an inch of soot.

"What is going on?" I mumble. My eyes close and I rest against the cool ground, the air doesn't feel as bitter cold as it did a moment ago. I relax as everything starts to fall away, the adrenaline falling away. My animal form starts to fade to human. My claws turn into normal fingers and my teeth return to their normal state.

I hear a bellow and screaming coming from somewhere in the distance another rumble makes this place shake.

"She is back this way," a low booming voice calls out.

I open my eyes to slits once again and see Robert stick his face down by mine. His breath puffs out at me. He looks over me and sees the shirt has ridden up, showing the blooming bruise on my side. He carefully lifts me up into his arms. "Stay with me," he urges.

I nod but my lids fall shut and I can't seem to work out how to get them open once again.

"Out of the way nine tails," Natasha's voice grates.

Robert staggers, jolting me. I yip in pain.

"Careful," Natasha yells close by. "Where is Shade? Isn't he supposed to be protecting you?"

A rumble answers her and rocks come crashing down in the hallway that we had moved out into.

I shake my head in answer. I am struggling to stay awake, let alone pay attention to what is happening.

"Did you run into anyone on the way here?" Robert asks as he urges them to continue forward. "Let's get out into the open. I am not sure what is going on but it doesn't sound like the house is going to make it through it."

Natasha nods and continues moving, but throws back with just a glance. "No, I didn't run into anyone. They all got distracted with something that is happening on the other side of the compound. I thought you had made a distraction so I was going to come in and see if I could get to Alexia."

My head lolls back and my eyes shut. I am no longer able to continue watching where we go. The bouncing and jostling is getting to me and causing me to be dizzy. I keep passing out, not able to hold on the pain becoming too intense. One moment, we are in a rumbling decrepit home, another we are outside with blue skies above us.

"Just hold on a little longer, we have the horses ready to take us back. We will follow the path so it will be easier to get there faster," Robert calls to me, urging me to hang on.

That is the last thing I remember fully. The pain and dizziness become too much. I can only concentrate on that, and then when we get to the horses where the motion gets even more aggressive, I cannot hang on any longer and welcome the darkness that has been waiting at the ready.

CHAPTER 17

"**T**HIS NEEDS TO STOP." I groan as my eyes blink rapidly the daylight sears my retinas. I try to open them up slowly but am starstruck with the light once again. I hold an arm up to cover my face so that it is in the shadows and then try to open my eyes.

My eyes travel around the room I am in and notice I am back in the same room I woke up the day before. I feel the blankets and contemplate sinking back into the warmth and just making it all go away.

"Are you okay?" a small voice says from the end of my bed.

I give a start and quickly look over at the left edge of the bed but don't see anything.

"Up here." She waves.

I glance up and see her in her full fairy form with her wings fluttering behind her and sitting on one of the bed's columns. "Natasha, what are you doing up there?" My voice is raspy.

I try to sit up and am cut short by a sharp pain. I cough and can hardly catch my breath.

She flutters her wings quickly falling forward as she pushes me back down tucking the covers under me creating a cocoon. Her wings help her hover over me as she makes sure I am fine and tucked back in. "You had internal bleeding on your side as well as bleeding from the back of your head. You have to take it easy."

I nod slowly as the pain thumps in answer to her. "What happened?"

"What happened? You tell me," she says. She flies to the side and sits beside me on the bed instead of back to her perch. "I checked Shade isn't on you, where did he go? I thought he was supposed to protect you."

"They turned him human," I say in answer, my heart aching in pain as I felt truly alone for the first time.

"Blaise did this?"

"No. Not Blaise he wasn't there, he wasn't even a part of this. I mean he might have been at first but not for this I don't think. Hell, I don't know." I glance at her, feeling defeated.

"Who changed Shade to human?" she says slowly. Trying to keep her voice even and calm. "Don't get worked up just think it through if it's too much we can stop. But know that we have to do this eventually."

"You sound like Quintan now." I cough again, clearing my lungs. "It was Tom who orchestrated this all. He was upset that I killed Jade and wanted to get even. The spell, the damn spell he was so worried about so he turned the spell into a person to get rid of the problem and to finish me off." My voice cracks.

"There was no other person down there with you. Robert assured me of that." Natasha's face pinches in worry.

"No, he left. Something was different with him. He wasn't right." I bite on my lip.

"Where did he go?" I shrug in answer. "Something was chasing Tom and his men off. Whatever it was did not follow us though," she says as an afterthought. "Perhaps it was Shade and now he is going to the darkness where he originated from or to finish them off."

I hesitate. "Shade said something before he left me."

"Well, what did he say?" Natasha pushes.

"He said he will finish this." I try to remember if there was anything else, but cannot get close, the pain still too fresh.

"Finish what?"

"Could be to finish what I wanted originally, which was to find Blaise or finish this war. He wants to make this world pay. Who knows what that could entail? He was a part of me but we couldn't see into each others minds like that," my voice cracks.

Natasha throws her icicle hair over her shoulder. "Well, heal up, princess. You have a war to fight and mediate. You have people looking to you now, and you will need to tell them what to do next."

"I never asked for this, they can war alone without me. They don't need me for any of this. I want to go find Blaise and Shade. I just want to be left alone. You know what that feels like more so than any of them."

"Who said you can't do both?" Natasha waggles her eyebrows.

"You?" I ask.

"No, you are in charge so that means you get to make the rules. That means we can do both. If you want this to not go to war you will have to mediate with each side. Why not start with the dark side of things and look for the two people you are wanting to find first then deal with Tom and his pitiful band?"

"Tom, won't he cause problems for us? Shade might take care of him for us, or at least we can hope. Knowing my luck though I won't be that lucky."

"He most definitely will be something we will have to deal with. That is why I was thinking, let's start with the dark side that way. If he has the lights' ear, then we have more cards stacked in our favor, to either go to war or we have a better hand to play with. They will understand why we shouldn't continue with this bloodshed."

"I still don't know anything about my past," I complain.

"Perhaps that will be your next chapter. Remember most of these people fought with your parents, they would know more about where you came from, you can start there." She lets her hand rest against my arm over the top of the blanket. "Your place is with us here. But if you want to go back to your human world, I can see about making that happen as well."

"I can also help with that." Zeek pokes his head into the room.

My eyes settle on him. "How so?"

"I can explain the story you are wanting to know. The one of your past. I was called on by Jade and Tom. I was supposed to put you in a deep sleep where you could never wake. When I learned of who you were I of course did more research, our brotherhood doesn't stay alive with being stupid."

I ease against the blankets content with finally learning the truth of it all.

"I had learned who you really are. Jade and Tom took you that night their plan before your mother put a death curse on her was to rid the world of you but since they could not finish you off with out harming Jade they hid you away and siphoned your power for their own gain. The Light council was okay with this as long as they kept you on a leash. There were a few years when you were young that you believed all the lies or made up fantasy Tom would create but that became to much for even him to keep up when you started coming into your own, your powers. They put you under to keep them at bay and week. Even then you were a hell cat and fought against them. That is why I was called in to put you in a coma like state until they could come up with a way to get rid of you."

"But I woke up, or got a way some how." My fingers clench the blankets around me, I grunt as I pull myself up into a sitting position to better get a handle on the situation.

Zeek comes further into the room and closes the door so no others can hear the conversation. "With our deal we made when I saw you in the past I knew I must be the one to take this opportunity and have to help you. I had to do everything to the letter though. I did put you in a coma like state that you couldn't get out of but sent some thing to make sure that you could get out of the spell. They were also supposed to help get you out of the situation you were in, unfortunately I left the how of it up to them and they thought it would be fun to instead activate your powers and your creature. Hence the massacre. With the spell Tom gave you to make you forget any supernatural thing you saw it made remembering or keeping information intact hard."

"Tom will not let this go he will be back. We have to prepare."

"That is a lot to accomplish in such a short time. I suggest learning who and what you are along with anything you can about this world and then go from there." He shakes his head. "Shade can wait, it will take time for him to learn of this world as well. Tom will be regrouping and figuring out his next steps. Blaise is in the wind we have no idea where he could be. Working on yourself will help you understand the next leg of your journey and what needs to be done."

"Thanks, I will think on it. I just need rest for now." I yawn, my eyes and body begging for more sleep.

Natasha lies down next to me and holds me close. "We could always run away from everything," she whispers to me. "Away from Zeek and everything." She eyes him.

Zeek backs up, I hear his boots against the floor as he retreats. "Don't tempt me," I laugh.

That thought swirls in the back of my mind as I try to think through the chaos and begin to think up a battle plan and what to do next. For now I needed to rest and recover. There would be time to learn this town and what my true mother and father had planned for me. Once I felt better I would get back to training and learning, then no one would be able to take advantage of me again or make me do something I didn't want to.

Acknowledgments

Most importantly Thank You! To you the reader who is reading this story and any others you may read from me. I hope my characters are nice to you and show you a good time because they definitely put me through the ringer. I know if everyone listed here where not in my life I would not be where I am today.

There are so many people that I would love to thank! Because of these people who have touched my life I am here were I need to be doing what I love. Even if you are not personally mentioned here know that if you have helped me through my life, I thank you.

I would first like to thank my grandma or G-ma for short. She has helped me in so many ways, she has nourished my love of books and reading in ways no one else could. I will forever miss her and will one day meet her in a field of flowers.

Allen has been there through the bad times and the good. He is my rock and will help as well as follow me through anything. He is the very best part of me. Without him things would grow very dark very fast.

Selby who is my sister maybe not by blood but definitely in heart. She encourages me and pushes me to be great even when I feel less than.

Callie is the light of my life, my rainbow to my storm, my other half I never knew I needed. I don't know what I would do without her in my life.

I also want to thank the people who have helped me on the book. Kyla, Shelby, Johnathon, Kev, and Zack. The have helped make my dreams a reality and helped this book become not only a dream of mine but a reality.

I would also like to thank my aunts Becky and Dorrie who have always believed in me and pushed me in ways I didn't even know I needed. They are always on my side and know I can go the distance.

About Author

Raquel Gabrielle resides in Oklahoma with her husband, dogs and cat. She grew up loving stories so much that she even made up her own tales. Writing has helped her and continues to do so. Writing has always been there for her and something she will always fall back to when things get tough. She loves all things spooky and knows some of the best people come with a bite.

If she isn't writing or telling stories, you can find her hanging out with friends or traveling. She loves to see the world and all its wonders.

She mostly dabbles in Urban Fantasy or Paranormal Romance but has been known to go outside the box from time to time. For more information about her book and writing journey, you can join her

newsletter at www.RaquelGabrielle.com or on her Facebook author page Raquel Gabrielle

Coming Soon...

Don't miss the next novel in Raquel Gabrielle's A Soul Saga. Keep reading to read a blurb of what book two will bring:

Alexia Kremer is back and she is ready for things to start making sense. She stumbles across her mother's journal and pieces start to come together, just not from her own memory.
Blaise is still missing and there are more questions than answers when it comes to him. More importantly Alexia is getting the sense he doesn't want to be a part of her life as much as she thought originally. That is until someone else shows some interest.
Her animal is starting to show her teeth and make things interesting. Her wild side is not taking no for an answer and is not waiting on the sidelines anymore. She is angry and tired of waiting for things to make sense.
One thing is for sure through all of this and that is nothing is quite what it appears to be.